GORGO

"GORGO"
A King Brothers Production—An M-G-M Release

61/36

# GORGO

Edited
By
Philip J. Riley

Production Background
By
Bill Cooke

MagicImage Filmbooks is an imprint of
BearManor Media

BearManor Media
P.O. Box 1129
Duncan, OK 73534-1129

Phone: 580-252-3547
Fax: 814-690-1559

www.bearmanormedia.com

Pressbook Courtesy of Ronald V. Borst/Hollywood Movie Posters

Photographs Courtesy of Ronald V. Borst/Hollywood Movie Posters and the editor

"This is the Big One! The Story Behind Gorgo By Bill Cooke ©2014

Edited and designed by Philip J. Riley©2014

Special thanks to Erik D. Harshman


First Edition

The purpose of this series is the preservation of the art of writing for the screen. Rare books have long been a source of enjoyment and an investment for the serious collector, and even in limited editions there are thousands printed. Scripts, however, numbered only 50 at the most. In the history of American Literature, the screenwriter was being lost in time. It is my hope that my efforts bring about a renewed history and preservation of a great American Literary form, The Screenplay, by preserving them for study by future generations.

# This is the Big One!
## The Story Behind Gorgo

## By Bill Cooke

The early 1960s was perhaps the best time ever to be a kid in love with monsters. Classic horror films of the 30s and 40s were commonly found on television, in some cases hosted by a regional ham actor in thick clown-white makeup. The newsstands were veritable mosaics of fearsome faces peering from the covers of *Famous Monsters of Filmland* magazine and its imitators. As the decade wore on, plastic model kits of Frankenstein, Dracula, the Wolf Man and other fiends gave "weird" kids an option to the usual tanks and planes. But best of all, there were the plentiful monster movies that played at the local cinemas, splayed across coke-stained screens big enough to engulf imaginative young minds. One movie that all "Monster kids" of that era remember to this day with awe and reverence is *Gorgo*.

Released by MGM in 1961, *Gorgo* is that oft-told cinematic fable of the giant beast that threatens humanity. It may not be on par with the original *King Kong* or even the first *Godzilla*, but it is what you might call a minor *monster*piece. The story mixes familiarity with a couple of neat plot twists; the special effects are ambitious and oftentimes stunning; and the use of a man in a rubber dinosaur suit, a technique usually met with derision, is undoubtedly one of the best on record. But perhaps the reason that supersedes them all is that *Gorgo* is the rare city-stomping monster spectacle with heart.

By the time *Gorgo* hit theater screens across the world, the giant-creature cycle was winding down after nearly a decade of popularity. The trend was ignited in 1952, when RKO re-released the archetypal film of this type, *King Kong*, to theater screens across the United States. The 1933 classic about a 50-foot gorilla and its infatuation with a slightly over 5-foot blonde was a phenomenal success for RKO in its initial run; but this time the company had the benefit of television advertising at their disposal and was able to entice a whole new generation to venture out and experience the wonderment and thrills of "The Eighth

Wonder of the World." As a result, box-office far exceeded the original run, and TIME magazine heaped its praise by crowning *King Kong* "Movie of the Year."

Not surprisingly, Hollywood film producers picked up on the success story. The first to capitalize on the *Kong* revival was producer Hal E. Chester, who hurriedly made *The Beast from 20,000 Fathoms* for distribution through Warner Brothers in 1953. *King Kong* was a variant on the Victorian-era "Lost World" archetype, the idea that somewhere in the world there could be a lost plateau or unknown island where creatures from a by-gone era still exist; but the makers of *The Beast from 20,000 Fathoms* cannily tapped into more current cultural anxieties by using a technological catalyst—an atomic bomb—to bring a dinosaur into modern times. Released from an icy prison and dangerously irradiated by a nuclear-bomb test in the arctic, the film's star, a fictitious species called a "Rhedosaurus," swims down the Atlantic to reclaim its old stomping grounds, which just happens to be downtown Manhattan.

With its timely nuclear theme, the picture set a precedent for the genre, and before long theater screens were alight with all manner of animals, insects and dinosaurs that had been either magnified or unleashed by the nasty after-effects of atomic explosions. These ranged from the excellent *Them!* (another Warner Brothers release, this one about super-sized ants in the Nevada desert) and the thoroughly entertaining *Tarantula* (a scientist's radioactive serum causes the gigantism this time) to the sadly ridiculous *Beginning of the End* (Chicago under siege by sloppily matted-in grasshoppers). Interestingly, while the genre is an American invention, the most famous example remains the Japanese-made *Gojira* (1954) (retitled *Godzilla, King of the Monsters* for Western markets), a film that took its cues from *The Beast from 20,000 Fathoms*, but hit with a bit more profundity due to metaphorical resonance. It was at once unsettling and darkly poetic to watch a nuclear-spawned, fire-breathing dragon laying waste to the only nation that ever experienced the horrors of an exploded atomic bomb.

A late entry in the cycle, *The Giant Behemoth* (1959, aka *Behemoth the Sea Monster*) was produced in Great Britain and had a plot that closely mirrored *The Beast from 20,000 Fathoms*. Once again an oceanic dinosaur was aroused by nuclear testing and headed to a major city (this time London) for the usual parade of destruction around famous landmarks. Nobody could cry plagiarism, however, since both films were directed and co-written by the same man: Eugène Lourié, a French production designer with a scarcity of directing credits but who was already becoming typecast as a specialist in the genre. When King Brothers Productions got the impulse to produce their own giant-creature epic—the project that developed ultimately into *Gorgo*—it was only natural they called on the man with the proven track record.

THE BIGGEST THING SINCE CREATION!

The GIANT BEHEMOTH

Eugène Lourié (b. 1903, d. 1991) grew up in Kharkov, Russia, where even the turmoil of the 1917 revolution could not deter him from his favorite pastime: losing himself in the flickering, piano-accompanied fantasies of his local cinema. Three years later, the teenaged Lourié fled from Russia and sought refuge in a movie theater in Istanbul that often took in refugees. In time he was hired by the theater owners to paint posters for the lobby and manage their publicity campaigns. This was the young man's first step toward realizing his dream of living in Paris and studying art; however, once there, he found the lure of working odd jobs painting scenery and designing costumes for films too compelling to resist. Before long he was a production designer in the French film industry, working with some of the great directors of that time. He designed the sets for Max Ophuls' *Le roman de Werther* (1938) as well as Jean Renoir's *La Bête Humaine* (1938) and *The Rules of the Game* (1939). With the dark *noir* melodrama *The Long Night* (a remake of the bleak French film *Le Jour se lève*, and featuring Henry Fonda in the Jean Gabin role), Lourié made the transition to American films. In 1951 he designed the Franco-American co-production of *The Adventures of Captain Fabian*, starring Errol Flynn, and in the following year he had the pleasure of working with producer-director-star Charlie Chaplain on *Limelight* (1952).

But even as Lourié felt fulfilled as a designer, he knew he was capable of more. He would watch the films on which he labored and start to think how he would have directed them differently. In his memoirs, Lourié wrote:

"In many ways work as an art director or production designer prepares you for directing. In designing you have to visualize the action as well as the settings. [In France] we had very tight budgets for films and short schedules, which forced us to make thorough preparations. Very often I had to prepare detailed shooting scripts, breaking down sequences into individual scenes, indicating each change in the camera angle, dolly shots, pan shots, and so on. I usually prepared these shooting scripts with directors." [4]

Part of Lourié's duties as a production designer was to prepare a floor plan of the set with indications for camera and actor placement. Numbers on the floor plan coincided with numbers written into the script. "In preparing these detailed plans, I had to mentally direct the film." [4]

In the spring of 1952, Lourié was approached by producer Hal E. Chester of Mutual Films, who wanted Lourié to art direct several pictures he was planning. One of these was a mere outline that bore the title *The Monster from Beneath the Sea*. The scenario especially intrigued Lourié because of the imaginative nature of the subject matter and the artistic challenges it posed. Half-jokingly he suggested he would be willing to direct the monster picture if Chester and his producing partner Frank Dietz could not find anyone else. Much to Lourié's surprise, Dietz called him back in a few weeks and offered him the job. All of a sudden, Lourié found himself in charge of directing actors in addition to the visual planning he was accustomed to. Nevertheless, he never lost sight of who was the real star of the show—the monster.

As *The Monster from Beneath the Sea* went into preproduction, one of the most important tasks was to decide how they were going to bring a gigantic dinosaur to life on screen. There was already a history of techniques to draw upon. For his 1924 fantasy spectacle *Die Nibelungen*, director Fritz Lang realized a dragon by building a full-scale mechanically operated prop. The makers of the 1940 prehistoric epic *One Million B.C.* photographically enlarged ordinary reptiles, in addition to augmenting them with glued-on fins and horns. *Unknown Island* (1948) featured stuntmen parading around in embarrassingly stiff and unconvincing dinosaur costumes. In the end, Chester and Lourié opted for stop-motion animation, the method that had been so successfully employed for *The Lost World* (1925), *King Kong* and *Mighty Joe Young* (1949). A frame-by-frame animation technique involving jointed puppets, stop-motion animation is a time-consuming and potentially expensive process. Consequently, Chester could not afford the services of Willis O'Brien, the pioneering special-effects technician who had brought Kong to life. Instead, he hired O'Brien's apprentice on *Mighty Joe Young*, an eager young animator named Ray Harryhausen, who supplied a series of outstandingly accomplished effects sequences on a tight schedule and budget. Harryhausen went on to be the world's top stop-motion animator on films such as *The 7th Voyage of Sinbad*, *Jason and the Argonauts*, *Clash of the Titans* and many more.

*The Monster from Beneath the Sea* was bought by Warner Brothers and rechristened *The Beast from 20,000 Fathoms*. The film was a sleeper hit for the studio, grossing over $5 Million in its first year, and was instrumental in popularizing science-fiction films for the rest of the decade. Soon after the picture's release, Lourié attended a matinee showing with director Jean Renoir and remembered him reacting with wide-eyed wonder "Just like the youngsters" surrounding them. But the most surprising reaction of all came from Lourié's six year-old daughter. Very upset over the creature's death amid a burning rollercoaster, she cried, "You are bad, Daddy, bad. You killed the nice beast!" [4]

In the wake of *The Beast*, Lourié was offered the director's chair on a number of science-fiction productions, "all of them unbelievably bad." [4] One that he agreed to helm was *The Colossus of New York*, an ultra-low-budget production about a man whose brain is transplanted into the skull of an imposingly tall and eerie-looking robot. He was then approached by producer David Diamond, who was working on a co-production deal between Allied Artists and Eros Films of England. Their idea was to make another sea-monster movie, only this time it was to be about a radioactive, blob-like thing. To cement the deal, Diamond required a screenplay, quickly, and Lourié, in an attempt to appease the English financiers who were not very keen on the blob concept, counter-proposed with his tried-and-true dinosaur formula. He called on Daniel James, a blacklisted writer who contributed to the screenplay of *The Beast from 20,000 Fathoms* and was working in film under the alias of Daniel Hyatt. Together they dashed out a script in just 10 days. Said Lourié:

"I was plagiarizing myself and reluctantly gave the draft to David Diamond with the understanding that this script was a pro forma document to be used only to sign the producers' contract and would be drastically changed and developed in London where we had to start preparations at once. But the rewriting was never done." [4]

Made for considerably less money, *The Giant Behemoth* came across as a tacky rip-off of *The Beast from 20,000 Fathoms*, though it was not without moments of interest. The story succinctly moves along without a romantic sub-plot to slow things down, and some sequences have a nice gloomy—even scary—atmosphere to them. The producers

were able to hire Kong animator Willis O'Brien to oversee the stop-motion animation, but by this time O'Brien's age was catching up with him, and his technique lacked the fire and innovation it once had (not to mention the budget he had to work with was miniscule). In addition, one whole sequence—the monster's attack on a ferry boat—was achieved using an inarticulate prop head that did not come close to matching the look of the animation puppet. In later years Lourié expressed displeasure with the final film (he barely mentions in his autobiography) and was particularly disappointed in the special effects, which were executed without his supervision sometime after he had left the production.

Barely home from his work on *The Giant Behemoth*, Lourié was contacted by Frank and Maurice King, a pair of independent film producers who were anxious to make their own prehistoric-monster movie. For better or worse, it was becoming apparent to Lourié that he was getting a reputation in Hollywood as a director of dinosaurs.

The sons of Russian immigrants, Frank and Maurice ("Maury") Kozinski began their working life manufacturing slot machines and film projectors and running a chain of vending machines before forming their own film production company, King Brothers Productions, in 1941. A third brother, Herman ("Hymie"), was also part of the company, but served in a less active role. Frank was the most involved with film production while the other brothers focused on other money-making activities such as horse racing and playing the stock market.

The brothers were deeply attached to their mother, Sarah, who was a silent partner in the film company and met with her sons in the evenings to listen to their progress and offer advice. [5] Their early productions were 'B' movies and mostly in the *noir* category—gangster and crime dramas, such as *I Killed that Man* (1941) and *Rubber Racketeers* (1942)—and were normally distributed through Allied Artists or Monogram, the latter of which they owned a 25-percent share. [5] They made a big hit with *Dillinger* (1945) starring Lawrence Tierney as the infamous kingpin, and lost money on *Gun Crazy* (1950), an edgy drama about a couple on a crime spree that would later garner praise as a *noir* masterpiece and serve as a model for *Bonnie and Clyde* (1968). The brothers' love of the circus led to *Carnival Story* (1954), a big-top melodrama photographed in color and starring Anne Baxter; and they put a bit more money and effort into *The Brave One* (1956), a family film about a Mexican boy and his pet bull that was destined to fight in the ring. [1] Their re-editing and distribution of the Japanese-made monster-movie *Rodan* (1957) turned out to be a profitable venture for the brothers. An effects-laden picture about twin pterodactyls on the attack, it played extremely well to the children's matinee crowd, and the brothers were eager to tap that market segment and the science-fiction genre again.

Although Eugène Lourié was uncertain about being typecast as a sci-fi director, he liked Frank and Maury, and the brothers won him over with promises of a bigger budget, color cinematography and more time in which to develop a screenplay. With only slight reservations, Lourié "again took the tired dinosaur out of retirement"[4] and called on his writer friend Daniel Hyatt to assist with the script. Since the King brothers were working on a deal with Japanese financiers, Japan was chosen as the story's locale.

In their initial draft, titled *Kuru Island*, an oceanic earthquake unleashes a sea monster that is captured by a couple of pearl divers off said island and brought to the Tokyo Zoo for study. But in a surprising plot development, the creature's much-larger parent soon surfaces, trampling through the city in search for her stolen offspring. Perhaps because of their devotion to their own mother, the King brothers responded very enthusiastically to the parent/child idea.

Recalling the incident with his young daughter upon seeing *The Beast from 20,000 Fathoms*, Lourié decided to break from convention and allow the creatures to live. "Here was the occasion to repair my wrongs against the sea monster species!"[6] And so the story ends with both mother and child returning safely to the sea, leaving behind a shaken and humbled mankind.[2] The story additionally bucked 1950s genre trends by forsaking the nuclear theme. These were to be natural sea animals, not mutants created or riled by atomic-bomb testing.

Early into the planning of *Kuru Island*, Lourié decided he wanted to use a man in a rubber suit rather than rely on time-consuming stop-motion animation. This was in favor of Frank King's bizarre initial idea to manufacture a giant inflatable rubber balloon and float it around the city streets. "The man in the skin," as Lourié called it, was the method preferred by Japanese filmmakers in productions such as *Godzilla* (1954) and *Rodan* (1957), and since the King brothers were planning to co-produce the film with Japanese investors and shoot it in Japan, it made sense to go that route. Also influencing this decision was Lourié's less-than-satisfying experience with the special effects on *The Giant Behemoth*. The director confided:

"I really don't have a special interest in stop-motion. You have to use certain means that are most appropriate for the visual effects you are trying to achieve. Stop-motion is a technique that makes a lot of things possible but can also make things very difficult.

"By using a man in the skin, I felt I would be in control of the whole operation without inviting anxiety over work done out of the studio."[6]

Just as Lourié and Hyatt were completing their screenplay, the deal with the Japanese financiers fell through, suddenly necessitating a change in the story's locale. Their next stop was Paris, a prospect that excited the brothers because of all the famous landmarks (the Eiffel Tower, Notre Dame, the Arc de Triomphe) they could level. Lourié went so far as to sketch some of these sequences for them on paper—including one they requested of the beast actually climbing the Eiffel Tower à la *King Kong*—before finally talking the brothers out of the idea. To Lourié, Paris made no logical sense because the parent sea monster would have to wade over a hundred miles up the Seine in order to get there. Berlin, Madrid and Rome were considered, too, before everyone settled on London, where the landmarks were recognizable enough and production facilities were most accommodating. But the change in setting was just the first of many revisions that the screenplay—now titled *Gorgo*—would undergo. According to Lourié, "The problem with *Gorgo* were my producers. The story as originally conceived was far more poetic. But the King Brothers butchered the idea entirely."[6]

Wanting to beef up the story's action, the King Brothers commissioned Robert L. Richards (writing as John Loring) to doctor the script. Lourié opposed many of the changes, finding them to be illogical, but was overruled. He especially disagreed with the many added scenes of military attacks on the parent creature, feeling that no animal, no matter how big, could survive such an onslaught. Thanks largely to the Japanese, this kind of approach had become common for the giant-creature genre. According to Lourié:

"When I asked the King brothers for the reasons for this rewrite the answer was, 'But Gene, it is to your advantage. As you will direct this film, you will have an enriched screenplay. Believe us—two brains are better than one!' I was committed to direct. And while directing tried my best to bring some logic to the embarrassing developments of the new story."[4]

In the revised script (still credited to Lourié and Hyatt), the Pacific island of Kuru becomes Nara Island off the coast of Ireland. Joe Ryan and Sam Slade are partners in a ship-wreck salvaging operation and are dredging up treasures around Nara when an undersea earthquake shakes things up. While making repairs to their ship, Joe and Sam get into a conflict with McCartin, a shifty local authority who's been hoarding treasure and doesn't want the salvagers' competition. They also form a friendship with a lonely orphan, Sean, who tells them a legend about Ogra, a sea monster that once defended the island from Viking invaders. This proves to be useful exposition when a prehistoric sea animal, disturbed by the undersea volcano, comes ashore and threatens the village. Joe and Sam smell opportunity and agree to capture the animal for a sizable sum. Acting as bait inside a bathysphere (a situation lifted from *The Beast from 20,000 Fathoms*), Joe is nearly killed when the creature attacks, but the animal is successfully netted and subdued. Snubbing the scientific community, our heroes take a better-paying deal from Dorkin's Circus in London. Little Sean stows aboard their ship and comes to London with them, expressing concern for the beast's welfare and even attempting to free it. As the creature (now known as Gorgo—a reference to both the real dinosaur species Gorgosaurus and the mythical gorgon), is being exhibited, a much larger parent makes its presence known—first leveling Nara Island, then evading a fleet of battleships before attacking London to reclaim her own.

A comparison of the screenplay with the final film reveals several key bits were never filmed, no doubt because of the expense. For example, in the early part of the story, Sam and Joe were to dive among an elaborate graveyard of Viking ships (In the film the wreck is modern and barely seen) where they are first hunted by a killer whale and then attacked by a giant octopus (!) that lives inside one of the wrecks. After the men struggle with the tentacles for some time, 'Baby' Gorgo makes its first appearance, obscured by a cloud of the cephalopod's ink. None of this ambition made it to the screen. In fact, Gorgo's first appearance is one of the lamest moments in the film, lacking any sort of suspenseful buildup and made worse by a blurry, underwhelming shot of the monster.

Another scripted scene called for 'Mother' Gorgo to attack a lighthouse. If filmed, it would have paralleled a similar situation in *The Beast from 20,000 Fathoms*. [3] But perhaps most ambitious was 'Baby' Gorgo's battle with a circus elephant—a scene that would have overtly recalled *20 Million Miles to Earth* (1957) and its standout sequence of an alien creature's deadly confrontation with an elephant at the Rome Zoo. *20 Million Miles to Earth* featured amazing stop-motion animation by Ray Harryhausen; how Lourié's crew planned to pull off such a tussle using men in suits might have been very interesting to see, if not unintentionally hilarious. All that remains of this dropped bit in the finished film is a brief shot of a static elephant (an obvious model) during 'Baby' Gorgo's failed attempt to escape its circus compound.

As with *The Giant Behemoth*, Lourié felt no obligation to provide a romantic complication to *Gorgo's* storyline, and the King Brothers didn't see a need to add one in their rewrite either. Consequently, *Gorgo* is more bare bones and direct in its intentions than most films of this type ever dare to be. Other than a fleeting appearance by a snarky woman reporter and 'Mother' Gorgo herself, there are no female characters in the film whatsoever. Children of the time, who came to see a monster toppling buildings and were eager to get on with it, more than likely didn't complain about the lack of human interest.

But for adults, *Gorgo* is perhaps too simplistic for its own good. The main characters of Joe Ryan and Sam Slade are very sketchily drawn. Basically they function as a binary Carl Denham, the filmmaker-adventurer who captured *King Kong*—though Denham was a much more interesting character. The *Gorgo* screenplay offers a bit more character meat than the film, going to some lengths to present Joe as the "heavy" of the two; but many of his expressions of callous greed were removed from the final film, which dilutes the differences between him and Sam to the point where it's difficult to tell the two apart. Sam's slightly softer character is meant to act as Joe's guilty conscience, though interestingly (and confusingly) it is Sam who first plants the idea of exploiting the beast in Joe's head. Joe's heavier nature only truly comes out in the film when he shows sudden anger toward Sean, ordering him to go below deck after an incident with the netted creature. The moment feels odd because the character is otherwise affable toward the boy. Perhaps if Joe had retained his edge in the final film, his selfless attempt to rescue Sean from danger would have had a lot more impact. As it is in the finished product, there isn't a real sense of evolution in the character.

Sam develops even less. In one scene he's presented as being driven to drink by the guilt of exploiting the creature, though he hadn't shown any signs of being guilt-ridden prior to this. His drunken attempt to free the creature leads to Joe slugging him. Later, as they prepare for the final confrontation with the mother beast, the two men simply drop their differences with a smile. This is the full extent of the characters' relationship arc. If Joe and Sam linger in the memory whatsoever it's due to the presences of the likable actors who play them: Misters Bill Travers (as Joe) and William Sylvester (as Sam).

Bill Travers (b. 1922, d. 1994) came from Newcastle and was the younger brother of actress Linden Travers, who's most remembered today for playing the bitter mistress to a caddish judge in Alfred Hitchcock's The Lady Vanishes (1938). Mr. Travers followed in his sister's footsteps, developing his acting chops on stage before landing small but noticeable roles in films at the dawn of the 1950s, including The Wooden Horse (1950) and The Browning Version (1951). He found favor with director George Cukor, who cast him as Benvolio in the 1954 film version of Romeo and Juliet, and later gave him a major role in the MGM production of Bhowani Junction

*Christopher Rhodes, Bill Travers, William Sylvester*

(1956)—a historical drama set in India during the time of Great Britain's withdrawal. Travers felt special affinity for the project, as he had served for six years in the Chindits, a British "special force" in India. Coincidentally, the author of the source novel, John Masters, had been Travers' Brigade Major there.[7]     Another early triumph for Travers was Wee Geordie (1955), in which he starred as a young Scottish man who overcomes scrawniness to become an Olympic hammer thrower. The success of these two films paved the way for a contract at MGM, and soon Travers was enjoying a steady stream of films, including *The Barrets of Wimpole Street* (1957) in which he acted alongside his future wife, Virginia McKenna. The pair appeared together on screen numerously, most famously in *Born Free* (1966) as George and Joy Adamson, a real-life couple who raised a lion cub to adulthood. A pop-culture phenomenon of the sixties, the film had a huge impact on Travers, who spent the rest of his life closely involved in wild-animal welfare projects and films that promoted the cause.

William Sylvester (b. 1922, d. 1995) was born in the same year as Travers, but hailed from the other side of the pond—Oakland, California, to be exact. As a young man, he was bitten by the acting bug, but had to take a hiatus to serve in the Navy throughout World War II. After the war, he settled in England, where he joined the Royal Academy of Dramatic Art. He started winning film roles in the early 1950s, memorably playing a villain in *The Yellow Balloon* (1952), though later he would be known for playing affable and upright characters—commonly American. After *Gorgo*, Sylvester played the skeptical hero in the low-budget horror-thriller *Devil Doll* (1964), a seedy variant on the "living ventriloquist's dummy" tale. In 1968 he landed perhaps his most famous role, that of Dr. Heywood Floyd in Stanley Kubrick's *2001: A Space Odyssey*. The second act of Kubrick's episodic film is told from Sylvester's point of view; and it is through his character that we experience the marvel of mankind's future technologies as he travels from a space station to the moon. In later years, Sylvester had a recurring part in the short-lived American science-fiction television series *Gemini Man* (1976), in which he played the boss of an invisible secret agent, and he won occasional small roles in feature films, such as *The Hindenburg* (1975) and *Heaven Can Wait* (1978).

As the wise little boy Sean, Vincent Winter played an important role in *Gorgo* by boosting the movie's kid appeal, as well as adding a welcome human element. If Sam is occasionally Joe's guilty conscience, then Sean serves

13

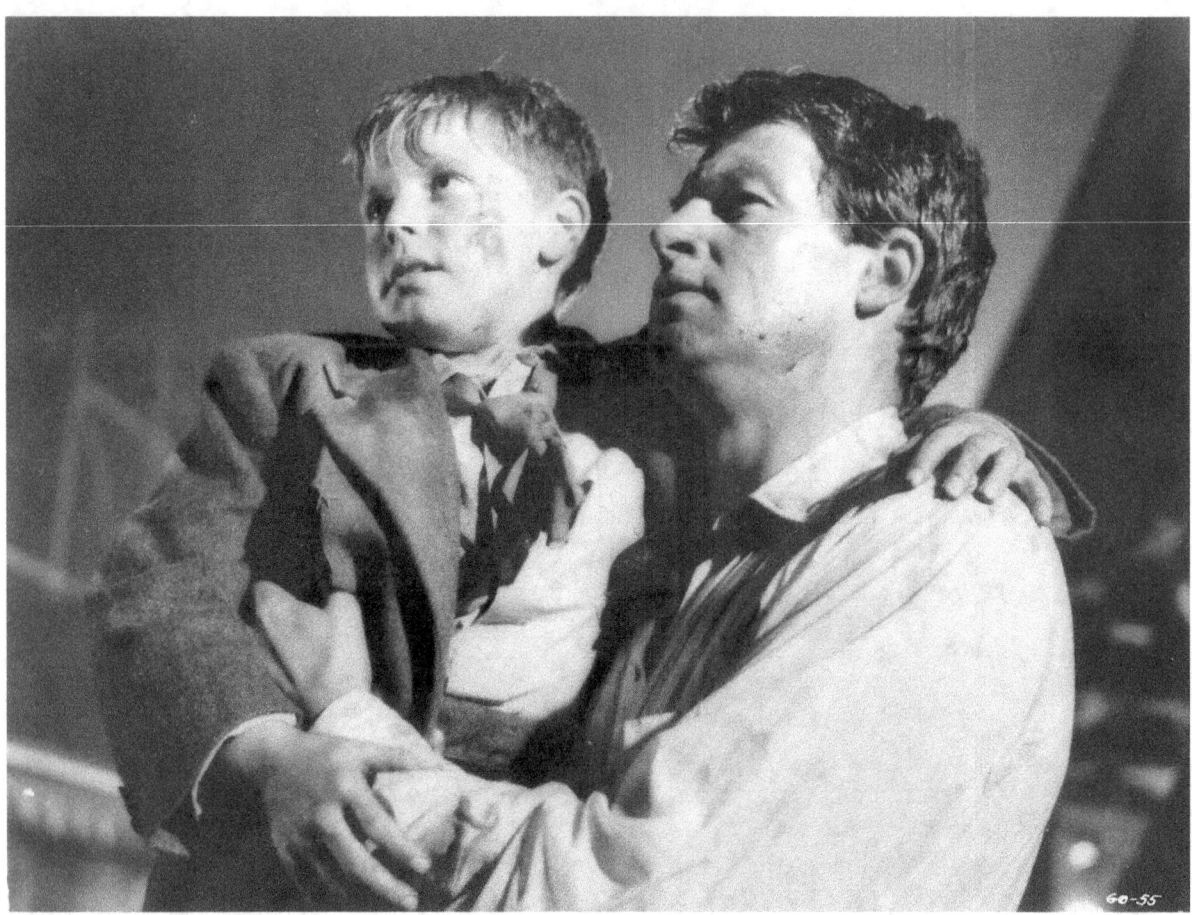

Vincent Winter, Bill Travers

that purpose for both men. Continually he reminds his entrepreneurial guardians that by capturing and displaying Gorgo for mass entertainment, they've done "a bad thing... a *terrible* bad thing." Also, as an orphan, Sean serves as a human counterpart to 'Baby' Gorgo—a parallel that becomes dramatically apparent as 'Mama' Gorgo devastates the city trying to find her baby while Joe concurrently searches the rubble for Sean. In both unfolding situations, a parent (or in Joe's case, a parent figure) desperately seeks reunion with a child.

Born in 1947 in Aberdeen Scotland, Vincent Winter was cast in a major role in the British film *The Kidnappers* (1953, aka *The Little Kidnappers*) at the age of five and had to be coached his lines verbally since he could not yet read. According to director Philip Leacock, "He had a memory like a computer; he would do his own lines aloud and then silently mouth everyone else's words." [8] The film was about two children who find a baby in the woods and attempt to secretly care for it, as they would a pet. Both Winter and his co-star John Whiteley were awarded special mini-Oscars for their "Outstanding Juvenile Performances."

More roles followed, and in 1955 he appeared in *The Dark Avenger*, an adventure vehicle for an aging Errol Flynn. Flynn was reportedly so taken with Winter that he toyed with the notion of adopting the boy. After his stint on

*Gorgo*, Winter became a contract player with Walt Disney and appeared in a number of family films throughout the sixties, including *Grayfrier's Bobby* (1961) and *The Three Lives of Thomasina* (1964). Advised that making the transition from child to adult actor could be fraught with difficulties and disappointments, Winter switched to a career behind the cameras later in life. He worked in various capacities, usually as a production manager or assistant director. Some of the higher-profile pictures he worked on included *Superman* (1978), *Indiana Jones and the Temple of Doom* (1984) and *The Color Purple* (1985).

Vincent Winter died in 1998 at the age of 51. As Sean in *Gorgo*, he functioned as a surrogate for not only Lourié's own daughter (who famously chastised her father for killing *The Beast from 20,000 Fathoms*) but for all child audience members who similarly identified with the misunderstood beast. Much of the emotional punch of the ending has Vincent to thank, as he looks wonderingly at the reunited creatures and remarks, "They're going back now... back to the sea."

His performance was admirably restrained, considering the potential for sentimentality that both he and Lourié could have wrung from it. Nevertheless, not everybody was a fan of the boy's role in the picture. In his excellent survey of 1950s science-fiction films, *Keep Watching the*

*Skies*, film historian Bill Warren felt Sean was "unreal" and further wrote, "Sean is one of those children's roles written by people who do not understand children, who seem to feel that because kids are young, they are more in touch with nature, or with animals." [9]

Surprisingly, Eugène Lourié was not a fan of Winter either, but his grievances were more about the actor than the character. "I had an idea to use another boy," the director claimed. "But this boy Winter had a little bit of experience—and he was an old ham already." [10]

Regardless of one's opinion of Sean or Vincent Winter's portrayal of him, there's no denying his influence on the genre. In the coming years, children (usually boys) would become increasingly common characters in giant-monster movies, particularly those produced in Japan. In *Gammera the Invincible* (1966), a little boy formed an emotional bond with a giant fire-breathing turtle; and in *Godzilla's Revenge* (1969), giant monsters became metaphors for schoolyard bullies when a lonely, ostracized kid fantasized about adventures on an island swarming with monsters. The trend saw its latest incarnation in the big-budgeted Hollywood production, *Super-8* (2011), in which a group of kids confronted a colossal alien menace.

Arguably the most important stars of *Gorgo*, however, are the monsters—and while the "man-in-suit" method is not ideal for a dinosaur, due their anatomical differences with the human body, the approach had its advantages. For one thing, Lourié would be able to direct the special effects on set rather than wait months later for animation to be completed. Like Godzilla, Gorgo was to be a bipedal dinosaur, sort of like a Tyrannosaurus, which was completely wrong for an ocean-dwelling animal, but scientific accuracy clearly wasn't on anyone's minds.

In spite of there being two creatures in the script, only one costume was built. While this decision certainly helped streamline the production process, it's disappointing from a viewer's perspective. It seems an infant would have less developed features than an adult animal, and a different look might have given each beast some individual character.

Lourié originally wanted a lightweight costume to allow faster and more flexible movement from the actor within. He consulted with Nicolai Wilke, a Russian special effects technician, who was too ill to join the production but helped Lourié come up with sketches of the monster and ideas about how it should be built. Nevertheless, the British technicians had their own ideas about Gorgo's construction, outfitting the headpiece with heavy hydraulics that allowed for mouth, eye, fin and tail movements. Each hydraulic movement was independently operated from a push-button box inside the costume. A mold was made from an 8-foot clay sculpture, and several thick rubber "skins" were manufactured for safety in the event of rips. The final costume was so hot and heavy that a person could only bear to be in it for short periods of time. Consequently, Gorgo was portrayed by three stuntmen who switched out every couple of hours on the set. One

Property of National Screen Service Corp. Licensed for display only in connection with the exhibition of this picture at your theatre. Must be returned immediately thereafter.

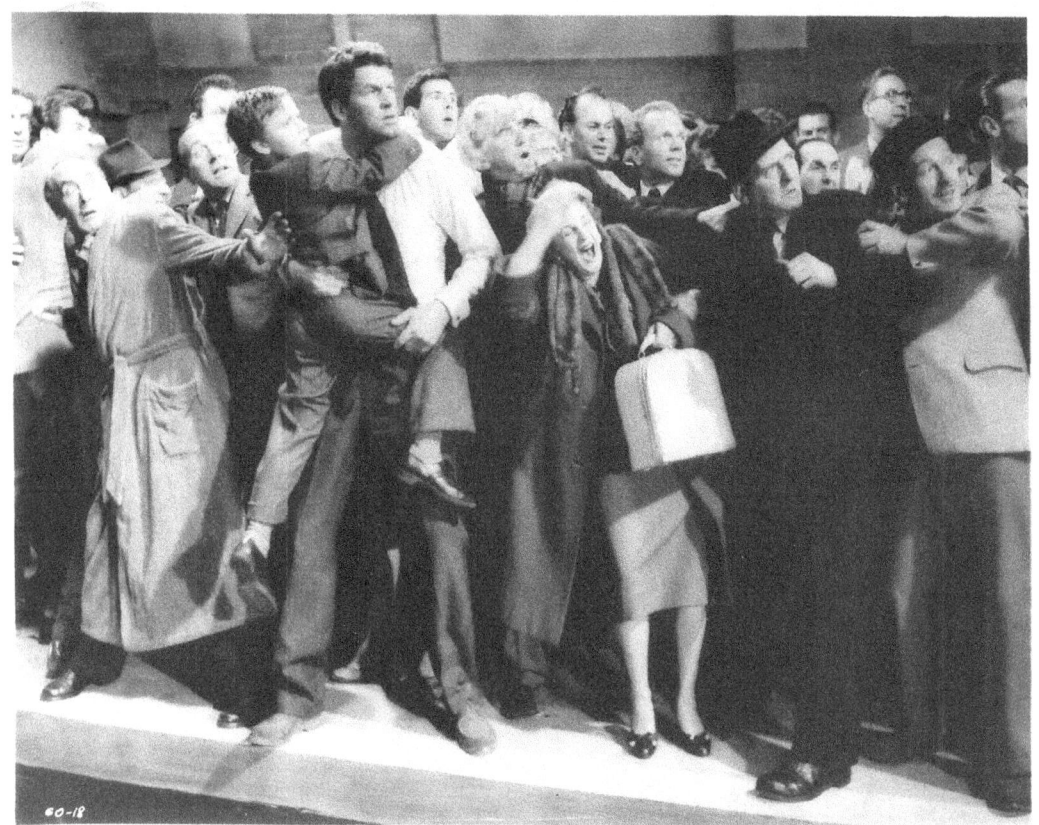

"GORGO"
A King Brothers Production — An M-G-M Release

Copyright © 1961, Metro-Goldwyn-Mayer Inc. Permission granted for Newspaper and Magazine reproduction. Made in U.S.A.

61/36

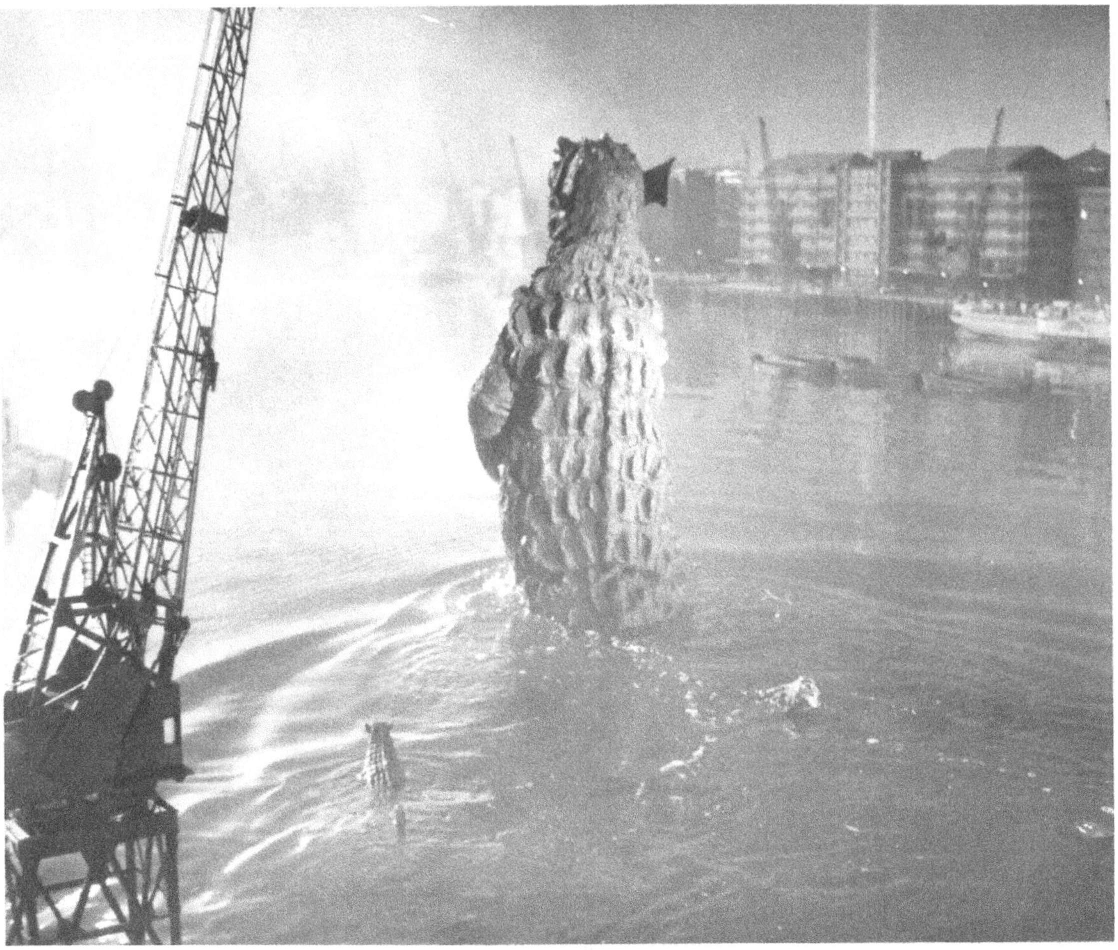

of them was Mick Dillon, a former jockey who got into stunt work for films in the 1950s. He doubled for Ringo Starr in *Help!* (1965) and played other monsters on occasion, including a walking carnivorous plant in *The Day of the Triffids* (1963) and a Dalek (which looks something like a walking trashcan) in *Dr. Who and the Daleks* (1965).

The final result of the Gorgo costume is a mixed bag. While the suit has its faults and limitations (a certain clumsy stiffness, an unconvincing "hinge-door" mouth), the filmmakers at least do a commendable job of giving it weight and power by consistently filming at a high frame rate (called "over-cranking"). The creature also has tremendous visual appeal: the face is fearsome and coldly reptilian; the claws are oversized and curved, like huge backhoe shovels; the scaly textures of its alligator-like hide are full of convincing detail; and the ear fins that wiggle from time to time are oddly endearing. Gorgo's design may have been inspired by Godzilla, but the aesthetic is impressive and holds its own against the so-called "King of the Monsters."

*Gorgo* commenced shooting in September of 1959 with Freddie Young serving as director of photography. Young was one of Britain's most renowned cinematographers, having been at it since 1928 and involved in an astounding number of great films: *49th Parallel* (1941), *Ivanhoe* (1952) and *Lust for Life* (1956) to list just a few. Immediately after his work on *Gorgo*, Young photographed director David Lean's historical epic *Lawrence of Arabia* (1962)—widely considered one of the most beautifully shot widescreen films—and continued his association with Lean on *Doctor Zhivago* (1965) and *Ryan's Daughter* (1970), winning Oscars for all three. His work on *Gorgo* has been difficult to judge fairly over the years because of the proliferation of bad prints and murky video copes. It's clear, however, that his eye for dramatic compositions and feeling for atmosphere served the production well. Part of the effectiveness of the man-in-suit monster must be attributed to Young's dramatic, low-key lighting of it. Early scenes set at sea and on the island have a gritty quality, not just from the inherent film grain of the fast Eastmancolor stock he was saddled with, but from the double printing of smoke over originally bright and sunny footage. Meant to give the locale a misty quality, the effect isn't always successful and tends to cheapen the look of the film at times.

The Nara Island scenes of *Gorgo* were filmed at Bullock Harbour and Coliemore Harbour near Dublin, while the remainder of the picture was shot in London and on the soundstages of MGM's studio in Borehamwood. The largest stage was reserved for the 200-foot long Thames River set, which contained a pool of water three feet deep and included realistic miniatures of waterfront buildings and the Tower Bridge. Art director Elliot Scott was allotted just $75,000 to create all the miniature sets and breakaway buildings, including Big Ben, the Houses of Parliament, Piccadilly Circus and Battersea Funfair. [12]

"*Gorgo* was almost like a circus act," Lourié mused. "You had to have a series of 20 acts, and each one had to be stronger than the previous one." [6] Of all the film's many "circus acts" the biggest and most impressive was the collapse of the Tower Bride from 'Mother' Gorgo's wrath—a special effects showpiece made additionally exciting by fast cutting between multiple camera angles and hair-raising sound effects. "It took 10 weeks to build the set," claimed Maury King, "and Gorgo ruined it in 10 minutes. We couldn't have done a second take if we had wanted to!" [13]

Filming on the waterfront set proved to be especially grueling for the performers in the Gorgo suit. For one scene the water was set on fire, and had to be a harrowing situation for the stuntman wading between the walls of flame. The filming wasn't without its unexpected moments of levity, however. Lourié recalled:

"The 'river' was not very deep, just knee high water. It was a comical scene, because the stunt man who played the beast had trouble walking through the water with the big, clumsy dinosaur's feet. So we cut the costume, and from the knees down were human legs with tennis shoes. It was a very strange beast!" [10]

In addition to the rubber suit, a small marionette was created for a couple of faked underwater shots, and huge, full-scale parts of Gorgo—the head, claws and tail—were built to be shot with the actors on location and in the studio. The full-scale claw was used in a wonderfully atmospheric publicity still where it was poised above two men in a small fishing boat. In the film, the claw descends to smash the boat in two, but the shot is disappointingly fleeting. Almost perfectly matching the look of the costume, the head was motorized to allow for mouth and eye movement. The blood-red eyes were illuminated like headlamps, as they were for the costume—a visually dramatic if unrealistic touch. For scenes of 'Baby' Gorgo being transported, a tarpaulin helped disguise the fact that the torso and lower limbs were missing.

One scene called for the full-scale Gorgo prop to be paraded around London on the flatbed of a truck. Lourié expected that he would be hiring a sizable crowd of extras to line the streets, but the King brothers nixed that plan, thinking the mere sight of their mighty monster would attract all the people they needed—free of charge. The plan backfired, however, when the filmmakers were forced to shoot at the crack of dawn on a Sunday morning—the only time the London authorities would grant permission. Multiple cameras were set up to catch the crowd's reactions, including one hidden inside the Gorgo prop itself. Sadly, though, not many people were up and about at 7 a.m. on a Sunday morn; and the few scattered pedestrians that happened to be at Piccadilly Circus and Trafalgar Square when Gorgo whizzed by looked either unimpressed or confused by the spectacle. Later on, Lourié tried to fix the problem the best he could by presenting the scene as a news story on TV and staging additional reactions from people inside pubs.

But aside from this one unfortunate incident, the London authorities and British armed forces were extremely accommodating to the filmmakers, even agreeing to mobilize military equipment on their behalf. As Lourié remembered it:

"We could move large motorized units in front of the Parliament Building and film the approaches of to the Tower Bridge on different nights. Tanks were crossing suburbs of London! We could take over entire city blocks to stage scenes of panic and desperation." [6]

These scenes of mass panic are perhaps Lourié's strongest work as a director. The situation of crowds fleeing down city streets had recurred in all of his dinosaur pictures, but with Gorgo he finally had the number of extras needed to effectively convey a city thrown into total chaos. An especially horrifying sequence shows curious bystanders being engulfed in flames; while in another, a hoard of people packs into a subway terminal moments before the monster's weight collapses the roof upon them (an idea that would resurface in Guillermo Del Toro's giant-creature epic Pacific Rim, 2013). As panic reaches a fever pitch, an end-times prophet shouts for us to "Repent!" as he's swept away by a wave of people and finally crushed to death. A little girl drops her doll in the street as her mother pulls her along. The "lost toy" was a symbol that recurred in some form in all three of Lourié's dinosaur pictures.

After wrapping on 24 days of principal photography, it was time to concentrate on the many optical effects shots required to complete the picture. Gorgo's special photographic effects were supervised by Tom Howard, one of the field's top talents. As a young man, Howard worked in the special effects department of Alexander Korda's Denham Studios, where he created a travelling matte process for color film and helped provide eye-popping visuals for Korda's Arabian Nights spectacle The Thief of Bagdad (1940). Because the war forced Korda to complete the film in Hollywood, Howard ended up not receiving a credit or even a mention when the film won an Oscar for special effects. He won his first Oscar for his work on David Lean's romantic ghost tale Blithe Spirit (1945), and for nearly two decades served as Director of Special Effects for MGM's

studio in England. With MGM, he oversaw and provided photographic effects for the biblical epic Quo Vadis (1951), the World War II adventure Where Eagles Dare (1968), the haunted house thriller The Haunting (1963) and the science-fiction masterpiece 2001: A Space Odyssey. He won his second Academy Award for his work on George Pal's fantasy-musical Tom Thumb (1958) for which he developed a moving split-matte process dubbed "Automotion." Howard described the effect for film historian John Brosnan:

"This is split screen work where the split moves within the screen as the scene is progressing. Instead of finding a convenient split-line, you split down anything... you split down the front of a face... or anywhere at all. You can make a man move around himself without a travelling matte." [11]

Howard used the effect on Gorgo to more realistically combine elements of the man-in-monster suit, collapsing miniature buildings and footage of people running in terror. Reportedly the film contained over 80 optical effect shots. Unfortunately the haste of cranking out so many optical effects led to some transparency of composited images and fringed edges on blue screen work. "There was simply no time to make corrections," Lourié regretted. "The optical department could not run it through more than once." [6] Some of the more successful composites include the mother monster's destruction of a dazzlingly neon-lit Piccadilly Circus (a funny scene, as the creature knocks down a sign advertising her offspring), and a shocking, almost surreal moment when a ton of rubble from one film element falls on top of another element of harried bystanders.

MGM's publicity department hyped Automotion upon Gorgo's release, but didn't bother looking into what it actually was and touted it as the process the filmmakers used to give the monsters realistic movement. (They probably assumed it was something similar to "Dynamation," the term coined for the animation effects in Ray Harryhausen's films.) Additionally, in one press release the publicist misspelled the word as "Sutomotion," and ever since people have confused the process in Gorgo with "Suitmation," a term that is now popularly used for the technique of men in rubber monster suits.

In his memoirs, Lourié recalled one of the "trickiest" shots to pull off was when the two monsters were finally shown together. The challenge was that there was only one 'Gorgo' costume, plus the animals were supposed to be drastically different in height.

"In the scene of the two monsters making their way to the waterfront among the burning buildings, the master shot was of the 'mother' moving, shot against the smaller-scale miniature set of the waterfront. The 'baby' was shot separately on blue backing, reduced, and printed onto the master shot by a traveling matte process. In the same shot we added views of panicky, running people, shot on the studio back lot and fitted exactly into a predetermined place on the frame." [4]

Gorgo's production costs ran $650,000 but the film ended up costing $2 million when distribution was added in—a pretty big sum in those days. Overall, Lourié was proud of their accomplishments. "The film in fact contained a multitude of difficult trick shots made mostly in unusual haste; amazingly, only very few had some technical flaws." [4]

On December 11, 1959, the Hollywood Reporter announced that filming had completed and the King brothers were returning from London to edit the picture in the states. The cutting fell to Eric Boyd-Perkins, a British editor who worked on a slew of British horror films throughout his career, including *The Two faces of Dr. Jekyll* (1960), *Curse of the Mummy's Tomb* (1964) and *The Wicker Man* (1973). One of the biggest challenges Boyd-Perkins faced with *Gorgo* was stitching together the many scenes of military retaliation against the parent monster. These included a full-on assault from Navy battleships, rounds of tank and mortar fire, plus heavy bombardment from RAF fighter jets. To curb costs, Boyd-Perkins had to cobble together these scenes using stock footage of military drills and actual warfare. The footage came from various sources, and the color-faded and scratchy quality of much of it stands out. In spite of this, Boyd-Perkins does a commendable job of keeping the pace lively. Some of the stock footage already appeared in the King brothers' Americanized version of *Rodan*. In later years, Lourié got hold of a print of *Gorgo* and recut the film for his own personal enjoyment, removing all the military intervention bits, which he detested. "Everything was so much better," he told writer Paul Mandell, "even to the point where it was understandable!" [6]

Another problematic element to the editing was the insertion of a broadcast reporter's running commentary throughout 'Mother' Gorgo's attack on London. The character (played by Maurice Kaufman, who had a bit part as a min-sub commander in Lourié's *The Giant Behemoth*) was an 11th hour addition after location photography had already wrapped. At first the reporter's presence is helpful in giving voice to the people's apprehension as the mother beast approaches; but when he keeps popping up in the middle of every set-piece with no shortness of breath or any explanation of how he got there so fast, the situation quickly becomes ridiculous. The actor was filmed in a studio in front of a blue screen and optically inserted into the action. Sometimes perspectives between him and the backgrounds don't even match. It begs the question: why

on earth did the King brothers feel the need to insert this unnecessary element at the last minute? Perhaps they were aping Raymond Burr's memorable newspaper-reporter character from *Godzilla King of the Monsters* (1955), or maybe they thought it would add dramatic weight to punctuate every visual effect with journalistic hyperbol.

One of the most important artistic contributions to a monster movie is its music score. Back when special effects lacked total realism, it was often the music that smoothed over the rough patches and instilled a sense of wonder in the viewer. It was certainly the case with *King Kong*, for which composer Max Steiner made us feel a myriad of emotions—from terror to sadness—for what was essentially a rubber puppet, all through the power and sweep of his groundbreaking, Wagnerian score. Happily, *Gorgo* has an especially strong and dramatic underscore by Italian composer Angelo Francesca Lavagnino.

*Angelo Francesca Lavagnino*

Born in Genova to a musically gifted family, Lavagnino (b. 1909, d. 1987) studied violin and composition at the Conservatory of Milan and composed numerous concert works—including three symphonic poems, a violin concerto and an opera—before he started working in film in the mid-1940s. He got into film scoring partly for financial reasons, but also because he had an intense interest in the art form. In 1950, he met Orson Welles, who was then trying to finance and make films in Europe, and was hired by the eccentric director to score his adaptation of Shakespeare's *Othello* (1951), as well as his fantasy on the character of Falstaff, *Chimes at Midnight* (1965). For the strange John Wayne pseudo-western *Legend of the Lost* (1957), Lavagnino memorably created an eerie, dream-like tone for the picture's Sahara desert settings. During the span of his career, Lavagnino scored for every genre imaginable, including westerns (*Requiem for a Gringo*, 1968), ancient historical adventure-fantasies known as "peplum" (*The Colossus of Rhodes*, 1961), horror (*Castle of the Living Dead*, 1964), science fiction (*The War of the Planets*, 1966) and even travelogue documentaries (*Lost Continent*, 1955). Lavagnino's score for *Gorgo* is one of his best and most dramatically varied. It is distinguished by a gentle seafaring theme, played in the opening titles and elsewhere by an accordion, an instrument that has historical associations with the sea. Debussy's *La Mer* appears to be an influence in the underwater sequences, where impressionistic woodwind figures and hypnotic effects from harps and vibraphone lend a sense of mystery to the deep. For sequences involving the monsters, Lavagnino unleashes the full might of the orchestra, characterizing the monsters with frenzied brass motifs and setting a tense, percussive pulse beat to the London finale. When the creatures are reunited in the end, the composer returns to his romantic, maritime theme, only now it's taken up by full symphony orchestra. This lush, final rendition is enough to make a grown man cry—which is quite a feat, considering how inexpressive the monsters otherwise are.

The score was recorded by members of the esteemed London Symphony Orchestra under the baton of Muir Mathieson, a prolific conductor of British film scores. Lavagnino wrote 47 minutes worth of music for *Gorgo*, of which only 37 minutes was used. When record producer David Schecter recorded a suite from the score for a 1998 compact disc, he found that the written scores were in Lavagnino's own handwriting, which seemed to indicate he did his own orchestrations. This is unusual because film composers are normally under the gun and have to rely on orchestrators to make their deadlines. Schecter also noted:

"Not only did the producers unmercifully edit *Gorgo* when Lourié finished it, but Lavagnino's score was also ripped to shreds, with whole cues dropped from the film, others drastically reduced in length, and too many of them drowned out by unbearably loud and unremitting sound effects. Lavagnino said he was asked to write a lot of music for the film, so he must have been discouraged when much of what he had been asked to provide was later excised. The music listed on the cue sheets bears little resemblance to what's in the film, which implies that the movie's soundtrack was edited even after the cue sheets were compiled." [14]

Prior to the film's opening in the West, the King brothers launched a monster-sized marketing campaign, announcing to the Hollywood Reporter that they were spending a record $280,000 on promotion. The dramatic poster art, painted by Joseph Smith, showed Big Ben and other London buildings falling to the might of 'Mother.' The title of *Gorgo* was done in the carved-in-stone, three-dimensional style that Smith had employed for *Ben-Hur* and which became the rage for historical epics throughout the 1960s. Ads were emblazoned with the promises, "Like Nothing You've Ever Seen Before!" and "This is the BIG one!" Lobby cards came in two versions: those that showed

Gorgo in all its glory and those that hid the monster 's face behind hyperbolic text.

To ensure people in small towns got the word, Maury and Frank King sat down with NEA Hollywood correspondent Erskine Johnson for a playful interview that was distributed to newspapers across the United States. Their main goal was to promote *Gorgo* as a wholesome family picture and paint the monsters as "lovable." Frank asserted, "We wouldn't dare make a movie without the Code Seal of Approval; our mother wouldn't let us. Our mother is right—you gotta have heart!" When Erskine reminded the brothers about their former run of less-than-wholesome gangster pictures, Frank admitted to the crime, but that their mother had been very unhappy with them. "That's why we switched to movies about togetherness and movies with heart. Our big Gorgo is really sweet until it gets mad." Chomping on a fat cigar, Maury added, "And little Gorgo is cuddly as a panda bear. Our mother loved it!" The rather strange and silly talk ended with Maury's assertion that "This picture has more heart than *King Kong*. You will feel sorry for big and little Gorgo just like you felt sorry for King Kong!" [15]

Drumming up a little extra pre-release buzz, Frank King sent several female models out into the streets of New York with picket signs that read "My hero, Gorgo!" and "Rock Hudson – No! Gorgo – Yes!"

Winning the approval of children was vital to *Gorgo*'s success. To help stoke small-fry excitement, King Brothers and MGM licensed 'Mother' and 'Baby' to Charlton Publishing Company for a series of colorful comic book adventures. The first issue debuted at a time when giant monsters were common characters in comic books, having taken the place of vampires, zombies and other horror subjects deemed too scary for kids once the Comics Code Authority was formed in 1954. A small, Connecticut-based operation, Charlton had recently enjoyed a profitable run with their comic-book adaptation of the giant-ape flick *Konga* before they snatched up the rights to *Gorgo*. MGM plugged the comic in press books that were sent to theaters prior to the film's release. They advised theaters to display the books in their lobby and sell them for "extra profits." [16]

Written by Joe Gill, the first issue was a succinct adaptation of the movie screenplay and, interestingly, retained the giant octopus scene that was omitted by the filmmakers. Subsequent issues pitted 'Mother' and 'Baby' against an assortment of colorful foes, including giant squids, dinosaurs, aliens and a Castro-like dictator. The comic ran for 23 issues, 10 of which were drawn by Steve Ditko, a shy, hard-working illustrator who specialized in horror and mystery books throughout the 1950s, and who made pop-culture history by co-creating Spider-Man and Dr. Strange for Marvel, remarkably in the same year that he

was drawing *Gorgo*. As time went along, Ditko humanized the Gorgo creatures through his expressive art, by giving them oddly human-like anatomies and taking time away from the action to show 'Mother' and 'Baby' in scenes of playful affection.

Additionally, Charlton published a paperback novelization of *Gorgo* through their Monarch Books division. Monarch, which specialized in cheap-thrill page-turners like *The Gang Girls* and *Payola Woman*, churned out a number of movie tie-ins at the time; and the one thing they all had in common (besides being cheaply done) was their authors' propensity to go off on enthusiastic and seamy departures from the original storylines. Published in July of 1960, *Gorgo* was written by Carson Bingham, a pseudonym for Bruce Cassiday, who was then an editor at Argosy magazine. To interject sex into a sexless story, Bingham/Cassiday had to invent a major new character: a hot young Nara Island native named Moira, who falls for Sam Slade (the story's narrator) and enjoys several steamy encounters with him, including this one at the beach...

"Take me, Somhairle," she whispered. "I demand to be taken." She clutched my hand in hers and I pressed her body, warm and quivering, to mine. Somehow I found the button to the dungarees she wore, and unbuttoned them, and slipped the clothes off her trembling flesh until there was nothing between us but the warmth of our bodies. She strained and twisted and clutched at me in the ecstasy of her stabbing, tearing pain, and with the unfeigned sincerity of innocence, she abandoned herself to me. And for me it was like dying and being reborn. It was a dizzying climb to a cloud of ecstasy such as I'd never experienced before. When the tumult and madness between us finally subsided, we lay there, breathless and sated and content, surrounded by the essence and magic of our love."

*Konga, Reptilicus, The Brides of Dracula* and others received the same dirty treatment from the Monarch stable of hack writers. But from a marketing standpoint, this was a seriously messed up affair. Most of the people who snatched up the monster-movie tie-ins were not of the intended "raincoat" crowd, but were innocent children who got an unexpected peek into adult kinkiness if they ever decided to crack the spines. Even more bizarre, those kids may have gotten a whiff of something unexpected, too, as Monarch was then experimenting with perfumed paper and liked to give each book a special "theme" scent (for example, they supposedly infused western novels with a leathery odor). Recently a member of the Classic Horror Film Board, an online forum of horror-movie devotees, recalled that his *Gorgo* paperback smelled a lot like bubble-bath soap!

*Gorgo* premiered on December 24, 1960—not in England where it was made or the U.S. where the distributor resided, but in the major cities of Japan. The Hollywood Reporter reported that the film opened to "the biggest business of any film to play the chain theaters in Kobe, Kyoto and Osaka in the past 12 months." On February 10, 1961, the picture opened in the United States at the Fox Theater in Philadelphia, just before nationwide bookings started rolling over the George Washington Birthday holiday. According to The Hollywood Reporter, "Biz was among the biggest of any Metro release in five years." When the film finally opened in England, it was rather stupidly slapped with an 'X' Certificate rating by the British Board of Film Classification (BBFC), which restricted anyone under the age of 16—only the film's intended target audience—from attending!

Critical reaction to Gorgo in the United States was generally good. The New York Times was one of the picture's most enthusiastic advocates, declaring, "For awesome technical wizardry and the boiling crescendo of its climax—the most hair-raising close-up of metropolitan panic we've ever seen on film—this is probably the best outright monster shocker since King Kong." Variety appreciated the film's exploitation potential and "the painstaking physical artistry" of Tom Howard's technical contributions, but felt the picture failed "in its attempt to add "a new human dimension" and that its "attempt to squeeze in some sort of message about man's mercenary motivations at the expense of his appreciation of the finer things in life (such as respecting the love of a dragon for her offspring) is largely abortive." Variety commended Lourié for the staging of the military assaults against Gorgo—praise which no doubt annoyed the director, who was opposed to such sequences in the first place.

Years after the dust settled on a decimated London, Lourié claimed, "It was a big pleasure" to make Gorgo. He found the shooting of the crowd scenes and the destruction of miniatures enjoyable, but he was less satisfied with the monster and how it was achieved with a man in a suit. He had to admit, "Frame by frame animation makes the animal more alive." [10]   And for that reason (and probably a host of others), he considered The Beast from 20,000 Fathoms his personal favorite of his dinosaur trilogy.

Gorgo was the last feature film that Eugène Lourié directed. He continued to work in films as an art director and production designer, contributing sets to Samuel Fuller's eccentric sixties melodramas Shock Corridor (1963) and The Naked Kiss (1964). He also brought his experience to special-effects heavy productions like Crack in the World (1965) and Krakatoa: East of Java (1969). The King brothers followed Gorgo with another children's fantasy, Captain Sindbad (1963), an Arabian Nights fantasy intended to compete with Ray Harryhausen's superior efforts in that realm. The brothers tried their hand at producing a TV series—the India-set boys' adventure, Maya (1967), based on their 1966 feature film of the same name—before they got out of films altogether by the turn of the seventies.

In spite of Gorgo's success at the box office, a sequel was never produced (not very surprising given that Hollywood rarely made sequels back then), nor did it stoke much interest in giant creature films from Hollywood or Great Britain. In Japan, however, it was a different story. Gorgo's solid performance there helped inspire Japanese film studios to crank out a steady stream of giant monster pictures over the next decade—so many, in fact, that Japan soon took over as the specialists in this genre.  Gorgo's influence can be felt in a number of these films. Nikkatsu Corporation's Gappa: The Triphibian Monster (aka Monster from a Prehistoric Planet, 1967) recycled Gorgo's basic plot, with the addition of two parent creatures on a warpath to reclaim their baby from exploiters. Toho's Son of Godzilla (1967) continued the theme of a parent/child bond between giant monsters; and in 1993's Godzilla vs. MechaGodzilla, the situation repeated itself with a bit more seriousness when the star dragon tore up Kyoto to find a newly hatched 'Baby' of its species. The film even mimicked Gorgo's ending when the two monsters turned their backs on humanity and returned to their "home" in the ocean depths.

Unfortunately, problems with copyright led to MGM losing control of Gorgo during the age of home video. For years, bad quality copies of the film made from washed out prints appeared on VHS and DVD, perpetuating the notion that Gorgo was a shoddy, ugly film. VCI finally managed a decent restoration in 2013 for their high-definition, Blu-ray edition, which came closer than ever to approximating what people saw on the big screen back in 1961. In recent years Gorgo has popped up in some unexpected places. It was good-naturedly lampooned by the cable series Mystery Science Theater 3000 in 1998; and in 2009, filmmaker Benjamin Craig paid affectionate homage with his comedy short Waiting for Gorgo —in which a young lady investigated a secret department of the Ministry of Defense, sworn to protect England from monster attacks.

Gorgo was a cornerstone in the giant-creature genre. It brought a grand finish to a decade of such films in the West, while helping to launch a revival of creature features in the East. It will always be remembered with reverence by fans of these films and hopefully will continue to inspire awe in youngsters who are exposed to it today. 'Mother' and 'Baby' may have left a shattered nation and gone back to the sea, but they will always be remembered for the tremendously exciting time they gave us on movie and television screens big and small. They were like nothing we ever saw—indeed.

Bill Travers as Joe Ryan
William Sylvester as Sam Slade
Vincent Winter as Sean
Christopher Rhodes as McCartin
Joseph O'Conor as Professor Hendricks
Bruce Seton as Professor Flaherty
Martin Benson as Mr. Dorkin
Maurice Kaufmann as Radio Reporter
Basil Dignam as Admiral Brooks
Mick Dillon as Gorgo

*Directed by* Eugène Lourié Produced by Wilfred Eades
Herman King *Written by* Robert L. Richards Daniel
James Eugène Lourié  *Music by* Angelo Francesco La-
vagnino *Cinematography* Freddie Young *:* Eric Boyd-Per-
kins *Distributed by* UnitedStates: Metro-Goldwyn-Mayer
- *United Kingdom:* British Lion-Columbia Ltd Release
dates *United States:* 29 March 1961 *United Kingdom:* 27
October 1961 Running time 72 min. *Country* United
Kingdom *Language* English, Irish

## NOTES

[1] *The Brave One* was written by Dalton Trumbo, who was then blacklisted and writing under the alias Robert Rich. The film won that year's Academy Award for Best Original Screenplay. Interestingly, the King brothers were later sued by independent film producer Edward Nassour for plagiarizing one of his own never-realized projects: *Ring Around Saturn*, which was based on a very similar story by stop-motion animator Willis O'Brien and was to feature an animated bull, as well as a dinosaur.

[2] It may have seemed innovative at the time that the monsters were not destroyed by the authorities, but the first major film of this type, the 1925 production of Arthur Conan Doyle's *The Lost World*, ended similarly. In that much earlier film, Professor Challenger captured a living brontosaurus and brought it back to London for exhibition. The animal broke free and caused a bit of mayhem in the city streets before falling off the Tower Bridge and swimming away down the Thames.

[3] Purely for publicity reasons, the producers of *The Beast from 20,000 Fathoms* bought the rights to a Ray Bradbury short story, "The Foghorn," which had recently appeared in the Saturday Evening Post. A quick scene of the monster toppling a lighthouse was added to tie in with the Bradbury story, which otherwise bore no resemblance to the film.

## SOURCES

[4] *My Work in Films* by Eugène Lourié, Harcourt Brace Jovanovich, Publishers, 1985, pp. 222 – 246.
[5] Interview with Eddie Muller, Warner Archive podcast, August 2, 2013, Warnerarchive.tumblr.com
[6] *Of Beasts and Behemoths Part III*, article by Paul Mandell, *Fantastic Films*, May 1980.
[7] Obituary: Bill Travers by David Shipman, *The Independent*, April 1, 1994.
[8] Obituary: Vincent Winter by Tom Vallance, *The Independent*, Nov. 23, 1998.
[9] *Keep Watching the Skies*, 2nd Ed., by Bill Warren, McFarland & Company, Inc., p. 351.
[10] Interview with Eugène Lourié, *They Fought in the Creature Features* by Tom Weaver, McFarland & Company Inc., 1995, pp. 207-210.
[11] *Movie Magic: The Story of Special Effects in the Cinema* by John Brosnan, Plume Books, New American Library, St. Martin's Press, 1976, p. 86.
[12] *The Making of Gorgo* by Deborah Del Vecchio, *Chiller Theatre Magazine* #6, January, 1996.
[13] *Gorgo*, edited by Jeff Rovin, Movie Monsters #1, Dec. 1974.
[14] *More Monstrous Movie Music*, compact disc liner notes by David Schecter, Monstrous Movie Music, 1998.
[15] *Film Makers Create Monsters With Heart* by Erskine Johnson, *Daily Capital News*, Jefferson City, Mo., January 31, 1961; *Movie Firm Makes Lovable Monsters* by Erskine Johnson, *The Odessa American*, Odessa Texas, February 24, 1960.
[16] *Ditko Monsters: Gorgo!*, edited by Craig Yoe, IDW Publishing, 2013, p.16.

## ACKNOWLEDGMENTS

The author would like to thank the following for their help in researching this article:
John Charles, Richard Harland Smith, Tom Weaver.

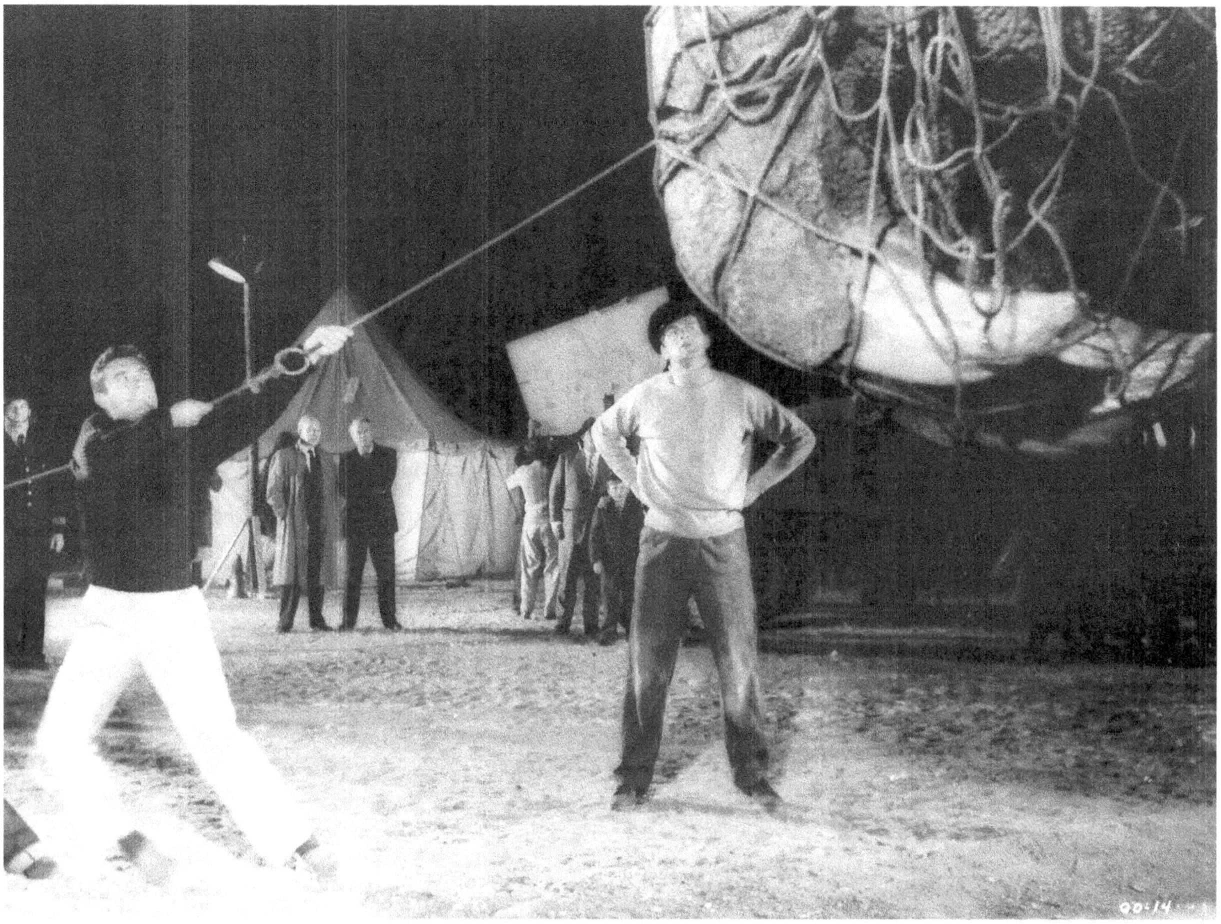

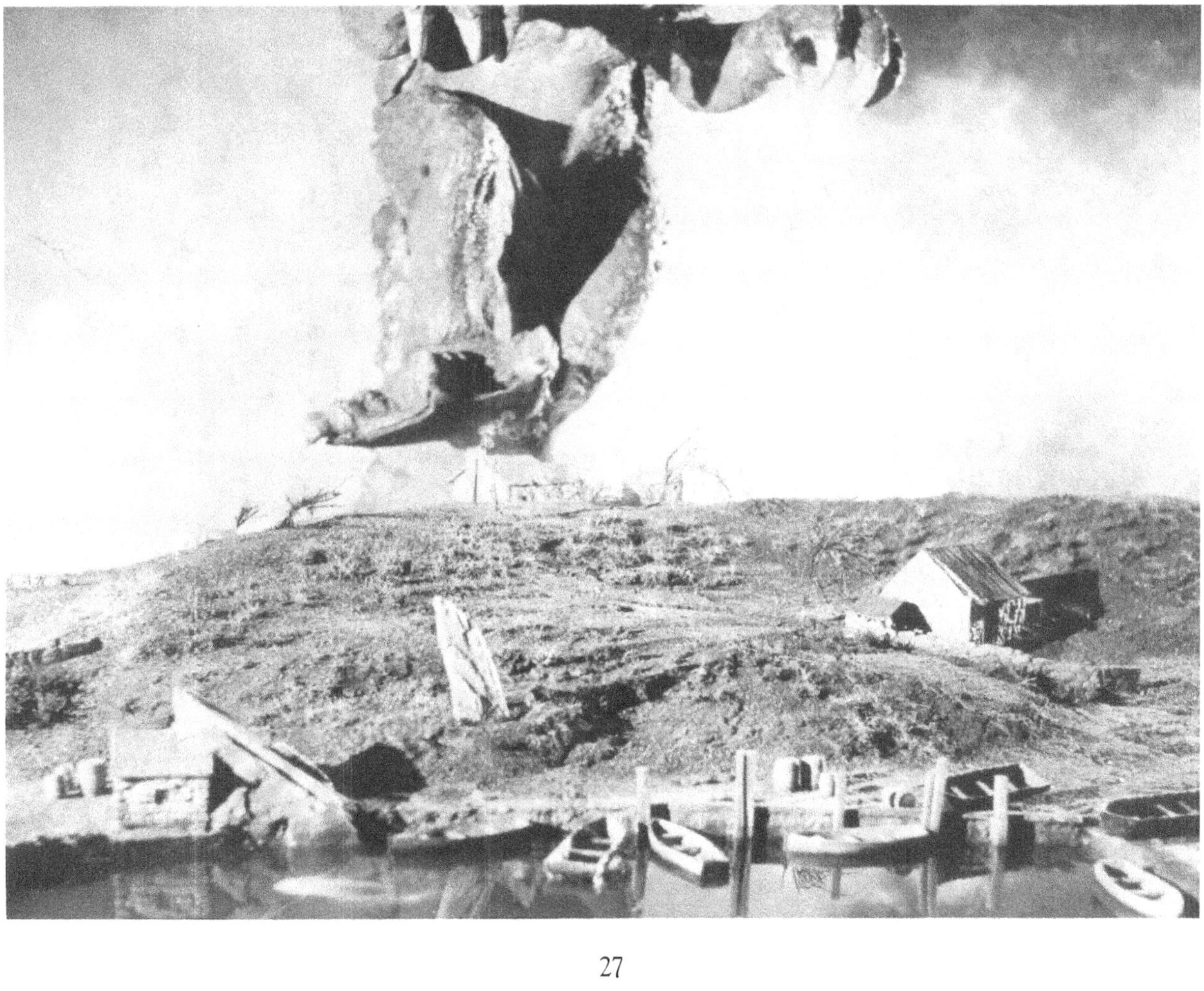

LIKE NOTHING YOU'VE EVER SEEN BEFORE!

METRO-GOLDWYN-MAYER Presents

A KING BROTHERS Production

GORGO

Starring
BILL TRAVERS · WILLIAM SYLVESTER

With
Vincent Winter · Bruce Seton · Joseph O'Conor · Martin Benson · Barry Keegan · Dervis Ward · Christopher Rhodes

Screen Play by
JOHN LORING and DANIEL HYATT

Original Story by
EUGENE LOURIE and DANIEL HYATT

Directed by EUGENE LOURIE · Produced by FRANK KING and MAURICE KING

TECHNICOLOR

" G O R G O "

Original Story

and

Screenplay

by

Eugene Lourie

and

Daniel Hyatt

KING BROS. PRODUCTIONS, INC.
8383 Sunset Boulevard
Hollywood 46, California

OLdfield 6-3110

16

# " G O R G O "

FADE IN:

1    A SERIES OF SHOTS - THE SEA                    1

in its more majestic aspects, with occasional vistas
of distant towering shorelines.  SUPERIMPOSED TITLE
and CREDITS.

                              FADE OUT:


FADE IN:

2    EXT. OCEAN - DAY                               2

The sea is a flat, ominous, oily-calm.  The sky is a
curiously sinister yellow, with the sun burning redly
through it.  A flight of birds goes over, flying low
and fast and purposefully.  Occasional odd, rolling
turbulences erupt upon the unnaturally flat surface of
the sea.


3    FULL SHOT - SS "TRITON" - SAM, BOSUN, OTHERS   3

Sam is at the rail, looking down anxiously at the water.
Slung on deck and lashed down we may see a small but
rugged and compact bathysphere.  Further forward is a
small group of crew members, chief of whom is the BOSUN.
They are huddled together, looking at the sea and the
sky, gesticulating and muttering among themselves.


4    GROUP SHOT - BOSUN AND CREW                    4

as they talk in low voices, looking at the sea and the
sky.  They SEE:


5    WHAT THEY SEE:                                 5

The glow of the sun is weaker now.  The eruptions disturbing the surface of the sea are more pronounced now,
and are accompanied by muffled rumblings, like claps
of distant thunder.

6  BACK TO SCENE             6

The Bosun detaches himself from the group and starts
aft.  (He is Irish - a touch of Brogue).


7  MED. SHOT - SAM             7

Sam glances anxiously at the strange manifestations of
sea and sky, as the Bosun comes up.

        BOSUN
   Sam..
      (as Sam looks)
   The sea's lookin' terribly
   ugly - the men are gettin'
   edgy..

        SAM
   So'm I..

They look down at the water.  Air bubbles are coming
to the surface near the ship.  A companionway leads
down to the water.

        BOSUN
   He's been down a good half hour.

        SAM
     (grunts)
   Him!..He'll stay down 'til his
   air runs out if he's latched
   onto somethin'..

They look anxiously at the ominous sea and sky.


8  UNDERWATER SHOT - JOE          8

with aqualung, swim fins - his face unidentifiable because of his face plate.  The air bubbles stream upward
as he breathes.  At his belt hangs a small pry-bar,
a machinist's hammer - and he is using a wrench.  For
he is working on the hulk of a sunken freighter -- a
wartime wreck.  For much of the bridge and super-
structure has been torn away, as though by shell fire,
exposing the chartroom.  It is here that Joe is working,
loosening the deck bolts of the gyro-compass.


9  EXT. DECK OF TRITON - SAM, BOSUN (CREW IN BG)

as they watch the air bubbles, and then the worsening
sea and sky.

           (CONTINUED)

9    (CONTINUED)                                          9

                         BOSUN
              I know these waters, and I never
              seen the like o' this...

                         SAM
                    (in sudden decision)
              Get me a lung - I'm goin' down
              and bring him up.

The Bosun hurries out of scene.  Sam rapidly strips off
his upper clothing, is about to kick off his shoes -
when Joe pops to the surface of the water, clambers onto
the companionway.  Looking, Sam SEES:

10   WHAT HE SEES:                                        10

He flips back his face plate, and we see his face for
the first time.  He is grinning broadly, as he starts
up the companionway.

                         JOE
              We're in!..Swing out the forward
              boom and let's get a cable over
              the side..

11   EXT. DECK OF TRITON - JOE, SAM

as he steps onto the deck.

                         SAM
              Are you kiddin'?

Sam indicates with a gesture of his head the sky and
the sea.  Joe casually follows his glance.  They SEE:

12   WHAT THEY SEE:

The situation has definitely worsened.  The darkening
yellow sky is oppressive and threatening.  The eruptions from the depths are more intense, the accompany-
ing underwater rumblings more ominous.

                         JOE'S VOICE (OVER)
              I see it..

13   BACK TO SCENE

Sam stares at him.

                                        (CONTINUED)

13      (CONTINUED)                                              13

                          JOE
                Listen.  There's a ten thousand
                dollar gyro-compass down there
                on that rustbucket, and I'm stay-
                ing here until I get it.

With a sweep of his arm Sam indicates the sea and sky:

                          SAM
                Joe!  Use your head!

                          JOE
                       (grinning)
                You tell me all about it when
                you're spending your share of
                the loot back in Brooklyn.

They look back towards the sea again, and then their
eyes widen at what they SEE:


14      WHAT THEY SEE:                                           14

A mile away, the ocean bulges up in a dark, angry
swell.  A thunderous explosion rips the surface,
hurling clouds of steam, ashes and fiery stones -
a thousand feet high in the sky.  The black shape of
a new-born volcano appears, belching out streams of
flaming lava.


15      BACK TO SCENE                                            15

                          SAM
                Holy Mother..!

Joe is yelling frantically at the Bosun.

                          JOE
                Get the anchor up!

The Bosun races for the donkey engine.


16      GROUP SHOT - THE CREW                                    16

        at the rail, yelling in terror at what they SEE:


17      WHAT THEY SEE:  EXT. OCEAN - DAY - MED. CLOSE SHOT - 17
        (SPECIAL EFFECT)

White-hot stones pepper the surface of the dark water.
Clouds of steam and ashes darken the sky.

18    FULL SHOT - THE DECK - SAILORS, BOSUN    18

The anchor chain is rattling through the hawse pipe, the Bosun at the winch. Two other sailors go tearing along the deck, aft.

19    MED. SHOT - JOE, SAM    19

Joe dashes to and up the companionway to the bridge. As he goes, he yells at Sam, his voice hardly audible above the thundering of the volcano:

> JOE
> Batten her down!

20    INT. BRIDGE - JOE    20

as he races in, frantically jangles the engine tele-graph, then yells into the speaking tube:

> JOE
> Full speed! Give it all you've
> got!

He spins the wheel, centering it, waiting for the ship to gain way. Then he looks off towards the volcano, SEES:

21    WHAT HE SEES:    21

The entire horizon is blackened by an expanding cloud. A new swell appears and is ripped open by another crater in a violent explosion of steam, ashes and flames. A gigantic wave forms around the volcano.

22    EXT. OCEAN - DAY - MED. CLOSE SHOT - (SPECIAL    22
EFFECT)

The wave moves forward, blood-red in the strange glare of the sun.

23    EXT. SS "TRITON'S" DECK - DAY - MED. CLOSE SHOT    23

terror-stricken sailors.

24    EXT. OCEAN - DAY - (SPECIAL EFFECT - MINIATURE) -    24
LONG SHOT

The SS Triton picked up by the wave like a helpless toy. For a moment she is tossed to the crest, then she slides into the trough and is buried under an even mightier wave.

25    EXT. SS TRITON'S DECK - DAY - MED. SHOT    25

A foaming wall of water engulfs the seamen.

26    EXT. OCEAN AND THE NEW VOLCANO - (SPECIAL EFFECT) -    26
LONG

In the red twilight, the eruption continues.

27    SERIES OF SHOTS    27

The TRITON being driven, battered, all but overwhelmed by the tremendous seas; on the bridge, JOE
and SAM fighting the wheel - even between them they
are scarcely able to hold it, and at one point both
of them are thrown, smashing against the bulkhead.
Sam is on his feet at once, dashing back to the wildly
spinning wheel. But Joe is hurt. Sam yells something at him which we cannot hear above the storm.
Joe is trying groggily to get to his feet. (These
should be INTERCUT with the following:)

28    MOUNTAINOUS WAVES    28

29    SMOKE EXPLODING FROM THE CRATER    29

30    MOUNTING WIND AND SPRAY    30

31    HUGE SEAS BREAKING OVER THE LIGHTHOUSE    31

32    FINAL SHOT - THE TRITON    32

as she looms up, carried on the crest of a monstrous
wave. Dimly seen through the driving spray is the
shoreline of NARA ISLAND, towards which she is
heading.

FADE OUT:


FADE IN:

33    EXT. DECK OF TRITON - JOE, SAM    33

as they walk slowly towards the companionway which
leads down to the water - looking over the ship.

(CONTINUED)

33    (CONTINUED)                                           33

We see evidence of damage aboard the Triton - a stove-
in-lifeboat, battered and twisted funnels, perhaps a
damaged stack, etc.  The day is damp, gloomy.

                    JOE
          How long you figure - to get
          her in shape?

                    SAM
          Sprung plates in the bilges -
          salt in the fresh water tanks...
          and the mess on deck...Three or
          four days...

                    JOE
               (nodding unhappy
                agreement)
          Yeah...Well, let's get ashore and
          see what they got...

They turn at the companionway.

                                        DISSOLVE TO:


34    EXT. BAY AND LAUNCH - JOE, SAM                        34

Joe at the wheel, as they proceed at slow speed
towards the shore, taking it all in.  They SEE:


35    WHAT THEY SEE:                                        35

The beach, village, installations, and the destruction of the storm.  Men, women and children, many
with their clothes torn, are poking about in, or
attempting half-heartedly to clear away the debris
and wreckage.  They seem stunned.  The DOCK, also
damaged, and its WATER TANK.


36    BACK TO SCENE:                                        36

                    JOE
               (nodding off
                towards shore)
          They got a dock, anyway - and
          water...

                    SAM
               (following his
                glance)
          Pretty hard hit, looks like...

                                        (CONTINUED)


37

36    (CONTINUED)                                              36

Now Sam sees something in the water:

                         SAM
         Joe...

Joe follows his glance.  They SEE:

37    WHAT THEY SEE:

An ugly, reddish-brown stain, coming from seaward
with the tide, is invading the waters of the bay.
And floating on the surface are several fish, about
the size of cod - but not like any cod ever seen before.  They are grotesque and hideous.  One has
burst open, as though it had come from the enormous
pressure of great depths.  One, right alongside the
boat, has a disproportionately huge head, with long,
rapier-like teeth, and four rudimentary legs.

38    BACK TO SCENE:                                           38

as Sam hauls this particular fish inboard with a boat
hook.  He and Joe look at it with a mixture of un-
easiness and disgust.

                         SAM
         I never seen nothin' like that
         before...You?

                         JOE
         No...

                         SAM
                    (tossing the
                    fish back)
         Whole ocean bottom must be tore
         up...

                                        DISSOLVE TO:

39    EXT. DOCK - JOE, SAM - DAY                               39

as they walk towards shore.  A group of ISLANDERS
is working to repair the damage to the dock.  They
glance surreptitiously towards Joe and Sam.  When
the latter draw abreast of them:

                                        (CONTINUED)

                         JOE
              Hi...Is there a harbor master
              we can talk to?

Some of the men don't even look up from their work.
A couple stare at the two strangers stonily for a
moment, then one of them mutters something in Gaelic,
and they too go back to their work.  Joe and Sam exchange a glance.

                         JOE
              Gaelic..

                         SAM
              Don't sound like "welcome" in
              any language...

But before they can make any decision, they see
McCARTIN coming towards them.  He is a big, bluff
fellow (Burl Ives type), with a flaming red beard
and a hearty affability that doesn't quite ring
true.  He speaks with a slight Irish inflection, but
as though he had been educated in England.

                         McCARTIN
              Hallo..I was just coming out
              to your ship..

                         JOE
              I'm Joe Ryan..
                   (nods towards Sam)
              Sam Slade - my partner..

                         McCARTIN
                   (as he shakes hands)
              My name's McCartin..I'm sort of
              head man around here - tempo-
              rarily..

                         JOE
              Then I guess you're the man we're
              lookin' for..

                         McCARTIN
              Right..
                   (gestures off)
              Well let's go over to my shack,
              shall we?

He has indicated a low, cottage-like building a few
yards away at the end of the dock.  They start towards
it.

40     REVERSE SHOT - THE THREE          40

as they come up.  The "shack" seems, on closer in-
spection, to be something rather more than that -
there are iron bars on the windows, and McCartin
uses a key to a very modern and substantial lock in
the front door, as he says:

>                    McCARTIN
>           Salvage vessel, are you?

>                    JOE
>           Yeah..

>                    McCARTIN
>                 (a look)
>           I thought so..

He holds open the door, as we

                    QUICK DISSOLVE TO:

41     INT. SHACK - THE THREE          41

The three are seated at a table that McCartin uses as
a desk.  There is a door leading to another room.
McCartin is pouring drinks.

>                    McCARTIN
>           Irish - all I have..Hope you
>           like it..

>                    JOE
>           The best..

They drink.

>                    McCARTIN
>                 (leaning back)
>           Well now.  How did you come
>           through the storm?

>                    JOE
>           Could have been worse..Three
>           or four days before I'm sea-
>           worthy though..

>                    McCARTIN
>                 (looking pained
>                 and thoughtful)
>           Oh...That makes it a bit awkward..

                    (CONTINUED)

41    (CONTINUED)                                                    41

Joe and Sam exchange a glance.

                         JOE
              For who?

McCartin makes like the decent fellow who has some bad
news to break and doesn't quite know how to do it.

                         McCARTIN
              Well you see - I'm an archeo-
              logist by profession - that's
              why the government put me in
              charge here..

                         JOE
              Ireland?

                         McCARTIN
              Eire - yes..And I don't mind
              telling you that being difficult
              with strangers isn't the part of
              the job I like best..

                         JOE
                   (leans forward,
                    his eyes hard)
              What's this all about?

McCartin looks at the two for a moment, as though
reaching a decision to let them in on a big secret,
then he rises:

                         McCARTIN
              I'll show you..

He goes to the other door, the other two following,
opens it, and they enter.

42    INT. STOREROOM - THE THREE                                     42

as they enter.  The place is a repository for a con-
siderable collection of Viking and old Irish relics -
swords, battle-axes, sheilds, helmets - even the prow
of a ship.  All show the effects of their long exposure to the sea, but most are quite recognizable.
Against one wall is a tall steel safe - also surprisingly modern.

                         McCARTIN
              Ever see stuff like that before?

                                              (CONTINUED)

                          SAM
              Only in the funny sheets..

                          JOE
              Viking, looks like..

                          McCARTIN
              That's right..About a thousand
              years ago the Vikings took over
              this island as a base for raids
              against the mainland.  Eventually
              they were driven out - there was
              a big sea battle, right off shore..
              Historians didn't know much about
              it, really, until a local fisher-
              man snagged his net, and decided
              to dive down and free it..
                      (indicating the
                       ship's prow)
              He came up with this..

The ship's prow is carved in a hideous representation
of a monster's head (close, but not too close, to our
own monster).

                          SAM
              What kinda stuff was them Vikings
              drinkin'?

                          McCARTIN
              That one's Irish - one of the
              ships that drove out the Vikings..
                      (indicating the head)
              He was their mascot - there's still
              some sort of legend about it - like
              Saint Patrick and the snakes..

                          JOE
                      (he's waiting for
                       the point)
              So they sent you out.  Then what?

                          McCARTIN
                      (looking pained again)
              Well that's it, you see..The stuff
              has no real value - except to us
              eggheads - but..
                      (a thought)
              I don't suppose you have a permit
              to come in here?

                                        (CONTINUED)

42    (CONTINUED)                                        42

Joe and Sam exchange a glance.  In the open door behind
them has appeared a boy, about twelve, SEAN.  He has
been staring at the two strangers, but now he glances
surreptitiously and somewhat contemputously at McCartin.

                    JOE
          Permit?  No..

Now McCartin notices the boy.  He is unaccountably
irritated.

                    McCARTIN
          What do you want?

                    SEAN
               (sullenly)
          You told me to come clean up.

                    McCARTIN
          Later - I'm busy..

The boy turns and leaves.

                    JOE
          So what's this permit business?

                    McCARTIN
               (unhappily)
          That's the problem..Silly of course
          - but since this turned up, no
          ship's allowed at Nara Island for
          more than twenty-four hours without
          a permit from Dublin..

                    JOE
               (irritated)
          Look friend - we got driven on
          this island - we didn't come here
          on any pleasure-cruise!

                    McCARTIN
          Oh I realize that..But you know
          how it is with us civil servants -
          we take our orders..If we don't..

With a pained smile, he passes his finger across his
throat.  Joe and Sam glance at each other - they
realize they'd better hold their tempers until they
can think this through.  Joe turns to McCartin with
a shrug:

                                        (CONTINUED)

42    (CONTINUED - 2)        42

> JOE
> Okay - I'm afloat anyway..
> How about fresh water?

> McCARTIN
> (all cordiality)
> Of course!  Come in to the dock
> - any time!..

> JOE
> We'll do that...

He and Sam turn to go.

> McCARTIN
> Another spot of the Irish?

> JOE
> No thanks..

They exit.  McCartin looks after them, calculatingly,
as we -

DISSOLVE TO:

43    EXT. BAY - JOE, SAM, BOSUN - DAY        43

in the LAUNCH, heading back to the Triton.

> SAM
> You believe him - about the
> permit?

> JOE
> Hell no!

Their attention is caught by something they SEE:

44    WHAT THEY SEE:        44

Four island boats, looming out of the gloom and mist.
They are rather like life-boats, rowed by four men
each, Islanders.  In the bow of each boat is a skin-
diver, with his equipment.  The Islanders are resting
on their oars.  All are looking at the strange strain
in the water, the dead fish, and can be seen con-
ferring among themselves.

45    BACK TO SCENE:                          45

> SAM
> Somethin's eatin' him..Wonder
> what?

> JOE
> (looking towards
> the boats)
> I don't know..But we might swing
> a little more weight around here
> if we found out..

Sam glances at him, then looks off at what Joe is watching.  They SEE:

46    WHAT THEY SEE:  LONG SHOT - THE FOUR BOATS    46

as they head out into the bay.

> DISSOLVE TO:

47    EXT. BAY - JOE, SAM, BOSUN - DAY          47

IN THE LAUNCH.  They are moving at about half-speed,
parallel to the shoreline, and about a hundred yards
off it.  Now the launch rounds a point of land.  The
Bosun, at the helm, sees something ahead.  He half
turns towards the other two, keeping his voice low:

> BOSUN
> Hey, Joe...

Joe and Sam look at what the Bosun is pointing out.
They SEE:

48    WHAT THEY SEE:                        48

Around the point of land is a deep indenture of the
shoreline, forming a good-sized cove.  Roughly in the
middle of this cove, are the four BOATS previously
seen, with their OCCUPANTS - the divers with their
face plates, going down.  Each wears at his belt a
pouch-like sack.

49    BACK TO SCENE - (ANOTHER ANGLE - DIVERS IN B.G.)    49

> JOE
> (to Bosun)
> Slack her off, Bos'...

> (CONTINUED)

The Bosun throttles the launch down, approaching the
divers in a circling maneuver.  The men in the boats
are eyeing the launch with suspicion.

                         JOE
                      (hailing)
             Havin' any luck?

The men in the boat look at each other, but don't
answer.

                         JOE
                      (to the Bosun)
             You try 'em..

                         BOSUN
                      (disgustedly)
             Ah - they speak English as good
             as you or me - they don't want
             to, is all..

The Bosun is a native of Ireland, with some brogue.
He hails the boats in Gaelic.  The Islanders mutter
among themselves, then one of them hails back, briefly
and sullenly.  The Bosun translates:

                         BOSUN
             They say they got no time to be
             talkin' to strangers - McCartin
             does the talkin' on the Island..

Joe and Sam look at each other.  But suddenly their
attention is brought back to the Islanders by a
commotion among them.  Three divers have just come
to the surface, clamber hurriedly into their boats,
talking to the others.  Now, as they talk, the
Islanders are peering down into the water, as though
looking for something, waiting for something.  The
Bosun explains:

                         BOSUN
             One of the divers didn't come
             up - they're sayin' he's gone..

                         JOE
                      (puzzled by
                      the word)
             Gone...

There is more talk among the Islanders.  The Bosun
explains:

                                        (CONTINUED)

49    (CONTINUED - 2)                                        49

> BOSUN
> They got to go down to find
> him..But they're scared of
> somethin'..

50    NEW ANGLE                                              50

During this, Joe's launch has circled in slowly to
within fifty feet or so of the boats.  Now reluctantly a couple of divers go into the water.  All
watch and wait tensely.  One of the divers is up
again in a matter of seconds.  He shakes his head -
he has found nothing, and he is obviously more than
reluctant to go down again.  There is a long wait for
the other diver.  Then suddenly he pops to the surface, only a few feet from Joe's launch, yelling incoherently, tearing his face plate off, as he takes
the few frantic strokes he needs to reach the launch.
He is beside himself with fear, his eyes wide with
some nameless horror.  Joe and Sam reach down to help
him into the launch.  He is babbling something, but
it comes out only gibberish.  Then suddenly his eyes
turn up, and he collapses in the bottom of the boat.
Sam bends over him, turning him over.

> SAM
> He don't seem to be hurt...

Meanwhile, from their boats, the Islanders stare
sullenly.  Joe is beside Sam, who is trying to re-
vive the diver.  The diver's breathing is shallow
and rapid.  He moves convulsively - and something
drops out of the pouch at his belt.  Joe's eyes widen
as he sees what it is.  His hand dives for it, taking
care that the Islanders from their boats can't see it
as he holds it out to Sam.

> JOE
> (tensely)
> Sam..!

Sam looks up from the diver, then looks at what Joe
is holding in his hand.  He SEES:

51    WHAT HE SEES:  INSERT                                  51

JOE'S HAND, holding four or five ancient gold coins.

> JOE'S VOICE (OVER)
> So that's what's buggin' McCartin..

52     BACK TO SCENE                                    52

Sam and the Bosun stare at Joe.

                     JOE
                (his tough grin,
                mimicking McCartin)
      "No value except to us eggheads,"
      huh...We're gonna make us some
      loot before we leave here..!
      Real loot!

Sam looks at him sharply, but before he can reply,
there is a convulsive shudder from the diver - and
then he lies still. Sam, and then Joe, look quickly
down at him, Sam bending his head to listen for a
heart beat. Then he looks up at Joe.

                     SAM
      He's dead..

                     JOE
      Dead...How?

                     SAM
      You saw him come up...You ask
      me - he died of fright.

They stare at each other as we...

                                DISSOLVE TO:

53     EXT. BAY - JOE, SAM, BOSUN (IN LAUNCH) - EVENING     53

In the b.g. can be seen the dim outlines of the
Triton, but blacked out, as the launch pulls away.
Distantly over the water comes the SOUND of the Triton's bell - three bells - nine-thirty p.m. The
Bosun steers, forward. In the stern sit Joe and Sam.
They are in swimming trunks, and in evidence is their
diving gear -- aqualungs, flares, harpoon, fins,
face-plates, etc. The launch is running at slow
speed, quietly. Joe is watching behind for signs of
pursuit. Sam does not look too happy. Voices are
urgent but low.

                     SAM
                (bursting out
                at last)
      This is crazy! A guy was lost
      down there today -- not even a
      trace! Another guy saw somethin'
      that scared him to death..!

                                (CONTINUED)

53   (CONTINUED)                            53

> JOE
> (turning on him,
> his voice harden-
> ing)
> Look.  You don't wanta go down -
> don't go.

> SAM
> (grudgingly)
> I'm goin' down all right..I'm
> goin' down to see that you get
> a chance of comin' up!

Joe grins his fond acknowledgement of Sam's concern:

> JOE
> Sure - with a hatful of gold...

Sam snorts as we...

DISSOLVE TO:

54   EXT. COVE - JOE, SAM, BOSUN - EVENING        54

A couple of lines, attached to the launch, go down
into the water.  They are, as we shall see, attached
to the weighted containers, now resting on the
bottom, into which Joe hopes to load his loot.

> JOE
> (to Sam)
> Set?

Sam nods, lights one of his magnesium flares, quickly
ducks it into the water to hide the glow, and they
both slip into the water.

55   A SERIES OF UNDERWATER SHOTS                55

As Joe and Sam swim down.  Sam carries the flare, Joe
the harpoon gun.  In B.G. we may see the lines that
go down to the container they hope to fill with loot.
Schools of fish scatter before them.  Reaching the
bottom, they swim slowly towards the remains of the
Vikings ship.  Imbedded between rocky formations,
these remains look like a strange cemetery of gigantic
ribs.  A carved figurehead is sometimes picked up by
the moving light of the flare, looking alive with
its swaying mane of seaweeds.  There is a sudden
darkening of the waters, as though a shadow were passing over them.  They look up, SEE:

56    WHAT THEY SEE:    56

A giant whale killer has passed over them, and now
turns back.  He senses prey, but he is wary, circling.

57    BACK TO SCENE    57

Joe and Sam have drawn closer together, watching the
thing.  They too are wary, but they are not afraid.
They are only figuring the best way to handle the
situation - whether to get ready to fight, or wait
for the thing to go away.  Joe moves slowly along
the edge of the rock-formation, watching the whale.
CAMERA MOVES with him.  Now he looks over towards
Sam - and suddenly realizes that Sam isn't there.
He turns sharply, SEES:

58    WHAT HE SEES:    58

From the cleft in the rock a huge tentacle has emerged
to wrap around Sam.  Sam is desperately trying to get
his knife into play, but now another tentacle emerges
and whips around him.

59    BACK TO SCENE - ANOTHER ANGLE - THE TWO    59

as Joe charges in, CAMERA MOVING with him.  Sam has
dropped his flare, and it now lies a little distance
below on the rocky bottom.  As Joe comes in, another
tentacle whips out for him, and now we can see the
huge, dirty-green body of the thing and its great,
staring, saucer-eyes.  But Joe does not make the
mistake of trying to avoid the tentacle.  He fights
only to keep his arms and gun free, and rides in with
the snake-like arm, intent only on getting in close
enough for a killing shot.  Sam by now is almost helpless.  With a half-imprisoned arm, he is trying to
cut through a truck tire with a jackknife.  Another
tentacle has coiled around Joe, but he drives in.
And now, straight between the eyes of the thing, he
fires.  There is a dull, muffled explosion (the exploding tip of the harpoon).  The great octopus
shudders violently, its color changes rapidly from
the dirty-green to a reddish-brown, its tentacles
loosen and become limp, and, as the two men struggle
free, in its death agony, it emits a great, jetting
cloud of black ink, all but obliterating the scene.
Joe and Sam pull back a little, close together.

60    CLOSE SHOT - JOE               60

his anxious face seen through his face plate, looking
at Sam.

61    TWO SHOT               61

as Sam, exhausted, nevertheless gestures that he's
okay. Now the two look around, looking upward
through the murk, the killer whale not forgotten.
They SEE:

62    WHAT THEY SEE:               62

dimly through the darkly clouded waters, a shadow
passing over. The whale has not forgotten them.

63    BACK TO SCENE               63

as Joe gestures caution. They are in no shape for
another fight at the moment. From his belt, Joe gets
another charge for the harpoon gun, loads it. From
somewhat below, the flare glows dimly. Then suddenly
there is a tremendous, thrashing turmoil in the water
above them. They look up quickly, SEE:

64    WHAT THEY SEE:               64

Through the murk and the wildly turbulent water, they
can see only something fantastically big and vague,
like a great thundercloud. The water is whipped to
fury. Then all at once there is a great jetting gush
of blood that crimsons the water all around, blotting
out everything in a swirling red haze.

65    BACK TO SCENE               65

as the two cling to the rock formation, staring up-
wards, staring at each other.

                             DISSOLVE TO:

66    EXT. BAY - JOE, SAM, BOSUN - NIGHT     66

The launch is heading down the bay, the Bosun forward
at the wheel, Joe and Sam in the stern. Joe gets
cigarettes and matches out of a jacket, gives one to
Sam, takes one himself, lights them. His hand is
shaking a little. Sam looks at him briefly. Both
men take deep drags. Then Joe finally says softly:

                             (CONTINUED)

66    (CONTINUED)                                          66

                        JOE
            What did you see, Sam?

                        SAM
                   (a little un-
                    steadily)
            I don't know...But I sure don't
            ever want to see it again!

Now distant and muffled, but carrying distinctly over
the water from the shore, we first HEAR THE SOUND of
Island voices in a mournful dirge.  Joe and Sam look
off towards the SOUND, then at each other, as we...

                                      DISSOLVE TO:


67    FULL SHOT - THE TRITON - JOE, SAM, BOSUN, OTHERS -   67
      NIGHT

The Bosun is supervising members of the crew as they
struggle to get a heavy water hose aboard from a water
tank on the dock.  The work is going on under the
ship's deck lights.  Over the scene comes the SOUND
of the dirge.  Joe and Sam stand at the rail watching
the work of the crew.  Then Joe turns, looking off
towards the shore and the SOUND of the dirge.  He SEES:


68    WHAT HE SEES:                                        68

The movement of torches on the beach indicates some
sort of purposeful Island activity, although it is
only dimly seen from this distance and in the darkness.  And, of course, the SOUND of the dirge covers
all.


69    BACK TO SCENE                                        69

                        SAM
            You think they know something?

                        JOE
            How could they?

Sam shrugs.


70    ANOTHER ANGLE - JOE, SAM, SEAN                       70

Normally alert-looking and intelligent, on this
occasion Sean's mood seems subdued - but not enough

                                      (CONTINUED)

70   (CONTINUED)                                                    70

to overcome his boy's fascination at doings in the
world of men aboard a big ship.  He is just stepping
rather hesitantly off the gangway, looking around
him, his eyes wide and serious.  Joe and Sam have not
seen him.  He glances towards them, sizing them up,
then moves slowly towards them, his eyes roving,
taking in the sights as he goes.  Joe turns irritably,
staring into the night, towards the shore.  The SOUND
of the chanting registers briefly:

                        JOE
          How long is that gonna go on!

                        SEAN
                    (quiet, serious)
          That's for my father.

Joe and Sam turn quickly, looking at him.  They glance
at each other, then back at the boy.

                        SAM
          For your father...?

                        SEAN
          Yes.  This mornin' it happened.
                    (his eyes dropped)
          He's dead.

Joe and Sam throw each other a quick glance.

                        SAM
                    (softly)
          Your father was the diver that...
                    (doesn't finish)

                        SEAN
          Yes.
                    (the eyes drop
                    again)

                        SAM
                    (a look at Joe)
          Oh...I'm sorry...

There is a beat as Joe and Sam look at each other.

                        SAM
                    (gently)
          What's your name kid?

                                        (CONTINUED)

70      (CONTINUED - 2)                                          70

                              SEAN
                    Sean..I work for McCartin.
                         (grimaces to show
                         his distaste for
                         McCartin)
                    He wants to see you...It's a fine
                    rage he's in..

Sam and Joe glance at each other.

                              JOE
                    Oh it is, is it..
                         (to Sam)
                    Maybe we better see what this
                    joker's got on his mind..

They turn to go, like two men ready and willing to
accept a challenge.  But they pause as Sean speaks.
For the first time the boy is smiling a little:

                              SEAN
                    About the permit now...He was
                    pullin' yer leg...

Joe and Sam look at each other, then start out, as we...

                                        DISSOLVE TO:


71      EXT. BEACH - McCARTIN - ISLANDERS                        71

McCartin is clearly in a foul humor about the whole
recent course of events.  Some Islanders are hauling
a boat towards the water.  Their efforts bring them
a little closer to McCartin than suits him, and he
barks at them in Gaelic, taking out his general spleen
on them.  The Islanders only glance at him sullenly.
Joe and Sam enter, followed watchfully by Sean.

                              JOE
                    I hear you got a beef...

McCartin turns on the two men:

                            McCARTIN
                    So you were snooping around out
                    there, were you?
                         (as Joe and Sam
                         glance at each
                         other)
                    My divers told me the whole thing..

                                        (CONTINUED)

                         JOE
              And I suppose they told you
              to give us that jazz about
              a permit...

                         McCARTIN
                      (angrily)
              Are you dubting my word?

                         JOE
              You're damn right!

McCartin takes a step towards them.  Joe and Sam are
set for him.  But McCartin has enough worries without
tangling with these two.  Sullenly:

                         McCARTIN
              All the same, after you load
              your fresh water, you leave.
              Tonight.

                         JOE
                      (testily)
              The sooner the better.

McCartin looks at him - this is certainly a change in
Joe's attitude.  As a diversion, Joe turns to Sean,
gestures towards the activity on the beach:

                         JOE
              What are they doing?

                         SEAN
                      (simply)
              'Tis a wake they're holdin'...
              That, and the thing we do when
              a man is lost - for Ogra - the
              sea-spirit, that is....

                         McCARTIN
                      (turning on the boy)
              Go on with you - with your non-
              sense!

McCartin makes a half-threatening move towards the boy
who breaks off, staring at McCartin with flat expression.

                         JOE
                      (guardedly)
              What's this about a sea-spirit?

                              (CONTINUED)

71      (CONTINUED - 2)                                                  71

        McCartin starts walking slowly towards the activity
        as he talks, the others going with him, CAMERA FOL-
        LOWING.

                              McCARTIN
                            (testily)
                It's a legend, I told you - that
                a sea monster helped them beat
                off the pagan Vikings...Huh!
                They're no better than pagans them-
                selves - Father Donnelly would
                never allow it - but he only gets
                out here twice a year...

72      EXT. VILLAGE AND THE FISHING BOATS - NIGHT -              72
        GENERAL VIEW

        activity on the village street and around the boats.
        Men are making fires on the beach.  Others are moving
        toward boats with torches.

73      EXT. ROAD LEADING TO THE VILLAGE - EVENING - MED.         73
        LONG SHOT

        A group carrying torches pass in the direction of the
        bay.

74      EXT. WATERFRONT AT THE VILLAGE - NIGHT - MED. SHOT        74

        The boats being launched, the oarsmen taking their
        places.  In each boat, two men carry torches, one in
        the bow, one in the stern.

75      EXT. VILLAGE WATERFRONT - NIGHT - LONG SHOT               75

        The boats start forward, crossing in FRONT OF CAMERA.

76      EXT. BAY - NIGHT - VERY LONG SHOT                         76

        GENERAL VIEW of the bay, framed by bonfires on the
        distant shoreline.

77      EXT. BAY - NIGHT - MED. SHOT                              77

        The leading boat.  The torch-bearer in the bow is an
        older man - a strong, weathered face - a local
        PATRIARCH.

78    EXT. BAY - NIGHT - CLOSE MED. SHOT - (ISLANDERS'    78
      P.O.V.)

      Waters of the bay, lit by the flaring torches, as
      seen from the slowly moving boat.


79    FULL SHOT - BAY - BOATS - NIGHT                     79

      The boats, in line, are starting to cross the bay in
      the arc of a circle that would eventually take them
      back to shore.  From shore, the KEENING comes over.


80    UNDERWATER SHOT - LOW ANGLE                         80

      CAMERA IS SHOOTING UP from the depths, from the direc-
      tion of the outer bay, towards the lights some little
      distance away.  CAMERA PANS SLOWLY over the flickering
      lights until suddenly is revealed the enormous head of
      the MONSTER, rising from the depths.  The head sways,
      seeking, looking upwards towards the lights.  Then the
      great bulk of the monster is revealed as it moves
      towards the lights.


81    ANOTHER ANGLE - MONSTER                             81

      as it moves in among the flickering, distorted shafts
      of light coming down from the surface of the water.
      It moves its head this way and that, as it is attracted
      by the lights.


83    MED. SHOT - BOAT AND PATRIARCH                      82

      The old man rises in the bow.  He has a crucifix in
      his hand.  The torch light catches the crucifix, as
      he holds it.


83    MED. SHOT - ANOTHER BOAT - (FAVORING BOW TORCH-     83
      BEARER)

      He is quite young - not much more than a boy.  Suddenly
      he sees something in the water.  His eyes grow wide.
      Dropping his torch, he grabs a harpoon from the bottom
      of the boat, hurls it into the water.


84    EXT. BAY - UNDERWATER - (SPECIAL EFFECT)            84

      The harpoon hits the head of the monster.  The head
      moves.

85    EXT. BAY - MED. CLOSE SHOT    85

the Islanders, all looking now, terrified by what they see.

86    EXT. BAY - CLOSE SHOT - (ISLANDERS' P.O.V. -    86
SPECIAL EFFECT)

The huge head of the monster appears from the water.

87    EXT. BAY - MED. SHOT - (COMBINATION SHOT OR    87
MINIATURE SPECIAL EFFECT)

The monster rises from the water, lifting the boat. The men are thrown out.

88    EXT. BAY - (COMBINATION PROCESS, MINIATURE -    88
FOREGROUND)

the men in the churning water. The bulky monster turns. With a violent movement of its tail, it smashes the boat.

89    EXT. BAY    89

The men in another boat are attracted by the SHOUTING of the wounded men.

90    EXT. BAY - LONG SHOT- (SPECIAL EFFECT)    90

The monster rises from the water. It moves towards one of the Islanders. The Lighthouse and Radio Tower in b.g. show its relative size.

91    EXT. BAY - CLOSE SHOT    91

The man tries desperately to swim away. He looks backward terrified.

92    EXT. SHORE OF THE BAY - MED. LONG SHOT    92

People, aroused by the cries from the bay, rush toward the water's edge. Some carry torches. Joe, Sam, McCartin, Sean, among them. The keening peters out.

93    GROUP SHOT - JOE, SAM, McCARTIN, SEAN                93

    at the water's edge as they stare fearfully out over
    the bay.  They SEE:

94    WHAT THEY SEE:                                       94

    At first they can only make out the wildly dancing
    torches of the boats.  Then they see the first boats
    driving frantically for shore.

95    BACK TO SCENE                                        95

    as they look at each other fearfully, then back out
    over the bay.  They SEE:

96    WHAT THEY SEE:                                       96

    Now, in the distance, they see the towering shape of
    the monster.

97    GROUP SHOT - JOE, SAM, McCARTIN, SEAN - (FAVORING   97
    SEAN)

    His eyes are wide, but more with a kind of awe than
    fright.  His voice has something of the same quality.

                    SEAN
         Ogra!

    Joe and Sam shoot him a quick glance, then look back
    out over the lagoon.

98    EXT. BAY - MONSTER - BOATS AND ISLANDERS            98

    as the monster advances towards the fleeing boats.
    In the nearest one, a couple of Islanders desperately
    throw harpoons.

99    EXT. BAY - THE MONSTER - (MINIATURE)                99

    The harpoons hit the monster, but they are unable to
    penetrate its scales.

100   EXT. BAY - CLOSE SHOT                               100

    One Islander takes careful aim.  The harpoon is thrown.

101     EXT. BAY - MONSTER'S HEAD - CLOSE SHOT -          101
        (MINIATURE)

        The harpoon hits close to the eye and imbeds itself
        between the scales.  The wound is bleeding.  The
        monster tries to shake it off.

102     EXT. BAY - MED. LONG SHOT - THE MONSTER -         102
        (MINIATURE)

        With a terrifying cry the monster moves forward,
        violently beating the water with its tail.

103     EXT. BAY - LONG SHOT - (COMBINATION MINIATURE AND  103
        LIVE ACTION)

        The monster advances between boats.

104     EXT. BAY - MED. CLOSE SHOT - (SPECIAL EFFECT)     104

        The gigantic tail smashes the boats, scatters men and
        debris in the churning water.

105     EXT. BEACH - JOE, SAM, McCARTIN, SEAN             105

        aghast at what they have seen.  McCartin draws his
        revolver, starts firing.  Sean's reaction to this is
        interesting - he scracely glances at the frantically
        firing McCartin, continues to stare out at the mon-
        ster with a kind of hypnotic fascination - almost as
        though he knew that such puny efforts to harm the
        monster would be useless.

106     ANOTHER ANGLE - (MONSTER IN B.G.)                 106

        Some of McCartin's fire is effective - except that
        it bounces off the monster as it would off a tank.
        In fact, we might HEAR THE SOUND of the ricocheting
        bullets.  The monster only roars, paws with a talon
        as though at bothersome mosquitoes, keeps on coming.

107     BACK TO SCENE                                     107

        as McCartin throws down his empty gun, runs out of
        scene.

108     EXT. BAY                                          108

the maddened monster, as he pursues the remainder of
the fleeing boats.

109     EXT. BEACH                                        109

panic, as men, women and children run for their lives.

110     EXT. BEACH - NIGHT                                110

as the monster comes out of the water onto the beach.
Women and children, and some men scatter before it.

111     NEW ANGLE                                         111

Joe, then Sam grab burning brands from a bonfire,
start towards the monster, flourishing the flaming
brands. About a dozen Islanders, grasping his intent, follow him with their torches. With his fixed
gaze, Sean watches all this. Undeterred by the sight
of the flaming torches, the monster continues to advance. Joe and the others dare go no nearer. On an
inspiration, Joe hurls his torch. It hits the monster on the wounded eye, and he bellows in pain.
Although it is a terrifying SOUND, there is a pathetic
quality too, as of the cry of any animal in anguish.
At this, Sean averts his eyes, in sympathy for the
beast. Now the other men follow Joe's example,
hurling their torches. Some of them strike the monster, but do no further damage. The men wait. The
monster hesitates, bewildered. Then it turns again
towards the water, sending the embers of a bonfire
flying in every direction with a flick of his tail.
He goes into the water, and slips out of sight beneath the surface. The group stares after the dis-
appearing beast, as we...

                                          DISSOLVE:

112     EXT. McCARTIN SHACK - McCARTIN - OTHERS - LONG SHOT - 112
        DAY

McCartin is standing in the doorway, surrounded by a
couple dozen Islanders - among whom we may recognize
the BOATMEN and DIVERS of previous sequence. SEAN
stands on the fringe of the crowd. We do not hear the
exchange distinctly, but it is clear that the men are
sullenly angry, and McCartin is trying to calm them

                                          (CONTINUED)

112    (CONTINUED)                                          112

down.  Most of the men have sea bags with them - they
are set for travel.  JOE and SAM come into scene,
CLOSE IN CAMERA, watching the scene.

                    SAM
                (a tight little
                grin)
            Now there's a man looks like
            he's really got a problem...

                    JOE
                (slowly, thinking)
            Uh huh...And I bet he'd pay
            through the nose if you could
            solve it for him...

Sam looks at him, as the thought registers.  Joe gives
him a grin, and both move over towards the crowd,
CAMERA MOVING with them.  The men turn towards them,
a little sullen, a little defiant.  A SPOKESMAN ad-
dresses Joe:

                    SPOKESMAN
            We'll be wantin' passage on your
            ship, Mister...
                (a glance towards
                McCartin)
            When His Nibs gets around to
            givin' us our pay...

                    McCARTIN
            Now hold on - you'll get your
            pay, if you like - but there'll
            be no taking passage on any ships!

                    JOE
            Why not?

There is a murmur of approval from the men.

                    McCARTIN
            For God's sake, Ryan!  Look - come
            in here and let me talk to you.

                    JOE
                (a glance at
                Sam)
            Sure...

He and Sam start through the crowd.

113    INT. SHACK - McCARTIN - JOE - SAM    113

as they enter. SEAN tries to squeeze in after them,
McCartin aims a blow at him, as he snaps:

> McCARTIN
>
> Get out!

Joe grabs his arm, growls:

> JOE
> Take it easy!

McCartin glares at him a moment, but now that the
immediate crisis is over, the fight goes out of him
and he wilts. He closes the door.

> McCARTIN
> (nodding towards
> the men outside)
> The whole thing'll go to smash
> if they leave - my divers - my
> boatmen - the lot of them!

> SAM
> (dryly)
> Me, I kinda see their point...

> JOE
> You got any other reasons you
> don't want 'em to leave?

> McCARTIN
> What do you mean?

Joe has taken the gold coins from his pocket, holds
them out:

> JOE
> Like - maybe they'd talk too
> much?

114    INSERT JOE'S HAND    114

with the coins.

> McCARTIN'S VOICE (OVER)
> (choked)
> Where did you get those?

115    BACK TO SCENE                                          115

                         JOE
                The same place you did...

McCartin stares at the two - he knows they've got him,
but he doesn't quite know how.

                         JOE
                Suppose we could get rid of
                that thing for you?

                         McCARTIN
                      (hope stirring
                      in his eyes)
                The beast?  You think you can?

                         JOE
                Maybe...

Joe nods off, towards the storeroom, as he says:

                         JOE
                Let's take another look in
                there...

McCartin gives him a sharp look, but he crosses and
opens the door.  The three enter.

116    INT. STOREROOM - JOE, SAM, McCARTIN                   116

        as they enter.  Joe looks around, deliberately - then
        springs it.

                         JOE
                      (nodding towards
                      the safe)
                Open the safe.

McCartin freezes, speechless.  Joe looks at him, then
at Sam.

                         JOE
                      (to Sam, nodding
                      towards the men
                      outside)
                Well, we can always make a few
                bucks takin' those guys back
                where they came from...

There is a kind of strangled sound from McCartin.
Then he crosses and opens the safe.  Inside are heaps

                                        (CONTINUED)

116    (CONTINUED)                                          116

of the gold coins - plus gold chalices studded with
precious stones - the works.  Even Sam catches his
breath.  But Joe keeps playing it cool.

                    JOE
          Nice...

He reaches in, picks out one of the best of the
chalices.

                    JOE
                 (to Sam)
          How about this - for a down pay-
          ment?  You like this one, Sam?

                    SAM
          Not bad...

                    McCARTIN
                 (his voice choked)
          You're out of your mind!  A thing
          like that is priceless - and how
          do you think you're going to dis-
          pose of it!

                    JOE
          You musta figured a way - I bet
          we can...

                    McCARTIN
          You filthy blackmailer!

Joe backhands him, fast and hard, across the mouth.

                    JOE
                 (growls)
          We'll get your beast for you -
          but mind your lip.

McCartin's hand has gone to his bruised mouth.

                    JOE
          You're gettin' off easy, friend...
                 (indicating the safe)
          You're in no spot to squawk - even
          if we grabbed the whole thing...

Joe tucks the chalice under his jacket, turns towards
the door.  McCartin is whipped, all the way around,
and he knows it.

                                        (CONTINUED)

116 (CONTINUED - 2)                                      116

                    McCARTIN
                    (sulkily)
          When will you start?

                    JOE
          Now - why not?

He and Sam exit, McCartin glares after them, as we...

                              DISSOLVE TO:

117   EXT. DOCK - JOE, SAM, OTHERS - DAY                 117

      as Joe and Sam walk slowly, thoughtfully, back towards
      the Triton.  In b.g. can be seen the group of Islanders,
      staring after them.

118   TWO SHOT - JOE, SAM                                118

      as they walk, CAMERA MOVING with them.

                    SAM
                    (pursuing a
                    conversation)
          ...Maybe we can get it in the
          shark net -- but how do you
          figure to kill a thing like
          that?

                    JOE
          I dunno...Dynamite...

                    SAM
                    (thoughtfully)
          Joe...
                    (as Joe looks at
                    him)
          You ever think how much that thing
          could be worth - alive?

Joe stares at him a moment, then they grin at each
other.  But before they can pursue the thought further, they are startled to hear:

                    SEAN'S VOICE (OVER)
          Mister Ryan...

119   ANOTHER ANGLE - JOE, SAM, SEAN                     119

      as the boy comes up to them.

                              (CONTINUED)

119    (CONTINUED)                                              119

                              JOE
                           (grinning)
                    Just call me Joe...

The boy's face and voice are solemn:

                              SEAN
                    You'll be tryin' to catch him?
                    Ogra?

Joe and Sam exchange a quick, amused glance.  Then:

                              JOE
                    Yeah - stick around...

But the boy only stares at him, then turns away, back
down the dock.

                              JOE
                           (kidding him)
                    Not afraid, are you?

But the boy turns seriously towards him.

                              SEAN
                    No...But 'tis a bad thing you're
                    doin'...A terrible bad thing...

He goes slowly back down the dock.  Joe and Sam look
after him, then at each other, amused, but puzzled
too, as we...

                                        DISSOLVE TO:


120    EXT. DECK OF TRITON - JOE, SAM, McCARTIN, BOSUN,      120
       OTHERS - DUSK

The Triton is out in the bay again, a half mile or so
off shore.  Two heavy booms are extended out over the
side.  Steel cables run through snatch-blocks on deck,
and up through blocks on the booms, and back to a steam
winch.  By this means a great steel net is slowly being
fed over the side.  The Bosun is operating the winch.
The other drum of the winch is rigged to another,
smaller boom, to serve the bathysphere, which sits on
deck, in a position to be lowered over the side in its
turn.  The door is swung open, and Joe, Sam and McCartin
stand beside it.

121     BACK TO SCENE                                121

Although there is certainly no friendliness between
Joe and Sam on the one hand, and McCartin on the
other, McCartin is at least resigned - a thief who
has had to make the best of a bad bargain.

> McCARTIN
> (turning to the
> bathysphere)
> You really think you'll catch
> him with that?

> JOE
> With the lights, I figure it'll
> act kinda like a lure - it was
> the torch light from the boats
> brought him up last night...

> SAM
> If that don't work, we'll try
> somethin' else...

At this point the SOUND of the rigging and winch stops,
and Joe looks over towards the Bosun.

> JOE
> Okay, Bos?

> BOSUN
> Okay.

Joe, about to step into the bathysphere, turns to Sam:

> JOE
> I'll be on the phone to you
> the whole time...

He enters the bathysphere, and the heavy door clangs
behind him. Sam turns towards the winch, CAMERA
MOVING with him. He takes his place, puts a pair
of earphones with attached speaker that connects with
the bathysphere, and speaks:

> SAM
> Ready any time you are...Okay...

Sam lets in the clutch on his winch, the bathysphere
is raised from the deck and swung on its booms over
the side.

122     INT. BATHYSPHERE - JOE                   122

as he stands at one of the thick glass view plates.
He also wears earphones.  We see water outside come
up over the view plate, and the bathysphere is submerged.  Joe switches on the interior lights.

JOE
(on phone)
Gimme about fifteen fathoms...
Then I'll tell you...

123     A SERIES OF SHOTS (UNDERWATER)               123
thru                                               thru
126     The bathysphere descending on its heavy steel cable;   126
the water growing darker; occasional schools of fish
swirling around it, or a big grouper or similar
large fish nosing towards it curiously; at the point
its powerful exterior lights go on, piercing the
darkening waters around it.  INTERCUT WITH:

127     A SERIES OF SHOTS - INT. BATHYSPHERE - JOE        127
thru                                               thru
131     as he watches intently through the view plates.  At   131
one point he snaps on the exterior lights.  Looking
out through the view plates, he SEES:

132     WHAT HE SEES:                                       132
thru                                               thru
135     The darkening waters, now illuminated by the ex-     135
terior lights, as they descend; the schools of
fish, etc.

136     MED. CLOSE SHOT - SAM                          136

at the winch.  He speaks into the phone:

SAM
Fifteen fathoms...

137     INT. BATHYSPHERE - JOE                        137

JOE
Take her on down...Slow...

He is watching through the view plate.

138    UNDERWATER SHOT - THE BATHYSPHERE                  138

as it slowly descends.  Now it is within forty or
fifty feet of the bottom, which we dimly see, faintly
illuminated by the bathysphere's lights.

139    INT. BATHYSPHERE - JOE                             139

as he looks through the viewplate, SEES:

140    WHAT HE SEES:                                      140

the slowly approaching ocean floor, as the bathysphere descends.

141    BACK TO SCENE                                      141

                       JOE
              Okay - hold it...

Looking through the viewplate, he SEES:

142    WHAT HE SEES:                                      142

only the vague outlines of the ocean floor, the
schools of fish moving through the beam of light
thrown by the bathysphere.

143    BACK TO SCENE                                      143

                       JOE
                  (becoming more
                  tense)
              Gimme slow engines, Sam - four
              or five knots...Head her down
              the bay...

144    UNDERWATER SHOT - STERN OF TRITON AND PROPELLER    144

as the propeller, idling to hold way against the
tide, now revs up, and the ship begins to move forward.

145    UNDERWATER SHOT - THE BATHYSPHERE                  145

as it moves slowly against the background of the ocean
floor, its cable at a slight angle due to the forward
motion of the ship.

146   INT. BATHYSPHERE - JOE       146

as he peers through the viewplate, tensely.  He SEES:

147   WHAT HE SEES:       147

the dim outlines of the ocean floor, moving slowly
past.

148   MED. CLOSE SHOT - SAM       148

> SAM
> (into phone,
> tense)
> See anything?

149   INT. BATHYSPHERE - JOE       149

as he looks through viewplate.

> JOE
> Not yet...

QUICK DISSOLVE TO:

150   EXT. BAY - THE TRITON       150

as she moves slowly forward.  She is quite far out in
the bay, about opposite the point of land which leads
to the cove.

151   INT. BATHYSPHERE - JOE       151

> JOE
> Where you now, Sam?

152   MED. CLOSE SHOT - SAM       152

> SAM
> Just off the point...Nothing,
> uh?

153   INT. BATHYSPHERE - JOE       153

> JOE
> No...Keep goin'...

He peers through the viewplate.  Suddenly he tenses
at something he SEES:

154   WHAT HE SEES:                                    154

a huge, vague, ill-defined shadow out in the darkness,
beyond the range of the lights.

155   BACK TO SCENE

                           JOE
                 (sharply, on phone)
       Stop engines!

He is now watching closely through the viewplate.
Suddenly his eyes grow wide. He SEES:

156   WHAT HE SEES:                                    156

the monster, as it comes slowly out of the darkness,
into the light. It is not coming in a rush - if anything it seems a little confused, swaying its great
head back and forth in the light. But it is coming
straight on towards him nevertheless.

157   BACK TO SCENE                                    157

                        JOE
                  (tensely)
      I see him...! Stand by with
      your net..!

158   UNDERWATER SHOT - THE MONSTER                  158

as it approaches the bathysphere, more purposefully
now, almost like a fish coming to investigate a lure.

159   INT. BATHYSPHERE - JOE                         159

                        JOE
      Take me up - but not too fast -
      I don't wanta lose him...

160   UNDERWATER SHOT - THE MONSTER                  160

as it makes a sudden, swift rush at the bathysphere,
its jaws open. The bathysphere starts up, but it is
a moment too late. The monster has one of his great
talons over it, and now he attempts to take it in his
teeth, mauling it, somewhat like a clumsy puppy trying
to get his mouth around a bone that's too big for it.
The bathysphere sways in his clutch.

161   INT. BATHYSPHERE - JOE               161

We can hear the dull, scraping clang of the monster's
claws and teeth as it mauls the bathysphere. In the
resulting wild swaying of the bathysphere, Joe is
staggering, trying to keep on his feet. Through the
viewplate, we are now looking right into the monster's
mouth - almost down his throat, so to speak. Joe is
yelling desperately into the phone:

> JOE
> Pull up! PULL UP!

162   EXT. DECK OF TRITON - SAM          162

at the winch. He is desperately giving it all its
got, but the winch drags and shudders, bogging down,
the cable slipping but not coming up.

163   UNDERWATER SHOT - THE MONSTER       163

At the bathysphere, mouthing it. Now he gets a good
grip, and his great jaws clamp down.

164   INT. BATHYSPHERE - JOE              164

thrown partly to the floor of the tilted, swaying
bathysphere, his face drawn with fear as he looks up
on the cue of a rending SOUND and sees a spurting
sheet of water coming through a crack that the monster has made in the bathysphere. He struggles frantically to his feet, grabbing the phone, the water
spraying over him, beginning to slosh in the bottom
of the bathysphere.

> JOE
> Sam! SAM! PULL!

165   EXT. DECK OF TRITON - SAM          165

at the winch, sweating as he tries, with no success.
The steel cable from the winch to the boom is vibra-
ting like a bass string, and the boom is groaning.
Sam yells into his phone:

> SAM
> That's all she'll take - she'll
> snap the cable!

166    INT. BATHYSPHERE - JOE                        166

     as the water sprays in, sloshing and rising on the
     floor as the bathysphere sways and rocks, and the
     fearful SOUND of the monster's mauling comes over.
     Joe takes a quick, frightened look towards the view-
     plate, then yells into the phone:

                    JOE
              Then drop your net!

167    EXT. DECK OF TRITON - BOSUN                    167

     as he slams off his brake, and the cables to the net
     start paying out with a rattling roar.

168    UNDERWATER SHOT - THE MONSTER                  168

     as it gnaws at the bathysphere.  The net descends.  It
     touches the monster.  The monster reacts, slashing at
     it with his talon.  It is the beginning of his undoing.
     His talon is caught in the net, like a cat's claw in
     a wire screen.  Now he releases the bathysphere,
     striking out at the net with his other talon.  It also
     becomes enmeshed.

169    INT. BATHYSPHERE - JOE                         169

     as the bathysphere, released by the monster, eases in
     its violent motion.  Joe rushes to the viewplate,
     looks out, SEES:

170    WHAT HE SEES:                                  170

     the monster struggling savagely, becoming more and
     more entangled in the net.

171    BACK TO SCENE

     as Joe yells into the phone.

                    JOE
           Snug up!  Snug up!  We've got
           him!

172     UNDERWATER SHOT - THE MONSTER                              172

as the net tightens around him, and he tries to fight
it.  The bathysphere starts rising out of scene.

                                        DISSOLVE TO:


173     EXT. DECK OF TRITON - JOE, SAM, BOSUN, McCARTIN -    173
        MONSTER

The Bosun is at his winch.  McCartin looks on from
b.g.  Standing well in the clear are Sam and Crew
Members stationed near heavy cables with shackle
bolts which, at the other end, are attached to ring
bolts in the deck.  Joe, still wet from his bathysphere experience, stands at the rail, supervising
the lifting of the netted monster.

                        JOE
                    (calling to
                     Bosun)
                Come on up - easy...


174     EXT. TRITON AND SEA - (MINIATURE)                       174

The net with madly struggling monster is being
slowly pulled up.


175     EXT. TRITON DECK - MED. LONG - MINIATURE AND         175
        TRAVELLING MATTE

The net with struggling beast is being pulled and
now swings in the air above the deck line.  Joe
gives order to swing in the outrigged boom.

                        JOE
                Swing 'er in...


176     EXT. TRITON DECK - MONSTER IN F.G.                      176

The monster is being moved toward the deck.  Joe
crosses to pick up one of the cables:

                        JOE
                Let's get ready with those
                shackle bolts...

Sam and crew members move to execute his order, as we...

                                        DISSOLVE TO:

MONTAGE

177    TRITON RADIO ANTENNA                                    177

and over it the SOUND of rapid Morse code.


178    RADIO TOWER - (LIKE RCA)                                178

Other RADIO TOWERS come in, SUPERIMPOSED - the SOUND
of Morse code from many keys, building.


179    INT. U.S. TV STUDIO - NEWSCASTER, CAMERAMAN             179

                          NEWSCASTER
              The headlines of the entire
              world are being monopolized...


180    A SERIES OF SHOTS:  (STOCK WHEN POSSIBLE)              180

    a)  Crowds around a New York newsstand, snatching
        papers.

    b)  Workers in a plant, crowding around a radio
        loudspeaker.

    c)  Crowds in Moscow, around a newspaper kiosk.

    d)  Crowds outside a TV store, listening and
        watching the TV set in the window (the screen
        to be seen or not, as desired).

    e)  Crowds around a Paris newspaper kiosk.

    f)  London crowds - a newsvendor with his sign:
        "MONSTER OF NARA ISLAND!"

    g)  Crowds in Times Square looking up at the
        Times Building lighted newsticker.

                          NEWSCASTER'S VOICE
                        (continuing over above)
                   ...by the news of the capture of
                   a fantastic monster, seemingly
                   prehistoric origin, off the coast
                   of Ireland.  Puzzled scientists
                   are already speculating that the
                   monster may have been released
                   from some vast suboceanic cavern
                   far beneath the earth's crust, by
                   unprecedented volcanic eruptions,
                   which occurred in the area last
                   week...

                                        DISSOLVE TO:

181     INT. BRITISH TV STUDIO - BBC NEWSCASTER                    181

                    BBC NEWSCASTER
            ...Some scientific authorities
            are suggesting that the whole
            thing is merely an elaborate
            Irish hoax.  Nevertheless...

                                        QUICK DISSOLVE TO:


182     FULL SHOT - THE BAY - FLYING BOAT                          182

        as it comes down to a landing, heading towards the
        dock.

                    BBC NEWSCASTER'S VOICE
                        (over)
            ...The Irish Government are send-
            ing two of their top paleontolo-
            gists to claim the creature for
            Ireland - if it does exist...

                                            DISSOLVE TO:


183     EXT. DECK OF TRITON - JOE, SAM, McCARTIN, FLAHERTY,    183
        O'BRIEN

        The Triton is anchored in the bay.  Joe and Sam are
        standing at the companionway which leads down towards
        the water.  CAMERA IS HIGH to catch FLAHERTY and
        O'BRIEN, followed by McCartin and his guards, as they
        come up.  At this point the RADIO OPERATOR enters,
        hands Joe a radiogram form.  Joe scans it hastily,
        grins broadly, glances at Sam, stuffs the radiogram
        in his pocket.  The both men are shaking hands with
        Flaherty and O'Brien, as introduced by McCartin.

                                            DISSOLVE TO:


184     EXT. DECK OF TRITON - THE GROUP -(MONSTER IN B.G.)     184

        as they stand, in appropriate order, around the now
        thoroughly shackled monster.  The beast rumbles
        occasionally, and glares, but seems to have achieved
        a certain resignation to its captivity.  The two
        scientists are looking the monster over, conferring
        briefly in lowered voices.  Now Flaherty turns to Joe:

                                        (CONTINUED)

184    (CONTINUED)                                              184

                          FLAHERTY
          I was just saying to my colleague
          - it is almost unbelievable!  I
          wonder if you realize, Captain
          Ryan, the enormous scientific
          value of this discovery!

                          JOE
                    (a glance at Sam)
          I think we do, Professor Flaherty.

                          FLAHERTY
                    (looking at the
                    monster)
          Incredible..!
                    (then back to Joe
                    and business)
          Well, then.  I shall wireless the
          University of Dublin at once to
          make proper preparations to re-
          ceive the animal...

                          JOE
                    (nodding)
          I see...

Sam looks increasingly puzzled as the scene goes on,
but Joe is bland.

                          FLAHERTY
          You will proceed to Dublin...
                    (adding hastily)
          Of course you will be properly
          compensated for your services...

                          JOE
          Oh - sure...

                          FLAHERTY
                    (including O'Brien)
          We will meet you there...
                    (afterthought)
          Unless you would like to have
          one of us go with you...

                          JOE
          No need...

                                              :(CONTINUED)

184   (CONTINUED - 2)                                    184

> FLAHERTY
> Very good.  Ah - one thing.  The
> animal's skin should be kept wet
> with water -- a continuous stream
> of water.  That is important.

> JOE
> I'll take care of it...

> FLAHERTY
> Yes...And when do you intend
> sailing, Captain?

> JOE
> Tonight, if it's okay with you.

> FLAHERTY
> Excellent - the sooner the
> better...
> > (putting out
> > his hand)
>
> Well, then.  We shall expect
> you within a few days.

Joe, Sam, and the two scientists shake hands, and the
scientists start down the gangway.  McCartin follows.
Joe turns toward Sam - to find that Sam is looking at
him with a thoroughly sour expression.

> SAM
> University of Dublin..!  Com-
> pensated for your services!
> Big deal..!

But Joe is grinning as he pulls the radiogram from
his pocket.

> JOE
> From Dorkin's London Circus.
> > (reading)
>
> "...guarantee thirty thousand
> pounds against fifty percent of
> the gross..."

He hands the radiogram to Sam.  Sam glances at it
briefly, grins broadly.

> JOE
> Set a course for London...

Both are grinning broadly, as we...

                                          DISSOLVE TO:

185    FULL SHOT - OPEN SEA - TRITON - NIGHT    185

She is out of sight of shore. There is a moderate
sea running, and she is pitching some, and throwing
spray at her bow. She shows running lights, a single
deck light forward.

186    EXT. MAIN DECK OF TRITON - THE MONSTER - NIGHT    186

in his net. The numerous steel cables which hold
down the base of the net are snugged down and taut
now. The netted monster is partially illuminated
by the deck light, which is located aft of him. But
forward on the other side of him, there are areas of
deep shadow. A canvas canopy has been rigged above
him to keep off the sun during the day, and one of
the ship's fire hoses plays a stream of water on him
from above, the water running down aft into the
scuppers. It is the middle watch, and the ship is
quiet. We hear the muffled thudding of the engines,
the splashing water and the rhythmic dash of spray
from the bow; the faint, groaning labor of the ship
as she plows through the seas; the creaking of a
swaying boom; the rattle of a block, and the clanking
of the monster's net. (This whole sequence to be
played for eeriness and not maximum suspense.) The
monster too is quiet, hunched down into itself,
almost as though dozing. Then suddenly it raises its
head as though it had heard or sensed something.
Now, rising under its net, it turns slowly towards
the shadowed area on the other side of it.

187    REVERSE SHOT - THE MONSTER    187

as he looks down at the shadowed deck. Then, from
under a tarpaulin lashed over some oil drums, emerges
Sean. First he sticks his head out, looking around
cautiously. But it is not for fear of the monster,
as we shall see. Now he crawls out, stands looking
up at the monster, contemplatively. The monster
looks down at him in much the same spirit. Then
Sean says something, softly, in Gaelic - the impression
is of a salutation, or expression of respect. The
monster rumbles, but the boy still shows no fear. He
looks swiftly about him, sizing up the situation of
the monster and the net, then steps forward and to
one side, where the nearest shackle bolt is located,
and starts trying to loosen it. The monster turns,
so that he again is facing towards the boy, towering
above him, and edging forward. The boy is oblivious
of this, engrossed with the shackle bolt, though

(CONTINUED)

187    (CONTINUED)                                                187

    making little progress.  He does not notice the
    flickering beam of a flashlight moving up behind
    him.  But it is on this cue that the monster
    strikes.  It is impossible to tell whether he is
    striking at the light or directly at the boy, but
    the fact remains that the talon is descending over
    the boy, as the monster roars.  Sean has whirled
    to see Joe with the light, thus does not see the
    descending talon.  Joe is just in time to yank the
    boy back before the slashing talon rips into the
    net where the boy was.

188    ANOTHER ANGLE - JOE, SEAN - (MONSTER IN B.G.)            188

    The monster roars and snarls, slashing.  Joe and
    Sean are on the lighted part of the deck.  Himself
    shaken by the experience, Joe has the boy tightly
    by the arm and is shaking him till his teeth rattle,
    as he yells:

                JOE
            What the hell do you think
            you're doing!

    There is a suspicion of tears in the boy's angry
    eyes, from the pain of Joe's grip, and the general
    situation.  Sam hurries in, followed shortly by the
    Bosun, attracted by the commotion and the roaring
    of the beast.  Sam growls at Joe:

                SAM
            Hey - take it on the slow-
            bell...

    Joe releases his grip, the boy rubs his arms.  Joe
    and Sam exchange a glance.  In the b.g. the Bosun
    looks on curiously.

                SEAN
            (sullenly)
            I came to let him go.  Back to
            the sea.  Where he belongs.

                JOE
            (still sore)
            Oh, you did, did you!

                SAM
            (more gently,
            curious)
          Why?

                              (CONTINUED)

188    (CONTINUED)                                          188

> SEAN
> (flaring)
> To save your silly skins for
> ye - that's why!

Joe and Sam exchange an amused, tolerant glance,
Joe's anger mollified.

> JOE
> (not meaning
> it)
> I got a good notion to toss you
> right over the side.

> SEAN
> You wouldn't be sendin' me back?

> JOE
> You little stinker, you know
> I can't send you back.

> SEAN
> Now there you're showin' some
> sense...

Joe and Sam grin at each other.

> JOE
> (to Sam)
> Well, we better get the new
> hand a bunk and some grub...
> (to Bosun, indi-
> cating the mon-
> ster)
> Bos', put a watch on that thing.
> Twenty-four hours.  And give him
> a rifle.

> BOSUN
> (approving)
> Right now, Joe!

> SEAN
> (looking up slyly
> at Joe, wondering
> if he'll bite)
> I could be watchin' him for ye,
> now...

The Bosun rings and exits, as Joe looks down at the
boy with a rueful grin, seeing through him:

> (CONTINUED)

188   (CONTINUED - 2)                     188

> JOE
> Yeah - you'd be great!  Come
> on...

The three exit, the boy looking back at the monster.
CAMERA MOVES IN on the monster.  It rumbles, as we...

> DISSOLVE TO:

189   EXT. DECK OF TRITON - BOSUN, CREW MEMBER -   189
(MONSTER IN B.G.) - NIGHT

as the Bosun brings the crew member in, indicating
the monster, handing the man a rifle.

> BOSUN
> ...And if he makes so much as
> a move, start shootin' and run
> like the devil!

The man grins, and the Bosun exits.

> DISSOLVE TO:

190   INT. CABIN - JOE, SAM, SEAN - NIGHT       190

The boy is slipping into his bunk.  O.S. we HEAR the
monster rumble.  All turn momentarily towards the
SOUND, listening.  Then:

> SAM
> Tell me somethin' kid...Did any-
> one ever see that thing before?

> SEAN
> And why should anyone have to
> be seein' it to know it's there?

Joe and Sam exchange a glance of resignation to the
kid's credulity, then Joe turns to put out the light,
as he says gruffly:

> JOE
> Go to sleep.

They exit.

191    EXT. DECK OF TRITON - JOE, SAM - NIGHT                    191

    as they come out on deck, make their way forward.
Suddenly Sam hesitates and stops, looking over the
rail.  Joe follows his example.  They SEE:

192    WHAT THEY SEE:                                            192

    the dark sea, as it streams back along the side of
the ship, but strangely streaked with a white,
gleaming irridescence.

193    BACK TO SCENE - (HIGH ANGLE - SEA IN B.G.)               193

    as Joe and Sam look down.

                JOE
         Phosphorus...

                SAM
           (shaking his
           head)
         It's comin' from the scuppers...
         It's the water off the animal...

                JOE
         So it's still sea water...
           (grinning)
         You seein' spirits too?

    At this point there is a rifle shot, followed immedi-
ately by a piercing scream that dies out in a kind
of gurgle.  Joe and Sam stare at each other, then turn
and race forward.

194    EXT. DECK OF TRITON - JOE, SAM, BOSUN, CREW              194
       MEMBERS - (MONSTER) - NIGHT

    as Joe and Sam race in, followed by the others.  A
small portion of the net has been torn.  Near it
lies the watchman, badly mangled, clearly dead.
Joe grabs up the fallen rifle, fires a couple of
shots towards the monster as he yells:

                JOE
         Secure that net!

    The Bosun and other crew member frantically whip the
loose cable through strands of the net, backing away
as the monster roars, but hanging onto the cable,

               (CONTINUED)

194   (CONTINUED)                                                    194

pulling it tight.  Joe meanwhile bends over the dead
man.  Sean enters the scene.  The silent reproof -
the "I told you so" - in his eyes, causes Joe, when
he sees him, to burst out:

> JOE
> I thought I told you to stay
> below!

The boy looks down at the dead man, then at Joe.  Joe
shoots a glance at Sam.  A couple of other crew members
have entered the scene, murmuring to each other, staring
down at the dead man.  The Bosun has come over beside
Joe.  Joe straightens up, looking down at the dead man,
speaking to the Bosun:

> JOE
> (quietly)
> Get him ready for burial...

Now he turns gruffly to Sean:

> JOE
> Go on back to your cabin...

The boy turns and exits.  Joe and Sam look after him.
Sam looks worried as we...

> DISSOLVE TO:

195   EXT. LOWER THAMES - DORKIN, BBC NEWSCASTER #2,        195
OTHERS - DAY

CAMERA IS CLOSE on a huge banner, similar to one we
will see at the Circus Grounds, of the beast, exaggerated and hideous, and lettering:

> Dorkin's London Circus
>
> Welcomes
>
> G O R G O !
>
> The Eighth Wonder of the World!

We hear the whistles and horns of ships from all over
the river, CAMERA PULLS BACK TO REVEAL that the banner
is displayed on a LAUNCH which is carrying Dorkin,
Newsmen, Customs Officials, etc. out to meet the Triton.

196  SKY SHOT - BBC HELICOPTER - DAY                          196

as it hovers over the river, BBC lettered on its side.


197  INT. HELICOPTER - BBC RADIO ANNOUNCER, CAMERAMAN -   197
(PROCESS)

the newsreel cameraman shooting the scene below as
the announcer speaks into his mike:

                    BBC RADIO ANNOUNCER
          ...and it is safe to say that
          London has not seen such ex-
          citement since V-E Day...


198  AIR SHOT - THE RIVER - (STOCK ?)                       198

SHOWING the gala atmosphere - decorated harbor
craft, etc.

                    BBC RADIO ANNOUNCER'S VOICE
                         (over)
          The ship is now approaching
          the dock, and directly we
          shall transfer you to her decks,
          and try to give you an actual
          view of the monster itself...


199  EXT. DECK OF TRITON - JOE, SAM, DORKIN, OTHERS -    199
DAY

The B.G. SOUNDS continue.  Joe, with a beaming Dorkin
at his side, is being besieged by NEWSMEN.  Flash-
bulbs pop.  The officials and Sam stand a little aside.
A TV camera and cameraman move past, accompanied by
BBC Newscaster #2, who approaches Dorkin.

                    BBC NEWSCASTER #2
          Mr. Dorkin, this is the BBC.  We
          understand that your Circus has
          contracted for the exhibition of
          this strange creature - perhaps
          you could tell our audience some
          of your future plans...

Dorkin is a brash character, a trace of Cockney.

                    DORKIN
          Plans?  Well - we've built a
          special tank - rushed the job
          through - and now we hope to
          just sit back and watch the money
          roll in!

                                        (CONTINUED)

199    (CONTINUED)                                                    199

                              BBC NEWSCASTER #2
                    I see...Now there is a report
                    from Dublin that the Irish
                    Government have instituted
                    legal proceedings to recover
                    the animal...

                              DORKIN
                    True enough.  It will go through
                    the courts, naturally, and in a
                    year or so we'll have a decision.
                              (broad smile)
                    Meanwhile - come and see Gorgo
                    at Battersea Park!

                              BBC NEWSCASTER #2
                    By the way - that name Gorgo --
                    has it any special significance?

                              DORKIN
                    Certainly!  The Greek Monster -
                    the Gorgon!  What could be more
                    horrible than a creature, the
                    mere sight of which could turn
                    a man to stone!

                              BBC NEWSCASTER #2
                    Oh, you've actually seen the
                    creature?

                              DORKIN
                    Not at all!
                              (a wave towards
                              the banner)
                    But I have the most accurate re-
                    ports - from the BBC!

                              BBC NEWSCASTER #2
                    Oh...

          The TV camera moves in, cutting off the scene, as flash-
          bulbs pop again, other Newsmen surge forward.

                                                  DISSOLVE TO:


200    EXT. DOCK - (TRITON IN B.G. - MINIATURE) - JOE,        200
       DORKIN, FLAHERTY, HENDRICKS, OTHERS - NIGHT

          The hubbub of the day is over, and the ship is quiet.
          But we hear the angry voice of Professor Hendricks:

                                                  (CONTINUED)

200    (CONTINUED)                                                200

                          HENDRICKS' VOICE
                        (over)
              ...A creature unique in the history
              of evolutionary biology!

CAMERA PANS to the group of Joe, Dorkin, and the two
Professors:  SAM and SEAN stand a little apart.

                          HENDRICKS
              And you turn it into a circus
              freak!  It's outrageous!
                        (a glance towards
                        the bitter Flaherty)
              Quite apart from the fact that
              you stole it!

        JOE                                    DORKIN
That's a matter                        But Professor Hendricks -
of opinion!                            when the courts decide...

                          FLAHERTY
                        (cutting them off)
              But even worse at the moment -
              you know absolutely nothing
              about the animal!  It's ex-
              tremely dangerous...

                          JOE
                        (cutting in)
              We've handled him so far...

                          FLAHERTY
                        (going on)
              ...it may even carry disease -
              bearing parasites or unknown
              bacteria...and you take it into
              the heart of a great city before
              any observations can be made -
              before any tests - without the
              slightest thought of what the re-
              sults might be!

                          JOE
              Look - what do you want from us?

                          HENDRICKS
              First, the opportunity to make
              a complete study...

                          JOE
              Sure - if it doesn't interfere
              with business...

                                          (CONTINUED)

200   (CONTINUED - 2)                                   200

                    DORKIN
              (hastily placating)
Believe me, gentlemen - once we
have the creature installed at
Battersea, you'll be given every
facility!

                 FLAHERTY
You insist on taking the animal
into the city?

                  DORKIN
              (a shrug)
Arrangements have already been
made...

                HENDRICKS
I suppose you've thought of the
need to give the animal a tranquilizing drug while you transport it...
              (as Joe and Dorkin
              look blank)
Because if you haven't, you'd
better.

                  DORKIN
              (ingratiating)
Perhaps you gentlemen could do
that for us...

                HENDRICKS
              (a look at Flaherty,
              then, coldly)
Very well - we'll be back in the
morning...Goodnight.

They turn to go.  Joe is frowning.


201    CLOSE SHOT - SEAN                           201

There is a strange little smile on the boy's face,
as he watches the Professors go.

                            DISSOLVE TO:

202    LONG SHOT - NARA ISLAND AND BAY - NIGHT    202

There is a swirling fog, and somewhere a foghorn
sends out its periodic, mournful hoot.  In f.g. is
a lighthouse with its revolving beam, and near it
a radio shack and radio tower.  This is a somewhat
higher point of land, which accounts for the location of the lighthouse and tower.  There is a light
in the radio shack.  In b.g. may dimly be seen
through the fog a few lights of the village and
dock.

203    INT. RADIO SHACK - McCARTIN - RADIO OPERATOR -    203
    NIGHT

McCartin is going over a sheaf of radiograms.  The
operator is at his set, receiving and taking down a
routine message.  Suddenly McCartin raises his head,
listening.  Now the operator hears it too - o.s., a
SOUND like the rising rush of a huge wave.  McCartin,
followed by the operator, goes to the window to look
out.  They freeze in horror at what they SEE:

204    MAMA MONSTER    204

a great, gray shape, at first indistinct, rising
from the water.  Then appears the head.  It is tremendous.  This is shown against the b.g. perspective of the lighthouse and radio tower and shack.
She has risen in all her giant majesty, and now sways
her great head, almost as though searching for some
clue or scent.  She gives an angry, hair-raising,
earthshaking roar, and starts for the shore.

205    INT. RADIO SHACK - McCARTIN, OPERATOR    205

as they make a dash for the door, and with fear.

206    MAMA MONSTER    206

as she clambers up onto the point of land, swaying
her head.

207    EXT. RADIO SHACK - McCARTIN, OPERATOR - (MAMA    207
    MONSTER IN B.G.)

as they run for their lives, the operator now in the
lead, looking back for a terrified glance at Mama
Monster towering above them.

208     MAMA MONSTER                                    208

on the point of land, her head moving, searching. Now
she turns towards the sea, on the other side of the
point from which she emerged. The beam of the lighthouse falls on her, passing over her. The foghorn
(which is in the lighthouse) hoots. Mama Monster
growls angrily, lashes out with her huge tail,
striking the lighthouse. The structure begins to
crumble. The light goes out, and the foghorn stops
abruptly in the middle of a blast.


209     TWO SHOT - McCARTIN, OPERATOR                   209

running. Looking back, they see the lighthouse falling. It is falling directly towards the radio tower,
near the base of which they are.


210     MAMA MONSTER                                    210

as she turns her head towards the destruction. The
lighthouse crashes into the radio tower, and the tower
begins to crumble.


211     TWO SHOT - McCARTIN, OPERATOR                   211

as they run madly to get out from under the falling
tower. The operator makes it, but McCartin is too
late, and is crushed by the tangle of steel.


212     MAMA MONSTER                                    212

turning back towards the sea. Behind her a great cloud
of dust rises from the rubble of the lighthouse. She
slips down into the water. A faint phosphorescent
streak, fading off northward can be seen at her point
of entry.

                                        FADE OUT:


FADE IN:

213     EXT. STREET - DAY - CLOSE SHOT - (TRAVELLING)   213

Two men in white, with white helmets and flame-throwing
gear. CAMERA DOLLIES BACK REVEALING that they are
riding in a jeep, on the flank of a huge platform
(a trailer, similar to that used for moving houses)

                                        (CONTINUED)

213 (CONTINUED) 213

on which the monster is being transported. The monster is in its net, securely chained to the platform, apparently asleep. The platform is liberally decorated with signs similar to the one we saw at the dock. The BLARE of the Circus Band is HEARD, and the CHEERING of crowds. As the procession moves on, the Circus BANDWAGON comes into scene, directly behind the platform, the Band playing lustily.

214 EXT. STREET - THE HEAD OF THE PROCESSION - DAY 214

In an open car are JOE, SAM, DORKIN - the latter particularly expansive. Now, coming into scene behind it is another open car. CAMERA MOVES IN. In it is a driver, police official, Professors Hendricks and Flaherty, Sean. Now Sean's attention is caught by something. He looks up.

215 EXT. STREET - DAY - MED. TRAVELLING SHOT - (THEIR 215
P.O.V.)

The rooftops as seen from moving car. The rooftops are jammed with people.

216 EXT. STREET - DAY - VERY LONG SHOT FROM ABOVE - 216
(ONLOOKERS' P.O.V.)

SHOOTING DOWN FROM THIS VANTAGE POINT we see for the first time the transfer operation in its majestic totality. Police on motorcycles; open car with our principals; jeeps with City officials; and the platform. On it, the monster. The slow-moving procession passes by. The wide street is cleared of pedestrians. All adjacent houses are closed by lines of policemen, holding back the huge crowds.

217 EXT. STREET - DAY - MED. SHOT 217

CAMERA DOLLIES SLOWLY on the row of policemen holding back the crowd in one of the adjoining streets. They look at the procession with intense interest.

218 EXT. STREET - DAY - MED. LONG SHOT 218

the procession passing...

DISSOLVE TO:

219     EXT. ENTRANCE TO THE CIRCUS - NIGHT - LONG SHOT     219

The procession now passes the gates of the circus.


220     EXT. CIRCUS - NIGHT - A MONTAGE OF SHOTS OF CAGES     220
AND ENCLOSURES OF WILD ANIMALS - MED. CLOSE SHOT

The wild animals are greatly disturbed. They move
about uneasily. The tigers and lions are snarling.
The elephants stomp their feet nervously.


221     EXT. CIRCUS - LONG SHOT - (SPECIAL EFFECT)     221

FEATURING the monster's tank and enclosure. The
tank is a circular concrete bowl in the ground,
about a hundred and fifty feet in diameter, its rim
a raised concrete parapet about four feet above
ground. In the center is an artificial rock, similar
to that of polar bear tanks. It is filled with water,
with a standpipe for constant flow and circulation.
It is about twenty feet in depth, so that - as we
shall see - the top of the parapet comes just below
the monster's forearms when it stands at full height.
Mounted on steel posts embedded in the parapet at
about twenty foot intervals, and about twenty feet
high, is a network of high tension wires - about
five strands of them, or four feet apart. They are
attached to the posts by heavy porcelain insulators.
Surrounding all of this, and about twenty feet back
from it, is an eight foot fence to keep the spectators back from the tank and the wires. But now there
is a twenty foot opening in both fence and wires, to
permit the monster to be placed in the tank. Through
the opening in the fence, the truck-platform is
backed towards a ramp leading to the tank. A crane
is lowering the animal to the ramp. JOE directs the
operation by hand signals, as Sam and Bosun stand by.


222     EXT. CIRCUS - NIGHT - CLOSE     222

The crane operators are tensely watching.


223     EXT. CIRCUS - NIGHT - CLOSE     223

Professors Hendricks and Flaherty, Sean, Police
Officials and Dorkin are watching.

224    EXT. CIRCUS - NIGHT - MED.               224

A daring workman suspended on the chain lowering the
animal directs the speed of the crane.

225    EXT. CIRCUS - NIGHT - MED. - (SPECIAL EFFECTS)    225

The animal still entangled in steel nets is lowered
to the inclined ramp.

226    EXT. CIRCUS - NIGHT - MED. CLOSE - JOE, DORKIN,    226
BOSUN

Dorkin gives an order to an assistant.  The assistant
rushes out of the SHOT.

227    EXT. CIRCUS - NIGHT - MED.               227

A group of workmen armed with long clippers.  The
assistant runs in, gives order.  The workmen move
toward the animal.

228    EXT. CIRCUS - NIGHT - MED. CLOSE - (SPECIAL EFFECTS) 228

Workmen cautiously approach the animal, start to cut
the steel net with their clippers.

229    EXT. CIRCUS - NIGHT - PROFESSORS HENDRICKS,    229
FLAHERTY, SEAN, POLICE OFFICIALS, DORKIN - MED.
CLOSE

They are watching the dangerous operation.

                    HENDRICKS
                (to Flaherty)
         The tranquilizier seems to be
        working - so far...

230    EXT. CIRCUS - NIGHT - MED. CLOSE - (SPECIAL EFFECTS) 230

Workmen approach the tremendous head of the animal.
Its eyes are closed.  Is it asleep?...The workmen
start to cut the steel net around the animal's head.
Joe, Sam and Bosun move in, pulling back the cut
strands of net.

231   EXT. CIRCUS - NIGHT - MED. CLOSE                    231

A group of newsmen.  One of them, runs forward, lifts
his camera.  Shoots flash picture.

232   EXT. CIRCUS - NIGHT - MED. CLOSE - (SPECIAL EFFECT)  232

Aroused by the flash, the animal roars, snaps the
last treads of the steel net.

233   GROUP SHOT - JOE, BOSUN, WORKMEN                     233

as they fall back.  Joe yells over his shoulder:

                         JOE
              Bring up those flame throwers!..

234   GROUP SHOT - PROFESSORS - SEAN, POLICE OFFICIALS,   234
      DORKIN

as they watch fearfully.

235   EXT. CIRCUS - NIGHT - ELEPHANT - MED.               235

Reacting to the thunderous ROAR of the monster, the
elephant moves about violently.

236   EXT. CIRCUS - NIGHT - CLOSE                         236

The stake holding the elephant's foot to the ground
pulls loose.

237   EXT. CIRCUS - NIGHT - MED.                          237

The beast still aroused by the flash and for the
first time free from the steel net, lashes about,
ROARING.  A truck is in its way.  It turns it over.

238   EXT. CIRCUS - NIGHT - CLOSE                         238

The truck pins down three workmen.  The monster
marches across it.

239   EXT. CIRCUS - NIGHT - MED.                          239

The beast moves forward.

240     EXT. CIRCUS - NIGHT - MED.                          240

The enraged elephant charges.


241     EXT. CIRCUS - NIGHT - MED. LONG - (SPECIAL EFFECTS)  241

With all its might the elephant charges the monster.
Its tusks plow into the massive body of the beast.


242     EXT. CIRCUS - NIGHT - ANOTHER ANGLE                 242

The beast staggers under the impact, then turns toward
the attacking elephant, beating the ground with its
tail.


243     EXT. CIRCUS - NIGHT - LONG HIGH SHOT - (SPECIAL     243
thru    EFFECTS COMBINING LIVE AND MINIATURE)               thru
253                                                         253

The struggle of the giants.


254     EXT. CIRCUS - NIGHT - MED. - (SPECIAL EFFECTS)      254

The beast sinks its teeth in the neck of the elephant
and lifts all of 5 tons of him, then throws him down
and tears at the elephant with its steel talons.


255     REACTION SHOTS                                      255

of horrified spectators.


256     GROUP SHOT - JOE, FLAME-THROWERS                    256

The flame-throwers running forward, urged on by Joe,
gesturing frantically, yelling, but almost unheard
over the ROARING of the beast.


257     ANOTHER ANGLE                                       257

as they approach the monster.  The monster, his talons
on the dead elephant, sways his great head, looking
around as though he's in a mood to take on the whole
bunch.  The men give a couple of bursts of the flame-
throwers.  The monster roars.  But the men are too
far away.  Joe yells at them, they move forward, give
the monster a close burst.  The monster bellows in
anguish.

258    REACTION SHOTS          258

of spectators.  Sean is visibly suffering.

259    GROUP SHOT - JOE, SAM, FLAME-THROWERS (MONSTER)    259

The monster begins to retreat, bellowing in pain,
guided and urged on by bursts of the flame-throwers.
Bosun moves in beside Joe.

260    ANOTHER ANGLE          260

The beast suddenly turns, avoiding the fire, heading
for the ramp.  It looks as though it's all over.
There is a relaxation of those in scene.  And then,
like a bolt of lightning - so quick and unexpected -
the great tail flicks.

261    MED. CLOSE - THE BOSUN          261

as the tail hits him a terrible, full smashing blow.
He is sent flying, CAMERA FOLLOWING, and he never
moves when he lands.  JOE rushes in, followed by SAM.
They kneel beside the Bosun, but it is clear from
the outset that he is dead.  Sam and Joe's eyes meet.
Sam gives him a long, level look.  Then both turn to
SEE:

262    ANOTHER ANGLE - JOE, SAM, SEAN    262

as the boy stands looking solemnly down at the Bosun.
Sam looks at Joe again, but Joe will not meet his
eyes.

                  DISSOLVE TO:

263    EXT. CIRCUS - NIGHT - MED. LONG - (SPECIAL EFFECTS)  263

The animal is alone.  It moves uneasily in its new
surrounding.  The openings in both fence and wires
are now of course closed.  The monster raises up to
full height at the parapet, reaches out and grasps
the lowest strand of wire.  Instantly there is a
bright, crackling flash.  The monster bellows in pain,
backing off, climbing up on its rock.  Then it lifts
its head and emits a long plaintive ROAR.  At a little
distance, Sean watches.

                  DISSOLVE TO:

264     EXT. SEA - NIGHT                                    264

A full moon looms large above the horizon.  Then, in
f.g. there is a great roiling of the waters, and the
head and shoulders of MAMA MONSTER appear - against
the b.g. of the moon, and almost blotting it out with
her huge size.  She ROARS, on a long, rumbling note,
like thunder.  Then she starts sinking beneath the
sea again.  We note the phosphorescent "track" in the
water.

                                        DISSOLVE TO:


(Following montage sequence to express the feeling
of popular excitement and a land-office business.)


265     EXT. SIGN - DAY - CLOSE                             265

The beast.  CAMERA DOLLIES BACK and REVEALS that it
is being painted by men from a hanging board on a
huge advertising sign.  The sign dominates a panorama
of London's business district.  The picture of the
beast is greatly exaggerated, emphasizing its more
hideous features.  And huge lettering proclaims:
GORGO!  The Eighth Wonder of the World!  Dorkin's
London Circus.

                                        DISSOLVE TO:


266     EXT. NEWSSTAND - LONDON - DAY - MED. CLOSE          266

A display of papers.  The headlines and photographs
all carry the story about the beast.  CAMERA DOLLIES
BACK to INCLUDE a crowd of eager bystanders.  A line
of school-children passes, led by their teacher.

                                        DISSOLVE TO:


267     EXT. CIRCUS ENTRANCE - DAY - MED. LONG              267

Another line of school-children in front of circus.
There is an excited jostling crowd waiting at the
ticket office.

                                        DISSOLVE TO:


268     EXT. CIRCUS - FULL SHOT - DAY                       268

The crowd in front of the monster's enclosure.  They
are in a gala mood.  Vendors of all kinds circulate
among them, and attendants are having a hard time
keeping order.

269     MED. SHOT - FEATURING MONSTER                    269

The monster gives the impression of being bewildered
and unhappy.  He shrinks back from the milling, gaping
crowd.  He gives a plaintive bellow, and the crowd
roars in delight.  The monster shrinks from the sound.
A little apart, SEAN watches, darkly.

                                        DISSOLVE TO:


270     EXT. CIRCUS GROUNDS - NIGHT                      270

On the outskirts of the throng gathered near the monster exhibit, Joe drives an expensive foreign make
automobile.  Joe notes the queue at the monster exhibit with some gratification.  He moves the car alongside a circus wagon.  When he emerges, we see that he
is elegantly attired.  He moves to the wagon.


271     INT. CIRCUS WAGON - NIGHT                        271

The interior of the wagon is very small.  A few bunks.
A small table.  Several chairs.  A single bulb for
illumination.  Within are Sam and Sean, the latter in
bed and asleep.  Sam sits at the table, a bottle and
glass in front of him.  He is not drunk but he's had
a few.  From time to time from O.S. come the eerie
bellows and roars of the circus animals.  It is summer
and the door is partly open.  Sam looks up as Joe
enters.  For the first time they are ill at ease with
each other.  Both keep their voices down, not to waken
the boy.

                          JOE
                Uh - I was goin' into town...
                I saw the light...

                          SAM
                Have fun...

                          JOE
                I thought you might like to go
                along - have a coupla belts...

                          SAM
                I'm havin' a coupla belts...
                     (a barb in it)
                How's business?

                                        (CONTINUED)

                    JOE
               (defiantly, sensing
               the barb)
          Great!
               (a beat; then:)
          Aw Sam, quit buckin' it!
               (waving his arm
               at the wagon)
          Get out of this dump!  Live a
          little!  I got a whole suite
          at the Claridge!..

                    SAM
          This suits us...

Suddenly there is a deafening roar of animals from
O.S.  Sam listens, rises and goes to the small window
and looks out, then turns to Joe.  There is accusa-
tion in his tone.

                    SAM
          The animals are going crazy.
          Something's gonna happen, Joe.
          I can feel it!  The Bos' is
          dead -- who's next?

                    JOE
          I'm as sorry about the Bos'
          as you are -- It was a tough
          break, that's all...

                    SAM
          He's got a wife in Galway.
          That'll make it just fine --
          knowing it was only a tough
          break!

                    JOE
          So send her a thousand bucks.
          We can afford it.

                    SAM
          Sure.  But he's dead.  And there's
          gonna be more tough breaks - be-
          fore this is over.

                    JOE
               (cynically, ges-
               turing to Sean)
          You've been listening to your
          new buddy too much.

                              (CONTINUED)

271     (CONTINUED - 2)                                          271

                              SAM
                         (disheartened;
                          soft)
                    No.  I been listenin' to myself.

But before Joe can make an angry rejoinder, a wall phone
rings.  Sam answers it, being nearest.

                              SAM
                    Hello...Yeah, just a minute...

He nods at Joe, indicating it's for him, as he says:

                              SAM
                    The Professor...Says he's been
                    tryin' to find you...

                              JOE
                         (as he crosses)
                    This time of night?
                         (on phone)
                    Hello...Oh?...Okay, if you say
                    so...I'll bring Dorkin...Yeah.
                         (hangs up; to Sam)
                    He's found out somethin'...You
                    wanta come along?

                              SAM
                         (meaningfully)
                    I think I better...

Joe gives him a quick look, as they turn to go.

                                        DISSOLVE TO:


272     INT. DINOSAUR HALL - PROFESSORS HENDRICKS, FLAHERTY   272
        - NIGHT

The big room is in heavy shadow.  At one end of it,
under a single light, Professor Hendricks stands on
a fifteen foot ladder, comparing the skull of a
dinosaur with a photograph he holds in his hand.  At
the foot of the ladder, looking up at him, is Flaherty,
who stands beside two or three large blow-up photographs of baby monster.  A KNOCK is HEARD.  Hendricks
and Flaherty exchange a glance.

                              PROFESSOR
                    Come in...

                                        (CONTINUED)

272    (CONTINUED)                                                      272

JOE, SAM, DORKIN enter, looking down the shadowed
hall, seeing the two scientists.  They start towards
them.  Professor Hendricks starts down the ladder.
There is a distant coolness on the part of the scientists, particularly towards Joe.

                        JOE
                   (trying to be
                   light)
          Well - we got a problem?

                        FLAHERTY
          At least you can't say we didn't
          warn you that a problem might
          arise...

                        PROFESSOR
                   (seriously)
          The creature you've captured,
          Captain Ryan, is not an adult
          specimen.

                        SAM
          You mean - it isn't full grown?

                        PROFESSOR
          No...In fact we believe it's in
          rather early infancy...

All look at each other, then:

                        SAM
                   (slowly)
          Are you tryin' to say there may
          be a full-grown one of these
          things somewhere?

                        FLAHERTY
          It's a fair assumption.  Where
          there are offspring, there are
          generally - parents.

They stare at each other a moment as this sinks in.
Then:

                        JOE
                   (softly)
          How big would a full-grown one
          be?

                                              (CONTINUED)

272    (CONTINUED - 2)                                    272

                          PROFESSOR
                        (considering)
                An approximate guess...
                        (he points off)
                Does that give you an idea?


273    FULL SHOT - THEIR P.O.V. - THE BRONTESAUR EXHIBIT    273

        The exhibit shows a small skeleton scarcely larger
        than a crocodile -- mounted below a monster thirty
        feet high at the shoulder.  They ENTER the SHOT,
        stare at the two skeletons.

                            JOE
                        (trying to grasp
                        it)
                That would make it nearly two
                hundred feet tall!

                          FLAHERTY
                        (solemnly)
                At the very least...

                            JOE
                Ah, who do you think you're
                kidding!
                        (a gesture to
                        include Dorkin)
                If this is some kinda gag to
                put the heat on us...

                          FLAHERTY
                        (cutting in)
                The "heat" as you call it, Captain
                Ryan, may already be on...
                        (a glance to
                        include Hen-
                        dricks)
                Obviously the proper authorities
                must be notified at once...

        But as Hendricks nods his agreement, Joe bursts out:

                            JOE
                You mean you want to stir up a
                whole hornet's nest just for a
                few calculations you've made on
                a piece of paper?  Nuts to that!

                                          (CONTINUED)

273    (CONTINUED)                                          273

                          PROFESSOR
                           (icily)
               I am afraid, Captain Ryan, that
               the decision is no longer in
               your hands...

Joe is glaring at him, as we...

                                          DISSOLVE TO:


274    EXT. ADMIRALTY BUILDING - DAY                        274

       It is identifiable by its Marine sentries, etc.  CAMERA
       MOVES IN, and we...

                                          DISSOLVE THRU TO:


275    INT. ADMIRALTY COMMUNICATIONS ROOM - ADMIRAL,        275
       HENDRICKS, FLAHERTY, OTHERS

       Camera is SHOOTING down a long bank of uniformed Naval
       RADIO OPERATORS, seated at what looks like an elaborate
       switchboard.  From the murmur of their VOICES, we may
       gather that each of them is sending in a different
       language.  In f.g., the Admiral and the two scientists
       stand behind an OPERATOR.

                          OPERATOR
                       (turning to Admiral)
               Nara Island still doesn't answer,
               Sir...

                          ADMIRAL
                       (slightly impatient)
               Then check with Communications
               Monitor - find out why...

                          HENDRICKS
               I realize, Admiral Brooks, that
               it's -- what shall I say -- a
               fantastic situation - but...

                          ADMIRAL
                       (humoring them
                        with a smile)
               One expects the fantastic of you
               scientists these days...

                                          (CONTINUED)

275    (CONTINUED)                                                      275

                              OPERATOR
                           (to Admiral)
                    Monitor reports there has been
                    no communication with Nara
                    Island for a week, Sir...

Hendricks and Flaherty exchange a glance.

                              FLAHERTY
                    A week..!...

                              ADMIRAL
                           (his little smile)
                    You're concerned, eh?  Well, what
                    do you think?

                              HENDRICKS
                           (looking at him
                            quizzically)
                    Tell me Admiral Brooks - have
                    you ever seen the animal that
                    captured?

                              ADMIRAL
                    I'm afraid I haven't had the
                    time...

                              HENDRICKS
                    Then perhaps you should take the
                    time.  And when you do - remember
                    it first appeared at Nara Island...

                              OPERATOR
                    No answer yet, Sir...

The Admiral is looking at the two scientists, more
seriously now, as we...

                                                     DISSOLVE TO:


276    INT. ADMIRALTY COMMUNICATIONS ROOM - OPERATORS        276

CAMERA is MOVING down the line of Operators, hearing
each one briefly in a different language; HOLDS on an
Operator:

                              OPERATOR
                    ...The British Admiralty...All
                    ships in the area seventeen de-
                    grees west longitude, thirty-
                           (continued)

                                            (CONTINUED)

276    (CONTINUED)                                           276

                              OPERATOR (cont'd)
                    three degrees north latitude.
                    Please report any unusual sight-
                    ings or conditions in vicinity
                    of Nara Island...This is priority
                    A...
                              (starting to repeat)
                    A message from the British Admir-
                    alty...


277    A SHIP AT SEA - (STOCK) - NIGHT                       277

       She is about six thousand tons, proceeding at reduced
       speed through fog.  Her WHISTLE is HEARD - a fog warn-
       ing.


278    INT. WHEELHOUSE SS ETTA LORING - CAPTAIN, MATE,       278
       HELMSMAN - NIGHT

       The ship is proceeding through a swirling fog.  The
       SOUND of her whistle, blasting its fog warning, comes
       over at regular intervals.  The wheelhouse is lit only
       by the light of the binnacle and the radar screen.
       The RADIO OPERATOR comes in, hands the Captain a
       message.  The Captain glances at it:

                              CAPTAIN
                    Thanks...

       The Operator nods and exits.  The Captain crosses and
       hands the message to the Mate.

                              CAPTAIN
                    From the British Admiralty...

       The mate glances at it.  Both move over to look at the
       radar screen.  The screen is clear.  The Captain moves
       off, crosses the wheelhouse to peer out the starboard
       side, the foggy glow of the green running light fall-
       ing on his face.  Looking down at the water, he SEES:


279    WHAT HE SEES:                                         279

       An odd, phosphorescent streak in the water that the
       ship is passing through.

280   BACK TO SCENE                              280

A puzzled look comes over the Captain's face.  The
Mate calls to him.

                    MATE
          Captain...

The Captain crosses to the Mate, and both look at the
radar screen.  A line of blips has appeared on the
screen.  The Captain and Mate study it for a moment,
then the Captain says something to the Helmsman.

                    CAPTAIN
          Drop it off a couple of points...

The Helmsman moves his wheel, dropping the ship off
to starboard a couple of points, as shown on the
overhead photo-reflector of the binnacle.  The Captain
and Mate watch the radar screen.  The blips move off,
but then move in again.  After a moment, the Captain
speaks to the Helmsman again, his attitude more abrupt
this time.

                    CAPTAIN
          Two more points!

Again the blips move away on the radar screen - but
now they move in again with terrifying swiftness.
The Captain yells frantically at the Helmsman.

                    CAPTAIN
          Down your helm!  Hard right!

The Helmsman puts his wheel down in a hard right turn.
The ship heels slightly at the abruptness of the turn.
Then suddenly the whole ship - and wheelhouse - heave
upward, slanting at a steep, crazy angle.  The Captain
and Mate are sent flying across the wheelhouse, yelling incoherently as they are slammed against the starboard bulkhead.  The Helmsman is fighting to hang onto
the wheel.  A great wall of water rises and comes
crashing down, obliterating the screen, as we...

                                   DISSOLVE TO:


281   INT. ADMIRALTY OPERATIONS ROOM - ADMIRAL, HENDRICKS, 281
       FLAHERTY, OTHERS - DAY

The three are standing before a large table, the surface of which is a map the kind you can move miniature
boats around on.  IN B.G. various Naval Personnel go
about their duties.  The Admiral is leafing through a
large volume, and now reads from it:

                                   (CONTINUED)

281  (CONTINUED)                                          281

                          ADMIRAL
          ...The Etta Loring, out of Boston,
          Massachusetts, USA...Registered
          at six thousand tons...

He looks at the other two, and he is no longer humor-
ing them:

                          ADMIRAL
          Six thousand tons!..Do you really
          believe that such a thing is possi-
          ble?

                          FLAHERTY
          The ship's gone.

                          FLAHERTY
          And it was on exactly the same
          course as the ship that brought
          the baby animal from Nara Island...

                          ADMIRAL
                       (trying to smile)
          You must credit your beast with
          a remarkable aptitude for navi-
          gation...

                          FLAHERTY
          They were running water over it -
          at my suggestion...The water may
          well have left some sort of -
          track...

                          ADMIRAL
                       (a moment of
                        thought, then:)
          Frankly, gentlemen, until a few
          moments ago, I thought you must
          be - exaggerating...Now I'm not
          so sure...
                       (pointing at the
                        map)
          It happens I have a destroyer in
          the vicinity.  I shall dispatch
          it at once...

                                        DISSOLVE TO:


282  FULL SHOT - DESTROYER - DAY                          282

     as she swings in a tight arc, changing course.

283   AIR SHOT - THREE PLANES          283

in echelon, then fanning out.


284   PLANE COCKPIT - (PROCESS) - PILOT      284

as he talks into his radio phone.


285   BRIDGE OF DESTROYER - SKIPPER, FIRST OFFICER,   285
      HELMSMAN - DAY

They are looking up at the skies, and the First
Officer is talking into a radiophone.  We HEAR the
distant drone of plane motors.

                         DISSOLVE TO:


286   INT. ADMIRALTY OPERATIONS ROOM - JOE, SAM, DORKIN,  286
      PROFESSOR, FLAHERTY, ADMIRAL, OTHERS

There is some bustle of lesser Navy personnel -
telephone operators, etc. - but there is no great
tension as yet, for, as we shall see, the Navy, as
personified by the Admiral, is quite confident of
its ability to carry out its mission.  The Admiral
himself is provided with radiophone, and is in direct
contact with the scene of operations.  He indicates
positions on the map as he speaks:

                 ADMIRAL
      ...Our aircraft are certain they
      have sighted a creature answering
      your description in this area...
          (indicating on map)
      Here...But when they approached,
      the creature submerged...We are
      waiting for a further report now...

Sam points to the place on the map which the Admiral
has indicated.

                 SAM
          (darkly)
      That's a lot closer to London than
      it was this morning...

                 ADMIRAL
          (smiling)
      Oh, it is definitely following
      your indicated course for London
      ...which makes it all the easier -
      we know exactly what areas to cover...

287     INT. PLANE COCKPIT - PILOT - (PROCESS) - DAY          287

The Pilot is looking over the side of his banking
craft, speaking into his radiophone.

288     BRIDGE OF DESTROYER - SKIPPER - FIRST OFFICER,        288
HELMSMAN - DAY

The First Officer is listening on his radiophone, now
he speaks briefly into it:

> FIRST OFFICER
> Right...
> (to Skipper)
> They've sighted something, Sir -
> four points off the starboard
> bow...

> SKIPPER
> (to Helmsman)
> Four points starboard...

289     FULL SEA SHOT - THE DESTROYER                         289

as she sweeps in a sharp, fast, canting arc on her new
course.

290     BRIDGE OF DESTROYER - SKIPPER, FIRST OFFICER,         290
HELMSMAN

The Skipper and First Officer are both on the wing
of the bridge, looking through binoculars.  Suddenly
we see their tension.  The First Officer says something to the Skipper:

> FIRST OFFICER
> That's it, Sir!

The Skipper nods.  THEY SEE:

291     WHAT THEY SEE -(AS THROUGH BINOCULARS)                291

Mama Monster.  Her tremendous bulk is emerging from
the water, dripping, until about a third of it is dis-
closed.  Her great head moves from side to side, again
in that seeking, searching motion.

292    BACK TO SCENE                             292

As the Skipper and First Officer lower their binoculars, stare at each other for a moment.  Then the Skipper speaks to the First:

                   SKIPPER
        Fire number one turret...

The First hurries across the bridge to a phone.

293    THE DESTROYER                           293

firing.

294    THE MONSTER                            294

as the shells raise great geysers of water around her.  She roars in anger.

295    THE DESTROYER                           295

firing.

296    THE MONSTER                            296

a bright, flash as a shell hits her.  She bellows in pain and anger, flailing with her talon.

297    THE DESTROYER                           297

firing.

298    THE MONSTER                            298

as she is hit again.  She rears, bellowing, then swiftly slides beneath the water.

299    BRIDGE OF DESTROYER - SKIPPER, FIRST OFFICER,    299
        HELMSMAN

The Skipper is looking through his binoculars.  He turns briefly to give an order to the First, who relays it into his phone.

                           (CONTINUED)

299  (CONTINUED)                                                299

                         SKIPPER
                Cease fire...

                         FIRST
                     (into his phone)
                Cease fire...

The First crosses to the side of the Skipper. Both
look through binoculars.

They SEE:

300  WHAT THEY SEE:  (THROUGH BINOCULARS)                       300

     the roiling water, faintly crimsoned with blood,
     where the Monster has disappeared.

301  BACK TO SCENE                                              301

     As the Skipper and First lower their binoculars,
     smile at each other.  The First is signalling on
     the engine telegraph.

                         SKIPPER
                We'll just go over and have a
                look I think...

                         FIRST OFFICER
                Yes sir...
                     (crosses, speaks
                      to Helmsman)
                Port two points...

302  FULL SEA SHOT - THE DESTROYER                              302

     as it slackens speed, turns leisurely towards the
     spot where the monster disappeared.

303  PLANE COCKPIT - PILOT - (PROCESS)                          303

     as he banks his plane, looking over the side, talking
     into his radiophone, smiling broadly.

304  INT. ADMIRALTY OPERATIONS ROOM - JOE, SAM, DORKIN,    304
     THE PROFESSORS, ADMIRAL

     as the Admiral listens, smiling on his radiophone.

                                        (CONTINUED)

304     (CONTINUED)                                              304

The others watch him.  The Admiral turns to them,
smiling:

                    ADMIRAL
          ...They report at least two
          direct hits...By the way, your
          description of the creature
          was no exaggeration - they say
          it was almost as big as the
          destroyer herself...

                    SAM
               (dubiously)
          "Was?"  They killed it?

                    ADMIRAL
          It has disappeared beneath the
          sea...They are sweeping the
          area, but it has almost cer-
          tainly been killed...

There is a general relaxing, the Admiral is about to
rise from his seat, when he hears something on his
radiophone.  He sinks back into his seat, his face
pale.  The others are looking at him.  There is sudden
tension over the whole room...


305     PLANE COCKPIT - PILOT - (PROCESS)                        305

The pilot is looking down over the side of his craft
as before, but now there is horror on his face, as
he yells into his radiophone.

He SEES:


306     WHAT HE SEES:                                            306

The monster rising out of the sea, directly alongside the slowly cruising destroyer.

307     BRIDGE OF DESTROYER - SKIPPER, FIRST OFFICER,     307
        HELMSMAN

        as they stare for a moment in horror at the rising
        monster. We see her two wounds, which, however, to
        her seem no more than a couple of irksome scratches.
        There is a mad dash to the other side of the bridge,
        as one of her huge talons comes crashing down...

308     FULL SEA SHOT - DESTROYER AND MONSTER     308

        as the monster brings her other talon into play,
        rolling the ship over, bottom up, then smashing at
        it, forcing it under the water. The stern raises
        as she rapidly begins to fill, and then the ship
        slides swiftly beneath the sea, leaving only a great
        bubbling turbulence of the waters. The monster roars
        her raging triumph.

309     PLANE COCKPIT - PILOT - (PROCESS)     309

        as he stares down in horror, yelling into his radio-
        phone.

310     INT. ADMIRALTY OPERATIONS ROOM - JOE, SAM, DORKIN,     310
        THE PROFESSORS, ADMIRAL

        Everyone is frozen, the room is deathly still. The
        Admiral sits stunned. When he finally speaks, it is
        as though in a dream.

                     ADMIRAL
            Capsized...Sunk...With every man
            aboard...

        There is a stunned silence. It is Sam who suddenly
        breaks it. He is on his feet, staring at Joe and
        Dorkin.

                     SAM
            All right! Now what?

                     DORKIN
                  (nervously)
            It - it's terrible...But what
            can you do?

                     SAM
            Turn the thing loose! What else?
            Take him back to the sea! While
            you've still got a chance!

                            (CONTINUED)

310   (CONTINUED)                                  310

> JOE
> What's the matter with you!
> This is the twentieth century!
> We can certainly find a way
> to handle an overgrown lizard!

Sam stares at him. Then, abruptly he turns and exits.
The group watch him go, look at the Admiral. The
Admiral has been looking hard at Joe, angered by his
brash outburst, and Joe drops his eyes. Now the
Admiral turns to the group, smiles a little, regain-
ing some of his confidence.

> ADMIRAL
> There's no doubt we can stop
> the creature...It's only that -
> this has been something of a
> shock...

Professor Hendricks is deep in troubled thought, the
Admiral is turning to issue orders to a subordinate,
as we...

> DISSOLVE TO:

311   INT. CIRCUS WAGON - SAM, SEAN                  311

Sam has a bottle, holding it by the neck, and he is
thoroughly drunk. Sean is watching him with a kind
of curious solicitude, as Sam stands looking out the
window. He SEES:

312   WHAT HE SEES:                                      312

The baby monster in its tank.

313   BACK TO SCENE                                    313

as Sam turns, looks at Sean blearily, drunkenly knowing.

> SAM
> You knew alla time, didn't you?
>    (as the boy looks,
>     not getting it)
> You knew it was more'n just a
> big lizard!..All their science -
> all their civ'l'zation - you
> knew more'na whole bunch of 'em...
>     (in sudden decision)
> Well le's go!

> (CONTINUED)

313     (CONTINUED)                                              313

                         SEAN
                    (knowing, trying
                     to divert him)
                 Go, Sam - where?

Sam heads, only a little unsteady, for the door.  Sean
hurries after him.

314     EXT. CIRCUS WAGON - SAM, SEAN - NIGHT                    314

        as Sam comes out, followed by the boy.  Sean is des-
        perately worried, is trying to kid Sam out of it:

                         SEAN
                 Sam now - what would you be
                 doin'?

        Sam ignores him, takes a last, long pull on the bottle,
        emptying it, hurling it away from him, starting for
        the monster's tank.  Sean makes a grab at him:

                         SEAN
                 Sam!..

315     EXT. CIRCUS GROUNDS - JOE'S CAR

        driving up.

316     INT. CAR - JOE - (PROCESS)                               316

        His eyes widen as he SEES:

317     WHAT HE SEES:                                            317

        Sam is picking up a two-by-four from a scarp lumber
        pile left over from the forming of the tank.  He
        heads again for the monster's tank, Sean tugging at
        him, pleading.

318     EXT. CIRCUS GROUNDS - JOE                                318

        as he slams on the brakes of the car, jumps out,
        and starts on a dead run for the monster's tank.

319     EXT. MONSTER CAGE - SAM, SEAN - NIGHT                    319

as the boy tugs at Sam, pleading, knowing his intention now.

> SEAN
> Sam! Don't! He'll kill you!

> SAM
> Whassa difference - one more...

As though to confirm Sean, the monster GROWLS spine-chillingly. But in spite of the boy's attempted interference, Sam flails at the first strand of wire with the two-by-four. There is a bright blue, crackling flash, and the two-by-four begins to burn. Sam is about to take another swing, when JOE comes in. Sam turns, dropping the two-by-four. There are no preliminaries.

> JOE
> All right! You been askin' for
> it...

He lets fly. But in spite of the booze - or perhaps because of it - Sam is a tough cooky tonight. He moves well, taking the blow on the shoulder, and crosses with a right that sends Joe sprawling. Sam turns, lurching back towards the wires. But Joe is up again, spins him around. He catches Sam a quick one, and Sam goes down. Sean reacts to this - by stepping in fast and giving Joe a hard right to the belly. Joe grunts - both from surprise and from momentary loss of wind. He stares at the defiant boy. But before he can do more, Sam is in again. In the subsequent exchanges, always with the imminent danger that one or the other will come in contact with the wires, it's touch-and-go for a minute or so, until Joe realizes that he's got to be careful. He waits his chance, then catches Sam flush. And another. And another. Sam is down, and out like a light. Sean has been agonized, but able to do nothing. The monster has been intermittently ROARING. Now Joe stands over Sam, breathing hard. Sean is down beside him, tears in his eyes, trying to rouse him. He looks up at Joe. For a moment, Joe's face has softened. But then he reaches down, hauls Sam up and gets him over his shoulder, starts off with him, without a word. A chastened, tearful Sean follows.

                                        DISSOLVE TO:

320  LONG SHOT - WIDE ANGLE - THAMES ESTUARY - NIGHT        320

as searchlights sweep over the waters of the estuary
*from the land.*  SOUND of patrolling planes.


321  INT. TV STUDIO - BBC NEWSCASTER                        321

                        BBC NEWSCASTER
            ...It is now regarded as certain
            that the creature is approaching
            the Thames Estuary.  Following
            the disaster of this afternoon -
            the loss of a destroyer with all
            hands...


322  LONG SHOT - BATTLE SQUADRON - NIGHT - (STOCK)          322

A battleship and a couple of cruisers (or what is
available) patrolling at sea.

                    BBC NEWSCASTER'S VOICE (OVER)
            ...The Admiralty has deployed major
            forces of the North Seas Fleet off
            the mouth of the Estuary in an
            attempt to locate and destroy the
            monster even before it reaches
            the coastal defenses...


323  INT. BRIDGE OF BATTLESHIP - ADMIRAL, AIDE, OTHERS -  323
     NIGHT

The Admiral is on the phone:

                        ADMIRAL
            What's your present situation?


324  INT. SUB NET CONTROL ROOM - LIEUTENANT, ENSIGN,       324
     OTHERS - NIGHT

The Lieutenant in charge is on the phone.  A RATING
is turning into "Lock" position one of a number of
large wheels that operate the nets.  Lights flash on
a panel.  The Lieutenant is looking over at this:

                        LIEUTENANT
            We're just closing the last of
            the submarine nets now, sir...
            Yes sir.

He starts to hang up.

325     SKY SHOT - PLANES - NIGHT                          325

A group of night-fighters, as they commence patrolling the outer waters of the bay.


326     PLANE COCKPIT - GROUP LEADER - (PROCESS)          326

as he looks down at the waters below, adjusting his
radiophone.  He SEES:


327     WHAT HE SEES:                                      327

The waters below, clear and undisturbed.


328     BACK TO SCENE                                      328

                    GROUP LEADER
                     (on phone)
              ...Visibility about ten miles...
              No sir - all serene...


329     INT. BATTLESHIP BRIDGE - ADMIRAL, AIDE, OTHERS -   329
        NIGHT

                      ADMIRAL
                     (to Aide)
              Get me submarine patrol, sector
              two eight...

The Aide picks up a phone.


330     SUBMARINE - AT SEA - (STOCK) - NIGHT               330

partially submerged.


331     INT. SUBMARINE - SUB CAPTAIN, RADIO OPERATOR,      331
        SONIC TECHNICIAN

Across the screen of the sonic recorder passes a
regular squiggle, like an electrocardiograph, emit-
ting a regular "beep-beep".  The radio operator
stands by with his portable phone, an open circuit.
The Sub Captain is at the periscope, slowly rotating
it.  He SEES:

332    WHAT HE SEES:                                          332

the sea, as seen through the periscope, in a 360
degree turn, revealing nothing.

333    BACK TO SCENE                                          333

as the Radio Operator gets a call:

                    RADIO OPERATOR
           Yes Admiral Brooks...
                (to Captain)
           Captain...

The Sub Captain is already moving to take the phone.

                    SUB CAPTAIN
                (after a moment
                of listening)
           No Sir - nothing...

334    INT. BATTLESHIP BRIDGE - MED. CLOSE - ADMIRAL          334

                    ADMIRAL
                (on phone)
           What are your sonic readings?

335    INT. SUBMARINE - MED. CLOSE - SUB CAPTAIN, SONIC       335
       TECHNICIAN

as the Sub Captain, with his phone, moves over to the
sonic recorder.  At a look from the Captain, the
Sonic Technician increases his volume.  The "beeps"
become more insistent, but still come in a regular,
almost soothing rhythm.

                    SUB CAPTAIN
                (on phone)
           The same, sir - no change...Yes
           sir...

He starts to hand the phone back to the Radio Operator.

336    INT. BATTLESHIP BRIDGE - ADMIRAL, AIDE, OTHERS -       336
       NIGHT

The Admiral is handing a phone back to the Aide.  There
is a thin little smile on his face:

                              (CONTINUED)

336    (CONTINUED)                                          336

> ADMIRAL
> Well gentlemen - perhaps we
> shall have a quiet night
> after all...

337    INT. SUB NET CONTROL ROOM - LIEUTENANT, ENSIGN,      337
OTHERS

The Lieutenant is just starting to light a pipe, and
others are starting to take out cigarettes on his
cue, when the quiet of the room is shattered by the
clanging of electric gong.

> LIEUTENANT
> The nets!

But the Ensign has already picked up a phone:

> ENSIGN
> (on phone)
> Yes...Yes...One moment...

He is about to hand the phone to the Lieutenant, when
the gong suddenly stops, and a puzzled expression comes
over the Ensign's face.  He speaks again into the phone:

> ENSIGN
> Hello...Hello...
> (to Lieutenant)
> The connection is gone...

> LIEUTENANT
> (a little irritably)
> Well what did they say?

> ENSIGN
> The nets have been torn...And
> then the connection was gone...

The Lieutenant grabs up another phone:

338    INT. BATTLESHIP BRIDGE - ADMIRAL, AIDE, OTHERS -     338
NIGHT

The Admiral is on the phone, his face pale.  The others
register their concern.

> ADMIRAL
> ...I see...No, there's nothing
> further you can do now...

(CONTINUED)

338     (CONTINUED)                                               338

He hands the phone back to his Aide, speaking to all:

                    ADMIRAL
          The creature's got through, some-
          how - smashed the nets...
                    (to Aide)
          Get me Army Headquarters in London!
          As quickly as you can!

                              DISSOLVE TO:


339     INT. ARMY OPERATIONS ROOM - HENDRICKS, FLAHERTY,     339
        GENERAL, OTHERS

Action is centered around a huge table-map of London
and environs.  Also in evidence is a large radar
screen; a message center, with several RADIO and TELE-
PHONE OPERATORS talking, ad lib; Army and Navy staff
OFFICERS; a select group of NEWSHAWKS (no photographers).
Military Aides are placing red pin-flags in the map,
and there is a general atmosphere of tension and
anxiety.  The General is on the phone:

                    GENERAL
               (abrupt, irritated)
          ...I don't care how important it
          is - you must interrupt!  It's
          imperative that I speak to the
          Minister at once!..


340     EXT. NO. TEN DOWNING STREET - NIGHT                  340

Lights are on, and there is a quiet but tense crowd
standing outside.


341     INT. ARMY OPERATIONS ROOM - MED. CLOSE - GENERAL     341

on the phone:

                    GENERAL
          We believe the creature is fol-
          lowing the course of the river,
          sir...Atomic weapons would be
          out of the question in any popu-
          lated area...Tanks, of course...
          Yes we're counting heavily on the
          missiles as soon as we know where
          to deploy them...It's a matter of
          improvising at the moment, but
          we'll manage, sir...

342     EXT. STREET - NIGHT                                    342

        CAMERA is CLOSE on a SIREN, howling.  CAMERA PANS to
        reveal that the siren is mounted on a jeep, now
        racing away, which is escorting a column of TANKS,
        heading for the Tower Bridge.  People on the street
        watch them pass.

343     ANOTHER STREET - TRUCKS - NIGHT                        343

        as, loaded with troops, they careen on towards the
        Tower Bridge.  People watch.

344     EXT. STREET - NIGHT                                    344

        Two MPS on motorcycles, their sirens open, roar up to
        an intersection, leap off their bikes which are placed
        in such a way as to block off traffic.  A MAN in a
        car which is being held up sticks his head out of the
        window to see what's going on.  The column of tanks
        thunders by.

345     ANOTHER INTERSECTION              .                    345

        MPs on both sides of the street block off the cross-
        street as troop-trucks roar through.  People on foot
        and in halted cars watch.

346     EXT. TOWER BRIDGE - MED. LONG - (MINIATURE?)           346

        The bridge is closing as a Naval ship passes through.

347     EXT. TOWER BRIDGE - MED. LONG                          347

        A column of tanks and military vehicles waiting for
        the bridge to come down.

348     EXT. TOWER BRIDGE                                      348

        Soldiers are running, gaining their position on the
        upper level of the bridge.

349     EXT. APPROACHES TO THE TOWER BRIDGE                    349

        Tanks moving in position.

350     EXT. APPROACHES TO THE BRIDGE - ANOTHER ANGLE          350

Soldiers with bazookas, a walkie-talkie, unloading
from trucks, taking position.

351     EXT. UPPER PLATFORM OF THE BRIDGE                       351

A military patrol, watching.  All are tense.

352     EXT. RIVER - LONG SHOT - THEIR P.O.V. (MINIATURE)       352

A huge dark head appears.  It is seen dimly, at a
distance.

353     EXT. UPPER PLATFORM - CLOSE                             353

The leader of the watching patrol blows a whistle.

354     EXT. UPPER PLATFORM - CLOSE                             354

Officer gives order.  Siren sounds.

355     EXT. - CLOSE UP                                         355

Sergeant and a young soldier, peering in the dark.
The soldier has a walkie-talkie.

356     EXT. TOWER BRIDGE - CLOSE - NIGHT                       356

Officer giving order.

357     EXT. TOWER BRIDGE - MED.                                357

Soldier receiving order shoots flare-gun.

358     EXT. SKY - NIGHT                                        358

A parachute of the flare opens, flare-lights are
falling down, illuminating the river.

359     EXT. RIVER - (MINIATURE)                                359

The head of the monster can be seen illuminated by
the green light of the flare, but briefly, fitfully.

360     EXT. BRIDGE - MED. LONG                    360

        Soldiers start to shoot with tracer-bullets. We see
        the sergeant and the young soldier at previous scene.

361     EXT. RIVER - (MINIATURE)                   361

        The monster's head, surrounded by tracer-bullets,
        disappears under the water.

362     EXT. BRIDGE - DOLLY SHOT                   362

        On a row of tense faces of soldiers peering in the
        darkness.

363     EXT. BRIDGE - MED. LONG SHOT               363

        The bridge is now down and the military units are
        moving forward in a rush. Orders are given and
        the tanks start to turn facing the river.

364     DETAIL SHOT                               364

        Tanks turning towards the river. Another flare is
        lighting the scene.

365     EXT. CLOSE - A GROUP OF SOLDIERS          365

        Lit by the green light of the flare. Suddenly an
        expression of unbelievable fear on the faces of the
        soldiers. (The sergeant and the young soldier are
        in this group.)

366     EXT. LONG - WHAT THEY SEE: (MINIATURE)     366

        Out of the water, with unbelievable speed, comes the
        monster.

367     EXT. BRIDGE - MED. LONG - (MINIATURE) - TRAV. MAT.    367

        Soldiers in FG firing. The monster rising in BG,
        advancing.

368     EXT. BRIDGE - MED. CLOSE                 368

        SOLDIERS retiring in good order. A tremendous crack-
        ing sound is heard.

369     EXT. LONG SHOT - MASTER-SCENE -  MINIATURE +      369
        SPLIT SCREEN

        The monster is standing up and is twisting the steel
        girders, tearing the cables, breaking the towers of
        the bridge.  The parachute flares are falling and
        illuminating the scene with greenish lights.

370     TO INTERCUT WITH:                                  370

        Stones falling on group of soldiers.

        Tank is smashed by falling stone towers.

        The iron railing breaks under falling debris, soldiers
        rolling in water.

        BACK TO:

371     LONG SHOT - MASTER SCENE                          371

        Monster's paws break the bridge.  Tanks and soldiers
        are precipitated into the dark water.

        INTERCUT WITH DETAIL SHOTS:

372     MED. LONG                                        372

        The pavement of the bridge caves in and the cluster
        of soldiers and vehicles are precipitated down into
        the turbulent waters.

373     CLOSE                                            373

        The Sergeant and young soldier of previous scene,
        falling down amidst twisted girders.

374     MED.                                              374

        A tank rolls down in the water with falling debris.

375     EXT. AT THE FOOT OF THE BRIDGE - NIGHT - MED.      375

        Shocked and wounded soldiers coming from the direc-
        tion of the bridge, meeting with other soldiers and
        tanks arriving to take positions.

376    EXT. RIVER - VERY LONG SHOT    376

Monster finishing the destruction of the Tower Bridge
in BG, and turns towards shore.

DISSOLVE TO:

377    INT. ARMY OPERATIONS ROOM - GENERAL, HENDRICKS,    377
FLAHERTY, OTHERS - NIGHT

In an atmosphere of growing tension, the General is
on the phone while an AIDE places a pin-flag repre-
senting the monster on the map at the Tower Bridge.

> GENERAL
> (on phone)
> Yes sir...The Tower Bridge - the
> power of the thing is fantastic!..
> We're doing that, sir - I have a
> call in to the Admiralty...

An Aide is approaching with another phone:

> AIDE
> (quietly)
> Here is the Admiralty now, sir...

> GENERAL
> (on phone)
> Very good, sir...

He hangs up, takes the other phone from the Aide.

DISSOLVE TO:

378    EXT. RIVER - LONG SHOT - NIGHT    378

A Navy gasoline BARGE moving into position. It is
lit by the glow of the sky, and on its side is
lettered: DANGER - HIGH OCTANE.

379    EXT. BARGE DECK - NAVAL OFFICER, SAILORS - NIGHT    379

The sailors stand by a series of deck valves (wheel
type - a foot and a half or so in diameter). The
Officer stands a little apart, waiting to give the
order to open the valves. But all are staring tense
and awe-struck at what they SEE:

380    WHAT THEY SEE:                                              380

       MAMA MONSTER, as the looms out of the murk, walking
       in the river.

381    REVERSE SHOT - MAMA MONSTER                                 381

       as she moves forward.  In BG can be seen the gasoline
       BARGE.

382    EXT. BARGE - CLOSE SHOT - NIGHT                             382

       As the Officer brings down his hand with a sharp
       command.

383    EXT. - CLOSE - SAILORS                                      383

       The sailors start opening the valves.

384    EXT. - CLOSE                                                384

       The gasoline gushes down out of a series of pipes
       and expands on the surface of dark water.

385    EXT. - LONG SHOT - BARGES IN FG, MONSTER IN BG              385

       Officer gives order.

386    EXT. - MED. LONG                                            386

       Sailors, having finished their operation, swiftly
       abandon barges.

387    EXT. - MED. CLOSE                                           387

       Monster advances in water.

388    EXT. WATERFRONT                                             388

       The group of sailors and officer run towards an em-
       placement and hide behind sandbags.  Officer watching
       tensely the river.

389    EXT. - LONG SHOT                                            389

       The monster advances in the river.  Sailors and offi-
       cer in FG.  The officer is ready to give signal when
       the monster will reach a certain point.

390     EXT. WATERFRONT - ANOTHER PART OF THE RIVER -          390
        MED. CLOSE

        Group of young men are watching with interest, half-
        hidden between two barges.


391     EXT. RIVER - NIGHT - LONG SHOT                         391

        The monster still approaching.  The Officer in the FG
        gives signal.


392     EXT. - CLOSE SHOT                                      392

        Sailor fires a flame-thrower.


393     EXT. RIVER - MED. CLOSE                                393

        The fire of the flame-thrower shot starts the gasoline
        fire.


394     EXT. RIVER - MED. LONG - NIGHT                         394

        With tremendous speed the fire moves on, like a
        flaming curtain.


395     EXT. RIVER                                             395

        The flames are approaching the monster.


396     EXT. RIVER - CLOSE SHOT                                396

        The beast stops hesitatingly in front of approaching
        flames.


397     EXT. - MED. SHOT                                       397

        A slap of the monster's tail throws the fire on the
        barges.  The barges catch fire, the men perish in
        the flames, one of them runs away on fire, like a
        living torch.


398     EXT. CIRCUS GROUNDS - BABY MONSTER                     398

        as it stands in its tank, emits a cry.

399     EXT. RIVER - MED. LONG                          399

The call of the Baby Monster is heard.  Mama Monster
turns around -- stops the retreat, ROARS an answer.

400     EXT. THE SANDBAG EMPLACEMENT                    400

Officer and sailors watching in fascination.  The
officer has the field telephone in readiness.

401     EXT. RIVER                                      401

Mama Monster moves forward, crossing curtain of flames,
moves towards the shore.

402     EXT. SHORE                                      402

The monster starting ashore, amidst burning barges.
(The gasoline is about burnt out by now.)

                                        DISSOLVE TO:

403     INT. TV STUDIO - BBC NEWSCASTER                 403

                    BBC NEWSCASTER
                  (his face and voice
                      strained)
                The Ministry of Civil Defense has
                declared a state of emergency for
                all areas of London within three
                miles of the Thames River...

404     A SERIES OF QUICK SHOTS                         404

(Over all, the glow in the sky - the sound of SIRENS)

a)  A woman's face, framed in a window.  She screams
    at what she sees, and breaks away.

b)  Half a dozen people on apartment (poor section)
    roof - horrified at what they SEE:

c)  WHAT THEY SEE:  The great silhouette of the mon-
    ster in its approach to Piccadilly, the glow of
    fire behind it.  (A long, high angle to be taken
    from the very beginning of the Piccadilly sequence
    which follows).

d)  BACK TO SCENE:  as the people turn, running fran-
    tically for a skylight which leads down from the
    roof - fighting to get down.

                                        (CONTINUED)

404    (CONTINUED)                                            404

e) Another group of people, crazy with fear, fighting each other to get out of an apartment house
door onto the street.

405    EXT. STREET - POLICE SOUND TRUCK                       405

as it cruises slowly, while three or four individual
persons go tearing by in panic:

                        SOUND TRUCK PA
            The streets must be kept clear
            for military and defense per-
            sonnel!..

f) A small group of people running in blind panic.

g) Two policemen try to stop a group of fleeing
people - the people rush on, ignoring them.

h) A fire truck screams down a street - people
scatter madly out of its way.

                        SOUND TRUCK PA (OVER)
            If you are without shelter, go to
            the nearest Underground and stay
            there...

                        BBC NEWSCASTER'S VOICE (OVER)
            All unauthorized persons are re-
            quested to stay in their homes,
            or whever they are, and keep off
            the streets.  If you are in a
            car, leave it where it is and
            take shelter.  I repeat - military
            authorities request all persons
            to keep off the streets...

                                        DISSOLVE TO:

406    EXT. STREET - (NOTE:  BEST SHOTS TO BE SELECTED)       406

People are running in wild, blind panic.  Looking
back, they SEE:

407    WHAT THEY SEE:                                         407

The MONSTER advancing on them, half obscured in a
towering cloud of dust.

408    BACK TO SCENE                                         408

Specifically we see:

a)   We HEAR the wail of emergency (Air Raid) sirens.
      A frantic MOTHER is hauling a BOY along by the
      hand. But he is reluctant, looking back in
      happy delight. She screams at him.

b)   A HUCKSTER'S push cart is turned over in the
      street, its contents spilled every which way.
      People fall over it as they run blindly.

c)   A young WORKMAN is running with a small child in
      his arms. His WIFE, in a shabby housecoat, runs
      after him.

d)   AN OLD WOMAN is being almost literally dragged
      along by her frantic daughter.

e)   TWO TEDDY BOYS outstrip a well dressed MAN,
      oblivious of all thoughts but safety. The MAN
      has lost his hat.

f)   A FANATIC stands in the street, his arms raised,
      shouting. He is twisted and then knocked down
      by the surging crowd, his sandwich board flying
      out, people falling over him.

                          FANATIC
                    (half-incoherent)
             It's Armageddon!..Your sins have
             found you out!..It's the prophecy
             fulfilled!..

But by now he is overwhelmed by the crowd.

                                      DISSOLVE TO:

409    INT. ARMY OPERATIONS ROOM - GENERAL, HENDRICKS,    409
      FLAHERTY, OTHERS

The General is on the phone. An Aide moves the monster pin-flag on the map towards Piccadilly. The
General is irritable under the intense strain:

                         GENERAL
             ...Near Piccadilly...There's no
             way of telling where the thing
             will turn next - what are your
             dispositions?

410    EXT. PARLIAMENT AREA    410

As a line of MISSILES moves forward. In BG are the
Parliament Buildings and Big Ben. A mile or so away,
the sky is lit by the glow of fires caused by the
beginning of Mama's destruction in the city. The distant scream of fire trucks is HEARD. The commanding
COLONEL speaks into his headphone:

> COLONEL
> We're moving into position now,
> sir...

411    ANOTHER ANGLE    411

The MISSILES wheeling into position. A SERGEANT is
frantically waving his orders of direction.

412    INT. ARMY OPERATIONS ROOM - GENERAL, HENDRICKS,    412
FLAHERTY, OTHERS

> GENERAL
> (on phone)
> ...Let me know the moment you are...

He hangs up, turns to the two scientists:

> GENERAL
> How much voltage do you estimate
> would be required to electrocute
> the animal?

Hendricks and Flaherty exchange a glance, then:

> HENDRICKS
> Two million - three million volts...

Flaherty nods assent, as Hendricks continues with a
tight little smile:

> HENDRICKS
> That's only a guess - there's not
> much precedent to go on, sir...

The General is already on the phone:

> GENERAL
> Get me the Battersea Power Station...

> DISSOLVE TO:

413    EXT. CIRCUS GROUNDS - THE MONSTER TANK - NIGHT          413

With the aid of a huge crane and intricate rigging,
a PYLON, its great porcelain insulators glistening,
is being raised slowly but surely straight up in
the air from what had been a prone position.  A
second PYLON starts up.  Activity is feverish.  Linemen are preparing wires.  Everyone is working -
HENDRICKS and FLAHERTY are helping with connections
at the master panel.  SAM and some of the Circus
ROUSTABOUTS are sweating and straining as they roll
out the huge spools of high-tension wire.  SEAN tries
to help.  Even DORKIN is doing what he can - helping
to unload fittings and connections from a truck.

414    EXT. CIRCUS GROUNDS - MED. - SAM, SEAN - NIGHT          414

as, with a ROUSTABOUT, he strains at his task.  Then
he stops, at something he sees.  Sean looks too:

415    ANOTHER ANGLE - JOE, SAM, SEAN                          415

as Joe enters.  Joe glances at the boy, he and Sam
stare at each other for a moment.

                    JOE
                 (defiantly)
          So I was wrong!  So you were
          right!

Sam just looks at him, then turns back to the work.
After a moment Joe goes to work too.

The pylons are now up.  The Linemen are stringing
their wires.  Joe and Sam are sweating as together
they haul out a length of heavy wire.  No words
between them.  Joe looks around casually.

                    JOE
          Where's the kid?

Sam merely nods off, towards the spot where he had
last seen Sean.  Joe looks, then stops.

416    ANOTHER ANGLE                                           416

as they both look.  The boy is nowhere to be seen.
Then, looking around, they SEE:

417    WHAT THEY SEE:                             417

        at a considerable distance, SEAN, heading towards the
        glow in the sky.  Looking back, he sees that he has
        been spotted, puts on a burst of speed, disappears
        into the shadows.

418    BACK TO SCENE                                 418

        as the two look at each other.  Then, both with the
        same instant thought, they dash off after the boy.

419    PAN SHOT - JOE, SAM                       419

        as they run.  Looking, they SEE:

420    WHAT THEY SEE:                             420

        SEAN, as with goat-like agility, he hooks himself
        up onto the tail of a passing Army truck.

421    BACK TO SCENE                               421

        as they stop in a moment of frustration, realizing
        that pursuit on foot is now useless.  Then they veer
        off and run for Joe's car.

                                         DISSOLVE TO:

422    PICCADILLY CIRCUS                         422

        High shot on Piccadilly Circus in its unusual state.
        You can feel the catastrophe that grips the city.
        Busses and cars abandoned helter-skelter.  Groups of
        panicky people are running from the direction of
        Leicester Square.  Sinister cracking noises, flicker-
        ing light of burning fires; gusts of smoke and dust
        from debris.  Looking back, they SEE:

423    WHAT THEY SEE:                             423

        MAMA MONSTER, silhouetted against the glowing sky,
        surrounded by clouds of dust, towering over the re-
        mains of the residential area she has destroyed and
        from which the people have fled, advancing to the
        SOUND of crashing, snapping masonry and timber.

424     INTERCUT WITH DETAIL SHOTS SUCH AS:       424

Among the passing people - a Mother is running with her little daughter. The girl has a doll in her arms.

425     CLOSE       425

In the violent movement of running crowd, the doll is snatched from girl's hands; she tries to pick it up, but is pulled away by her Mother. The doll is being run over by passing people.

426     AN OLD WOMAN CAN'T RUN ANY MORE       426

A man (her son) helps her, tries to calm her, to re-assure her. They are looking backwards, are terri-fied.

427     THEIR P.O.V. - EXT. STREET (SOHO DISTRICT) - MINIATURE       427

Mama Monster is raging, destroying blocks of houses. Flames, stirred by the wind, accompany the destruc-tion.

428     EXT. STREET (SOHO DISTRICT) - MINIATURE AND TRAV. MAT.       428

Panicky people flee infront of the advancing monster. A corner house is being crushed. A man hurtles from a window.

429     EXT. CORNER OF A NARROW STREET - (SPECIAL EFFECT)       429

Bottlenecks form in the narrow street; forward move-ment is almost impossible. The sinister noise of cracking house - then! WALLS ARE CRUSHING DOWN, BURYING THE PEOPLE.

430     EXT. ANOTHER PART OF A NARROW STREET - (MINIA-TURE AND TRAV. MAT.)       430

People try frantically to pass. A house in BG. splits open. The gigantic paw crushes the debris.

431     EXT. CRUSHED HOUSE - MED. CLOSE - MINIATURE AND SPLIT SCREEN       431

The gigantic paw passes, crushing the debris and people, dead and alive.

432     EXT. STREET - (SPECIAL EFFECT - H. SPEED)                432

A house crushes, stones and debris falling down
directly in the lens.

433     INT. CAR - JOE, SAM - (PROCESS)                          433

as Joe drives, Looking ahead, they SEE:

434     WHAT THEY SEE:                                           434

The Army truck, with SEAN. It is blasting a siren,
clearing a way for itself. But already Joe and Sam
are getting into the congestion of the fleeing crowds.

QUICK DISSOLVE TO:

435     EXT. STREET - CAR - JOE, SAM                             435

attempting to force a way through. But already the
crowds have thickened so that progress is very
difficult. As he approaches an intersection, other
cars reach it first, and are stalled by the congestion ahead. Joe's car is now stalled also, and
so are other cars that have pressed in behind him.
There is no going either forward or back. The truck
has disappeared.

436     THE STREET - FROM THE CAR                                436

People streaming by on both sides. A man presses
his face to the glass window, yelling something unintelligible, and gesticulating, about the danger
ahead, and then is gone, carried on by the crowd.
Seeing their predicament, JOE and SAM start to get
out of the car.

437     EXT. STREET - CAR, JOE, SAM                              437

as they pile out of the car. But they have under-
estimated the force of the crowd. Instantly they
are caught up in it. They fight their way against
it.

438     ANOTHER ANGLE - JOE, SAM                                 438

as they fight and literally claw their way against
the tide of the crowd. Joe scrambles up on top of
an abandoned car. He SEES:

439    WHAT HE SEES:          439

In BG the MONSTER moving on her path of destruction.
In FG, in a little square, is a fountain with a
statue and pedestal. Perched on the pedestal, above
the wildly fleeing crowds, is a tiny figure - SEAN,
watching the havoc.

440    BACK TO SCENE:          440

as Joe starts to scramble off the top of the car,
yelling at Sam:

            JOE
    I see him!

But Sam has been swept back by the crowd, irresistibly,
like a leaf on a fast stream. Seeing this, Joe takes
advantage of a momentary break in the crowd where he
is, makes with the open field running.

441    REVERSE SHOT          441

Joe running - struggling - running again. CAMERA PANS
with him to reveal SEAN on the pedestal. The boy sees
him, his eyes widen, but before he can make any decision, Joe grabs him - none too gently - and hauls him
down, as he says:

            JOE
       (half mad - half
       glad)
    You little knothead!

Almost instantly they are caught up in another surging
crowd, swept along with it.

442    EXT. STREET - (LEADING OFF SQUARE) - JOE, SEAN    442

as they are swept along by the crowd, out of the
square and into the street. Looking back, they SEE:

443    WHAT THEY SEE:          443

The little fountain is crushed by falling debris.

444    EXT. STREET - JOE, SEAN, CROWDS - NIGHT    444

in BG is a subway entrance. The frantic crowds are
jamming towards and into it, seeking safety, and Joe

                    (CONTINUED)

444    (CONTINUED)                                          444

and Sean are carried along in spite of themselves.
An agile old MAN elbows his way expertly past them.
All are reacting to the SOUNDS of destruction,
looking back in horror.  They SEE:

445    WHAT THEY SEE:                                       445

In the distance, a towering cloud of dust caused by
the destruction, shot through with flickering flames,
as bursting gas lines fire the debris.

446    BACK TO SCENE                                        446

as Joe and Sean are forced by the frantic crowd into
the subway.

447    INT. STAIRS OF THE SUBWAY - NIGHT - MED.             447

People rushing down the stairs, Joe and Sean among
them.

448    INT. SUBWAY PLATFORM - NIGHT - MED.                  448

Whirlpools of people crowd in.  Joe and Sean among
them.  The boy is almost torn away from Joe by the
press of the crowd, and Joe grabs at him, picking
him up.  The boy clings to him - for the first time,
he's scared.

449    INT. ENTRANCE PAVILION - (SHOOTING TOWARD THE        449
       STREET - SPECIAL EFFECT)

The monster approaches.  A man with a battered suitcase tries at the last moment, with horrible futility,
to protect himself by holding the suitcase over his
head.  The kiosk collapses crushing the people beneath it.

450    INT. SUBWAY PLATFORM - NIGHT - MED. - JOE, SAM       450

All freeze, looking up in terror.  A woman with a
shopping bag drops it, unconscious of the act in her
fear, and the contents spill, unnoticed, on the platform.  A terrifying noise...

451    INT. SUBWAY PLATFORM - CEILING - (SPECIAL EFFECT)    451

The arched ceiling of the subway starts to cave in.

452    INT. SUBWAY PLATFORM - NIGHT - MED.    452

Bricks and debris shower down on the stunned crowd.
Joe, with Sean, jumps down and runs along the rails
toward the tunnel.

453    INT. SUBWAY - NIGHT - (SPECIAL EFFECT)    453

The gigantic talon breaks through the ceiling.  Then
moves on.

454    INT. SUBWAY TUNNEL - NIGHT - MED.    454

A subway train approaches the platform.

455    INT. SUBWAY TUNNEL - CLOSE    455

The motorman sees something ahead, tries to apply
brakes.

456    INT. SUBWAY TUNNEL ENTRANCE TO PLATFORM - (SPECIAL    456
EFFECT)

It is too late.  The train still moving is hit by an
avalanche of collapsing arches.  Bubbling water
escapes from broken main.

457    INT. SUBWAY PLATFORM - NIGHT - MED.    457

Moaning people covered by debris of broken glass,
bricks and dark bubbling water.

458    INT. SUBWAY TUNNEL - JOE, SEAN    458

They are more or less in the clear - only a few other
people have managed to make it.  They are running,
splashing through the rising water.  Suddenly the
boy stumbles.  When he tries to go on, he obviously
has a badly sprained ankle, at least.  Joe looks back,
sees the situation, goes back and grabs the boy up in
his arms, running on.

459   EXT. LONDON STREET - NIGHT             459

     as Army AMBULANCES, accompanied by armed MOTORCYCLES,
     race through the street, their sirens howling. Pan-
     icked CROWDS are running in the opposite direction.

                               DISSOLVE TO:

460   EXT. PARLIAMENT AREA - MISSILES, OFFICER AND MEN   460

     In BG the bank of missiles is being turned slowly
     towards the river direction, and the fiery glow in
     the sky. In FG the commanding COLONEL speaks into
     his portable phone:

                    COLONEL
             We're ready here, sir...
                (glancing at his
                watch)
          Any estimate as to time of alert?

461   INT. ARMY OPERATIONS ROOM - GENERAL, OTHERS     461

                    GENERAL
                 (on phone)
           No, but stand by...

462   INT. SUBWAY TUNNEL - NIGHT - MED. - JOE, SEAN   462

     Joe is moving with difficulty in rushing water. He
     sees a ventilation shaft. They head for it.

463   INT. SUBWAY TUNNEL - NIGHT - CLOSE         463

     Joe has the boy hang around his neck as he starts
     up the emergency iron ladder of the ventilation
     shaft.

464   INT. VENTILATION SHAFT - NIGHT           464

     SHOOTING DOWN the narrow shaft. Joe and Sean climb-
     ing. Below them, in the tunnel, the water is rising
     in whirlpools.

465   EXT. CORNER AT THE SQUARE AT WESTMINSTER ABBEY   465

     In BG a missile rack, starting to turn. In FG the
     COLONEL, on his phone. His eyes are turned towards
     the firelit sky, his face is tense, but his voice
     is quiet and businesslike:

                           (CONTINUED)

465     (CONTINUED)                                                465

                              COLONEL
                    We're zeroing in now...Yes sir,
                    I shall.


466     EXT. MISSILE RACK - CLOSE                                  466

        The missile rack is turning and adjusting the range.


467     EXT. ANOTHER MISSILE RACK IN THE VICINITY OF THE           467
        PARLIAMENT BUILDINGS - MED.

        The missile rack is turning, adjusting the range.


468     EXT. HIGH SHOT FROM THE BIG BEN                            468

        From different corners of the square the long rays
        of searchlights are moving, criss-crossing, con-
        verging.


469     EXT. AT THE MISSILE RACK - CLOSE                           469

        A Captain tensely watches.  He SEES:


470     EXT. LONG SHOT - FOG - NIGHT                               470

        Lit by red flickering flames (off stage) looming out
        of smoke and murk - Mama Monster.


471     EXT. STREET - JOE, SEAN - NIGHT                            471

        as they struggle up out of the shaft, looking around
        them.  They SEE:


472     WHAT THEY SEE:                                             472

        MAMA MONSTER looming up in the distance behind the
        Tower of Big Ben.  From the opposite direction is
        HEARD the CRY of Baby Monster.  At the same time the
        beam of a searchlight strikes Mama.  She ROARS, turns
        directly toward the Tower.  Another beam of LIGHT
        strikes her.


473     EXT. MISSILE RACK - CLOSE                                  473

        The Captain looks off, apparently gets his signal
        from the Colonel, turns and orders to fire.

474     EXT. MISSILE RACK                                474

First cluster of missiles are fired.

475     EXT. MAMA MONSTER - CLOSE                        475

The missiles fly by the head of the monster like
fiery hornets.

476     TWO SHOT - JOE, SEAN                             476

as they watch.  Joe is awestruck.  The boy is too,
but there is an element of pain in his reaction.

477     EXT. ANOTHER MISSILE RACK                        477

At the given signal, the missiles are fired.

478     EXT. MAMA MONSTER AND BIG BEN                    478

One of the missiles explodes close to the monster's
head.  It makes the beast furious and she approaches
and is partly hidden by Big Ben.

479     EXT. SEARCHLIGHT                                 479

The searchlight operators adjust the beam trying to
follow the movements of the monster.

480     EXT. BIG BEN                                     480

The moving beam of light hits Big Ben and the monster
partly hidden by it.

481     EXT. MISSILE RACK                                481

Another cluster of missiles is fired.

482     EXT. MONSTER AND BIG BEN                         482

The missiles deflected by the Big Ben explode in the
air.  Mama Monster is infuriated.  With her front paw
she takes hold of Big Ben and starts to shake it.

483    EXT. MISSILE RACK                                      483

The soldiers have difficulty in aiming their missiles
- monster being partially hidden by Big Ben.  They
fire.

484    EXT. MONSTER AND BIG BEN                               484

With missiles exploding around and searchlights trying to pinpoint the monster.  Big Ben is shaking,
then starts to break.

485    EXT. SEARCHLIGHT PART                                  485

The men are looking with awe at the destruction of
the best known London Landmark.

486    EXT. MONSTER AND BIG BEN - MED.                        486

With shattering noise Big Ben is falling down (the
debris flying directly toward the lens)

487    TWO SHOT - JOE, SEAN                                   487

as they look up in horror at the falling Tower.
Clearly it is going to fall quite near them, but
their backs are literally against a wall.

488    EXT. MISSILE RACK                                      488

Missile rack and men buried under the avalanche of
falling stones.

489    EXT. MONSTER AND RUINED BIG BEN                        489

Mama Monster moves forward destroying the Parliament
Building.

490    EXT. PARLIAMENT BUILDING                              490

With a triumphant roar the monster is stepping on
the ruins of the Parliament building.  The searchlights, now stationary and at crazy angles, light
the scene of destruction.  Mounting cloud of dust
obliterates the scene.

491    MED. SHOT - JOE, SEAN          491

      Utterly shaken by what they have seen, powdered with
      the dust that swirls around them, they start to
      clamber over the debris that now chokes the whole
      area, Joe carrying the boy.

                          DISSOLVE TO:

492    EXT. CIRCUS GROUNDS - NIGHT       492

      A kind of COMMAND POST has been set up near Dorkin's
      office.  There are a couple of tables with temporary
      telephone connections, a field switchboard and oper-
      ator (Army).  An Army COLONEL is on the phone.  In BG
      is the Baby Monster's enclosure, surrounded by its
      network of high tension wires.  A cordon of police
      surrounds the area to keep out unauthorized persons -
      though actually all but the hardiest have fled, and
      the main function of the police is to keep back the
      ever present news and camera men. Opposite the tables
      is a temporary panel with voltage and amperage dials.
      A couple of electricians who have made the final
      hook-ups, are showing the set-up to PROFESSORS HEN-
      DRICKS and FLAHERTY.  SAM stands a little apart, look-
      ing off, anxious about Joe and Sean.  All look off
      tensely as the CRY of Mama Monster is HEARD, quite
      near.  The Baby Monster replies.  The Colonel, listen-
      ing on the telephone:

                    COLONEL
                 (on phone)
          The circuits have just been
          completed, sir.

493    EXT. AT THE ELECTRICAL CONTROLS    493

      The Colonel gives a sign and the contacting switch
      is lowered.  The needles of the dials jump.

494    INT. CONTROL ROOM - POWER HOUSE - NIGHT - MED.  494

      In background we see a series of switch levers and
      dials.  The operator picks up the phone, listens,
      replies, then reaches for one of the switch levers.

495    INT. CONTROL ROOM - POWER HOUSE - CLOSE    495

      He throws the switch.  Needle on dial flashes up to
      50,000 volts.  Operator throws a second switch.

496    EXT. COMMAND POST - NIGHT - MED.          496

This is the point where the main cable meets the web of lines about the beast's enclosure.  The wire hums.

497    INT. CONTROL ROOM - POWER HOUSE - CLOSE      497

Operator continues to throw switches.

498    INT. GENERATOR ROOM - POWER HOUSE - FULL SHOT    498

The generator's hum suddenly accelerates to a ROAR, as they are turned on to full speed.

499    EXT. COMMAND POST - NIGHT - CLOSE         499

PROFESSORS watch the dials connected to the web.  The needle rises to full capacity.  HENDRICKS speaks to the COLONEL.

                  HENDRICKS
          Four million volts and full
          amperage...The wires can't
          take any more...

500    EXT. APPROACH TO THE CIRCUS GROUNDS - NIGHT    500

Mama Monster approaches the circus grounds.  She uproots huge trees at the Battersea Park.

501    EXT. - THE GROUP                    501

As they hear the crashing approach of Mama Monster. Looking off, they SEE:

502    EXT. - CLOSE                      502

of Mama Monster, towering, approaching.  Converging searchlights.

503    MED. CLOSE - SAM                  503

Looking off, he starts forward at something he SEES:

504   WHAT HE SEES:     504

JOE and SEAN approaching.  They show the strain and wear of their hazardous trek back to the Circus Grounds.  Joe carries the boy.

505   ANOTHER ANGLE - THE THREE     505

as they come together.

> SAM
>
> He okay...

> JOE
> (a tight little
> grin)
> He'll live...

He puts the boy down.  Sam puts an arm on the boy's shoulder for a moment, he and Joe exchange a quick smile - the three are together again, emotionally as well as physically.

506   EXT. ANIMAL CAGES     506

Tigers and lions, roaring in fear and rage.

507   EXT. - FULL SHOT     507

The group at the Command Post in FG.  Mama Monster in BG.  Approaching, she cries to the Baby.

508   EXT. - BABY MONSTER     508

As it cries back.  It approaches the smaller network of wires that surround its tank.  There is a flash -- Baby is hurt -- slipping back into the tank.  But it starts back again.

509   EXT. MAMA MONSTER - COMMAND POST IN FG     509

Reacting to the cry, moves forward.  The sound of approaching planes.

510   EXT. SKY     510

The fighter planes approach.

511    EXT. - CLOSE                                      511

The pilot of the fighter plane looks down and puts his plane in a dive.

512    EXT. - HIS P.O.V.                             512

A general view of the circus grounds, the Baby Monster's enclosure and the approaching Mama Monster, as seen from the diving plane. Mama Monster is approaching. Then the two missiles shoot out (from under the frame), they are close misses, exploding behind the monster. The plane swiftly turns and climbs.

513    EXT. - FULL SHOT                               513

As Mama Monster approaches the high tension wires, another fighter plane is diving. Two more explosions shatter the earth around the monster.

514    EXT. - CLOSE                                      514

Mama Monster touches the high tension wires. Blinding electrical sparks.

After a pause - caused by the shock - Mama Monster advances into the wires, slashing at them with her talons. There is another blinding flash of electricity. Mama Monster screams in pain, her whole body shudders. The Baby Monster cries back at her.

515    EXT. - REACTION SHOTS                        515

(particularly JOE, SAM, SEAN) - horrified yet awestruck.

516    EXT. BABY MONSTER                           516

tries to break through the wires.

517    EXT. - MAMA MONSTER - GENERAL VIEW        517

Bellowing in pain and rage, she tears into the wires, smashing one of the pylons. The "hot" wires flash and crackle.

518    EXT. - MORE FIGHTING PLANES AND DIVING                518

519    EXT. - ONE OF THE FIGHTER PLANES                      519

hits the pylon with its wings and is falling down in
crazy loops.

520    EXT. - CLOSE - PILOT                                  520

tries to right his plane.

521    EXT. - HIS P.O.V.                                     521

in crazy gyrating movement, his plane is heading toward
the city gas tanks.

522    EXT. GAS TANKS                                        522

With a tremendous impact the falling plane explodes
the gas tanks. Flames start raging.

523    EXT. BABY MONSTER'S ENCLOSURE - LONG SHOT             523

Mama Monster throws down a whole section of wires
and pylons - in a blinding display of electrical
discharges.

524    EXT. - CLOSE                                          524

Twisted pylons and broken wires destroy the communication cars. The "live" wires sweeping around like
fiery snakes.

525    EXT. - CLOSE                                          525

A hot wire hits a car - a flash as the car is
destroyed.

526    EXT. BABY MONSTER'S ENCLOSURE - MED. LONG            526

The last wires are broken by the furious Mama Monster.
Suddenly the whole area is in semi-darkness lit only
by the flames from the burning gas tanks in BG. The
dark silhouette of Mama Monster is seen crushing the
sides of the Baby Monster's enclosure (to help the
getaway of the Baby Monster).

527     EXT. - CLOSE                                               527

*Reaction of Joe, Sam, Sean.*

528     EXT. BABY MONSTER'S ENCLOSURE - MED. DOLLY SHOT            528

The huge feet of Mama Monster are crushing the sides
of the enclosure.  Answering Mama's call, the Baby
moves closer to her - coming up the slide of rubble.
Camera travels with them - fires in BG.

529     EXT. - CLOSE - SEAN                                        529

as he looks on with wonder in his face.

530     EXT. - LONG SHOT                                           530

Lit by raging flames of gas tanks.  Mama preceding
the Baby - the Monsters move towards the river.

531     FULL SHOT - COMMAND POST - DORKIN, PROFESSORS,            531
        OTHERS

stunned and silent, the group watches the departure
of the MONSTERS, in BG.

532     GROUP SHOT - JOE, SEAN, SAM                               532

                        SEAN
                   (softly, looking
                  after the Monsters)
               They'll be goin' back now...Back
               to the Island...And the sea...

Joe and Sam look at the boy, who is still watching
the monsters, then at each other.  Now there is a kind
of wonder in their eyes, as they watch the monsters go.

533     EXT. RIVER - REVERSE - MONSTERS GOING AWAY                533

We can see only water.  The opposite embankment is in
fog, smoke, and dust - and gives impression of infinity.  The Monsters move forward.  Mama turns her
head, gives a final, rumbling ROAR, like distant thunder and like a warning.  Then both animals move off
and are swallowed up by the swirling, fire-lit fog...

                                        FADE OUT:


                    T H E   E N D

LIKE NOTHING YOU'VE EVER SEEN BEFORE!

A **METRO-GOLDWYN-MAYER**
## PRESS BOOK
Copyright © 1961 by Metro-Goldwyn-Mayer Inc. All rights reserved. Magazines, newspapers and radio stations granted customary use. Country of origin U.S.A. In furnishing this press-book, M-G-M does not thereby imply that this picture has been licensed for exhibition.

METRO-GOLDWYN-MAYER Presents
A KING BROTHERS Production

GORGO

IT'S ALIVE!

THE GREATEST MONSTER PICTURE EVER PRODUCED!

# A PRE-HISTORIC MONSTER VIRTUALLY DESTROYS MODERN LONDON IN MGM'S AMAZING "GORGO," THRILL-PICTURE OF THE YEAR!

*A giant pre-historic monster on the rampage in London destroys the famed Bridge Tower and other London landmarks in search for its offspring, which has been captured for exhibition. This is one of the spectacular thrills in "Gorgo," a King Brothers Production for Metro-Goldwyn-Mayer in Automation and color. Bill Travers, William Sylvester and young Academy Award-winner Vincent Winter head the cast.*

Still GO-4                                    Gorgo Mat 2-A

The havoc wrought on the modern city of London by a giant pre-historic monster which demolishes such famed landmarks as Big Ben, Westminster Abbey, the Houses of Parliament and the Thames' huge Tower Bridge will keep spectators of Metro-Goldwyn-Mayer's thrill-drama, "Gorgo," on the edge of their seats.

The story concerns adventurous partners Joe Ryan and Sam Slade (Bill Travers and William Sylvester) who are salvaging for sunken treasure off the coast of Ireland but instead come upon and capture an extraordinary monster which has been released from its underwater home by a volcanic eruption.

Taking with them young, orphaned Sean, whom they have befriended, Ryan and Slade place the monster, named Gorgo, on exhibition in a London circus. The little boy develops an attachment for the curious beast but is prevented from setting it free. But soon the monster's parent is reported headed toward London in search of its offspring. A destroyer attempting to intercept it is overturned by the 200-feet-long creature. Flame throwers, missiles and jet airplanes fail to halt its progress and a terrorized populace takes flight when the monster reaches London and forges a path of destruction. Does it find its child? And what happens to Ryan, Slade and the boy?

In addition to presenting some of the most breath-taking thrill scenes ever shown in a motion picture, "Gorgo" is also a human drama touching the heart in its depicture of Sean's affection for the imprisoned monster. The boy is played by Vincent Winter, who won an Academy Award for his moving performance in "The Little Kidnappers" and who again reveals an unforgettable appeal in the new film.

Produced for MGM by Frank and Maurice King and directed by Eugene Lourie, "Gorgo" was two years in preparation and filming. It was photographed in the new Automotion process and color largely on locations off the coast of Ireland and in the streets of London, with its startling special effects created by Tom Howard, a two-time Academy Award winner in this field.

John Loring and Daniel Hyatt wrote the screen play, based on an original story by Eugene Lourie and Hyatt.

*Bill Travers carries young Vincent Winter when hysterical crowds in the streets of London flee from a giant pre-historic monster which is destroying the city in "Gorgo," one of the most thrilling motion pictures ever made. A King Brothers Production for Metro-Goldwyn-Mayer, it was filmed in the new Automation process and color.*

Still GO-18                                   Gorgo Mat 2-B

## BRIEF SUMMARY

Packed with thrills as well as heart appeal in its story of a lonely boy who develops an affection for an extraordinary prehistoric monster, "Gorgo," new King Brothers Production for Metro-Goldwyn-Mayer, is one of the most remarkable and exciting science-fiction dramas ever brought to the screen.

Gorgo, the monster from which the picture takes its title, is captured after an undersea explosion releases it from its home beneath the ocean off the coast of Ireland and is taken to London to be exhibited. Another giant monster, Gorgo's mother, trails it to London and virtually demolishes the panic-stricken city in rescuing its offspring. Such famed landmarks as Big Ben, Westminster Abbey, the Houses of Parliament and the Thames' huge Tower Bridge are left in ruins by the mammoth beast's rampage.

During its captivity, Gorgo has but one friend in all the world—a little orphaned boy, also in need of affection. The boy is played by Vincent Winter, who won an Academy Award for "The Little Kidnappers," and who shares stellar honors with Bill Travers and William Sylvester.

Produced by Frank and Maurice King, the picture was directed by Eugene Lourie and was filmed in the new Automotion process and color largely on locations off the Irish coast and in the streets of London.

## CAST

| | |
|---|---|
| Joe Ryan | Bill Travers |
| Sam Slade | William Sylvester |
| Sean | Vincent Winter |
| Flaherty | Bruce Seton |
| Professor Hendricks | Joseph O'Conor |
| Dorkin | Martin Benson |
| First Mate | Barry Keegan |
| Bo'sun | Dervis Ward |
| McCartin | Christopher Rhodes |
| Admiral Brooks | Basil Dignam |

*Executive Producers: Frank King and Maurice King. Directed by Eugene Lourie. Screen Play by John Loring and Daniel Hyatt. Original Story by Eugene Lourie and Daniel Hyatt. In Automotion and color. A Metro-Goldwyn-Mayer Release.*

**THE ADDITIONAL SCENE AND PLAYER MATS, SHOWN IN THE COMPLETE CAMPAIGN MAT ON ANOTHER PAGE, MAY BE ORDERED SINGLY.**

### What Does Pre-Historic Monster Sound Like

What would a giant pre-historic monster, waiting for its missing offspring, sound like?

This was one of the out-of-this world problems faced by the King Brothers, producers of the new Metro-Goldwyn-Mayer release, "Gorgo," which tells a thrill-packed story of a giant monster which virtually destroys the city of London in an attempt to liberate its captured offspring.

Sound libraries in this country and England, where the picture was filmed, did not provide a solution, so the Kings decided to create their own sound for the pre-historic monster.

How? By using four of the biggest jet planes obtainable and recording the sound of the jets as it was bounced through a tunnel!

### "Actors," Made of Foam Rubber, Breathe and Cry!

Two of the most extraordinary "human" non-human actors play pivotal roles in Metro-Goldwyn-Mayer's thrill-drama, "Gorgo." They are two pre-historic monsters, a mother and its child. When the latter is captured the mother monster follows it to London and virtually destroys the city in rescuing its offspring.

Two-time Academy Award-winner Tom Howard created the remarkable special effects for the picture. The life-like monsters were made of foam rubber, fibre glass and hundreds of ingenious mechanisms. They breathed, cried, moved eyes, mouth limbs and tail, and during location scenes filmed on the streets of London caused a sensation, to say nothing of traffic jams.

Bill Travers, William Sylvester and Vincent Winters are the stars of "Gorgo," but the two monsters are the film's scene-stealers.

## TWO YEARS IN MAKING "GORGO" WAS FILMED OFF IRISH COAST AND ON STREETS OF LONDON

Hollywood's most unusual and colorful film producers are three brothers who made their first feature motion picture some two decades ago for $20,000 and recently devoted more than ten times that sum and two years to an ambitious project that may prove to be 1960's most unique movie.

The King Brothers — Maurice, Frank and Herman—are former newsboys, real estate investors, pin-ball machine moguls and self-made motion picture producers. The latest and biggest of their thirty-nine films is "Gorgo," a super-monster picture different from anything previously attempted in its field.

It tells the story of a baby prehistoric monster which is captured and exhibited in a London carnival. When the monster's mother misses its giant-sized baby, it follows the offspring to London and destroys most of the city before rescuing the infant monster.

The picture, released by Metro-Goldwyn-Mayer, stars Bill Travers, William Sylvester and young Vincent Winter, Academy Award-winning boy of "The Little Kidnappers." It was filmed in color and in the new Automotion process, with its startling special effects created by two-time "Oscar" winner, Tom Howard.

Filming took place on locations off the Irish coast, in the streets of London and in MGM's British studios. The monsters — Gorgo and Mama — were created from foam rubber, fibre glass and hundreds of ingenious mechanisms. They breathed, cried, moved eyes, mouth, limbs and tail. They didn't actually wreck London, of course — the demolishing took place in miniature sets — but it isn't likely the British will soon recover from the impact of their appearance on the streets of London.

When baby Gorgo — sixty-five feet long — was paraded over a seven-mile route past Piccadilly Circus, Regent Street, Trafalgar Square and Whitehall, traffic jams ensued. A more unexpected tie-up occurred at Battersea Pleasure Gardens, where gates had to be dismantled before 250-foot-long momma monster could enter.

Inside MGM's largest stage at Borehamwood, a detailed scale model of the Thames' Tower Bridge, Westminster and the Houses of Parliament were constructed at a cost of $75,000.

"It took ten weeks to build it," the King Brothers said. "Gorgo ruined it in ten minutes. We couldn't have done a second take if we had wanted to!"

## WOULDN'T YOU KNOW!

Connie Tilton, England's No. 1 stunt girl, has jumped from blazing buildings, leaped off London Bridge into the Thames, driven cars off precipices and jumped from speeding trains while pursuing her arduous motion picture career.

But she suffered her first injury during filming of "Gorgo," thrill-packed King Brothers Production for Metro-Goldwyn-Mayer, telling the story of a giant pre-historic monster which virtually destroys the city of London in its attempt to release its captured offspring.

And how did Connie sustain her injury? By falling downstairs in an interior scene of the picture filmed in a studio!

*Vincent Winter co-stars with Bill Travers and William Sylvester in "Gorgo," thrill-packed King Brothers Production for Metro-Goldwyn-Mayer. Twelve-year-old Vincent, who won an Academy Award for his performance in "The Little Kidnappers," plays a boy whose sympathy for a captured pre-historic monster leads to fantastic results when the animal's mother virtually destroys London in searching for its offspring. The picture was filmed in the new Automotion process and color.*

Still GO-46                     Gorgo Mat 1-B

*Bill Travers plays the adventurer who aids in the capture of a pre-historic monster in "Gorgo," an event which has horrifying results when the monster's giant mother virtually destroys the city of London in searching for its offspring. William Sylvester and young Academy Award winner Vincent Winter also star in the King Brothers Production for Metro-Goldwyn-Mayer, filmed in Automotion and color.*

Still GO-54                     Gorgo Mat 1-C

2

LIKE NOTHING YOU'VE EVER SEEN BEFORE!

SEE GORGO
Challenge The British Navy!
Destroy Waterloo Bridge!
Topple The Tower Of London!

UP FROM THE OCEAN'S DEPTHS TO TERRORIZE THE CITIES OF THE WORLD. NEITHER JETS, MISSILES, NOR ROCKETS CAN HALT THE HORROR OF ITS REVENGE!

METRO-GOLDWYN-MAYER
Presents
A KING BROTHERS Production

GORGO

What was the strange link between a little boy and this terror from the deep?

STARRING
BILL TRAVERS · WILLIAM SYLVESTER · WITH Vincent Winter · Bruce Seton
Joseph O'Conor · Martin Benson · Barry Keegan · Dervis Ward · Christopher Rhodes
SCREEN PLAY BY JOHN LORING and DANIEL HYATT · DIRECTED BY EUGENE LOURIE · PRODUCED BY FRANK KING and MAURICE KING
TECHNICOLOR

THEATRE

# STAR NOT MUCH TO LOOK AT, BUT HAS A HEART OF GOLD!

The feminine star of Metro-Goldwyn-Mayer's "Gorgo," new King Brothers science-fiction film has measurements like you never heard of. She is 250 feet tall, has a 100-foot bust and measures 150 feet at the hips. She's not much to look at but she has a heart of gold!

This particular star is Mama Monster, who comes to the rescue of her baby, Gorgo, after he has been captured and placed on display at a London sideshow. In rescuing Gorgo, Mama Monster sinks the British navy, paws its air force out of the sky, spits missiles back at the firers and demolishes London—and a good number of its inhabitants—from the Tower Bridge to Battersea Pleasure Gardens.

The King Brothers, Maurice, Frank and Herman, who conceived the idea of "Gorgo" and his monstrous mother, contend that "Gorgo" in substance is a "message picture." The message is that people should leave nature alone.

In the story, if a couple of venturesome boatmen had not trapped baby Gorgo (only 65 feet tall!) after it was tossed to the surface by a sub-ocean volcanic eruption, and taken it away to be a sideshow freak, none of this would have happened. In fairness to the men, portrayed by Bill Travers and William Sylvester, it must be noted that had they known Gorgo had a mother, much, much larger, they probably would have let Gorgo swim back to its family depths.

Gorgo is described by the King Brothers as "the first man-made human beast." They explain it has human qualities in that it can weep, has an expressive face and, through roaring and wailing, can voice a message adequately understood in any language.

Gorgo and mother, with the general contour of a lizard or of a mythical dragon, are the biggest monsters of all time. By comparison, King Kong was a midget.

That's why "Gorgo" has a happy ending, with Mama Monster and little Gorgo escaping to their home at the bottom of the sea. There was just nothing powerful enough to stop them.

*A massive bathysphere, in which Bill Travers is seeking signs of a fearsome pre-historic underwater monster seems just a toy to the tremendous beast in this scene from "Gorgo," King Brothers production for Metro-Goldwyn-Mayer. It's a thrill drama in Automotion and color that will keep you on the edge of your seat!*

Still GO-38 Gorgo Mat 1-D

***What's in a title? Metro-Goldwyn-Mayer's "Gorgo," drama of giant prehistoric creatures, was coined by the King Brothers as a free-flowing contraction of Gargantua. It's also the Greek spelling for Gorgon, famed legend of the snaky-haired Medusa and her sisters.***

# CAPTURED MONSTER BROUGHT TO LONDON

*A fantastic pre-historic monster is captured and brought to London for exhibition in this scene from Metro-Goldwyn-Mayer's suspenseful thrill-drama, "Gorgo." Bill Travers, William Sylvester and young Academy Award-winner Vincent Winter star in the King Brothers Production, filmed in Automotion and color.*

Still GO-20 Gorgo Mat 2-D

# "GORGO" OFFERS STARTLING INNOVATIONS IN EVER-POPULAR MONSTER FILM KICKS

Monsters always have had an amazing appeal for motion picture audiences. Although they have taken varied forms and different dramatic devices, many have been box-office bonanzas and several have achieved recognition as screen classics.

Latest entry in this popular category is Metro-Goldwyn-Mayer's "Gorgo," a King Brothers production, and to make the obvious pun, it's a "king-size" picture with some startling innovations for monster films.

For example, there are two monsters. One, who plays the title role, is a baby, yet he is 65-feet long. The other, Gorgo's mother, checks in at 250 feet! Played against the spine-tingling and spectacular destruction of modern London is probably the strangest love story ever screened, the love of this monster mother for her child.

In fact, she is so determined to rescue her captured baby that she fights a modern warship, ignores machine guns, flame throwers and missiles, and spreads a trail of terror through the city, toppling the Tower Bridge, Big Ben, Westminster Abbey and the Houses of Parliament.

The human stars of "Gorgo" are Bill Travers, William Sylvester and young Academy Award-winner Vincent Winter. There are some 10,000 players in this picture, which was filmed in Automotion and color off the coast of Ireland and on the streets of London.

Monster movies weren't of such magnitude when the screen was young and they mostly dealt with known natural creatures. Away back in 1907, Edwin Porter, who had startled the world with his "The Great Train Robbery," dabbled in the monster dodge to some extent with a one-reel thriller called "The Eagle's Nest." In this pioneer film, a huge bird carried a baby high above a painted landscape. As a footnote to screen history, David Wark Griffith, then an actor, was the frontiersman who rescued the child.

Two years later, Winsor McKay, a newspaper cartoonist, exhibited the first drawn motion picture, called "Gertie the Dinosaur." In a fashion, this was the forerunner to the dinosaurs used by Walt Disney in the Stravinsky's "The Rite of Spring" segment in his "Fantasia" of a score of years ago.

As Hollywood grew older, it turned to the classics, such as Herman Melville's novel, "Moby Dick." Although Melville's mighty whale doesn't fall into the monster category as it is known today, it wasn't exactly a tame tadpole. John Barrymore starred in the first version in 1926, called "The Sea Beast," reminiscent of later-day titles of monster pictures. He repeated the role as "Moby Dick" in 1930, and the yarn was done again only a few years ago by Gregory Peck.

The daddy of today's screen monsters undoubtedly was "King Kong," the huge gorilla-like creature who startled and delighted filmgoers back in 1933. Some fifteen years later, "Mighty Joe Young," also an ape-like creature, took his niche among the greats of movie mammoths.

The monster-makers have dreamed up their creatures from the air, on the land and from the sea. Eugene Lourie, who directed and co-authored "Gorgo," previously directed "The Beast from 20,000 Fathoms."

Many monsters, of course, have been beasts in human form. The classic examples are "Frankenstein," the robot, as created by Boris Karloff, and "Dracula," the vampire made memorable by Bela Lugosi.

The all-time tops in purely human monsters remains "Dr. Jekyll and Mr. Hyde." John Barrymore first played the dual role in a silent picture and Fredric March won an Academy Award for his performance in the same story in 1932. This irresistible role also was played by Spencer Tracy in 1941.

*A fantastic pre-historic monster wades up London's Thames River and destroys the famed Tower Bridge as it invades the modern city bent on rescuing its offspring, which has been captured for exhibition. This is part of the breathtaking action of "Gorgo," King Brothers production for Metro-Goldwyn-Mayer. Bill Travers, William Sylvester and young Vincent Winter star in the thrill-drama, filmed in Automotion and color.*

Still GO-5 Gorgo Mat 2-E

# BILL TRAVERS' OWN LIFE PERFECT FOR A MOVIE ADVENTURE

As wild as some of his make-believe adventures have been on the motion picture screen, scarcely less fantastic have been the real-life experiences of internationally known film star, Bill Travers.

The tall, husky actor, shy and diffident by nature, is inclined to gloss over his exciting past. But from the time he joined the British Army at the age of seventeen, his life story has read like fiction. It doesn't have monsters in it, as does his latest motion picture, Metro-Goldwyn-Mayer's "Gorgo," but it doesn't lack much else.

In less than a year after entering the Army, Travers was on the northwest frontier of India, fighting with General Wingate's hit-and-run army behind enemy lines.

During one of Wingate's campaigns in Burma, he contracted malaria. Left behind in a small village, he stayed flat on his back in a friendly native's hut for two weeks. Then, determined not to surrender, he walked hundreds of miles through the jungle, disguised in a Chinese coolie jacket and hat. After three torturous months, he reached Allied lines.

Later, after being made liaison officer to United States forces in Burma, he waged war in the Kachin Hills north of Mandalay and then was sent to Ceylon in command of a native troop battalion. In charge of a small force ordered to harass the Japanese, he once parachuted into the Malayan jungle. When the war ended, he remained in the jungle to round up enemy war criminals.

After his discharge from the service and return to England, Travers was persuaded to try his hand at acting. His growing list of film successes have brought their own excitement, including making cinema love to most of England's screen beauties and such American favorites as Ava Gardner and Jennifer Jones. In real life, he is married to British actress Virginia McKenna.

Some of Travers' most interesting present day adventures are found deep beneath the ocean's surface. He is an avid skin-diving enthusiast. Incidentally, he was able to enjoy this underwater sport during the filming of "Gorgo." Portraying a salvage operator, he dives for sunken treasure off the coast of Ireland and discovers, instead, a strange pre-historic monster.

From that point on, one fantastic adventure follows another in the spectacular picture, produced by the King Brothers.

# WILLIAM SYLVESTER AMERICAN STAR WITH "BRITISH MADE" TAG

One of England's most popular stage and screen leading men is, strangely enough, as American as hot dogs and crackerjack. He is tall, handsome William Sylvester, a native of Oakland, California. Nine years ago, after attending the University of California and then seeing two years of South Pacific service with the U. S. Merchant Marine, he headed for London.

Today, a star in Britain, he will be seen on the American screen for the first time in "Gorgo," a King Brothers Production filmed in England and released by Metro-Goldwyn-Mayer. Since departing these shores, however, Sylvester has appeared in a dozen British pictures and nearly as many London stage productions. His one U.S.A. appearance was in the Broadway play, "Mister Johnson."

It was the advice of an actor friend that sent Sylvester overseas, once he had decided an acting career held more allure for him than his family's dry-cleaning business. The friend told him that the best way to become an actor was to become a student at the Royal Academy of Dramatic Arts in London. Sylvester quickly took the advice and almost as quickly was on his way up in his newly chosen profession.

*Popular British star William Sylvester plays an adventurer who aids in the capture of a giant pre-historic monster in "Gorgo," King Brothers production for Metro-Goldwyn-Mayer in Automotion and color. Also starred in the thrill-drama are Bill Travers and young Academy Award-winner Vincent Winter.*

Still GO-46 Gorgo Mat 1-E

"I did a few plays staged by fellow-Americans at the Royal Academy," he says. "Then I had a chance to play John, the Witch Boy in 'Dark of the Moon,' which was a big success in its West End production in London. It was a lucky break for me, coming so fast."

Since then, Sylvester has been seen in a number of West End hits, including "Streetcar Named Desire," "The Joshua Tree" and "Teahouse of the August Moon." In the last, he appeared for eighteen months in the Captain Fisby role enacted by Glenn Ford in the film version.

His British pictures haven't brought him to the attention of American audiences, but his home folk will have a chance to see him impressively in "Gorgo," an unusual science-fiction drama, in which he stars with Bill Travers and young Vincent Winter, boy Academy Award-winner of "The Little Kidnappers."

As a treasure-hunting adventurer, Sylvester succeeds with Travers in capturing a giant prehistoric monster freed from its underwater home by a volcanic explosion. They take the beast to London, where Sylvester and the boy regret imprisoning the monster and try to free it. When they are stopped, the beast's parent monster trails it to London and virtually destroys the city to rescue her off-spring.

4

155

Ad No. 406—600 Lines (4 Cols. x 150 Lines)
NOTE: This ad also available in 500 Lines (4 Cols. x 125 Lines) Order Ad No. 407

Ad No. 150—80 Lines

Ad No. 111
50 Lines (1 Col. x 50 Lines)

Ad No. 211—56 Lines (2 Cols. x 28 Lines)

7

157

# NATIONAL TV CAMPAIGN ZOOMS "GORGO" SKY-HIGH!

Sensational TV TRAILERS have been specially prepared to launch the massive national TV campaign on "GORGO". Selling "GORGO" via the air is a MUST for your campaign and this unusual and exciting material will HELP YOU DO THE JOB! Reprinted below are scripts of some of the TV trailers that are available (6 one-minute and 6 twenty-second video spots). The TV campaign will encompass many branch and other key cities through the country, and your local MGM Branch Manager has all the information on the campaign in your area. Also available to add box-office dollars to your playdate is a 16 mm version of the production trailer which runs 2 minutes. Plant (gratis) with your local TV stations. Additionally, RADIO TRANSCRIPTIONS similar in format to the TV trailers and equally effective, are available. Start lining up the best time availabilities on your local media now, and let your community know that "GORGO" is on the way!

*Contact your local MGM Press Representative for all materials.*

### 60 SEC. TV SPOT "A"

Up from the dread depths, rages "GORGO" the prehistoric terror-monster! . . .

Towering over the cities of the world! . . .

Defying the force of armies . . .

The might of navies . . .

And the fury of the jets!

Yet, one little boy had a curious sympathy for the awesome creature.

What strange secret does he know, that might have saved the world?

Incredibly realistic . . . Shockingly convincing!

No motion picture of our time has ever unleashed shock-spectacle of such scope and excitement!

This is the Big One! . . .

"GORGO"! . . . Astounding, on the giant screen . . . in blazing Technicolor!

### 60 SEC. TV SPOT "C"

Is this the end of the world? . . .

It's the Big One!

"GORGO" . . . The prehistoric terror-monster . . .

Spreading panic, as millions flee its mad vengeance against mankind! . . .

Can anything stop its march of destruction? . . .

Bullets! . . . Bombs! . . . Torpedoes! . . . Rockets! . . .

Like nothing you've ever seen before!

Never before, such terrific spectacle! . . .

Never before, such shocking excitement! . . .

Never before . . . such astounding realism! . . .

Because, This is the Big One . . . The Big One! . . . So gigantic it towers over the cities of the world! . . .

It's the Big One!

"GORGO"! . . . Storming the giant theatre screen in a cataclysm of blazing Technicolor!

### 60 SEC. TV SPOT "E"

This is "GORGO" . . . A gigantic prehistoric monster!

. . . And this is "Sean" . . . a little Irish boy, who was his friend.

Sean was the only one in the world who knew the secret of "GORGO" . . .

What was the strange link between this little boy and the awesome creature from the depths of time!

This is the Big One! . . . "GORGO"!

Like nothing you've ever seen before! . . .

Towering over great cities . . . Even defying the army . . . the navy . . . and the air-force!

Don't miss "GORGO" . . . The mystery monster from another age . . . but a friend to a little boy!

"GORGO"! On the giant theatre screen . . . in Technicolor!

### 20 SEC. TV SPOT No. 1

Is this the end of the world?

It's "GORGO"! . . . The prehistoric terror-monster! . . .

Wreaking terrible vengeance against mankind! . . .

"GORGO"! . . .

Astounding, on the giant theatre screen . . . in Technicolor!

### 20 SEC. TV SPOT No. 3

Big! . . . Big! . . . Big! . . . This is the Big One!

"GORGO"! . . . The most massive monster ever to attack mankind!

Horror in its path! . . . Terror in its wake! . . .

"GORGO"! . . . Like nothing you've ever seen before! . . . on the giant theatre screen . . . in Technicolor!

### 60 SEC. TV SPOT "B"

This is the Big One! . . .

"GORGO"! . . . Shocking! . . . Realistic! . . . Terrifying, on the giant theatre screen . . . in blazing Technicolor!

The most awesome sight ever beheld by human eyes! . . .

"GORGO"! . . . Horror in its Path! . . . Terror in its wake!

This is the Big One! (pause)

Neither the Army . . . Or the Navy . . . Or the Jets, can stop it!

What does it want? . . . Does this little boy understand?

What secret does he know about the terrifying creature that might save the world! . . . as millions flee the awful destruction of the vengeance-mad monster!

Like nothing you've ever seen before!

This is the Big One! . . .

"GORGO"! . . . Shocking! . . . Realistic! . . . Terrifying, on the giant theatre screen . . . in blazing Technicolor!

### 60 SEC. TV SPOT "D"

Like nothing you've ever seen before! . . .

"GORGO"! The gigantic prehistoric monster from the depths! . . .

In all the annals of science-fiction no sights and sounds, such as this, have ever inspired such exciting entertainment!

"GORGO" is thrilling adventure, uncovering a mystery from another age! . . .

Can anything stop it?

Impervious to the might of the army . . . the force of the navy . . . or the fury of the jets!

"GORGO" is also the story of a little Irish boy, with a curious sympathy for the awesome creature . . .

What strange secret does he know that might have prevented such havoc?

Yes . . . This is the Big One! . . .

Incredibly realistic! . . . Thrillingly convincing!

"GORGO"! On the giant theatre screen . . . in blazing Technicolor!

### 60 SEC. TV SPOT "F"

This is the Big One!

"GORGO" . . . The most massive monster ever conceived by science-fiction! . . .

The BIG One!

BIG in Action! . . .

BIG in Spectacle! . . .

BIG in Excitement! . . .

"GORGO"! . . . Like nothing you've ever seen before!

Defying bullets! . . . bombs . . . (pause) . . . even Torpedoes!

Yet one little boy had a curious understanding of the fantastic creature . . .

What strange secret does he know, that might have stopped "GORGO" on its path of destruction?

"GORGO"! . . . Like nothing you've ever seen before! . . .

This is the Big One! . . .

"GORGO"! . . . On the giant theatre screen . . . in Technicolor!

### 20 SEC. TV SPOT No. 2

Like nothing you've ever seen before!

"GORGO" . . . The Terror-monster!

Towering above the cities of the world! . . .

Defying the force of armies . . . The might of Navies . . .

This is the Big One!

"GORGO"! . . . On the giant theatre screen . . . in blazing Technicolor!

### 20 SEC. TV SPOT No. 4

This is the Big One!

"GORGO"! . . . . The prehistoric terror-monster from another age! . . .

BIG in Realism! . . .

BIG in Spectacle! . . .

LIKE NOTHING YOU'VE EVER SEEN BEFORE !

METRO-GOLDWYN-MAYER Presents

A KING BROTHERS Production

# GORGO

BILL TRAVERS · WILLIAM SYLVESTER

with Vincent Winter · Bruce Seton · Joseph O'Conor · Martin Benson · Barry Keegan Dervis Ward · Christopher Rhodes · screenplay by JOHN LORING and DANIEL HYATT

directed by EUGENE LOURIE · produced by FRANK KING and MAURICE KING

TECHNICOLOR

THEATRE

## MONARCH MOVIE EDITION

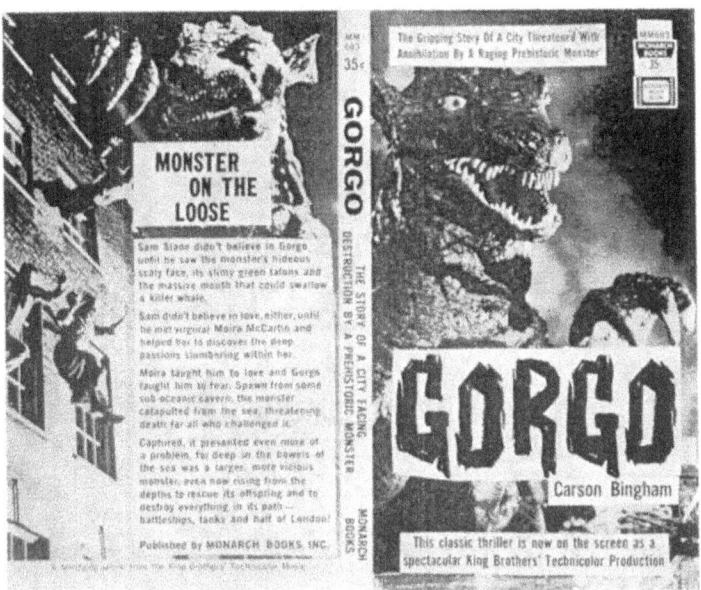

Monarch Books, among the largest paperback publishers, has planned one of the biggest book campaigns in their history for the special movie edition of GORGO. The book is going to be distributed to meet the opening playdates of the film around the country.

GORGO is being handed out at numerous promotion campaigns tying in the film with the book.

### YOUR PROMOTION CHECK-LIST

1. Arrange point-of-sale displays of books, posters, and movie tie-in stills at all Monarch Books outlets.

2. Plan eye-catching, full window displays with book, drug and department stores, utilizing 8 x 10 stills, posters and playdate.

3. Run a coop ad with distributor and/or stores selling the paperback edition.

4. Tie-up with local libraries. Set up counter displays using stills from the picture.

5. Set up lobby displays of paperback book, stills and posters.

For further information, write or wire:

MR. ALLEN ADAMS
Capital Distributing Company
Division Street
Derby, Connecticut

## FAMOUS MONSTERS MAGAZINE

GORGO is featured in "Famous Monsters of Filmland" Magazine's April issue, now on the stands. The full-color cover rendering of GORGO plus seven page story in text and photos contains full credit to the picture along with highlights of same. Contact local distributors and arrange newsstand posters, window cards and truck banners. For further information, contact:

MR. JAMES WARREN
Famous Monsters
1426 E. Washington Lane
Philadelphia, Pa.

### PROMOTE "GORGO" BOOKS

The trio of GORGO publications illustrated on this page offer rare opportunities for promotional effort. Make sure all book and magazine outlets give prominent display to each item since the cover of each is an eye-catching ad for the picture. These books suggest an outlet not usually open—the book pages of your local paper. Run a small ad announcing your playdate, tied in with the local distributors of the GORGO publications.

## CHARLTON COMICS

Magazine wholesalers will distribute this comic book movie edition across the country timed to the release of GORGO. For extra profits arrange for run of the film itself. Set off a prominent corner of the lobby for a table on which to display the books. In addition, contact local retail outlets for windows, store counter and newsstand displays, tie-in ads and other promotions. Do not overlook the magazine racks in drug stores and book shops.

To obtain comic books, contact your local magazine wholesaler. Your neighborhood comic book dealer can supply his name. Distributors will supply you with the GORGO comic book at a reduced rate. Use them as giveaways for the first 100 children attending your opening day, distribute them to schools and offer them as prizes in contests.

For further information, write or wire:

MR. ALLEN ADAMS
Charlton Comics
Division Street
Derby, Connecticut

### BOOKMARK

Take advantage of these three special GORGO editions by preparing and giving wide distribution to a bookmark. For this purpose, use 1-column mat #150 in the advertising section of this pressbook. Add theatre and playdate imprint and distribute through book store, newsstands, etc. You might also use them as giveaways in the week prior to your opening both in theatre and out in the streets.

12

159

## EXPLOITATION

### MOST CHILLING EXPERIENCE

Here's a simple but effective letter-writing contest that should get generous space. Through the local newspaper ask for letters describing in fifty words or less "My Most Chilling Experience." Award guest tickets to see GORGO to the ten best letters.

### FAVORITE THRILL PICTURE

Through TV, radio or a newspaper, ask for the longest list of "thrill" pictures, plus a letter stating "Why I Would Like to See GORGO." Limit letters to fifty words and award guest tickets to the ten winners.

### FLASH FRONT

Here's an opportunity to put up a real flash front. Use the posters and accessories available from National Screen to project the excitement and action of GORGO. Place lobby pieces around box-office and in inner and outer lobbies and on the sidewalk. Create a really colorful front that will draw all eyes to GORGO.

### LOCAL LEVEL HERALD

Use ad mat #L-301 to make up a herald locally. To lend further impact, have each herald numbered differently and announce a "lucky number" contest. Have a drawing each day for one week prior to playdate in theatre lobby, posting the winning number in a prominent position. Award guest tickets to the holders of the heralds

Through a TV or radio show or the local newspaper, "dare" people to sit through GORGO. People must "invite" themselves by writing postcard or letter stating why they would like to attend such a screening. Take photos of them "before" (smiling) and "after" (frightened) for newspaper art and story. An alternate method would be to have one person sit through picture by himself.

### STREET BALLYHOO

Dress a man in a "Gorgo Costume" and have him make the rounds of the busiest sections of town. He should be appropriately bannered and hand out calling cards inscribed "Gorgo Is Coming."

### STREET STENCIL

Make up a stencil reading "Gorgo Is Coming" and use it on every street corner in the downtown area, also, on fences, building sides and telephone poles. Do this ten days in advance of playdate thereby setting people to wondering who GORGO is and creating much interest.

### TOY SHOP TIE-UP

GORGO presents a fine opportunity for local level toy shop tie-ups. Suggest window displays built around stills and posters from the picture utilizing models of prehistoric animals. Enlarge on this by getting toy store to conduct an essay contest for children in which contestants write a brief historical and informative essay about the prehistoric beast of their choice. The writers of the best letters should get a set of educational toys with guest tickets awarded to the runners-up.

14

## 40 x 60 ACTION DISPLAY POSTER

PRICES

**BLACK AND WHITE**
**$9.00**

If wanted with easel add $1.00

When ordering please state playdate.

Order direct from:

**IDEAL PHOTOGRAPHIC CORP.**
**160 West 46th St.**
**New York City**

This 40x60 poster, mounted on heavy board, carries exciting scenes from GORGO. It projects all the startling elements of the picture itself. Use it as an advance lobby display and move it out front when the picture is current. You will find it makes an ideal window display and lends itself perfectly to merchant tie-ups. It may also be incorporated into lobby

## 8 x 10 COLOR STILLS (12 to a set)

Nothing sells a color film better than a color in your lobby. Here is an opportunity to sell all the colorful and exciting elements of "GORGO" with a full (12) set of beautiful color stills.

AVAILABLE FROM N.S.S.

THEATRE

Ad No. L-101
1 Col. x 2" (28 Lines)

Ad No. 114
14 Lines (1 Col. x 14 Lines)

A giant pre-historic monster
virtually destroys the city of
London in its search for its
offspring, which has been
captured for exhibition, in
"Gorgo," one of the most
Award-winner Vincent Winter.
It was filmed in the new Automotion process and color.

Mat 1-D

THEATRE

THIS IS
GORGO!

Ad No. L-102
1 Col. x 3" (42 Lines)

Ad No. 212—28 Lines (2 Cols. x 14 Lines)

Ad No. L-201—2 Cols. x 2½" (70 Lines)

Ad No. 208—200 Lines (2 Cols. x 100 Lines)

Two fishermen cannot believe their eyes when the claw of a
giant pre-historic undersea monster emerges from the surface of the water in one of the shock scenes of "Gorgo." The
picture tells the story of this monster which virtually destroys
the city of London in its search for its offspring, which has been
captured for exhibition. Bill Travers, William Sylvester and
young Academy Award-winner Vincent Winter head the cast
of the King Brothers Production for Metro-Goldwyn-Mayer,
filmed in Automation and color.

Mat 2-C

COMPOSITE AD AND
PUBLICITY MAT

# SPECIAL MAT NO. 1

15

6 SHEET

3 SHEET

ONE SHEET

# POSTERS and LOBBY CARDS

## ORDER FROM NATIONAL SCREEN

All advertising material in this pressbook, as well as all other newspaper and publicity material, has been approved under the MPAA Advertising Code as a self-regulatory procedure of the Motion Picture Association of America. All inquiries on this procedure, which is voluntarily subscribed to by the major motion picture companies, may be addressed to: Advertising Code Administrator, Motion Picture Association of America, 28 W. 44th St., New York 36, N. Y.

14 x 22 WINDOW CARD

11 x 14 LOBBY DISPLAY CARDS

22 x 28 CARD

INSERT CARD

PRINTED IN U. S. A.

The Gripping Story Of A City Threatened
Annihilation By A Raging Prehistoric Monster

MM603
MONARCH
BOOKS
35¢

MONARCH
MOVIE
BOOK

GORGO

Carson Bingham

This classic thriller is now on the screen as a
spectacular King Brothers' Technicolor Production

200     (CONTINUED)                                                    200

                         HENDRICKS' VOICE
                    (over)
                 ...A creature unique in the history
                 of evolutionary biology!

          CAMERA PANS to the group of Joe, Dorkin, and the two
          Professors:  SAM and SEAN stand a little apart.

                         HENDRICKS
                 And you turn it into a circus

## Part one: CATACLYSM

## Chapter 1

I HAD TRIED to argue Joe Ryan out of making that last dive with the aqualung to prowl the freighter hulk we'd found. But he was the boss, and what boss will ever listen to you?

In the thirty minutes or so since he'd gone down, the sky over the North Atlantic had turned a dirty yellow, like moldy lemon custard. The sea surface was flat and oily, without a ripple visible for miles. Something was going to happen. An ominous oppressiveness hung in the air. It crushed down on all of us, like a solid weight.

I turned and moved across the deck of the *Triton*, past the rugged little bathysphere we kept lashed amidships. When you're working the salvage racket, you use the best and latest equipment. The initial outlay costs an arm and a leg, but in the long run, class pays off. Even in a gambler's game like salvage, you only play the sure thing.

The Bos'n, a big, solid Irishman named Jack Finn, was leaning on the rail with three of the crewmen, staring off into the western sky. The crewmen, were a taciturn bunch of Gaels we'd signed on in the Galway Bay area. They never said much, and they were a superstitious lot. Whenever they had any serious talking to do, they did it in Gaelic.

As far as I could see, something was eating them now. They kept their eyes averted, squinting seaward, and they muttered among themselves in their own language.

A flock of birds headed toward the *Triton*, flying low and purposefully. They flew in a soaring V, knifing through the sulky sky. A strange, muted turbulence began to swell the surface of the unnaturally calm waters. Ominous lethargic ripples roiled the glassy surface.

"Boats," I called.

The big Irishman approached me with the solid widespread gait of a man who has spent most of his life on the deck of a ship. A cigarette hung out of the corner of his mouth, just under the nicotine stain on his upper lip. He was born with it there.

"What's up, anyway?"

Jack Finn raised an eyebrow and glanced at the yellow sky. He had his thumbs hooked in the belt of his dungarees, and his sweat-and-salt soaked skivvies bulged under his heavily muscled chest and forearms.

"The weather's getting foul." His words came out in a rich, true peat-bog brogue.

Motioning him after me, I crossed the deck out of earshot of the crew. We leaned over and watched a long spiraling trail of air bubbles that rose to the surface of the water next to the ship.

The Bos'n glanced at the watch on his massive wrist. "He's been down a half hour already."

"Damn fool. He'll stay till his air runs out if he thinks he can latch onto a buck's worth of salvage."

I glanced up at the sun where it glowed blood-red in the thick yellow overhang—the damndest thing I've ever seen. It was as if the whole sky was slowly smoldering to ashes.

"I know these waters, Mr. Slade," Jack Finn said softly, "and I never seen the like of this. Something funny's going on."

I nodded. Over his shoulder I could see the crewmen up front, peering into the heavy sky. One of them gesticulated wildly to an other. Unintelligible syllables of Gaelic drifted to me through the murky air.

"Boats," I said, "get over there and calm them down. They just might jump overboard and leave us high and dry."

Jack Finn grunted. "Superstition is all these Irishers got, Mr. Slade. But I'll do what I can."

Jack Finn moved away. I turned and peered over the rail again. There was no change below. The bubbles still curved upward, vanishing on the surface of the flat turbid sea. I could imagine Joe down there, his aqualung in position, peering out through his face mask. I wondered what he'd located. I closed my eyes and crossed my fingers. God, could we use a buck! We were in hock up to our eyeballs on this salvage rig, and if we didn't come up with some heavy scratch pretty soon, we'd have to run for Tahiti or be repossessed.

Thirty-five minutes, I mused. Not that I blamed Joe for making a thorough recon. It had taken us a week just to find the wreck. And now, with this damned storm coming up, we'd have to abandon it just when we were getting close. I cursed soundlessly and spat into the brackish water.

Just our luck. Just our lousy stinking luck.

As I stood there, the sky went dark. It was almost as if I were standing in a room filled with normal daylight while someone slowly drew all the blinds shut. It was the same feeling you get when you're going to pass out. And it was fast.

I looked up. The sky was night. The clouds were mushrooming like the smoke from an oil-well fire. The sun was gone. It was twilight and growing darker.

I tore myself from the rail and headed for my lung and fins. As I moved I pulled my skivvy shirt out of my dungarees and hauled it over my shoulders. I got out of my shoes and was unbuckling my pants when I heard a sound behind me.

I turned and there was Joe, standing dripping on the companionway, looking like come creature out of the deep.

He flipped back his mask and I could see an idiotic grin of greedy triumph on his sharp, narrow-cheeked features.

"We're in Sam!" he cried. "Swing that forward boom out. I want a cable over the side!"

I looked at him sourly. "You're kidding?" I nodded up at the sky and pointed to the water. "Look at that weather."

Joe turned. "It was getting a little rough down under," he admitted. "Damn it! Just when we get our hooks into something, Mother Nature screws it up for us!

"No use standing here and cussing. From here on, it's a one-way trip—straight down."

I could see Joe's hands knot into fists. His face got a strained, bitter look. His yellow eyes were as narrow as slits. I'd seen him that way before, in Korea, where we served together. He was a killer at heart. A dangerous man. Right now I knew he'd like to take on the whole damned North Atlantic Ocean.

"No sir!" he snapped. He wheeled on me. "Give me that cable hook. There's a ten thousand dollar gyrocompass down there on that rustbucket. I'm staying until I get it!"

"For God's sake, Joe! Don't be damned fool—you'll get us all killed!"

He wheeled and gripped the rail in frustrated rage. And as he stood there, glaring out at the sea, we both saw it happen. It was as if the whole ocean swelled like a blowout in a tire tube. The horizon bulged, and the ocean's surface lifted for what seemed to be miles. Then it drew back, separating, and in its center a huge ball of fire bloomed out like some rank, poisonous flower.

"My God!" Joe gasped. His jaw sagged.

The explosion came then. The *Triton* shuddered as the shock waves hit her steel plating. We saw steam shower out of the fireball—steam and ashes and molten rock. It seemed as if the big blob of erupting, exploding material from the earth's center rose miles in the sky. Possibly it was only a thousand feet or so. I'd never know.

The ocean settled back into its normal horizon line, and a cone-shaped mass of glowing red rock thrust itself up out of the turgid, boiling sea. Flames shot from the point of the cone, and red-hot flaming lava belched forth, flowing down its sides. When the molten rock hit the water, more steam swirled into the air, all but obscuring the newly formed volcanic crater.

"Boats!" Joe yelled. "Get the anchor up! Quick!"

"Aye aye," the Bos'n cried. He yelled orders to the crew and kept saying, *"Corraigh ort! Corraigh ort!"* He was telling them to hurry. He turned and raced for the donkey engine and kicked it instantly into action.

I stood there, frozen to the deck plates. I couldn't move a muscle. All I could do was gape at the cataclysm in the ocean. Clouds of steam and ashes fanned out in stinking, foul air boiled over the *Triton*. Red-hot stones hit the surface of the ocean about us with sizzles and hisses.

When I could wrench my gaze away from the awesome sight in front of me, I saw that Jack Finn had two crewmen helping him at the winch, hoisting the anchor chair through the hawse pipe. Throughout the din of the metallic rattling I heard Joe hollering at me.

I turned.

"Batten her down, Sam!"

Joe leaped up the companionway to the bridge. I moved then, released from whatever spell held me, and dashed about securing everything on deck. I never worked so fast in all my life. All the while it was getting darker and hotter and the air was turning more sulphurous. There was the smell of gunsmoke in the air, the smell of rotten eggs.

I joined Joe in the bridge room. He was yelling down the speaking tube and jangling the engine telegraph.

"Full speed! Give it all you've got!"

He flipped the wheel around eastward, waiting for the screw to grab hold. We both looked through the window at the newly-formed volcanic upthrust.

The entire horizon was jet black now—a continuous cloud of smoke, ash and lava. The sea was building up around the blackened cone, dancing wildly like an enchanted incarnation to some strange other-world melody. And then came the second blast—a thunderous, violent, eruption ejecting rock, fire and steam from the volcano's center.

"My God!" Joe cried. "Look!"

Around the bottom of the volcano, evenly formed and swelling majestically appeared a huge tidal wave, rising slowly and inexorable from the base of the cone, moving ponderously outward in an ever-widening circle.

The wave swelled turgidly, dull red in the strange unearthly glow of the sky. It flowed toward us like blood. The deck of the *Triton* shuddered under us as the engines pulsed. We began to move. But we were not moving fast enough. Behind us the huge comber moved steadily closer, rising into a massive mountainous crest, bearing down on us like the superhuman agency of some malignant sea devil.

The crewmen clutched the deck rails for support, to keep from being hurled overboard by the thrust of the wave. Jack Finn, his big burly body straining against his skivvies, held tightly to the mooring of the donkey engine, gazing up fearlessly and curiously at the avalanche of water approaching us.

"Joe!" I cried. "Here it comes!"

The *Triton* shuddered heavily, listed slightly, and then in a tremendous surge of power, hurled high into the air, like a catapulted plane from the deck of a carrier. It was as if some giant hand had grasped us and shot us out of the water. There was nothing around us but yellow-black air, and ashes and sizzling rocks. I saw sky, and more sky, and black clouds and smoke.

The wheel was spinning around, Joe's hands bleeding and ripped by his struggle to control it. I tried to move toward him, but the deck was the steepest hill I'd ever tried to climb. I could not move against it. I found myself flattened to it, pulled down. I slipped and fell; then my clutching fingers found the bottom of the wheel. I pulled myself up. The deck immediately reversed its angle, and I crashed forward into the wheel. I saw a pinwheel of dancing colored stars and my head spun.

Then we righted again. I saw the ocean about us, a mass of white- caps and waves forming a series of strange flat plateaus, arranged like moving escalator steps. And Joe and I were calmly holding onto the wheel, and it was not fighting us at all. Now we were headed in an easterly direction, exactly where we wanted to go. For one long, surprising instant there was silence all about us. The crewmen picked themselves up from the foredeck, shaking their heads. Jack Finn still clutched the donkey engine mooring. He looked around dazedly.

And then, with no warning, the sky vanished again. At our stern arose another mountain of water. If the first wave was a mountain, this was Everest. It bore down on us, towering and forbidding. We were done. Joe turned his greenish face to me, smiling sickly.

The deck shuddered, the engine gave a snarling screeching moan, and the *Triton* shook from stem to stern. We stood in a sea of water. The bridge room. The deck. Belowdecks. Salt water tore at my clothes, my eyes, my skin. I slipped and slid to my knees. One after the other Joe and I hit the deck, the bulkhead, the deck, the bulkhead. The *Triton* spun like a top, turning in every direction of the compass, completely out of control.

I tasted blood and salt. I tasted rust and sulphur. The world was a thick, green swirl. I turned over, sliding on metal. And then again I was at the wheel, trying to right the *Triton*.

Joe was stretched out on deck.

"Joe!"

He looked up dazedly. Blood oozed out of his cut forehead, passing over his filmed eyes. He crawled to me, trying to stand. The *Triton* veered around. We were headed in an easterly direction, speeding along swiftly and gracefully. I looked out over the bridge.

It was the damnest thing. We were being carried along the crest of a gigantic tidal wave, like a surfboard. I took my hand from the wheel. The *Triton* continued straight ahead, plunging along, turning neither to port nor starboard, piercing through a wall of gray spray sheeting up in front of us from the crest of the wave.

Joe was standing beside me, shaking his head groggily, staring out through the bridge window. All I could make out were vague shapes—whitecaps and spray intermingled.

By now the deck hands were getting to their feet and looking about them dazedly. Jack Finn shook himself dry, peering back at me. I gave him a nod. He grinned and waved a hand. But he did not let go of the donkey engine.

The spray vanished in front of us. Now I could see ahead of me.

"Joe!" I cried. "An island. Right there ahead of us."

He was gripping the wheel too, his face tense, his eyes slitted. "My God! We'll be driven on the rocks and smashed to bits!"

We were riding the second of the two tidal waves. I saw the first one ahead of us now, a vast, spreading blanket of water, crashing against a projecting spear of rock jutting out from the island. A lighthouse stood on the far tip end. As I looked, the first wave crashed against the base of the lighthouse, whipping on past it. To the right of the lighthouse lay a peaceful harbor, with sails and rigging of many ships plainly visible.

Even as we watched, horrified, from our grandstand seats atop the second wave, the first one hit the island. Water crashed over boat hulls, sent masts snapping in the air, banged ships against the long wood dock. Water shot up high in the air, jetting into a thing mist, leaving splotches of foam swirling about in its wake.

But the action of the first wave saved us. It hit the island and bounced back against our oncoming wave, cutting across it, dissipating its force. As we lay there outside the little harbor, we could actually feel the throb of the *Triton's* screws as they grabbed the water and took hold.

Wondering where we were, we brought the *Triton* slowly in toward the island.

As if it mattered any more where we were. It was enough to be alive after the fantastic beating we had taken.

I sank back against the bulkhead while Joe piloted the *Triton* toward the harbor, thinking that I'd love to give it all up for a job in a factory. The hell with the wide-open sea. I'd had it.

In spades.

## Chapter 2

NEXT MORNING, the water was calm enough for us to sail into the harbor of the island. It was misty and damp, but better weather than the day before. The island itself was a round, flattish hunk of rock and dirt, covered with the scrub brush and grass so familiar to the Irish Coast and its islands.

We anchored clear of the wreckage in the middle of the harbor.

"Not much of an island," Joe observed.

"Seems kind of spare," I agreed.

"Villagers must fish for a living."

"If you can call it a living," I grinned.

"How long do you figure it'll take to get the ship back into shape?" Joe asked, glancing warily at me.

I shrugged. "I checked with Jack Finn. You want to hear the bad news now?"

Joe grimaced. "Might as well."

"Sprung plates in the bilge," I ticked off one finger. "Salt in the fresh-water tanks. And a hell of a mess on deck."

Joe made a face.

"Three or four days, the way Jack figures it."

"That's the way the cookie crumbles." Joe waved his hands in mute resignation. "Come on. Let's get ashore and see what they've got in the way of supplies. We'll need fresh water."

We climbed down into the *Triton's* launch and Joe took the wheel. He guided it carefully, and as we drew closer to the shore, I could see the terrific damage that the storm and tidal waves had done. Broken pieces of masts floated in the water. Dead fish and waste swirled about us. I could see bits of sail and rope half-submerged.

The shore hadn't escaped damage either. Shutters hung lopsided on the houses of the village; and windows were broken, glass was scattered about. Roof had been smashed in by flying debris. Pools of water had washed up onto the shore and now stood reflecting the dull, misty gray sky.

As we came in, I could make out the townspeople poking in the rubble, trying to clear away the worst of the wreckage. Men with lined faces lifted their heads and stared at us with dull eyes. Women, their hair awry, their faces blank with shock and sorrow waited us with mute curiosity. Only the children seemed to be enjoying themselves, running around and throwing household objects about with carefree abandon.

"They got a dock, anyway," Joe said. "And water."

I looked over at the dock and water tank. The dock hadn't come through the tidal wave unscathed. It was broken in the middle, some of the planks torn up and hurled into the sea.

"Pretty hard it, looks like," I said. My eye caught sight of something in the water just out of reach of the launch. "Joe!"

He turned. An ugly reddish brown stain was drifting in from the sea, moving along lazily with the incoming tide. Dead fish floated in the midst of the red smear. They looked like cod, but they weren't like any cod I had ever seen before.

They were startlingly grotesque abominations. One of them had burst wide open, like an overripe watermelon. It was almost as if it had exploded from the enormous pressure of great sub-oceanic depths. Then I saw one that made me want to retch.

I pointed. Joe looked, and blinked.

It was a fish with a huge, malformed disproportionately massive head and long, rapier-like teeth, it had four rudimentary legs. It looked exactly like some creature from another planet.

I leaned over and hauled the monstrosity in with a boat hook. I held it in my hand, trying to keep my stomach from turning over. Something about it filled me with the dread of the unknown—along with the natural nausea anyone feels for a dead and stinking thing.

"I've never seen anything like that before. How about you?"

"Good Lord, no," Joe said, shuddering.

I tossed the fish back. I looked around at the red stain, and the debris drifted by.

"It was that volcanic explosion." I said. "It tore up the bottom of the ocean and released these deep-sea fish. No wonder they exploded. They're built for heavy deep-down pressure."

Joe guided the launch to the dock and tied up. We climbed out and hopped onto it. We passed a couple of men already at work on the planking. One of them glanced surreptitiously at us.

I'm no linguist, but I do know a couple of words. I tried to scramble a translation. "*Máistir poirt*," I said.

They merely stared at me and shrugged. Then one of them pointed vaguely toward the cliff past the village, muttered "McCartin." I looked in the direction he had pointed.

"Come on," I said.

"One thing I know, Joe. It wasn't the word for 'welcome.'"

The old man had gestured to a rocky promontory which housed a lighthouse, a radio tower, and a white cottage. A winding, switchback path led up to it from the beach.

We trudged up the trail cut in the rock, gazing from time to time at the panorama of the harbor that spread out before us. We could see the broken ships, the ripped up moorings, the floating debris and jetsam.

Finally we reached the cottage and knocked on the door. After a moment, it opened and we stood looking down at a freckled-faced youth about twelve years old, with green eyes and weedy carrot-colored hair.

"*Máistir poirt*," I said again in my best Gaelic, waiting expectantly.

The boy nodded, his eyes brightening perceptibly.

"'Tic the right place you've come to, then" To our relief, he spoke English—with a slight brogue. He pulled the door open wider, and stood aside for us to enter.

I looked at Joe and he winked at me. We walked in.

And got the surprise of our lives. We were in a big room with wide windows and plenty of light. But it wasn't an ordinary living room. It was a laboratory of some sort. I saw a microscope on a table, weighing scales, and some tools that looked like assaying equipment.

"The harbor master lives here?" Joe asked in astonishment.

"No, no!" the boy laughed. "My father. He's a government man."

I didn't get that. "Who is he? What's he do?"

"He's an archeologist," the boy said, pronouncing the word carefully as if he had been taught it with some pains.

"What's his name?"

"McCartin," the boy said promptly. "Kevin McCartin. I'm Sean."

We shook hands solemnly.

"What do you do around here to help your father, Sean? Work with these gadgets?" I pointed to the scientific equipment.

"Mostly I clean the things he finds."

Sean grinned widely, showing his big, strong front teeth. "You want to see them?"

"You bet we would."

We followed the red-headed boy into another room that was joined to this by a door. "It's the storeroom," Sean said with some pride.

The place looked like a junk shop. But what junk! I traded glances with Joe, then began checking off the items. These were artifacts, ancient antiques probably worth thousands of dollars to collectors. I recognized some of them—relics of ancient Ireland. Swords, battle axes, shields, helmets. There was even the prow of a ship. And some Viking things, too. Viking and Irish, and all of them showing the obvious effects of long exposure under water.

"Sam," Joe said softly.

I turned. He was pointing to a tall steel safe against the wall. He lifted his eyebrow in mute question.

"All this has been under the sea for, oh, a thousand years, they say," Sean observed proudly.

I touched the gargoyle prow of a ship. "Viking?"

"No Irish," the boy said excitedly. "But there was a sea-battle long ago, right off the bay here, with the Vikings. And we Irish drove them out and sank their ships! Fifteen years ago it was my father came here from Ireland to study the things brought up from sunken ships. I was born here."

I took a closer look at the ship's carved prow, and the gargoyle there sent shivers up and down my backbone. It was the personification of some ancient sea monster, with fierce eyes, a small mouth and lashing tongue, and with a frightening, supernatural look about them.

"Irish whisky carved this baby, I'd say."

Sean shrugged. "That's one of the ships the Irish lost,"

he admitted. Then he pointed to the gargoyle's face.

"And that's Ogra! He helped us. Oh, 'twas grand work Ogra did that day!"

I grinned. "Sounds like St. Patrick and the snakes."

The boy looked around at me and started to laugh. But then he caught sight of something in back of me, and his face froze.

I turned. Hulking behind me, slouched over like a giant of some kind, stood a huge man with a flaming red beard, red hair, and eyes as blue as bottle glass. He was glaring at us, his hands clenched into fists the size of cantaloupes, his shoulder muscles bulging through his shirt.

"What're you doing in here?"

I started to tell him, but he didn't let me. He turned on the boy. "Get out!" he snapped.

Sean gave him a quick look, and then slipped out past him, glancing back cautiously.

Joe stepped forward. "I'm Joe Ryan. This is Sam Slade, my partner."

The big red-bearded man grunted. "I'm McCartin. Salvage vessel, aren't you?

Joe nodded.

"I thought so," McCartin rasped. "You have a permit to be in these waters?"

Joe frowned, bluffing it out. "Permit? From who?"

McCartin's blue eyes narrowed. "From Dublin." He turned and gestured toward the relics on the walls. "My boy told you about it, didn't he?"

"Said something about sunken ships."

McCartin's eyes cleared. He took a breath. "I don't make the rules, Ryan. This stuff has no real value except to a scientist." McCartin grinned, but he wasn't really the type who could pull it off. "Ever since these ships have been found, nobody else's allowed at Nara Island for more than twenty-four hours without a permit.

Joe grunted. His yellow eyes began to smolder. "Look, friend," he said, "I'm not seaworthy, and I won't be for three or four days. I got *driven* on this island. I didn't come here on any pleasure cruise!"

McCartin's face was a blank. "I'm sorry. I don't make the rules. But that's the way it is.

I could see by the way Joe's body was hunching up that he was about to unwind and blow his cork. I stepped halfway in front of him, smiling amiably, and nodding acquiescence.

"That's fine, Mr. McClartin We're afloat now. How about fresh water? That's what we need."

McCartin looked at Joe, then at me. He considered a moment. Behind me I could tell that Joe was subsiding. He was breathing more easily now and I knew his yellow eyes were not quite so poisonous.

"Okay," McCartin said. "You can come in to dock for that."

I nodded. "Thanks."

We started out of the storeroom. "No hard feelings," McCartin called to us.

I saw Joe's face. He turned, his eyes hooded. "No," he said. "No hard feelings." He grinned. Not even a wold could do it better.

We went down the slope in front of the cottage, and were turning into the cliff pathway when suddenly, in front of us, stood Sean McCartin with a funny smile on his freckled face.

"Sean," I said. "What do you want?"

The boy's glance went over my shoulder up towards the cottage. From where we stood the cottage was cut off from view by a large rock outcrop.

"I want you to meet someone," Sean said, and called out behind him some words in Gaelic. It sounded like, *"Anois agus ni riamb, Moira"* —"Now or never *Moira!*"

Then my jaw sagged. I could not speak. For standing tight behind Sean, materializing there almost like a ghost, was the most gorgeous girl I've ever seen. She was about twenty, fully mature, with brilliant, flaming red hair. Her eyes were a dazzling sea-green. She was beautiful in a wild, unsophisticated way. She wore no makeup. She had on a man's shirt, without a bra, and it fitted tightly to her full, upthrust bust. Her hips flared out at her waist, where dungarees clung tightly to her thighs.

She was an ungodly beautiful girl, in a strange, eerie way.

"'Tis water you need?" she asked me in a singsong monotone, almost the tone someone uses who speaks English only by rote.

Joe moved forward, immediately letting his yellow cat's eyes run up and down her body. "'Tis that!" he said.

The girl's eyes turned to him watchfully. Oddly enough, I could see a sudden interest aroused in her. A slight flush suffused her throat and cheeks under his steady scrutiny.

"We will pay for it," Joe said. "Won't we, Sam?"

I shrugged.

Joe's eyes were predatory and eager. "Can you lead us to the water?"

"'Tis in a well. I shall fetch it to you."

"No!" Sean cried out fearfully. "If *he* ever finds out I've brought you to see these strangers, he'll kill me."

There was no doubt about who Sean meant by "he."

I reached out and grabbed Joe's arm. "Come on, Joe. Time's awasting. We'll be getting back to the ship ma'am," I continued, turning to Moira and nodding politely. "Send Sean down with some fresh water if you like. We'll pay him."

Moira nodded. Her eyes were level and calm. There was the cool of the forest and the depth of the sea in them. And they were looking straight into mine. I could feel something stir inside me down deep in my gut. Something

that had been dead a long time. Something that I thought had been killed by just such a pair of eyes, a long time ago.

The girl vanished the same way she had come, around the rock outcrop and into the cliffside underbrush. Sean plodded back up toward the cottage across the slope.

We hurried down to the beach. Joe let out a low whistle, and chuckled! "What a broad!" he sighed. "No wonder her old man keeps her under glass. She's set the whole island—or any other island—on its ear! What a build!"

She seems to be the wholesome type," I said quietly. "Not the kind you go for at all."

Joe leered at me, his yellow eyes slitted and glowing. "Wholesome! I saw that look you gave her, Sam. Don't be getting ideas about her! I don't want to have to wetnurse you through another assault rap!"

"You take care of your fleas," I snapped, "and I'll take care of mine."

Joe chuckled. "That bitch Anita you got hung up by in the States wasn't half the looker this tomato is, Sam. You got to admit that."

I didn't say anything. I was boiling. I thought I'd left all that behind me, wrapped up in a shopping bag in Port Arthur, Texas. But hell, you never leave a dame like Anita behind. She's always with you, hitching a ride in your belly somewhere, watching everything over your shoulder. Joe was right. No sense getting wound up in any dame the way I had, and sweat out another assault rap trying to clobber the guy she'd two-timed me with. Next time, if things went the way they had before, I'd be up on a murder charge.

And no way out.

The hell with it. I was through with women—for good.

We headed for the dock. "I hope that well water's as good as it sounds," Joe remarked.

I nodded. I was thinking about something else, something that puzzled me. "You believe McCartin about that permit Joe?"

Joe snorted. "*Hell* no!"

We were just about to board the launch when four island rowing boats loomed up out of the mist beside the dock. Each was manned by four oarsmen, and carried a skin diver complete with equipment including a pouch on the belt. The oarsmen were resting on their paddles now, studying the same strange red stain in the water we'd seen on our way in.

"They got the same feeling about that blood we did," Joe said.

I nodded.

"I wonder where they're diving," Joe muttered. "I think we'd swing a little more weight around here if we found out." He looked at me significantly.

We moved to the launch and climbed in. The four diving boats rowed on out past us through the mist, heading for the open sea.

We did our reconnoitering that afternoon, in the launch, with Jack Finn at the wheel. And we found the four diving boats in a deep, secluded inlet not far from the harbor, about a quarter of the distance around the small island.

Jack Finn throttled down the launch at a signal from Joe, and we approached the divers in a wide cautious circle. The sullen boatmen eyed us malevolently.

Joe grinned and waved a hand casually, playing the Personality Kid. "Having any luck?"

The men in the boat didn't answer.

"You try them, Boats," Joe told the big Irishman. "In Gaelic."

"Jack Finn snorted. "They speak English as good as we do. They just pretend they don't." But he went ahead anyway.

*Dia dhuit!* And he rattled off some fast Gaelic I couldn't follow. The boatmen snarled gutturals back at him. Jack Finn grimaced. "They got no time to be talking to strangers. McCartin does the talking on the island."

Joe shook his head. I was watching the divers, and I could see that something had suddenly agitated them. I pointed to them and asked Finn to translate their gabble.

The Bos'n listened, and I could see his stolid face animated with sudden interest. He shifted his cigarette slightly and spoke. "One of the divers didn't come up. They're saying he's gone."

I looked at the big Irisher, startled. There was something funny about his odd use of the word. "Gone?"

He cocked his head toward the group of boats.

"They've got to go down and find him. But they're scared of something."

"Scared?" I looked at Joe. His eyes widened. There was a sudden intuitive communication between us. The blood stains. The fish that had burst. The strange abomination with the four rudimentary legs.

We watched the dive. Two men jumped. The others watched tensely. Instantly the first diver came back up. He shook his head. The second did not reappear. After a moment there were more excited mutterings from the boatmen.

Then, abruptly, the second diver popped to the surface, only a few feet from our launch, yelling incoherently, tearing off his diving mask. He took two frantic strokes to reach our launch. The man was beside himself with fear, his eyes wide and beaming with horror.

I reached out at the same time Joe did, and we hauled him into the boat, his eyes turned up in his head, and he went limp on the bottom of the launch.

I leaned over him, twisting him so he was in position for artificial respiration.

He's not hurt," I said.

Joe went to work on the man. I could hear his breath-

ing, odd, shallow and rapid. His body twitched convulsively. As he lay there, with Joe working at him something dropped out of the pouch at his belt. Joe bent over, reaching down in the bottom of the launch.

"Sam!"

I leaned down, looking in Joe's hand, held low so none of the boatmen could see it. My eyes widened. He was holding three gold coins of ancient minting.. "That's what's bugging McCartin!" Joe hissed. "He's been looting this wreak. That's what he's keeping in his safe!"

I stared at Joe.

" 'No value except to a scientist'," Joe quoted drily. "Huh! We're going to make us some loot here before we leave, Sam! Real loot!"

I looked at him sharply, but before I could get a word out, the diver in the bottom of the boat gave a terrible twitch, gurgled out something that sounded like "arrachtach," and shuddered from head to toe. I reached out to touch him, but I knew the man was already gone.

Joe turned and felt the body. Finn's face was a frozen mask.

"He's dead," I said.

"Yes," Joe whispered. "But how?"

"You saw him come up," I said. "If you ask me, I think he died of fright."

Fright? What was there to be afraid of. *Arrachtach?* What did that mean? I turned to the Bos'n. "What's *arrachtach?*"

Jack Finn shook his head, avoiding my eyes.

"Monster," he whispered.

# Chapter 3

ABOUT AN hour later we'd pulled the *Triton* in to the dock, and I was working on a sheared deck plate bolt with a torch in my hands and a welding visor on when I heard someone call my name from the dock. "Mr. Slade! Mr. Slade!

I looked down at the battered planking and saw Sean McCartin's freckled face and wide green eyes. He was watching me with a serious, unblinking expression.

I flipped the torch off, laid it down, and lifted the visor of the welding mask. "Hi kid," I grinned. "What's up?

"I wish to speak to you," he said. "Alone."

I glanced around. "Shoot."

He shook his head. "I may be overheard."

Shaking my head at his tenacity, I walked to the rail and leaned over toward him. "Okay," I whispered loudly. "Nobody can hear us now. What is it?"

He cupped his mouth so no one could read his lips.

"My sister Moira wants to talk to you."

I stared. "Moira?"

"Yes. This afternoon. Quickly before you sail."

I shrugged. Moira? A tryst? I hid my grin. Probably wanted me to dive for three pairs of nylons in Macy's.

"Where?"

"The cove beyond the lighthouse." Sean gestured across the harbor past the neck of rock that shot out into the sea. "It is not seen from our cottage."

"I should hope so," I said, with feeling. I glanced around. It was still foggy. "Any particular spot?"

Sean gave me the details.

"Tell her four-thirty," I said. "Sixteen-thirty, Irish style."

I took the launch and pointed the prow toward the lighthouse. The fog was in heavier than ever and as I pushed through the ghostly mist, I could see dim phantom shapes of masts and rigging moving aimlessly by me. Dead silence hung over the sea. The harbor stank of death. Gulls swooped down for pecks at the floating, bloated corpses of fish cast up by the tidal wave.

I passed the rocky point, and steered in close to the cliffs on the side away from the harbor. There was nothing in sight—nothing but rolling fog and the choppy waters of the inlet ahead of me. The hum of the launch engine bounced back at me from the cliff's face. I kept going.

I saw the little beach. It was just as Sean had described it to me. Narrow, white and secluded. From here, even without the screen of convenient fog, nobody could see us. It was the perfect spot for a rendezvous. A steep cliff rose abruptly at the back of the sand strip. Through the fog I could see several vague black openings in the rock. Caves?

I beached the launch and secured it to a jogged rock. Then I crunched through the sand to the cliff. This was where Moira would be waiting.

But she was not there.

I sat down, lit a cigarette and stared into the fog. An eerie silence permeated the atmosphere, and the fact that I could not see more than six or eight feet in front of me began to work on my nerves. I suspected shapes of being people. The constant rumble of the surf assumed foreign sounds and became crunching footsteps, a human cough, a throat clearing.

Was the message actually from Moira? Or was this McCartin's little trick to ambush me? And if so, why? I shivered. My imagination was running away with me. Think sharp, Sam!

Then she was there. Like the wraith she was, she came out of the fog as if she mad materialized out of nothing. I recalled the way she had confronted us on the cliff path. Was she really human, I wondered, or was she the sea sprite I had first imaged her? Lord, the fog was really getting to me!

"Hello, Moira," I said.

"Mr. Slade," she said, approaching me, glancing about her. She held up a finger for silence. She cocked her head, then nodded. "There is no one. We are alone."

I tugged on my cigarette and watched the smoke curl up in front of me. It never occurred to me to offer her a smoke. "What's on your mind?"

She came over and sat down beside me. I could detect the fresh, outdoor, oceanic smell of her. She was beautiful in the swilling fog, her flaming red hair dew-flecked, her clear white skin moist and cool.

"I have come to ask a favor of you," she said softly, her voice husky and burred with a melodious brogue.

"Line forms to the right," I said with a laugh.

She turned her face to me, and her sea-green eyes were round and serious. "I do not joke, Mr. Slade," she said. "To you, nor anyone. You must promise me you will never let my father know I came to you."

"Rest assured," I said wryly. "And call me Sam."

"I am awkward with the English tongue," she said haltingly. "But 'tis the truth I must be telling. There is a heaviness in my heart that I must stay on Nara." She looked at me pleadingly.

"I get it. You don't like it here and you want to get away." I shook my head in disgust. I might have known it! Just another dame wanting water-taxi service!

"That's it, isn't it?" I went on, my voice beginning to rise. "You think we're running a passenger service to the mainland. Right, my charming colleen?"

Her mouth dropped open. She stared at me in astonishment.

But I was mad. Everybody who knows a guy with a boat invariably wants to hook a cheap ride. This broad with the wonderful body and the flaming red hair seemed to think she could buy a ride to the moon with a lift of the eyebrow and a rise of the breasts. Probably scented a short pleasure cruise to Galway Bay. The hell with that. I'd been suckered by enough dames in the past to know every angle of that game.

"Sorry, honey," I said. "No sale, like we say in the States."

The girl's cheeks flushed, and her eyes burned. Her breasts rose and fell angrily. She was Irish and she was quick-tempered, and now she was mad. I'd really riled her. That's me, Old Sam Smooth with the dames.

"'Tis a cheap hussy you think I am!" she cried. "I'm willing to pay my way, Mr. Slade. 'Tis no favor I'm asking. What do you take me for—a charity case?" Her eyes blazing, she jumped to her feet. "For your information, I would ask your captain, but I know exactly what he wants from me! Her cheeks crimsoned again. "I thought *you* were a gentleman, anyway. A worse mistake I never made!"

She wheeled from me and started running through the sand.

I moved fast. I spun her around, holding her stiffly in

front of me. I had to laugh.

"Calm down, Moira. I keep forgetting you're Irish. I have a wee bit of the ould sod in me, too. Come on, now. Sit you down. Let's talk it out, shall we?"

She dropped her eyes and moved away from me, but she was calm again. She sat down. I joined her.

"'Tis a long story," she said softly. "And I won't bother you with it. But I will tell you this: I must get of this devil's island before it's too late!" She closed her eyes and rock back. "Or maybe, in truth, 'tis already too late. I don't know."

The fog, the loneliness, the wind, the sea. I nodded. I knew what she meant. She was lonely for a normal life, a life among real live people, a life with young men about, not an island of ignorant villagers and indigent fishermen. Her father was an intelligent, educated man, and he had obviously tried to teach her all he could. She was a misfit here on Nara.

"Okay, so you want to see the world."

She turned her sea-green eyes to me. "'Tis not just curiosity, Samuel," she said, saying my name for the first time. Or, at least something that sounded like it. In Gaelic it's *Somhairle*.

I grinned. "What is it, then?"

"'Tis my father." She squinted through the fog, trying to pierce the veil of tiny droplets, trying to see something out in the watery cove. "A madman, he is, Somhairele," she whispered. "'Tis his mind that is affected. Ever since the—" her voice lowered,—"the drowning of my own mother."

"Drowning?" I stared at Moira. I'm sorry." "She walked into the sea, Somhairle, of her own accord, from right where we are sitting. Fifteen years ago, it was, when first we arrived. Walked into the sea in sear of him. Dórach Dolan." She closed her eyes and crossed herself. "Her lover, he was."

Hanky-panky, I translated. McCartin's wife fools around with another man, McCartin's finds out about it and sends his wife to her death. Or was that it exactly?

"Suicide, you say? Are you sure?

"She wanted to join Dórach," she said, turning her cool glance to me again. "Don't you see? My father—" her voice choked—he knew what was going on between them. But once Dórach was dead, he could do nought to prevent her from going to join him."

"Dórach was killed at sea?" I asked, trying to fill in the story.

"Yes. Killed."

"Shipwreck? Fishing?"

She shook her head. "Diving. 'Twas the monster."

I had to laugh. "The Loch Ness monster?"

Her sea-green eyes regarded me levelly. "Orga. The Monster of Nara."

I stared. I remember Sean's words. Ogra. The sea god.

"Some say," Moira went on, "that 'twas not the mon-

ster Ogra at all who carried off Dórach so that his body was never found. Some say 'twas Kevin McCartin who did him in down under the surface of the sea—with his diving equipment, no less—but whatever they say, they all know that 'twas, indeed, a monster of some variety who destroyed Dórach, and then my own mother. Whether it be the monster Orga, or the monster Kevin, if you would."

"What about Sean? Is he your half-brother? If all this happened fifteen years ago. . . ."

Moira nodded. "My father took up with another woman. Sean's mother, Maigréad. But she could not stand him either. She stowed away in a supply freighter." The sea-green eyes moved over my face. "You're the first ones here who haven't been thrown bodily off the island by my father." She looked down. "He is afraid we will follow the rest of them, you see."

She stared out to sea.

"And we will, you know. One way or another." She turned, and her eyes were misted with tears. "Will it be you, Somhairle? Or must I wait forever?"

There was little more to our talk, really, and after explaining as gently as I could that there was no chance of her going with us, I climbed into the launch and sailed back to the *Triton*. I was afraid of what might happen to this strange, clean, true girl if she ever got on board with Joe Ryan near. It was a bad situation. I wanted to help her, but I could not.

As I climbed on board, Joe met me on the foredeck.

"After chow we do some more looking," he told me. "I want to find out the truth about those gold coins."

He winked at me and slapped me on the back.

It was dark when we finally got in the launch and headed for the spot where the divers had died that afternoon. I cut the engine and turned to Joe.

"This is about it, isn't it?"

He nodded. I couldn't help shivering, not so much from the fact I was in my bathing suit in the night air which had suddenly turned clear and cold, but also from the fact I wasn't sure what we were going to come up with. Frankly, I didn't like it one bit. But I knew we needed the money, Joe and I. If we could get it here in some sunken wreak, why not?

We lowered two weighted containers to the bottom of the cove from the edge of the launch, and got into our lungs, fins, and face plates. Joe turned to me, indicating the big magnesium flare in the bottom of the launch. I nodded and picked it up.

"All set?" Joe asked, cradling the harpoon gun in his arm.

I nodded. I lit the magnesium flare and it whooshed into flame immediately. I plunged it down into the water to shield it from any prying eyes, and lowered myself after it. Joe followed.

The submarine world slipped eerily by us as we moved down through it. Weird shadows writhed in the distance among the kelp and fish. The strange illumination of the flare reached out about us, painting a warped, surrealist picture of a maritime graveyard. Imbedded between rocky formations, the stripped wooden ribs of ancient ships loomed up like reconstructions of dinosaur skeletons.

I could see a carved wooden figurehead close by me, and I swam toward it. It was a gargoyle, similar to the one decorating McCartin's storeroom. But it wasn't Ogra. It was a Viking representation of the same thing—a Norse god of the sea.

As I studied the grinning, hideous distorted face, I was aware of a sudden darkening of the water directly above me, as though a huge shadow of some kind were passing by.

I stopped. So did Joe.

We looked up. It was a familiar right—a killer whale, what scientists call *Orcinus*, the most aggressive and dangerous of aquatic mammals.

I held by breath. The killer whale could sense our presence, but it could tell exactly where we were. It passed over us, then gracefully arched back, moving warily and cautiously. It knew it could attack us, but it did not know how dangerous we were.

Joe moved toward me, and we both watched the big mammal. We had a problem: should we fight it with the harpoon gun, or just wait for it to go away? The shadow moved across us gain, and I could see Joe sidling over to the edge of the nearest rock-formation, still watching above. I backed up too, and felt the flat face of a rock comfortingly against my back; I stood there, keeping my eyes on the killer whale.

And then, before I could move, I felt something else—a clammy, rubbery tentacle slithering across my chest from behind. I looked down in horror. Somewhere in the rock formation behind me an octopus was hiding, waiting for one of us to move within range of its powerful tentacles.

I waved the flare about energetically, trying to attract Joe's attention. At the same time I slid my knife out of my belt and tried to angle it around so I could use it on the massive tentacle. As I fought to turn it, another rubbery tentacle slid out from behind the big rock and whipped around me. I could feel the tremendous power of the beast's vise-like grip. The rock edge pressed into my back.

My flare went spinning into the sand at my feet. Joe turned and started toward me. As he did so a third tentacle looped out to meet him, coiling around his body, rolling him in closer. He fought to keep his arms and harpoon gun free, riding in with the snake-like arm, intent only on getting in close enough for a killing shot.

I could not breathe now. I could only fight with the knife, dragging its cutting edge impotently across the touch flexible hide of the tentacle. But now my arm was half imprisoned by the pressure against it, and I could only manipulate the blade with my wrist and fingers. It was like trying to cut through a truck tire with a dull hackknife. The air was completely squeezed out of my chest. Blackness began seeping in at the edges of my brain. I struggled to keep my consciousness, knowing I would die if I passed out, but the continual pressure was like the weight of a building crushing me.

I saw Joe's face behind his plate, anxious and pop-eyed, as the fourth tentacle coiled about him, pulling him in closer to me in a two-way death embrace. It's all over, I thought. All over but the keening.

Then I heard the dull, muffled explosion as the tip of the harpoon went off. The shaft sank up to the hilt in the creature's gelatinous body. At the instant of explosion, I was suddenly aware of the sweet breath pouring into my chest again, of the slow ebbing of the pressure from my battered body, of the release of the monstrous grip on my flesh and bones.

Sobbing to get my breath, I reeled backward to the ocean floor, and saw the great octopus for the first time. Even as I landed on the sand, it shuddered violently, and the color of its body changed from a dirty-green to a spreading reddish brown. The dangerous, powerful tentacles collapsed and became limp like deflated sausage balloons.

In its death agony the beast emitted a massive, jetting cloud of black ink-like fluid which flooded around us, obscuring everything the flare had illuminated, and blacking out Joe's body.

I moved through the murk, stumbling.

The next thing I knew, I was staring into Joe's faceplate. He had lifted me from the sandy floor and carried me some distance. Beside us the flare burned its shimmering illumination. I could see the worried, concerned expression in Joe's yellowish eyes as they peered through the mask front.

I waved to him that I was okay, and pointed upward.

Joe nodded, and started to ascend. Then he turned and immediately gave me a signal for caution.

I glanced up. There, in the dirty, gradually clearing waters, the shadow of the killer whale passed over us again. It had still not forgotten the two of us.

Joe pulled another harpoon out of his belt and loaded the gun. I looked down across the rock formation close by and I could see the magnesium flare lying in the sand where I had dropped it still sending out its light.

Before I could move a foot toward it, the water around us shuddered violently, and a tremendous pulsating turmoil jolted everything. Schools of fish turned and fled into the darkness. The sand shifted on the ocean floor.

I stared into the murky, turbulent water above us. I could see something—not a whale, not an octopus, but something else—something fantastically huge and vague, like a great thunderhead, looming over us.

I backed up to the rock and hung on. The water about me swirled and ebbed, shuddering with the impact of the big thing moving about up there. Joe crept beside me, grasping for a handhold on a rock.

As we waited, the water about us whipped into a fury, and all at once there was a great jetting gush of blood as the thing attacked the killer whale. The entire sea around us turned a brilliant carmine, blotting out everything in a pinwheeling red haze.

Weakly we clung to the rock and gazed up at the red cloud. Then we looked at each other, and I hope never again see such a scared, awed, absolutely unbelieving expression on anybody's face as I saw on Joe's at that moment.

It took me a long time to breathe in enough courage to let go of that rock and swim up through the settling waters.

"What the hell did you see, Sam?" Joe asked me in a hushed whisper as we yanked off our aqua lungs in the launch.

"I don't know," I said, my voice shaking. "But I sure never want to see it again."

# Chapter 4

WHEN WE got back to the *Triton*, we found the Bos'n busy with the crewmen on the dock. They were working under a bright light shining from the deck of the ship. The men were sweating and heaving, trying to shake the huge water hose from the dock's water tank onto the deck of the ship. Jack Finn was cursing and bouncing around like a dog with fleas, alternately cursing and encouraging the straining Irishers.

We climbed on board, and Joe approached the Bos'n. "Boats!"

"Yes sir," said Jack Finn coming up.

"When the hell can you get us out of here?"

Jack Finn thought a second. "Two, three hours."

"Make it snappy," Joe said, and turned to go below. At that moment I looked toward the beach in front of the village, and saw a number of torches burning brightly on the sand.

"What's that?" I asked casually. Irish Clambake?"

Finn joined me at the ship's rail. Joe turned from the hatchway and came back.

Jack Finn shook his head. "Whatever it is, it's been going on for a couple hours. All the time you've been away."

As we watched, we could hear the muffled tolling of a church bell, booming monotonously and sonorously in the distance.

"Listen!"

I strained my ears, and then I could hear it too. It was a far-off moaning and humming, a gloomy lament, a wordless, keening cry in the night.

"Sounds like a wake," Joe said grimly. "That's a hell of a send-off for us. I'll be glad to see the last of this place!"

I heard someone behind me, and I turned. It was Sean McCartin. He too was watching the shore.

"'Tis a wake for the two divers who died this afternoon," Sean said softly. "One has not even yet been found.

Joe frowned. "What are you doing on deck, boy?"

Jack Finn interrupted. "I told him he could watch us, sir. I hope it's all right." He grinned. "The lad has a feeling for the *Triton* and the ocean, being an islander."

Joe considered a moment, and then nodded. "Okay. Be sure you git when I tell you git. We're sailing soon."

"Yes sir," said Sean. "But there is a message I came to deliver. In the excitement I've nearly forgotten."

Joe glowered. "What is it?

"My father wants to see you." Sean looked from Joe to me, and then his glance dropped. "'Tis a fine rage he's in."

"A rage is it?" Joe snarled. "Come on, Sam. Let's see what the devil this joker's got up his sleeve."

We didn't have to go up to the cottage. We found the big red-bearded man standing on the beach surveying the torchlight activity with a jaundiced eye. He had his large hands on his hips, and was scowling at a group of villagers hauling a rowing boat along the sand into the water.

As we cam up, we could hear him barking angrily in Gaelic, telling the men to keep away from him. All he got in return were sullen glances from the dour boatmen. Finally he turned away in disgust.

Then he saw us in the light of the flaming torches, and came stomping over.

"So there you are, you damned snoopers!"

Joe nodded. I was right beside him and I could see his arms tense up as if he were going to throw his fists at McCartin. I began to sweat. McCartin wasn't loved by the villagers, but we were loved even less. It would be a very fine bruhaha if it started. The thing we had to do was hold our tempers. I figured I was all right, but I could never predict Joe. I've seen him fracture a man's skull in a bar fight.

"So what's it to you?" Joe grinned wolfishly, his tone inviting trouble.

"I told you not to prowl the bay out there! My divers told me you've been smelling around, like a bitch in heat."

"Who's to stop us?" Joe asked, breathing heavily.

"Are you doubting I can?" McCartin cried angrily.

"Maybe I am!" Joe said.

McCartin moved impulsively towards us. But then,

as he got closer, I could see a flicker of indecision in his eyes. Obviously there was something else on his mind that was worrying him more than we were. I wondered for a moment what it was.

The red beard showed golden highlights in the torch flames. "After you load your water, you leave. Tonight."

"The sooner the better," Joe said testily.

McCartin stared at us in surprise. He couldn't figure out what had made such a radical change in our attitude.

Joe relaxed and waved at the torches on the beach. "What's all this?"

Sean was standing a little to the rear of us in the dark. He stepped up then, and said: "'Tis a wake they're holding. That, and the thing we do when men are lost. For Ogra, the sea-spirit, that is."

McCartin's eyes opened wide, and his cheeks blew out in rage. "You! Go on with you Get up to the house! This instant!"

Sean stared up at his father with a defiant expression and when McCartin moved toward him with a half-threatening swing of his big shoulders, the boy moved out of reach. Then he turned and began to go across the sand.

McCartin looked after his son, then turned and gazed at the torches stuck in the sand. "They're no better than pagans, none of them. Father Donnelly would never allow it, but he only gets out here twice a year."

McCartin looked at both of us, and then he moved off down the beach toward the cottage path. After a moment he was swallowed up in the gloom.

"Come on," Joe said. "Let's get back on board. I don't want to have to tangle with that creep again."

I started along after him, but then stopped, watching the activity on the beach. Some of the villagers were building bonfires on the shore. Others were moving toward the rowboats lined up at the edge of the water. They held torches as they climbed into the boats. From the cobble-stone streets of the tiny village, groups of men moved toward me with the flaming torches held high in the air. The black smoke from them curled up into the night air.

"Somhairle!"

I jumped. It was Moira McCartin, standing beside me on the beach. She had approached me while I was concentrating on the ancient pageantry about me. I wondered why she had come.

"You're leaving," she said.

I nodded, feeling embarrassment. She had wanted to come with us. But we were sailing on such quick notice, I doubted if we could arrange for her to come along. Besides, I didn't like to think what would happen if Joe began getting any bright ideas with her on board.

"Yes, Moira," I said. "Unexpectedly. We must sail tonight. Before morning."

I saw her looking up at me with those beautiful eyes, and in the flickering torchlight I could see tears forming around their edges.

"You're going without me."

I swallowed. "To take you would cause complications," I said lamely. "I don't want to be responsible for what might happen to you."

"The skipper," she said with a low laugh. "You are afraid for me." She turned her head and looked off at the water in the harbor. Bright flashes of firelight danced in her hair. "But I can take care of myself."

I reached out and touched her shoulder. "Moira," I said softly. "It would not work. You do not know Captain Ryan. When it comes to women, he is a man without scruples. Do you understand what I am saying?"

She nodded. "And do you understand what I am saying? That I do not care?"

I felt the annoyance building in me. Against Joe Ryan who had taken every girl he'd ever wanted, this slip of a thing. . . ?"

""Leave well enough alone, Moira," I said sharply. "Hear me?"

Her eyes flashed. She tossed back her head, and the red hair tumbled around her ears and throat. "I must go!" she said. "I'm begging you, on my knees, to take me with you! Can I do more>"

I grasped both shoulders now and began shaking her. I was angry at her, angry at myself, and most of all angry at Joe who made the whole thing impossible. I don't know what I was going to say, because I never got the words formed. At that moment I felt myself seized roughly from the side and torn from her. I went sprawling in the sand, hitting hard on my spine.

I shook my head to clear it. Kevin McCartin had returned from the darkness, and was now towering over his daughter, his bristling red beard wild and unruly in the torchlight.

"Slut!" he yelled at her, jostling her roughly. "Lousy little slut! Just like your mother. Can't keep the smell of a man out of your nose! Get back to the house!"

The girl cowered there, brushing her hair back out of her eyes, holding herself away from him.

Outraged at her silence, McCartin drew back his hand and flung it, open-palmed, into her face. Moira fell back screaming, going out full length on the sand, the dress she was now wearing pulled up around her thighs. She crawled to her feet, Digging at the same around her, crying out, sobbing with her shame.

I sprang for McCartin's throat. I wanted to strangle the man. I wanted to tear out his vocal chords. I wanted to rip that damn red beard off his face hair by hair and listen to him scream.

But I never got the chance. He was waiting for me figuring I'd be just the fool I was. As I leaped, he side-stepped me, and hacked down at my neck with his huge meathook of a hand. He slapped me into the sand, face first.

I came up spitting dried kelp and seashells. The big bastard was circling about, crouched, waiting for me to come at him again. I got to my feet warily and approached him. Both of us circled. I stepped closer and feinted at him. He didn't turn a hair.

By now the villagers were gathering in a disinterested circle, holding the torches high and watching us with flat, expressionless eyes. No one lifted a finger to help either one of us. I noticed that with sardonic delight. As for Moira, I heard her sobbing some distance off. I hoped she was all right.

I moved in again, drawing back my right arm for a roundhouse blow. The big man retreated a step, and held firm. Then I came around again, still moving in. McCartin took my cue and prepared to deliver a knockout punch to me. He stepped back with his right foot, swinging his arm for the blow.

It was a simple matter after that. What I did was to execute a more or less satisfactory Judo throw call *uki-goshi*. As McCartin swung his right arm to the rear and stepped back with his right foot. I moved rapidly toward him on my left foot, at the same time grabbing his left wrist with my right hand, and circling his waist under his upraised right arm with my left arm. We were hip to hip. I tightened myself to him, and rolled the big body over my left hip, turning to the right as I did so. McCartin wasn't familiar with the maneuver, and I toppled him over like a poleaxed steer.

He lay there stunned a moment, and a murmur of desultory approval came from the villagers standing nearby.

He shook himself doggedly, and rose slowly to his feet. But I wasn't alone now. As I waited for the big man to charge me, I was shouldered roughly aside from the rear, and Joe Ryan stepped up to face McCartin.

"Get up, McCartin," Joe said, "and beat it out of here! We've had enough trouble from you.

McCartin glanced across at me as he stumbled to his feet, and stared sullenly at Joe. Without another word he turned and vanished into the darkness.

I grinned at Joe. "You came just in time, pal."

Joe snorted. "You seemed to be doing all right, Sam." Then the yellow cat's eyes narrowed suspiciously. "What were you trying to do—prove yourself to that redheaded sea witch?"

I snorted and turned away, trying to get my breath. Moira was nowhere to be seen. Smart girl, I thought. But she'd better stay out of her father's sight. He'd be rough when he caught up with her.

The villagers were now going about their tasks again on the shore line. Joe and I watched them. Already several of the rowboats were moving across the harbor from a left to right direction. In each boat two men carried torches,

one in the bow, the other in the stern.

The leading boat was already halfway around the arc of a circle that would bring it back to shore across the harbor. The torch-bearer in the bow of the first boat was a dignified patriarch of the village, a leathery seaman with a strong, weathered face.

As the other boats fell into line behind him, he rose in the bow and held a crucifix up in his hand. Even from the shore the glittering reflection was plainly visible. He held it out in front of him, lifting his eyes to the skies.

Now, from around me, came the keening of the villagers' dirge. The sound of it swept out from the shore over the waters, and echoed back from the cliffs with an eerie hollow moan. Shivers ran up and down my spine. I could tell that Joe, standing beside me, was transfixed too, swept up in the haunting agony of human grief.

And then, suddenly, as we all watched, hypnotized by the unearthly flicker of the wavering torches, spell bound by the wailing, the piercing scream of a terrified youth in one of the boats cut through the sound. Everything stopped, abruptly.

For a frozen instant everyone in the harbor was silent, and there was no noise at all but the lapping of the water on the boat hulls. Then, in the vague torchlight, I could see a small figure rise in the third boat, and plunge a long heavy harpoon down into the water by the prow.

I glanced at Joe. He was frowning as he peered into the harbor. None of us could see anything more. All around, the villagers craned forward, listening, looking.

As we gaped, curious and startled by the agonized shriek that now repeated itself, the sea lifted up under the flickering procession of funeral boats, and a form that was neither water nor earth nor human reared into the air, sending the third boat high on its stern and toppling it over.

Rooted to the spot, I stared at what seemed to be a huge, massive shape writhing out of the water. Men and boat now plunged down, and the sea water churned about, foaming and sizzling as the torches plunged into it.

I could see the outline of a huge body, some twenty feet high, searching for something. The young boy's scream sounded again, for the third time. The huge bulky shape turned in upon itself, slashing at the second boat with a huge tail, which now became visible to us for the first time.

"My God!" I cried. "It's huge! As big as a house!"

We ran down to the shore now. Around us the villagers surged, eyes wide, mouths open, crossing themselves mechanically as they watched the fantastic, unbelievable visitation.

I saw Sean dart in front of me, and then Moira came running in from the cliffside. McCartin lumbered over, his eyes wide and aghast. The dirge was finished. A heavy, suspenseful silence closed down over us.

Men in the water began screaming for help. Cries of

"*Tarrthail, tarrhail,*" echoed in the harbor. The huge beast turned again, moving toward one of the swimming men. A boat sailed around in back of the big beast, and the torchlights in it cast the monster into profile. It was like some prehistoric saurian, a giant marine lizard of some kind left over from the Mesozoic era. I'd certainly never seen its like in any textbook.

The boats circled about now, headed for shore. I could see the monster loom up into the skies, looking around in curiosity, following the wavering lights with its beady eyes.

Sean McCartin danced up and down in front of me. "It's Ogra! he cried. "Ogra!"

Someone else took up the chant. Soon it was echoing all about us and the torches waved back and forth.

The monster moved to the nearest boat, reaching out for it with one of its upper limbs. At the end of the prehensile extremity were huge cleaning talons. It reached out with them, and closed on a boat. The boat was lifted and crushed like a toy in a baby's bathtub.

The boatmen in another craft threw harpoons at the beast. But I could see the harpoons glance harmlessly off the tough, scaly hide.

But now another villager, a superior marksman, tried for the head. The harpoon hit close to the right eye and imbedded itself between the scales. The wound instantly sprouted blood and the monster reared back, dazed suddenly, and tried to shake out the sharp, barbed harpoon.

For a moment there was an awed silence.

Then the monster lifted its bleeding head and emitted a terrifying roar that bounded back earsplitting from the cliffs across the water. And as it roared, it moved forward, violently beating the water with its massive, powerful tail. It flung boats to the right and left, extinguishing the torches, battering the crafts to kindling wood. Men's bodies ripped to pieces, smashed to shapeless flesh and bone by the power of the slapping tail, were tossed in all directions.

Now McCartin roared out, urging two of the villagers on. They were carrying rifles, and they started firing at the big beast.

"Shoot!" roared McCartin, "Shoot!"

Sean ran pell-mell across the sand, trying to stop them. "No, father! No!"

McCartin cuffed the boy out of the way and the rifles began again.

Bullets had no effect on the beast. It roared and clawed with its massive talons at the flying slugs, as if it were swiping at a bothersome swarm of mosquitoes. It kept coming toward us.

Flipping its tail to the left and right, the monster scattered the remainder of the fleeing boats, and now the men, women and children on the beach began to run past us toward the shelter of the village. Joe and I pushed our way to the front, grabbing up large brands from the bonfire, waving them toward the beast.

Some of the more able-bodied villagers got the idea, and began manipulating their own torches. I glimpsed Sean standing in the sand, frozen, fascinated, and not joining in. The look on his face was strangely sympathetic, a look of anguish. I couldn't see Moira at all.

We waved the torches at the huge beast as it leered at us from the edge of the surf. It thrust its head with the beady little red eyes down towards us, studying us curiously, like the ants we seemed to be. I could feel the hot stink of its breath as the immense head came closer. I fell back a bit, and so did those about me.

Then Joe tossed his torch at the beast's head. It hit the monster square on the wounded eye. Bellowing in pain, it let out a roar of anguish, as much as of anger, gush from its cavernous throat.

Other torches followed Joe's, and finally I let mine arc up at the beast's head. Flames leaped off the monster's scales, but did it no harm. The monster gazed at us all in a pathetic, wistful way, as if it did not know why it was being attacked, and then it turned and headed for the water. As it did so, it scattered the embers of a large bonfire, sending flames flying in all directions with a flick of its tail.

The monster lumbered to the surf, slid into the water and vanished under the smooth inky surface.

We stood immobilized for a long time afterward, trying to steady our nerves. But after the beast's disappearance, there wasn't a single ripple on the water.

"Good Lord, let's get out of here." Joe whispered.

I couldn't have said it better myself.

# Chapter 5

THERE WASN'T MUCH sleep aboard the *Triton* for any of us during what remained of the night, and we were hard at work on deck by early morning. I've never wanted to get out of a place so fast in my life. I had only one twinge of regret. I'd decided it would be best to forget about Moira. With McCartin ready to rip anybody to pieces who even glanced at her, I figured it wouldn't do to provoke him. He'd only take it out on her.

We'd been working no more than a quarter of an hour when we heard a loud commotion on the beach. I could see a group of McCartin's divers moving toward the dock. And right in back of them, gesticulating and angry, puffed Kevin McCartin himself.

Joe and I jumped onto the dock and met the group.

A stubble-bearded young man stepped forward and approached Joe. McCartin stood back, glowering at us.

"We'll be wanting passage on your ship, Mister," the young man said. He glanced around at McCartin sullenly. "When His Nibs gets around to giving us our pay."

McCartin moved around quickly and faced the group. "Now hold on, you men. You'll get your pay, if you like. But there'll be no taking passage on any ships!"

"Why not?" Joe asked.

McCartin whirled on us. "For God's sake, Ryan!" He started to  frame his words, and then he frowned at the men hovering near him. He grimaced. "Come on over to the house, you two. I want to talk to you."

Joe winked at me covertly. "Why not?"

The divers stayed on the dock while we followed McCartin. I saw Sean regarding us from a window of the cottage. I didn't catch sight of Moira, but I had the feeling she was watching, also.

We went into the cottage and closed the door behind us. McCartin faced us looking surprisingly worried.

"Let's lay our cards on the table, gentlemen," he said, beginning to pace up and down in front of his microscope and assaying equipment. "The whole thing'll go smash if they leave. All my divers. My Boatmen. The lot of them!"

I grinned wryly. "I kind of see their point."

Joe's yellow eyes gleamed. "You got any special reason you don't want them to leave?"

McCartin's beard bristled. "What do you mean?"

Joe reached in his pocket and took out the three gold coins that had fallen from the dead diver's pouch. He showed them to McClartin.

"Like, maybe you don't want them to talk too much?"

McCartin's face flushed. He moved back a bit, his lips tight, his fists clenched. He spoke in a strangled voice. "Where did you get those?"

Joe's teeth glinted, and his lips pulled tight in a wolf's grin. "The same place you did." He put the coins carefully back in his pocket. I could see the calculating look in his eyes, and I knew he was ready to sink the shaft. "Suppose we could get rid of that thing out there? Joe said.

"The beast in the harbor? You think you can? McCartin was startled.

Joe rubbed the side of his chin. "Maybe." I could see his eyes move across to the far door, the door to the store room. "Let's take another look in there," he said softly.

McCartin's eyes riveted on Joe's face. Then he wheeled abruptly, pulled the door open and we went in.

Joe pointed to the safe. "Open it up."

McCartin swelled and his face turned red. "Not on your bloody tintype! Look here, I've stood about enough of you!"

Joe shrugged elaborately, looking at me, nodding.

"Okay. I guess we can always make a few bucks for ourselves taking those diving birds back where they came from."

McCartin looked first at Joe and then at me, and bit his lip. Moving quickly, he spun the dial and flipped open the safe door. He stood back so we could see. Inside was a king's ransom in gold coins and gold chalices studded with precious stones. A fortune in salvage. I could feel the itch in my own palm. Joe had drawn to a bobtailed flush—and won! But he wasn't through yet. He was still as cool as a December morning.

"Nice," he grinned, reaching in. He picked out the biggest of the gleaming chalices. He brought it out, hefted it, admired it and showed it to me. "How about this, Sam, for a little down payment? You like?"

I tried to keep a straight face. "Not bad."

McCartin ground his teeth in rage. "You're out of your mind! A thing like that is priceless! And how do you think you're going to dispose of it? This stuff belongs to the government!"

Joe's mouth thinned to a tight little grin. "I'll bet you had some way figured. And if you did, so can we!"

McCartin advanced on Joe, his hands moving convulsively, "Filthy blackmailer!"

Joe dodged aside, and backhanded him savagely in the mouth. McCartin staggered, more surprised than hurt.

"We'll get your beast for you," Joe said. "But mind you lip!"

McCartin put his handkerchief to his bleeding lip and glowered at Joe.

"You're getting off easy friend. After all, you've in no spot to squawk, even if we grabbed the whole thing. Milking the government, holding out on them, for fifteen years?"

McCartin rubbed his cheek. "I've been here fifteen years, yes. But I didn't locate that wreck until two years ago. I'm merely accumulating this stuff for the proper time."

Joe laughed harshly. "I'll bet. The proper time for taking it on the lam!"

McCartin slammed the safe shut, and glared at us. "When will you start?"

"Now," Joe said. "Why not?"

We left McCartin eating his heart out, and went down the slope to the path. When we'd turned the bend away from the house, we found Sean and Moira waiting for us in the path.

"Mr. Ryan," Sean said.

Joe wasn't looking at Sean. He was looking hungrily at Moira. His cheek twitched. I felt a sudden surge of anger, but caught myself before I moved on him.

"Call me Joe, kid." Joe was staring at Moira.

Sean's eyes were big with pleading. "You'll be trying to catch him? Orga?"

"Yeah Sean," Joe said, reaching out and tousling the boy's hair. "Stick around for a good show."

"No!" It was Moira who spoke now, her sea-green eyes alarmed. She darted a glance at me, then faced Joe.

"You can't!"

Joe's face lit up. "You're worried!" He turned to me. "She's concerned over me, Sam!"

A flush crept into the girl's cheeks. "No," she said quickly. But 'tis a bad thing you're doing. I do not worry about you. I worry for all of us. The world . . . ." Her voice trailed off.

Joe grinned. "I don't get it."

"'Tis a manifestation of evil," Moira said rapidly. "Don't you see?'Tis the monster of the devil, making its appearance on earth to warn us all of the cataclysm. We have a saying: *Nuair atá tú go sóúil fulaing thú féin*. Do you understand what I am saying? Leave well enough alone. Heed the warning. Do not tempt the devil."

"Don't catch the monster?" Joe grinned. "Is that what you're saying?"

"Yes," Moira whispered. "Or it will be the death of us all. Mark my words."

With a glance at me, she turned abruptly from us and vanished around the rock outcrop. Sean glanced at us briefly and followed her.

I didn't say anything until we hit the beach. "What about all that? She's no dummy, you know. She may have something."

"Superstitious hogwash!" Joe snapped. "Now. How the hell do we catch it? With the shark net? And how do we kill a thing that flicks off harpoons like toothpicks?"

"I don't know," I said. "Dynamite?"

Joe's eyes glinted suddenly. "Sam," he mused. "You ever think how much that thing could be worth to us —*alive*.

I could almost see him counting the greenbacks. And somehow, even though I'm no angel myself, and I'd run guns to the Cubans with Joe, and smuggled contraband, I felt a shiver run up and down my spine. I somehow felt there was something inherently *evil* in everything that touched this operation. Or maybe I just had a powerful imagination.

Once we started working on the shark net, however, I forgot my twinges of apprehension, and plunged into the deckside activity. We'd finished with our repairs at the dock, and steamed out about a half mile to sea. It was here that we were rigging the big net.

We had our two giant booms out over the side, running steel cables from dead-end snatch-blocks on deck, up through the blocks on the booms, and back to the winch. From these cables we hung the huge steel net, and watched Jack Finn at the winch as he slowly lowered the shark net down into the water.

Joe and I put the finishing touches to the bathysphere operation. I'd rigged the cable of the 'sphere to a small boom, and had it in position to lower over the side. I was ready to climb into the 'sphere now. Joe and I had flipped a coin, and I won.

The 'sphere was a good idea, really. We'd decided the best was to flush out the monster was to attract it with a light of some kind. And the 'sphere has illumination inside, and powerful movable spots outside. That would bring out the beast, if anything would.

"Okay, Boats?" Joe called to Jack Finn.

Finn nodded.

Joe turned to me, and stuck out his hand. "Luck, kid."

I grinned and stepped inside the 'sphere. The heavy door clanged shut with a shudder, and I instantly felt the oppressive claustrophobia I always experience once I'm inside the damned thing. It's always the same feeling a professional actor get just before going on stage every night. I'll never get over it, either.

I put on the earphones and blew into the speaker phone. "Am I coming through, Joe?"

"Loud and clear," Joe said, his voice filtered and electronic and unnatural in the headset.

"I'm ready to dive if you are."

I could feel the gentle hum of the big deck winch as it started up, and then I could feel myself suspended slightly in the air, free from the rocking solidity of the deck. Up we went, until the bathysphere cleared the rails. Then I felt myself swing out over the ocean. Now I went down, and it was dark as the water closed over me.

I stood at the view plate and watched the water as I continued into the depths. It grew darker and I could feel the murky weight of the sea close in over me. I switched the interiors on and was instantly bathed in a glow of artificial yellow light.

"Give me about fifteen fathoms, Joe," I said into the phone. "Then I'll tell you."

Groups of fish swirled by, peering in at me, as the outer regions grew even darker. I saw the bulging eyes and protruding snout of a black grouper as it nosed around my view plate, and then it lazily swam off and disappeared. I flipped the exterior spotlight on, and the big beams cut into the water around me. The nature of the sea changed gradually down here. The life was of a different type. Light was an unknown thing. I could feel animal eyes staring at me, wondering what I was.

"Fifteen fathoms," Joe's voice crackled in the ear phones.

"Okay. Hold it."

I moved the exterior spotlight about. I could see nothing unusual.

"Give me slow engines, Joe. Four or five knots. Head her down the bay."

After a moment I felt a slight tremor on the cable holding the bathysphere, and then I began moving along through the water, tilted at a slight angle.

"Where are we, Joe?" I asked.

"Just off the point."

I kept the lights moving, and flushed out a few strange undersea fish, but nothing interesting. And then, about ten minutes after I'd been down, the big beam of light seemed to lift out something huge, vague, and ill-defined—a shadow in the dark, just beyond the range of the lights.

"Joe! Stop engines!"

I saw it! I saw it coming slowly out of the darkness into the light. It had seen me, and it was attracted to the light. It was not moving fast, but it was prowling about, confused, its tremendous reptilian head swaying back and forth in the water. But it kept moving toward me.

"Christ! It's here. Stand by with that net!" I yelled.

I could see the big head now, and the gleaming red eyes studying the'sphere. It extended its head then, somewhat like a fish investigating a lure. And when it did I could feel the tremendous power of the huge body movements. The 'sphere moved slightly, like a swaying pendulum. The huge, scaly, green face pressed up to the view plate, and I could almost *feel* the monster's slimy, rubbery, tough-plated hide.

"Take me up," I said cautiously into the phone. "But not too fast. I don't want to lose him."

Just as I spoke, I knew it was too late. The big head reared back, and then it darted right at the'sphere; the beast's jaws opened wide. The mouth wouldn't swallow the bathysphere, I gold myself nervously. I couldn't swallow me! But I was sweating and shaking. It looked in at me, puzzled. Then I felt the whole bathysphere shudder and lurch about. I realized what had happened. It had clapped one of its great talons over the'sphere to steady it, and was knawing at the metal with its mouth. I thought ludicrously of a puppy trying to get his mouth around a tennis ball that was too big for it.

I went down to my knees as the monster chewed at the big bathysphere, flicking it about in the water. I could see through the view plate now, and the powerful beam of the spotlight showed redness and fleshy pulp. I was looking right down the monster's open throat!

"Pull up! Pull up!" I shouted at the speaker phone.

The bathysphere trembled, jerked, heaved up, swayed and rotated. I couldn't keep my footing. I was being bounced from side to side of the 'sphere. The monster's inner mouth covered the view plate now, and I could hear the terrible sounds of steel tearing and rivets snapping and bolts shearing.

I was on the floor of the 'sphere and a jetting stream of water suddenly spurted in through a wide crack at the seam.

"For God's sake, Joe! Pull! Pull!"

The water was spraying all over me, and I couldn't stop it. I was wallowing in it now. It poured in faster as the seam widened. The monster was tearing the 'sphere to pieces with its powerful jaws.

I knew it couldn't be long now. I grabbed the phone again.

I don't know how many seconds elapsed, but I do know that after a moment the 'sphere stopped its agitation and hung limply in the water. Then the spotlight picked out the monster, and I clambered to my feet. I stood hip deep in water now, yelling frantically to be hauled up.

I started to move. And as I did so the spotlight from the 'sphere caught the monster. I could see that the shark net had descended over its back. And the monster reacting to the new enemy, had slashed at it with a powerful talon, letting go of me.

The monster was shaking the claw, trying to get it loose from the net. It was caught tight.

The monster was shaking the claw, trying to get loose from the net. It was caught tight.

The monster, anxious now, swiped at the net with its other talon, and became entangled from both sides.

"Snug up! Snug up the net!" I cried into the phone. "We've got him!"

Now, as I moved up through the water, I could see the net turning in around the monster, tightening up like a string purse. The monster was hopelessly entangled now, fighting frantically in a losing battle.

I felt the welcome relief of swift ascent. It was only a few moments before I climbed out of the 'sphere, shaken to the core, and saw that the fight was just getting under way on deck.

Jack Finn was working the winch. Joe was supervising the operation from the rail. Just as I climbed into dry clothes, I saw the huge net emerge from the water with the madly struggling monster inside.

"Swing her in!" Joe cried.

The boom moved the big monster in toward the deck and Joe yelled out: Get ready with the shackle bolts!"

Crewmen leaped to execute his orders, pulling tight on the cable running through the shackle bolts and attached on the deck to rim bolts. As they pulled in tightly, the netted monster was secured to the deck, enmeshed in its flexible steel prison.

We had caught the monster of Nara!

# Chapter 6

IT DIDN'T TAKE long for the news to get out. Nara was a lighthouse island, and it had a government radio tower. By nightfall the news was all over the world. I caught a radio broadcast in my bunk that night after dinner.

"Headlines of the entire world are being monopolized today by news of the capture of a fantastic sea monster, seemingly of prehistoric origin, off the coast of Ireland," the announcer trumpeted.

"Puzzled scientists are already speculating that the monster may have been released from some vast sub-oceanic cavern far beneath the earth's crust, by unprecedented volcanic eruptions which occurred in the area recently.

"Some scientific authorities, however, are suggesting that the whole thing is no more than an elaborate Irish hoax. Nevertheless, the Irish government is sending two of its top paleontologists to claim the creature for Ireland." The broadcaster's voice turned sardonic. "If it *does* exist."

I snapped off the set and grinned. It existed all right. I heard Joe snort disgustedly at the end of my bunk. He had come in and caught the last of the announcer's words.

"Listen to that damn crap!" he said. "That's people for you. Never believe anything until it's shoved down their throats."

I sat up on the bunk. "What's next Joe? What do we do with our catch now?"

Joe ground his teeth and cursed. "That radio operator up on the cliff sent the news out too fast. We've got to sweat it out right here until the government people show up. If we don't, they'll make it tough as hell for us to show it anywhere."

I groaned. "All that work—and nothing for it."

"We'll get ours, Sam, I promise it," Joe said grimly.

His eyes were slitted and I did not like the look in them.

"I hope something works out," I grumbled.

Joe turned and headed for the corridor outside the bunk. "I'm going to hit the sack," he said. In the morning we can get things moving."

"*Oíche mhaith agat!*" I said.

"Good night," I grinned. "I'm picking up the language fast."

"Sounds like good shark bait at that," Joe said with a leer.

I sat there a moment, yawning and thinking. I had been a long haul with Joe Ryan. I couldn't say I particularly liked him, but he was tough, and plenty handy with himself. He was a fighter who usually got what he wanted.

We'd served in Korea together, and that's where I'd learned diving and salvage. I'd never had any particular aim in life, and looked up Joe down in Texas where he was working on the Gulf in a greasy sack salvage operation. We worked together a while, and then a sleazy little Cuban named Joselito Fernandez got us onto a real good thing—bringing in shipments of arms to the rebels in Oriente Province, before Castro took over. We got zeroed in a couple times, and almost had our decks shot out from under us once, but we made out.

With the dough we couped from that operation, we bought the salvage rig and the bathysphere, and started out on our own. Once in a while we hit, but never really big. We had come up to the Irish coast to try for some of the convoy kills during World War II, and had just found a likely one when the big volcanic eruption took place. So here we were again, high and dry, without one cent in the bank, and a monster chained to the deck, ready to eat us all for breakfast.

Hell, there was no use brooding about it. We were hard-working guys who had never made it. Sometime we would. And when we did, so help me God, would live it up big!

I snagged a cigarette out of the pack, lit up, and went for a breather on deck. The stars were shining and it was a beautiful, clear night. I strolled to the foredeck where the monster was netted and chained down. A bright deck-light, located aft of the monster, was turned full on him, throwing the rest of the deck into shadows. A canvas canopy was rigged above the beast to keep the sun off its back during the day, and we had one of the ship's fire hoses playing a stream of water on it from above. This water was trailing over the deck and draining out into the harbor through the scuppers.

We figured it as best to keep the big thing wet. It was a sea beast, there was no doubt of that, yet it seemed partially amphibious. And it seemed to be doing all right so far. It had almost achieved a kind of resignation about its captivity. This helped morale on board ship, believe me. With that thing flailing about, God knows who we could get to ship with us.

The monster was hunched over now, dozing. I could see its green body, with the plated metallic scales and its gleaming water soaked skin. And then, as I stood there, I had surprised to see the monster suddenly raise its head as though it had heard or sensed the presence of something on deck.

It wasn't looking at me. It was looking back the other way, toward the bow of the ship. Now, rising under its hedge net, it turned slowly toward the shadowed area on the other side. I tried to squint into the darkness myself, but I could see nothing.

Then, before I could move, I saw someone come out from behind a tarpaulin lashed over some oil drums. It was Sean McCartin! I was just about to jump forward and throw him off the ship when I saw Moira, moving furtively and cautiously across the deck behind him. What the hell?

I was curious to make a move and tip my hand. I wanted to see what they had up their sleeves. Was this some kind of superstitious sacrifice to Ogra? The two of them crouched in front of the monster's big head, staring up at it. The monster looked at them, silent contemplative.

"*Fáilte romhat!*" murmured Sean. I recognized the words. "Welcome." Sean spoke the words with respect. Beside him Moira bowed her head in obeisance.

The monster rumbled and shook the net, but the two of them did not jump back. They looked at each other, and then I saw Sean cross over to the nearest shackle bolt which held the cable binding the net. He bent over and tried to loosen it.

Moira peered about the deck, seemingly keeping a lookout for her brother. The monster turned then, shifting its stance so it faced the boy; it towered above Sean and edged forward against the confines of the steel net. Sean shook the shackle bolt again.

I moved then, starting to come out from behind the deck light. But before I could say anything the monster struck with its huge talon. The blow did not catch Sean, but the net swung out, and its force knocked him to the deck. Moira cried out and jumped to him to pick him up.

At that instant, while I charged across the deck myself, the monster raised its huge talon again, and struck downward, now thoroughly aroused. The sharp, lethal edge of it grazed Moira's body, not tearing her flesh, but ripping her shirt and dungarees down the side like a huge razor.

Sean rolled out of range of the monster, and Moira was shaking with terror when I reached her and gathered her to me. Now the monster was roaring and snarling slashing at the net with its talons.

"What do you think you're doing?" I yelled at Moira. "You'll be killed!"

Now a voice called from the darkness beyond the deck light. I could recognize Jack Finn's husky basso.

"What's going on out there?"

"We've got it under control, Boats!" I called. "You can sit tight."

For a moment I froze there, curing soundlessly. I didn't want any trouble with Joe. If he knew these two members of the clan McCartin had come aboard, he'd have them keel-hauled. I was still holding the girl tightly, waiting for an okay from the Bos'n.

"Long as it's under control, Mr. Slade."

"Forget it."

I heard his footsteps moving away on the deck.

I looked at Sean. "You hurt?"

The boy was shivering. "No, sir."

I faced Moira. Her eyes were bright and wide and dilated. "How about you?"

I realized then that I was still holding her body tightly to mine, protectively. She looked into my eyes, and then away with embarrassment. She let her hands stray down from my chest, and I drew my arms from around her soft, yielding body. I felt a stir within me, and I backed away deliberately.

"I'm—all right," she said, her voice shaken. She looked down at herself, and in her modesty, pulled the ripped clothing closer around her. I could see part of her naked breast, and almost all of one long leg. I looked away.

"You two get off this boat fast," I said in a low urgent tone. "How'd you get here anyway?"

Moira stared at me defiantly, ignoring my question.

"You needn't look that way at him, Somhairle. 'Twas my own idea. This monster you've caught will only bring trouble to us all."

"Sure enough, if you keep trying to get close to him! He'll oblige you with a full-scale clawing!"

She bit her lip. Then she faced me again. "We rowed out here, if you must know. And we'll try again until we succeed."

I shook my head in resignation. "I have a feeling you will at that," I said. "Come on!"

"Come on where?" she asked me with a toss of her gorgeous red hair.

"I'm rowing you back to the beach."

"Sure and we can row ourselves, Somhairle," she snapped, turning to her brother. She took him by the hand. "Come on, Sean. We're finished here, for the time being."

And the two of them hurried to the rail, Moira all the time clutching the shreds of her shirt to cover her nakedness.

"Hold it!"

I came after them.

"And now what would you be wanting?" she asked impudently.

"I'm going with you. I want to be sure you *get* to the beach."

Moira chuckled then, her face breaking into an amused smile. "'Tis a determined man you are at that, Somhairle."

I helped them over the side, and we climbed down to the rowboat tied up there. We rowed in silence across the calm harbor, until we had reached the beach. Sean jumped out and tugged the prow up onto the sand.

"Okay, Sean, beat it. I intend to have words with your sister. You hear me?"

Sean looked questioningly at Moira. She gave him imperceptible nod, and then the boy turned and started loping across the beach to the cliff trail.

I helped Moira out of the boat. "Now would you like to explain to me exactly what you were trying to do?"

She turned to me and stared at me as if I were daft. "But to set him free, of course. 'Tis Ogra, the sea god. Did you not know that?"

I shook my head. "Frankly, it looks to me like some prehistoric link between the dinosaur age and ours."

"Scientific nonsense," said Moira, sniffing. "You sound just like my stubborn father."

We walked along the beach and sat down in a spot under the cliffs, sheltered and cut off from the village.

"Your father is an educated man," I said after awhile. "How did he ever come to devote his whole life to this desolate island? Nara doesn't even show on most maps."

She smiled secretly. "Haven't you guessed? 'Tis a simple thing after all. He was a brilliant archeologist, and he took a fine job with the Irish government. But he was always like he is now. Never could get along with other people. They finally sent him off to this desolate island where he didn't have to get along with anyone, to study the Viking and Irish wrecks. Fifteen years ago it was, and he's been here ever since."

"You've never been off the island?"

"Never since," she breathed, staring out to sea. My eyes were growing accustomed to the darkness, and I could see her profile, the lively red hair flowing down her neck, the strong clean cut of her nose, the line of her lips, the upthrust of her breasts against what was left of her shirt. There was even a gleaming patch of her milk-white skin, visible through the torn garment, and the gentle curve of her left breast which I could not help seeing. I pulled my eyes away from her, and looked once again at the masts bobbing up and down in the harbor. It seemed a much safer view to observe.

"This is no place for a girl like you."

She smiled. "What do you mean, like me?"

I looked in her eyes. She was watching me with amusement, with the arch look of a natural-born flirt, with the look of someone who wanted to be a woman but who had never had the chance to be.

"You should have men crawling at your feet, Moira. They would, you know, if there were any around here." I touched her chin and lifted her face. The stars twinkled in her eyes.

"There are men, Somhairle," she whispered. "The divers. The villagers who work for my father."

"Not the men you should have, Moira," I said, moving closer to her. "You should have princes, kings, men of wealth and power, and they would sit at your feet and tell you of your beauty and your charm."

" 'Tis the Blarney Stone you've kissed, Somhairle, that much is obvious to me." But her lips were wide and smiling and parted, and her teeth showed as she whispered.

"Who would kiss the Blarney Stone, Princess, if he had your lips to kiss?" I leaned and touched her lips with mine. They were cool and calm and she closed her eyes and we stayed together for a long moment. Then she drew her head away.

"Somhairle," she said, and the sound came from deep in her throat, blurred and husky. "That was nice."

"Very," I said, and I kissed her again. My arm slid around her shoulders now, and she turned slightly to me. Her lips moved against mine, and I could feel their growing warmth. The flesh of her body pressed against me, and though we were sitting side by side, we turned to each other, breast to breast. Her head went back slightly, and her hair fell down over my hand and wrist.

After a long time, I drew back. "That was wonderful, Princess. Princess Nara." I laughed.

"Oh, Somhairle!" she cried, and flung her arms around my neck, pulling me tightly to her this time, her lips clinging to mine, moving against mine, with awakened desire. Now her body moved in to mine, fitting itself curve to curve, to my own. She writhed under me, pulling me over on top of her, until I was face to face with her on the sand, and she was clinging to me with her warm, soft, aroused body. She was like a flower opening for the first time.

She had carried that body with her for twenty years, and she had thought she knew herself. But now she had suddenly learned that she did not know her body at all, nor what it yearned for, and she was more amazed at what it now told her, than she had ever been in her life.

"Moira," I murmured, tearing myself away from her lips for a moment. She lay there in the sand, looking up at me, her sea-green eyes slanted and oriental in the starlight. She gazed at me along her dark lashes, and her lair lay on the sand about her head, framing it like a halo.

In our embrace my hand had pulled at the shirt on her back, sliding it down over one creamy shoulder. Now, as I looked down at her, I was conscious only of the fact that the shreds of the shirt had parted over her breasts, and that one of them lay completely exposed, its white softness before my eyes. She saw my glance and she looked at me and smiled.

"Kiss me, Somhairle," she said softly, and as she closed her eyes I leaned down and I kissed her. A tremor shot through her body. She moved in the sand beneath me. She thrust her head back away from me, her fingernails digging into my back.

Then I touched her breast with my hand, and she closed her eyes, moaned softly and turned her head from me. The flaming red hair moved against my nose, tickling it. The smell of the fresh air came to me. It permeated my entire body.

"Somhairle," she whispered, as I held her there in a tight embrace. "I love you, Somhairle."

I closed my eyes. It wasn't fair. This lonely, woodland kid, who had never even seen a man like me before, thinking she was in love with me. It was one of those obscene, miserable things and I felt sick.

"No, you don't," I said. "You just think you do."

"Yes," she said. "It is the truth. I have asked my heart, and my heart has given me the answer."

I lifted her mouth to mine and kissed her again.

"You see," she said, looking into the sky beyond my head, "when you kiss me there is the ringing of bells in the air. There is soft music of the little people. There is the far-off singing of many voices. It is you I want, Somhairle. No one else. I know. A woman always knows?'

I held her to me, trying to forget what a slob and bastard I was to get her into a situation like this.

But she would have none of my excuses.

"Take me, Somhairle," she whispered. "I demand to be taken." She clutched my hand in hers and I pressed her body, warm and quivering, to mind. Somehow I found the button to the dungarees she wore, and unbuttoned them, and slipped the clothes off her trembling flesh until there was nothing between us but the warmth of our bodies.

She strained and twisted and clutched at me in the ecstasy of her stabbing, tearing pain, and with the unfeigned sincerity of innocence, she abandoned herself to me. And for me it was like dying and being reborn. It was a dizzying climb to a cloud of ecstasy such as I'd never experienced before.

When the tumult and madness between us finally subsided, we lay there, breathless and sated and content, surrounded by the essence and magic of our love.

Moira's soft, flame-red hair flicked across my face, and I opened my eyes. She was bending over me, her lips brushing my lips, her full, firm breasts teasing the flesh of my chest. I pulled her to me and desire swept through me again like that wild storm at sea.

"Moira!" I whispered hoarsely.

"Somhairle!" Her tongue was at my ear.

Then I rose to one elbow, my face flaming, my tongue dry. I sprang to my feet, and I turned to her, my eyes dry. I sprang to my feet, and I turned to her, my eyes blurred and hot. I snatched my shirt and pants and moved off down the beach hastily.

She sprang up to follow me. "Somhairle!" she cried in agony. "What have I done?"

"Nothing," I said. "It's what *I've* done."

"What have I said?"

I turned to her, my heart pounding. "It's *me*, Moira! I'm no good! I'm a lousy no-good son of a bitch, Moira! Do you understand that? It's what I did to you. You need a decent guy, a good man, Moira! Not me. Now get away. You make me sick!"

She staggered back from me as if I had struck her. "Sick?" she repeated, holding her hand to her mouth in despair. "I make you sick. When you mean all the world to me?"

I clutched at something invisible in the air between us. I had no idea what it might be.

"Sick!" I repeated.

"Somhairle!" she sobbed, and threw herself at me, grasping me around the shoulders, hugging me to her naked body as if her flesh would bring me back to her. "Hold me, Somhairle! You don't mean it!"

I ripped her from me, sent her reeling against the sand. "I do! Leave me alone! It's my misery now!"

She stood up again and stared at me, wonderingly, forlornly. "What did I do, Somhairle?" Tears glistened in her eyes.

How could I tell her that she had done nothing but love me, the finest thing in the world she could do? How could I tell her that it was my own shame that was angering me, for loving her? How could I tell her that I was not lying, that I *was* sick, that I could never love anyone pure and good and real like her.

The black waves of remorse rose before me and I stood alone in a black, empty void, and I was blinded by self-loathing. I slapped her face without seeing her. I heard her stagger back into the sand. She lay there sobbing out my name. She wept heart-brokenly like a child who had just been senselessly punished.

I turned on my heel and stalked off through the night.

## Part Two:  GORGO

## Chapter 7

TWO PALEONTOLOGISTS from the University of Dublin showed up early the next morning, landing in a government seaplane in the harbor. Nara didn't have a large enough flat spot to accommodate a land plane.

We watched Kevin McCartin's launch chug out to pick them up. After a short confab in the launch, which Joe and I watched with great interest through the ship's binoculars, McCartin grudgingly started up the launch and headed for the *Triton*.

We helped the three of them abroad, shook hands all around, made appropriately veiled comments to McCartin, and then led the newcomers to the monster's net.

One of the Dubliners was named Flaherty, the other one O'Brien. Professor Marious Flaherty was a tweedy man in his forties who smoked a pipe and took it out occasionally to move his lips in and out an dponder inexpressible thoughts. Professor Desmond O'Brien was a curly-headed, sandy-haired cherub with a baby's face who smoked a cigar and rarely said a word.

They studied the monster from all angles, muttering to themselves, peering with interest at the scaly plates, the huge, sharp talons, and the green luminescent color of the beast.

Flaherty took a notebook from his tween jacket and made marks in it, while he squinted through the wire mesh. Frankly, if I'd been the monster. I'd have been dammed embarrassed at all the attention. I'd have shaken the net just a bit, I think, to throw a scare into them. But our monster didn't move a scale. After a few minutes of this, Flaherty moved to where Joe and I stood watching. McCartin glowered at us.

"I've been saying to my colleague, Captain Ryan, this is almost unbelievable!" Flaherty took the pipe out and pressed his lips together. "I wonder if you realize the enormous scientific value of this discovery."

Joe grinned and looked at me. "Why, I think we do, Professor Flaherty."

Putting the pipe back into his mouth, Flaherty turned and gazed across the foredeck at the huge shape tied down in the shark net. "Incredible!" He turned to Joe. "Well, then I shall wireless the University of Dublin at once to make proper preparations to receive the animal."

Joe nodded. "I see."

I didn't quite like the tone of Joe's voice. It seemed as if he was laughing under his breath, as if Flaherty and O'Brien and all this folderol over the beast was a source of some hidden amusement. I was worried. I wondered if the excitement of the catch had unnerved him and jiggled some screw loose I didn't get it. Not at all.

"You will proceed, then Captain Ryan, to Dublin," Flaherty said. The gray eyes behind the thick glasses rested momentarily on Joe's hatchet-thin face and flat lips. "Naturally,compensation will be forthcoming for your services."

Joe gestured negligently. "Oh, sure."

I couldn't believe my ears. Joe, so casual about money?

"My colleague and I," Flaherty said, turning and waving a hand at the curly-headed cherub behind him, "will meet you at the harbor." Then he paused and gazed at both Joe and me. "Unless, of course, you'd like to have one of us go with you."

"Very good," Flaherty said, as if everything was settled. "Now, sir. One thing. The animal's skin should be kept wet with water. It is an amphibious reptile, but we don't understand too much about it. It will be best to keep a continuous stream on its back, just as you have been doing. I congratulate you on your intelligence and forethought." He looked vaguely at the distant horizon, considering. "When do you intend to sail, Captain?"

"Tonight," said Joe. There wasn't a flicker of expression on his face. "That is," he went on, "if it's okay with you."

Joe? Asking this egghead if it was okay with him? I couldn't believe my ears.

"Excellent," Flaherty said, nodding and beaming. "The sooner the better."

He stuck out his hand.

"Well, then. We shall expect you within a few days."

We shook hands all around again and watched them depart. As soon as they had cleared our decks, I turned to Joe.

"All right, Joe," I said. "Out with it. What's cooking?"

He turned an innocent face to me. "What are you talking about?"

I could see that whatever it was, Joe wasn't going to confide in me. At least, not right now.

I shrugged. "Okay. Keep it to yourself. I just hope it isn't one of your sneaky little deals that's going to backfire on us again!"

Joe grinned, clapping me on the back. "Have I ever let you down, Sam, Old boy?"

"No, not completely," I said. "And now's not the time to start."

He watched me as I moved away from him. I was mad and he knew it. Whatever it was he had up his sleeve, I hoped he could handle it.

I went below for a cup of coffee in the galley, and as I was drinking from the warm china mug I glanced out the starboard porthole. I was astonished to see two people rowing vigorously toward us in one of those hide-covered island boats call a "curragh." The energetic oarsmen were Sean and Moira McCartin!

I hurried on deck just as they had climbed aboard and stood inside the rail arguing with Jack Finn.

"Okay, Boats, I'll take care of this," I said, coming up fast.

Finn turned to me, pulling at his cigarette and studying me curiously with his blue eyes. "Okay, Mr. Slade. It's your party."

And he touched his cap and backed off.

"What are you two little fools doing on board the *Triton!*" I asked angrily. "Get ashore at once! I don't want Ryan to see you. Jump to it!"

Moira shook her head, her chin tilted high, her eyes hard with determination. "Not until you promise to let the beast go."

"Now listen here, you two!" I snapped. "I'm sick and tired of all this nonsense! I was fool enough to put up with you two last night, but if Captain Ryan finds out, he'll flog you to within an inch of your lives!"

"Partners, you are, is it not? Moira asked slyly in a sing-song voice, her beautiful eyes working me over calculatingly. "So?"

"Then the responsibility's as much yours as it is his," she said triumphantly. "It wouldn't do to have human blood on your hands, now would it, Mr. Slade?"

"Joe's the boss," I said. "We're partners, but he's the boss. There can be only one captain on a ship."

"Then 'tis him we shall have to see," shrugged Moira. "If you will be telling him."

I moved around in front of her to block her path. "If Joe ever dreamed you had come aboard this ship last night and tried to free the monster, he'll kill you! Believe me! It's a serious matter with him. Now get out of here before you have real trouble!"

" 'Tis here I'm staying till I see him! Moira said adamantly, shaking her head.

I longed to take her over my knee and paddle the daylights out of her. But she was a bit too big for that sort of thing. And I didn't think I could bring myself to do it, anyway.

I turned to Sean, to see if I could find reason there. "What's wrong with you two? This monster is a prehistoric discovery that may aid science immeasurably. Paleontologists from Dublin are expecting us to deliver it to them. Now you wouldn't want to set science back another thousand years would you?

"Science!" snorted Moira. "The beast is death. 'Tis like catching the devil by the tail. What do you do with it once you've got it?"

I groaned in frustration. "I'm not here to argue with you! I'm telling you to get off this ship!"

"Nought will I budge, Mr. Slade! 'Tis here I'll stand till I have my way!"

I lit a cigarette, eyeing her slyly. "Your father wouldn't have put you up to this?"

"Now why would he be doing that?" she asked with widened eyes.

"To cause us trouble. If the monster was released we'd likely leave Nara. He'd want that."

"Not at all!" she said. " 'Tis you he wants to have it! 'Tis you he wants to leave as soon as possible, and *with* the monster. Should it get free, his divers will leave the island. 'Tis you he wants to take the animal."

As I stood there glowering at her, I felt a sudden tremor of the steel deck plates underfoot. I turned startled.

It was the monster up on the firedeck, turning around restlessly, trying to make itself comfortable inside the net. A rumbling growl emanated from the shadows under the canvas. I walked away from Sean and Moira to check the guard we'd posted that morning.

His name was Pat Phelan, from County Kerry. I saw him sitting there by the monster, a lean, wiry young man with curly blonde hair, a rifle across his knees, looking nervously at the great green beast. He was breathing heavily, but with the rifle in his hands he seemed to feel safe. Safer than he should, I thought absently.

When I returned to the rail I saw we had a visitor. Joe.

He turned, smiling, to me when I cam up. "Sam, we've got guests. Did you know that?

"I was trying to get them off ship, Joe," I said briefly. "I don't think it's safe aboard."

Joe shook his head gently. "You don't seem to understand the duties of a host, Sam. We should make all our guests feel comfortable on the *Triton*. It's Moira's first time

aboard. We should show her around."

I froze. Joe was very close to Moira now, almost touching her. My flesh crawled. Joe Ryan had definite ideas about Moira. I felt sick suddenly, as if this had all happened before.

"The monster," Moira said swiftly, moving back just a step from Joe as he tried to take her arm. "You must free it. 'Tis not to be kept in captivity. Don't you see? 'Tis a manifestation of evil."

Joe smiled tolerantly, putting out his hand and patting Sean's head. "Oh, I don't see it that way at all, Moira. This is a great discovery for science, a tremendous advance for paleontology."

"You'll be taking the beast to Dublin, then?" Moira asked softly, crestfallen.

"Sure!" Joe said. "Come with me, I'll show you the ship."

He took her arm and pulled her close to him. She looked across at me, frightened at first. But then, when she saw my face, her expression instantly changed, and she deliberately snuggled up to Joe, lifting her chin in the air, flaunting her closeness to him, and playing it broad for my benefit.

" 'Tis a pleasure I couldn't afford to miss," she said, speaking in her heavy singsong brogue again, for my benefit. "Sean," she said as an afterthought, "go with Mr. Slade. 'Tis anxious he is to show you how to drive the ship."

As they moved out of sight she looked once over Joe's shoulder and made a face at me. She was playing with fire. I figured, let her get burnt.

I looked at Sean, and he looked at me. "Girls," he said with disgust. " 'Tis impossible to understand them."

I laughed and gave him a harmless punch in the shoulder. We started for the bridge where I intended to show Sean how to box the compass, when we heard another thumping and banging from the monster's roost up forward.

"Tell me something, Sean," I said. "Did anyone out here on Nara ever see that thing before?"

"Ogra? No."

"Then how come you're so familiar with it?"

Sean smiled and looked at me pityingly. "And why should anyone have to be seeing it to know it's there?"

He had me. I was about to admit it when the abrupt concussion of a rifle shot was followed by a piercing scream. The scream died out in a hideous bubbling gurgle. There was a tense, unbroken silence for about three seconds and then the deck was pandemonium. Crewmen appeared from all sides. We raced for the monster's net. When we got there Jack Finn had already arrived, with six crewmen.

The first thing I saw was the huge rent in the shark net, a gap that had been torn by the monster's powerful talon. My eye followed along the line of the rent to the outstretched form of Pat Phelan. His body was twisted oddly, and blood poured from it all over the deck. The rifle had been slung out of reach of the monster's talons. I picked it up.

"Secure that net!" I cried. Jack Finn began shouting orders to the crew.

"*Slabhra!*" shouted the Bos'n. "Cable!" One of the men rushed across the deck for the coil of steel cable. He was back in an instant. The seven of them then tried to whip the cable through the strands of the net, trying to weave the gaping hole together. The monster moved forward threateningly.

I fired four shots in toward the big beast. It moved back, growling and roaring. But it stayed back, afraid of the bullets buzzing about, even though they could not penetrate the tough outer hide.

I moved over and looked down at Pat Phelan's body. His viscera had been completely removed with one swipe of the monster's talon. Blood had spouted all over the deck plates.

I turned to Sean. He stared down at the corpse. When he looked up at me I could almost read the expression in his eyes."I told you so."

I turned away, angrily. Death, they had said. Death it certainly was. The death of two divers. The death of three men in third boat last night. And now the death of a crew member of the *Triton*.

I turned to Finn, who had just finished patching up the shark net. "Boats," I said quietly, "prepare this man for burial."

"Yes sir," he said, turning away so I could not see his eyes.

I didn't want to watch. I was sick at heart. I was fed up with this excursion of death, fed up with monsters and octopuses and killer whales, and everything that went with them. I was through.

"Where the hell is that sister of yours?" I asked Sean testily. He merely looked at me and shrugged.

"Stay up here," I told him, and went below. I knew Joe was showing Moira the ship, and I figured he had taken her down by the galley for a cup of coffee. Funny he hadn't heard the commotion on deck. Or perhaps he had, and didn't care to have Moira see it. Particularly since she wanted to get rid of the monster. It would only help prove her point.

I tried the galley, but there was no one there. Nor were the two of them in the crew's quarters. I retraced my steps, frowning. Where could they have gone? The engine room was no place for a girl.

I was passing the captain's cabin when a slight movement inside caught my eye. The door was open. I went over and peered in.

It was Joe and Moira.

They didn't see me. They didn't see me because they were too busy. I stood there a moment, watching them, disgust welling in me like a flood if nausea.

He had her down on the bunk, tight in his arms, and although he had not progressed past the preliminaries, he was certainly making fast and very sure time with her.

I was sick—fed up—with myself and Moira and Joe.

Then her eyes opened slightly, and over Joe's shoulder she saw me. Suddenly her eyes widened, and she pushed Joe off her. It was no effort. She could have done it before, but she hadn't.

"Somhairle!" she cried. *Somhairle!*"

She struggled to get up, trying, at the same time, to pull down the dress that had ridden up over her thighs, to push the open buttons of her blouse together.

Joe turned with a leer. "Hi, Sam. Didn't your mother ever teach you to knock before entering?"

"She did!" I snapped. "And now I know why."

Joe slid to his feet, fluid and catlike. Beneath his bravado he was eyeing me uncertainly. I must have shown a great deal of my anger on my face—more than I thought.

Moira was sitting on the bunk now, shaking her hair back and tossing it away from her face nervously. She watched me out of those grave, sea-green eyes. I could see that she wished she had never started fooling around with Joe.

"Okay, Sam," Joe said, moving toward me. "Show's over. I'd turn around and trot out if I were you."

"You've been asking for it for a long time, haven't you, Joe?" I was mad now.

His eyes were slitted. "*I* haven't been asking for it, Sam," Joe said softly. "Why don't you check out your facts with the little lady?"

Moira's eyes widened, and she glared at Joe. Then she turned to me. "No, Somhairle! she cried. "It isn't true! Somhairle!"

"It looked pretty damned real to me, Moira," I growled.

"*Real* is the word for it," Joe grinned wolfishly. "*Real good!*"

A red swirling cloud enveloped me, and I moved without thinking. I lashed out at him swiftly, trying to block his blows. But I must have telegraphed my punches, because he threw me aside, grabbed me by the waist and tossed me onto the bunk.

I bounced right off, going for his throat. He twisted aside and swung a blockbuster at my head. I saw it coming and ducked. But I tripped, and went down on the deck.

I lay there a moment, trying to grab a breath of air. Then I climbed to my feet.

Moira was holding onto Joe's arm, pleading with him, her eyes teary, her hair around her shoulders. Joe's face was wryly amused. His big, knotted biceps were straining, but I knew he wasn't interested in me right now. He could have thrown her off him in an instant with a minimum of effort. He didn't seem to want to. He knew a good thing when he had it.

Moira turned to me, her face red and wet. "*Somhairle!* You stop it! 'Tis a truce I'm asking.!"

I moved at Joe, unable to hold back.

Moira turned to me, pulling at my arm the same way she had clung to Joe's.

"Somhairle! By all that's holy!"

The girl. The green-eyed lovely shape of all that was wonderful in the world. She, pitted herself against two senseless, fighting, brawling males. I shook my head. I turned away. How did she always manage to shame me in the worst possible way?

I shook her arm off me and plunged through the doorway. As I moved down the passage outside the cabin door I could hear Joe's flat laughter, and Moira's angry scolding.

One of them was phony.

I figured it was Moira.

# Chapter 8

I watched Sean and Moira McCartin rowing back to the dock in that ridiculous curragh and I cursed myself for letting her make such a fool of me. I'm a pushover for a smart woman. I go all out for one and then I find out she's made of tinsel and papier maché like the rest. First that bitch Anita, with the soft, level eyes, the straightest girl in Texas. Sure. All the time shacking up with an oil rigger from the fields behind my back.

I'd almost killed him that night in the alley behind the hotel.

Now I wanted to do the same thing to Joe.

But it wasn't his fault. It was Moira's. She'd showed her hand, and I knew it was no good between us and had never been any good from the start. She was just a woman like all the rest of them, with the same tricks and the same lies.

Beneath my feet the deck shuddered from the impact of the monster's movement. I turned and looked across the deck at the big steel net under the canopy. The crewman on guard now was Michael Degan, and he saw me looking.

"Hello, Mr. Slade," he said, civilly enough.

"Keep your distance from that thing," I said. Hear?"

"Mr. Finn told me in the same words, he nodded unhappily. "The damned thing is a curse. If he's allowed to remain in captivity, Mr. Slade, evil will befall us all!

I started to shake my head with annoyance. But something in the man's eye held me. I said nothing.

" 'Tis the word," Michael Degan said, and lapsed into gloomy silence. He moved away from me and stood on the other side of the monster.

The monster's big head swiveled around and its red eyes glared at me. It moved slightly, trying to get comfortable under the weight of the net.

I shuddered. I could feel for it. I could feel the weight of that metal net on top of me, too. I was the monster, entrapped in a prison, not allowed my freedom.

"I know you, Ogra," I said "I know how you feel."

I'd spent six months in a Red prison camp during the Korean was. I'd never been so close to madness in my life before. It was a brand new experience to me, and a nerve-shattering one. I'd never hoped to escape. I'd spent every day wondering if I could last through another night inside my cell.

Life wasn't worth living under conditions like those.

I glanced across at the beast. It glowered at me. Ogra, I thought, you had it, old buddy. You'll never again see the bottom of the ocean.

Small wonder the beast had killed. Small wonder it flailed and maimed. Manifestation of evil? Maybe. Or maybe a manifestation of man's evil to man.

Maybe it was a warning, warning of destruction and disaster to come. Like with nuclear fission. Like with space exploration. Like with the hydrogen bomb.

Moira was right. I had to set the beast free. Too much was at stake if I didn't.

I'd put it up to Joe, man-to-man. With the death of Pat Phelan, maybe he'd face the issue and agree. What did we have to lose, anyway? There was no money involved.

I found Joe below, standing by the doorway to his cabin, reading a piece of paper. He glanced up when I approached and slipped the paper in his pocket. His yellow eyes watched me warily.

"She *is* a bit of a friendly type, isn't she?" I grinned.

Joe's mouth dropped open. Then he threw his head back and laughed. I knew he'd been sweating out my reaction to that tête-á-tête on his bunk. And in disarming him like that, maybe I'd gained an edge in my argument about Ogra.

"It's about the beast," I went on, before he had a chance to say a word. "Phelan was killed, you know. On guard."

Joe bit his lip angrily. "I know about Phelan. Its a dirty shame."

"We've got to let the damned thing go."

The yellow eyes narrowed, and probed me. "You lost your marbles, old man?"

I shook my head. "The beast is bad luck. The island people are right."

Joe snorted. "It's that girl, isn't it? She and her brother!

The islands are full of superstitious fools like them. They think everything on earth is a manifestation of good or evil. They're stupid pagans, Sam. I'm surprised you agree with them.

I shrugged, trying not to let him read my thoughts. If he knew I even entertained the idea of letting the monster go, he'd kill me. "I just don't like it," I said lamely.

"So you don't like it," Joe said and reached into his pocket for the piece of paper he had been reading when I came up. He broke out a great big grin. "Here, Sam. You're going to change your tune when you get a load of this. Came in by radio ten minutes ago. It's what I've been waiting for.

Curious, I took the sheet of paper.

"GUARANTY THIRTY THOUSAND POUNDS AGAINST FIFTY PER CENT OF GROSS TO EXHIBIT CAPTURED MONSTER AT DORKIN'S LONDON CIRCUS.

I stared at the wire, and then I looked at Joe. I could see what it meant, but my mind wasn't ready to accept the fact.

"Don't you see, you knothead! We're rich! We'll make a fortune with the monster! I've been dickering with these guys secretly." "But, Joe, " I stammered. "What about the University of Dublin? We promised them—"

"To hell with the University of Dublin!" snapped Joe. "Man, we're in!"

"But what about the Irish government? Won't they try to stop us?"

Joe's eyes narrowed craftily. "Who's to know until it's too late?"

I chewed on this for a moment. The plan had merits. And it did mean a lot of money in our pockets. But just the same. . . .

I thought of the dead divers. I thought of the three oarsmen torn to pieces in the harbor. I thought of Phelan on the deck of the *Triton*.

"Damn it, Joe! I said finally, "we can't do it! We've got to let the thing go and get away from this place. I don't want any part of it!"

"We're partners, Sam," he said quietly. "You want out now?"

"No! I want to bring you to your senses! This thing is a killer! Think what it would do if it got loose in London! My God, Joe, you'd be responsible for the deaths of thousands of people!"

"I've thought it through," snapped Joe. "If you want out, get out!"

He took back the wire and folded it carefully and tucked it in his pocket. I didn't like the intense, stolid expression on his face.

"It's that damned girl!" he burst out angrily. "How could you let her turn your head?"

"She doesn't mean a thing to me," I said defiantly. I wondered if I sounded as insincere as I felt. Even though I had lost her, I still wanted her.

"You're a fool!" Joe shouted. "You're really asking for trouble! She's just like that other one you got hung up with in Port Arthur!"

"Shut up!"

"No, sir! It's for your own good, Sam! She's trying to work on you. For anything she can get. She's like a bitch in heat. Hell, I should know, shouldn't I? Can't you see her game now?"

The blood boiled up in me. I knew he was right. That was what angered me. She was just playing both ends against the middle. She was using me. And yet I knew I had to do something to Joe for saying it. I knew he was a killer, but I had to attack him. I had to come to grips with him.

"Keep off Moira!" I yelled.

"She's a demon, a damned demon!" Joe cried. She's played you for a sucker! The worst kind!"

I leaped at his throat. Immediately I felt myself swung to one side, and my back smashed against the bulkhead along the passage. I slumped down on the deck. Joe was standing over me, his yellow eyes fiery, his hands knotted.

"Is this what you want?" he cried.

"Yes!" I yelled back. "That's what I want!"

I shot to my feet again, smashing my left into his face. He ducked back, but I caught his jawbone and I heard a crunch. My fist felt as if it had been smashed under a rock. Joe went back. He stumbled.

I leaped on him as he lost his balance, carrying him to the deck. I flailed at him blindly, not knowing what I was doing, and in turn I could feel him gouging at my eyes, tearing my shirt, hammering me unmercifully. We rolled over and over on the deck, smashing against the bulkhead to one side, and then thrashing back against the other.

I was blind. I was enraged. I couldn't think. There was no reason for us to be scrapping this way. What had ever possessed me? I was mad. He was right. The girl had turned my head.

Moira.

Then it all came clear, and I was sitting on him chopping away at his face, my knuckles slimy with blood.

I stopped. God, was I some kind of beast myself? And there was one other thing I hadn't thought about at all. What happened if I did get the best of Joe? Did I seize the ship. Did I become captain of the *Triton*.

Some subconscious awareness of my impossible position had stayed my hand at the last moment there. I had been too long at sea to depose any captain. I had plunged into a fight I couldn't possibly win. "Joe," I said.

He rolled his head, eyeing me through bruises.

"Joe." I got off him and stood up, shaking my head, trying to clear it.

He moved toward his cabin. I went after him, trying to frame some kind of an apology. We were partners, and he was the boss on board the *Triton*. How could I square myself?

I stood in the doorway, paralyzed.

Joe faced me, his eyes gleaming. He held a revolver in his hand. He had gotten it out of his things.

"Don't mess with me, Sam," he said tightly, drawing his lips back from his teeth in a grimace. "I'm going to take the beast to London. If you want to come along, come on. Glad to have you. But if you try anything funny. . . . Well, I *still* am captain on the *Triton?*"

There was only one thing I could say. I said it.

"Okay, Joe. You win."

For now, I said under my breath as I went above. For now. Because I had made up my mind. I was definitely going to free the beast. Whether it was because of Pat Phelan's death, or because of Moira's fear of the thing or because of the bad blood between Joe and me, I was going to free it. I didn't spend time trying to analyze my feelings one way or the other.

And I had a plan. It was simple and direct. I knew exactly what I'd do. I'd get the donkey engine going, attach a cable to the winch, and hook into the top of the monster's net. I'd have to trick him into his cabin, and barricade him up. Then I'd have to keep the crew under guard while I moved the cargo overboard.

I needed someone trustworthy to help me.

Jack Finn was out; he was loyal to Joe.

One of the crew? They were loyal to the Bos'n, far more so than they were loyal either to Joe or me.

Then I knew. Sean and Moira McCartin.

The trick was to get them aboard without creating a stir. The obvious thing to do was smuggle them on at night. And there was a way to manage that. Several hours later I climbed to the bridge room where I found Joe with a chart of the British Isles spread out on the table. He was bending over it, making penciled calculations.

He glanced up casually as I joined him. "Oh, hello, Sam. I'm just trying to lay out a course."

As if nothing had happened between us! Apparently he had no suspicion of my intentions.

I leaned over his shoulder. "When do we sail?" I asked.

Joe scowled and rubbed his chin. "Not before midnight, I'd say. The tides will help us from twelve-thirty to four. Why?" He turned and his yellow eyes flickered. "You got a heavy date or something?"

"Oh, I thought I might do some reconnoitering on the beach tonight," I drawled.

Joe struck a match and lit a cigarette. "One last fast one on the village mall," he chuckled. "Go on. I'll count

on you back at eleven-thirty. Finn can drop you on shore after chow."

"I don't know if I should make a big production out of it," I said, as if reluctant to complicate matters.

"No, no," Joe said, turning back to the charts. "Go right ahead. It may help get her out of your system for good."

I left him looking at his charts. And I was grinning to myself. He'd practically set it up for me, step by step. It would be the easiest thing in the world to do.

I'd have Moira get hold of her father's launch, by hook or crook. She could do it, if not alone, at least with Sean's help. Then I'd meet her and Sean at the cove, ride out to the *Triton*, secure Joe in his cabin, hold the crew off at gun point, and set the monster free. Most of the crew would probably want to help me, anyway.

It was a daring plan, but I knew that a daring plan had the best chance of success and I was determined to succeed. I knew if I didn't the damned monster would kill us all.

# Chapter 9

ABOUT FOUR O'CLOCK in the afternoon the village fishermen began coming back in from their day's stint. I hailed a likely looking lobsterman sailing a one-man curragh, and handed him a note I'd written to Moira. On the outside of this note I had written Sean McCartin.

"Sean McCartin," I explained to him carefully *"Tugair nóta ceo do Sean McCartin."* "Give this note to Sean McCartin." I deliberately wanted to keep it out of Moira's hands because I knew her father would be watching her like a hawk.

The lobsterman nodded, and I handed him a few silver coins which he pocketed immediately. He seemed visibly impressed. "Sean McCartin," he promised.

I kept making excuses to join Joe in the bridge room. About six o'clock I picked up the binoculars for the fifth time and scanned the rock promontory by the McCartin cottage. Then I saw it. One of Moira's blue shirtwaists was hanging on the clothesline, beside the thatch-roofed cottage. That was the signal I'd mentioned in my note: *Message received and will do.*

Everything was set. I was to meet her at the cove at 10:30 that night. So far so good. I went on deck then, and uncoiled a line over the stern of the *Triton*, securing it to a shackle bolt. No one saw me. I made sure of that.

It was about chow time, and I went down to eat with Joe and Jack Finn. I tried not to appear over-eager, but at the same time I didn't want to underplay it and appear to be engaged in something deep. I got Joe into a discussion about the Cuban revolution and we stayed carefully off the subject that was really bothering both of us.

At about 9:30 I looked in at Joe in his cabin and told him I was on my way to the beach. He came out to see me off in the launch, and warned Jack Finn to come right back and get the ship ready to pull out. I arranged to meet Finn on the dock at 11:30, even though I knew damned well I wouldn't be there. We waved to Joe, and he disappeared.

"Little last-night exercise?" Jack Finn asked me, grinning behind his cigarette as he steered the launch in toward the dock.

"Something like that," I said. "I wish I had your gift of gab in the mother tongue," I added a bit wistfully.

Finn laughed, his gusty voice booming out over the harbor. "You seem to be doing fine, Mr. Slade."

I waved a hand at him in dismissal as I hopped out onto the dock.

"Eleven-thirty," he called to me as he turned back to the *Triton*.

Even with my pocket flash I found it difficult going, climbing the rocky hill behind the village, and crossing over behind McCartin's cottage to approach the cove from the side. But I finally made it after bloodying up my hand once in a fall on the rocks.

I climbed quietly down the steep embankment behind the sand strip, and stood there brushing myself off.

"Ssst"

I looked carefully around. I couldn't see a thing.

"Somhairle!"

It was Moira all right, but where was she. I could see absolutely nothing.

Then I remembered the cave mouths. I moved over toward the cliff and poked the flashlight beam in through the openings.

She jumped out at me laughing. I staggered back. "Moira!"

"I knew you'd do it!" she cried. "I knew you'd help me! I'm ever so glad, Somhairle."

"Sh!" I said. "I don't want your old man poking his nose into this." I looked around. "Where's Sean?"

Her eyes were round in the darkness. "I thought you'd sent him off on some chore."

I shook my head. "You mean you didn't get my message?"

"I got it fine! 'Tis why I'm here. But Sean said nought about coming, too."

"I need you both," I said, trying to cover my concern.

Had McCartin found the note, and held the boy?

"Since dinner I haven't seen hide nor hair of him!" Moira went on.

"Perhaps he'll turn up later," I said. "Where is the launch?"

She smiled. Then she beckoned me with her finger and stood up, backing into the cave mouth. I followed. "Turn your light here."

I did as directed. The beam lit up the inside of a large natural cave, and I could now see something I had not guessed. The cave was connected to the ocean by a free-funning sluice of water. And just in back of Moira a shiny blue launch with the name *"Maighréad"* on it's prow bobbed up and down in the silence of the cave.

"Get in," I said. She climbed in beside me. "I don't know how you did it, but thanks."

" 'Twas as simple as stealing candy from a wee one. I have a way with Mulkerns."

"Who the hell's Mulkerns?"

"A favorite boatman of my father's" said Moira with a lilting laugh. I pointed the beam of light at her face, and saw her toss her head to one side flirtatiously.

"You little minx!" I had to grin. She'd done it as much for me as she'd done it for herself. How could I get angry because she'd enlisted the aid of this nonentity named Mulkerns?

I started up the launch and adjusted the engine down until it was muffled and low, and then moved the craft slowly out through the inlet and into the cove. Here the waves were rougher than inside the cave. The tide was coming in strong, but I headed the prow of *Maighréad* for a point a half mile from the lighthouse at the end of the cape, and kept pushing.

Moira didn't say much. She was obviously excited at the prospect of freeing Ogra. I had my hands full trying to navigate in the darkness without running lights.

As we passed the point of land on which the light hour sat, I breathed a sigh of relief. The worst of the journey was over. Now all I had to do was locate the lights of the *Triton* and head for them. There were no more obstacles in the way.

*Maighréad* was in the open sea now, and the heavy waves knocked us about a great deal more than they had in the protection of the cove. I made out the silhouette of the *Triton*, and headed confidently for it. I'd been going in that direction for several minutes, when suddenly my jaw dropped open.

"My God!" I cried. "Why, that lousy, double-crossing bastard!"

"Whatever is the matter?" Moira asked, turning to me with deep concern.

"The *Triton*!" I cried out, pointing. "It's moving out of the harbor! It's headed for the high seas! Joe's seen through my scheme and he's taking that damned monster to London without me!"

I was so shocked all I could do was sit there and stare.

Moira was immediately angered. "Well, then, we've just got to catch up to him!" she announced.

I pushed *Maighréad* to her limits, and we soared over the harbor waters after the fleeing *Triton*. One thing to McCatin's credit, he had good equipment. *Maighéad* really moved along. As we sailed, I cursed Joe Ryan enough to turn the air blue. I knew now why he'd been so cozy with me at dinner, why he'd gone along with my beach escapade. He'd guessed what I was up to, the slob!"

We did it, too. We did catch up with the *Triton*. I don't know how, but the fact is, we did. And apparently nobody saw us. The *Triton* herself made to much noise, and possibly the deck watches were too worried about the monster to hear anything else.

Certainly Joe had no idea of pursuit from me.

We reached the hullplates of the *Triton* about 11 p.m., and I immediately cut the engine of the launch and tied up to the trailing line which was still there. I showed Moira how to steer *Maighéad* so she didn't bang against the *Triton*'s hull.

"Wait here," I whispered to her, and climbed the line, scrambling hand over hand like an old-time sailor.

It was dark on deck, and I crouched there cautiously a moment, catching my breath. There wasn't a sound. I moved forward, then, coming out of a crouch, scanning the deck for the watch, and as I did so the whole world fell in on me, and I went down in a heap.

I came out of it blinking and shaking my head to clear it. I found myself flat on my back in my own bunk. I stared about me, not remembering a thing. Then I saw Joe and everything slid back into focus.

"Welcome aboard, old buddy," said Joe, his yellow eyes gleaming.

I lay back and stared at the deckhand. "You're mighty rough with the belaying pin."

"Pistol butt," said Joe. "You come sneaking up like that, you get treated like a sneak."

I glared at him. "Talking about sneaks what particular species are you?"

Joe shrugged. "You had to get smart and try to free the monster. You forced my hand. So I had to get a little smart and get the beast away before you could."

"Where the hell are we now?"

"Heading for London and Dorkin's Circus."

"Oh well," I said. "It was a good try."

Joe's eyes narrowed. "If it wasn't for that fool girl, Sam, I wouldn't have acted the way I did. She's the one poisoned your mind."

"Uh huh," I said.

"It was silly of us to fight over her in the first place,"

Joe continued. "And it was sillier of you to try to get back at me by dumping the beast overboard."

"It seemed like a good idea at the time."

"Because she poisoned your mind, Sam. My God, I'd think you had more sense than that! That woman's nothing but a common tart. She's laid everybody on the island at least once. I even had a roll in the hair with her myself the other night on the island."

"I don't believe it!"

"It must be obvious to you now, after seeing her with me in the bunk. That kid is a woman of the world. She's got what it takes, and she knows what to do with it!" Joe laughed.

I felt miserable. He was right. When I'd seen her there on the bunk with him, it had struck me forcefully how sensual and knowledgeable she was in Joe's arms. She must have had a lot of practice to be that expert.

"That's why she played me," Joe said finally.

I started up from the bunk, and then winced. My head throbbed with sudden pain.

"What do you mean?"

"I mean just that. Don't you see the plot? She's in it with her father. They want that monster for the money it'll bring them. Hell, she never was going to release the fool thing. That was all sweet jazz to tweak you by the ear, my boy! She was in it plain and simple to rob us of our thirty thousand and dump the loot from the circus into her father's lap."

I lay there staring at the ceiling. The story did have a ring of authenticity. It sounded more like the women I had known. And Moira was a woman. There was no doubt of that. I could still taste those lips, smell that hair, feel the soft silken skin of that naked breast.

"You're sure?" I scowled.

"You're damned right I'm sure. Dorkin wasn't the only one wanted us to go with him. There were several other shows trying to get us. McCartin was in touch with one of them, you can bet your boots. Wanted us to release the monster, so he could bring it in himself."

I snorted. "Maybe you've got something there, Joe."

"I'm only surprised she could pull the wool over your eyes. You must be losing your buttons. She was just a plan old lay, and you know it. Tell me the truth." Joe's eyes gleamed. "Did you have any trouble with her the first time you tried?"

I turned my face to the wall.

"Well?" Joe persisted. "If she was the sweet little innocent she pretended to be, do you think she'd bed down with you first time she had the chance?" Joe let that sink in. "Not on your tintype! No sir, Sam. She was just a little tart, and she got what she deserved!"

I sat up instantly alert. "Where is she now?"

Joe looked at me. "She got away."

"Sailed back in the launch?"

Joe faltered. "I think so."

I reached out and grabbed Joe's shoulder, wincing at the pain. "You sure?"

Joe nodded. "I think so. I cut her loose from that line you dropped over. God damn it, who cares? He was suddenly angry.

I closed my eyes. "Get out of here. Let me rest. I feel sick."

"Okay," Joe said, instantly sympathetic. At the door, he turned. "Oh," he said. "We've got a passenger."

I glanced at him, puzzled.

"Sean. He's stowed away on board. We just found him." Joe grinned. "Claims he wants to go to London to look for his old lady, name of Maigréad McCartin. Seems she ran away from McCartin with some freighter captain four or five years ago. He thinks she's in London."

That figured.

"Nice kid," Joe said, and stepped through to the companionway. "Better stuff than his sister, you can bet your boots!"

And he was gone.

I lay there and closed my eyes. But no matter how tight I squeezed them, I couldn't get the sight of that naked body out of my mind.

Not Moira's.

Anita's. I could see her again, lying on that unmade bed, her breasts gleaming and tanned from the Texas sunshine, her hair short-cropped and blonde, her eyes blue, her nose pug and freckled, her legs long and lovely, her mouth a crimson slash across her face. She lay there, her eyes closed, smiling, reaching her hands out to me, waiting for me to kiss her.

Only it wasn't me she was waiting for.

It was Rick Dumont, an oil-well wildcatter from the western part of the state. And he lay in the alley, more dead than alive. I'd found him in the lobby below, where I'd been waiting for him to come back to her, with the bottle of whiskey he'd gone to by.

While he lay there in his blood, gurgling through his broken teeth, I'd come into their room, looking at the girl who had promised to be mine forever, the girl who had promised to marry me, the girl who wanted her children to be mine.

I moved down over her, touching her body. In the darkened room she lay there, her eyes closed, either asleep or playing some kind of enigmatic game with her oil-well capper. I leaned down closer now, and I touched her naked breast with my hand. She squirmed delightedly.

"Oh Rick!" she sighed. "Touch me again."

I did. I touched her on the other breast. She gurgled with joy. "You can open your eyes now, Anita," I said softly.

"Oh Rick," she sighed, and then I saw her face freeze.

She did not open her eyes. "Rick," she said, suddenly panicky. "Rick!"

Then she opened them, hoping against hope that I would be Rick. Hoping against hope that her ears had deceived her.

But it wasn't Rick, and it wasn't her ears that had done the deceiving. It was she. Anita

The lousy little tramp.

"Rick is out in the alley, Nita," I said quietly. "I hope he's dead because he isn't going to be much good to you now."

The color drained from her face. She lay there mute and rigid. "My God, Sam. What do you mean?"

"I kicked him where he lives," I said casually. "And I hurt him bad right where he should be hurting."

"Sam," she whispered. She tried to turn over and cover her nakedness. I flipped her back on her shoulders and buttocks. She lay there and I could see the thin veil of moisture come out on her naked skin.

"I don't like to be suckered, Nita, baby," I said softly.

"Sam!" she rasped out, fear making her eyes bulge, her mouth writhe back from her lips. "I don't mean it, Sam! Forgive me, Sam! On my knees!"

"Bitch!" I snarled, feeling the black poison rise in me, feeling the sweat on my palms and the burning pain in my gut.

"Don't hit me, Sam!"

I grinned at her. "I wouldn't waste my muscle on you, Nita. You're nothing! *Nothing!* You hear?"

Tears streamed out of her eyes. She sniffled. "I'll do anything, Sam, anything!"

I looked at her, hard and long, looked at her face for the last time. "You've already done it."

And I went out there. She lay weeping and moaning. All she'd lost was one more man in a long string of men. Me, I had lost a lot more: my ego, my manhood, and all my illusions about women.

I shuttered now, feeling the throb of the *Triton* under me as she plowed her way through the Atlantic Ocean, around Ireland, heading for the Thames River and Dorkin's London Circus.

I shook myself awake and staggered up the companionway topside. I hung over the taffrail and stared at the *Triton's* wake. I was so outraged at my own stupidity for getting tangled up with that two-timing Moira bitch that I felt like beating my head against the deck plates.

I heard a step behind me. It was Joe. He came over and slapped me on the back. "You're looking better, Sam."

"Yeah. Feeling no pain. Thanks, old man, for bringing me to my senses."

"Sure," said Joe.

We both looked down at the water and I wondered if Joe noticed the same thing I did. There was a strange white, gleaming iridescence down there.

"Phosphorous," Joe murmured.

"It's coming from the scuppers. It isn't in the sea." I turned and looked at Joe. "It's the water off the monster."

I'll be damned," Joe said. "Must be something like human sweat, huh?"

I shrugged. And looked at the long trail of phosphorescence behind us.

# Chapter 10

EXCEPT FOR SEVERAL times during the next twenty-four hours when the monster seemed restless and thrashed around on deck, rousing us all to a full-scale alert, we passed an uneventful trip from Nara to the mouth of the Thames.

Joe and I were at the wheel, trying to come into the river, when we were interrupted by a tremendous blare of whistles and horns emanating from a group of ships bearing down on us from the river.

In the lead was a launch, bulging with a crew of newsreel cameramen, television crews, and a dozen well-dressed people I guessed immediately were British officials of some kind.

But the thing that really threw Joe and me was the huge banner unfurled on the yacht, showing a madman's conception of our monster, decorated with letters of gigantic size screaming:

DORKIN'S LONDON CIRCUS WELCOMES GORGO! THE EIGHTH WONDER OF THE WORLD!

"Who the hell is Gorgo? I asked, still not quite sure what was going on.

Joe shrugged. "That's show business, Sam. I guess it's our monster.

"Thought his name was Orgra," I grumbled.

We didn't have much more time for chatting. The convoy of cameramen, public relations men, radio broadcasters, and newsreel men tier up to us and boarded the *Triton* like a swarm of hungry locusts.

Over the babble and hubbub I saw a tall, dignified looking man with a top hat push himself forward and seek out Joe. We were standing on the ladder to the bridge, and Joe nudged me.

"Dorkin," he said.

He was right. "I'm Andrew Dorkin," the dignified man said in clipped, precise tones. They were a little too precise. Somehow I got the distinct impression that the man had Cockney origins in his background, origins which he had found it useful to cover up as much as possible in his public life.

"Captain Ryan?" Dorkin went on. He turned to me. "Then you'd be Sam Slade."

We shook hands all around. Before we could say anything more, an energetic, fluttery little fellow with gray hair pushed his way in between us and advanced on Dorkin. The little fellow was carrying a hand microphone, which he was already talking into.

"Mr. Dorkin," the man snapped out in staccato tones, "we understand that your circus has contracted for the exhibition of this strange prehistoric creature. Perhaps you could tell our listeners some of your future plans.

Dorkin beamed, and gazed about him. "Plans? Well we've built a special tank—rushed the job through in record time, in fact—and now we hope to just sit back and watch the money roll in!"

"I see," the little man said. "There is a report from Dublin that the Irish government has instituted legal proceedings to recover the animal."

"True enough," Dorkin admitted smoothly, "It will go through the courts, naturally, and in a year or so we'll have a decision." That tickled him somehow. He gave a broad smile. "Meanwhile, come and see Gorgo at Battersea Park!"

"By the way," the little man said. "That name Gorgo. Has it any special significance?"

"Certainly!"

I was glad to hear that. I glanced at Joe. He raised an eyebrow.

"The Greek Monster," Dorkin sailed on. "The Gorgon! What could be more horrible than a creature the mere sight of which could turn a man to stone! Been working all week on our billboards."

"Aha! Then you had actually seen the creature before today?"

"Not at all!" He waved toward the banner. "But I've had the most accurate reports—from you gentlemen of the press, radio and television!"

I don't remember much more of that morning, only enough to recall it as pure hell. But it wasn't over by a long shot. Dorkin had just given us a brief resumé of our triumphal entry into London, scheduled for the next day, when we were waylaid on the dock by a highly indignant group of gentlemen. I recognized one face. It was Professor Marius Flaherty, of the University of Dublin! Flaherty was eyeing Joe and me coldly, shaking his head. Joe was trying to pass it off lightly, but I felt like the worst kind of a heel. We *had* given the Dubliners the impression that we were going to give the animal to them. And now. . . .

A big heavily-built man with a stiff black mustache was chatting with Flaherty, but he broke off to approach us.

"Who's Dorkin? he asked testily.

Dorkin frowned and moved forward. "Here, my good man. What do you want? Dorkin glanced impatiently at his watch. "We're in quite a hurry, you know."

"Indeed," said the big man coolly, looking down his nose at Dorkin. Dorkin had the grace to flush. "I'm Professor Leroy Hendricks, of the University of London. My colleague, Professor Flaherty of the University of Dublin has flown in to London to join me in protest of the outrage! To deprive science of a creature unique in evolutionary biology! To turn it into a circus freak! It's too much, sir! Outrageous!" Hendricks narrowed his eyes and sniffed into his Anthony Eden mustache. "Quite apart from the fact that you stole it!"

Joe's face turned red. "That's a matter of opinion sir!"

Hendricks eyed Joe coldly. "And who are you?"

"I'm the guy who caught it."

"American, no doubt," murmured Hendricks, turning once again to Dorkin.

Dorkin was speaking smoothly. "But Professor Hendricks, when the courts decide—"

The volatile Irishman shook his head. "But even worse at that moment, you know absolutely nothing about the animal! Flaherty protested. It's extremely dangerous!"

Joe moved forward, angling in between Flaherty and Dorkin. "We've handled him so far!"

It may even carry disease-bearing parasites or unknown bacteria. And yet you take it into the heart of a great city before any observations can be made. Before any tests—without the slightest thought of what the results might be!"

Joe glowered. "Look, just what is it you want?"

Hendricks towered over Joe. I want the opportunity to make a complete study—"

"Sure," Joe nodded. "If it doesn't interfere with business."

Dorkin insinuated himself adroitly in the middle of the group. "Gentlemen, believe me, once we have the creature installed at Battersea, you'll be given every facility."

Flaherty stared at Dorkin. "You insist on taking the animal into the city?"

"Arrangements have already been made," Dorkin murmured, eyeing Flaherty from beneath his brows.

Hendricks turned to Dorkin with an air of resignation. "I suppose you've thought of the need to give the animal a tranquilizing drug while you transport it."

Joe and Dorkin exchanged puzzled glances.

"If you haven't," Hendricks went on, "you'd better."

Dorkin smiled triumphantly. "Perhaps you gentlemen could do that for us!"

Hendricks turned and looked sourly at Flaherty. Then he turned stiffly to Dorkin. "Very well. We'll be back in the morning. Good night."

We spent the rest of the day getting the *Triton* berthed at the docks on the Thames, and readying the huge flatbed trailer Dorkin had procured for the monster. We fell exhausted into bed at sundown and tried to snatch a night's sleep for the big day.

True to their promise, Professors Flaherty and Hendricks showed up early in the morning and administered the tranquilizers to Gorgo, who had spent the night shifting restlessly about on the deck of the *Triton*, confused and bewildered at the strange sounds of London about him. Needless to say, his own howls of resentment had likewise alarmed half of London.

At dawn we began the gigantic operation of lifting Gorgo and his net onto the flatbed. But the tranquilizers had apparently done their work well. Gorgo dozed in a somnolent state all the way through London. For emergency's sake, Joe and I had Dorkin hire some flame throwers to accompany us.

We set out finally, bands playing and flags waving, with Gorgo inside his net on the flatbed. I was astonished at the crowds we pulled. People leaned out of windows in every building and crowded the housetops. The streets were so jammed no traffic could move.

We drove up from the London Docks along the Thames past the Tower of London, past London Bridge, through Cheapside, along Fleet Street and Strand to Trafalgar Square, down Whitehall to Westminster Bridge and House of Parliament with Big Ben, past Buckingham Palace, Victoria Station, and on over the Chelsea Bridge to Battersea Park.

It was here that we finally pulled into the grounds where Dorkin's Circus was staked out. It was dusk when we entered the gates. All around us I could hear the growls and restless movements of the big wild animals caged about us.

Gorgo, meanwhile, hasn't let out a peep all day. He dozed in his huge shark net, seemingly at peace with the world. I hadn't seen a glint from those fiery, red eyes for a full eight hours.

I wondered about the wild animals, who were so suspicious of each other under normal circumstances. What did they think of Gorgo, a water-lizard freakishly snatched into this modern age from some pre-history.

I could smell the restlessness and the fear in the air. I began to have a foreboding of trouble and turned to Joe to say something, but Sean's big eyes caught me first. "The animals do not like Ogra."

I shivered. "You're right, Sean. But there's not much we can do about it.

Sean nodded agreement, and looked out at the cages we were passing. A lion bared its teeth, wrinkling up its nose and snarling at the monster. A tiger prowled back and forth, vaguely disturbed. At the end of the street an elephant, staked out in an open field, moved its huge feet up and down in a kind of nervous stamping.

196

I didn't like it one bit.

Then I saw the huge tank which had been constructed to house the monster. It was a beautiful job. I had to hand it to Dorkin. It was in the shape of a bowl, about a hundred and fifty feet in diameter, it rim a raised concrete parapet four feet off the ground. In the center stood an artificial rock just like the kind zoos have in polar bear tanks.

The giant bowl was filled with fresh water, with a stand-pipe for continuous circulation. The parapet was about twenty feet deep, so that it would come to the bottom of the monster's forearms when Gorgo stood at full height. A network of high tension wires, five strands of them four feet apart, were mounted on steep posts embedded in the parapet at about twenty-four intervals. Heavy porcelain insulators attached them to the posts.

About twenty feet back from this stood an eight-foot fence to keep the spectators away from the tank and wires.

A twenty-foot opening had been cut into the fence now, through which Gorgo was to be passed into the enclosure, and then up a ramp placed in front of the tank.

We stood by while the craneman got the big machine ready. Then the flatbed trailer was backed up to the opening in the wire fence.

Jack Finn came up to us. "Okay, Captain," he said to Joe. "The crane's ready. You better take over."

We walked out into the roadway, and Sean and I kept back away from the workmen. I looked around and saw the two flame throwers standing by. Dorkin himself stood on the opposite side of the giant bowl between Professors Flaherty and Hendricks.

Now Joe was monitoring the craneman to lower the chain over Gorgo's net. The chain man climbed out on the crane arm, and shimmied down the chain. As the hook at the end came down closer to Gorgo's net, the monster seemed to stir a bit, lifting its massive head and gazing up at the man. The chain man hooked into the net, and signaled to the crane operator.

The giant arm moved slowly skyward, and the net tightened around the quiet monster. Finally, the net left the flatbed and started through the air. I could see Gorgo's red, bright eyes. He had awakened and was looking about him.

"The tranquilizer seems to be working," I heard Hendricks say.

Flaherty nodded. "So far."

The crane swung the suspended animal over to a spot directly above the ramp leading to the pool. Joe signaled and the crane arm slowly lowered. The chain man, suspended above Gorgo's still body, took over from Joe, indicating the speed of the descent to the operator. Slowly, gently, Gorgo came to rest on the inclined ramp and the chain was pulled free.

A group of workmen ran in with huge metal clippers and started to cut the steel net from around Gorgo. I glanced across at Dorkin. The big man was watching with badly concealed apprehension.

I ordered Sean to join Dorkin, and I went over to Joe and Jack Finn. They would need me in the delicate operation of freeing the net from around the monster's head.

Up close I could see that Gorgo seemed to have dropped off to sleep again. Two men with clippers worked quickly and steadily along the animal's back. As they cut, the three of us pulled the big net aside, until most of Gorgo's body was freed.

Then it happened. Some stupid idiot of a cameraman dashed out of the crowd and shot a flash picture. The flash instantly roused Gorgo, whose huge beady red eyes opened and glared out at us. Now Gorgo roared, thrashing about, snapping the last threads of the steel net. Joe, Jack Finn and I ran for our lives.

"Flame throwers! Joe hollered. "Get those flame throwers!

I turned to watch. As I did so I felt the ground tremble beneath me. The elephant, staked out a hundred yards away, was stamping the ground again, as the animal had when we first rode by.

I cowered there, caught between the roaring of Gorgo, now thoroughly aroused, and the snarling and trumpeting of the angered elephant. I heard a great rending sound as if a tree had been snapped in two, and I squinted through the evening darkness toward the elephant's stakeout. The elephant reared on its hind legs, its front leg completely free! In its agitation, it had pulled the stake out of the ground. The elephant now began pounding toward me, drawn by the roaring of Gorgo.

Over my shoulder I saw Gorgo lashing about with its massive tail. Now, for the first time, Gorgo was actually free of the confines of the steel net. He moved out tentatively, down the ramp. The flatbed stood in his way. With a swipe of the tail, Gorgo turned the truck over.

The ground trembled again. The roars of the elephant and Gorgo drowned out all other sound. My heart was in my throat. I ran pell-mell for the safety of the roadway, and none to soon. All I could see were quickly moving shadows as panicked men dashed off into the darkness, trying to get as far away as possible from the enraged prehistoric monster.

I turned, cowering like a rabbit behind the safety of the cement bowl. Joe stood not far from me, cursing. And behind us stood Jack Finn, Sean and the professors. The enraged elephant, charging madly over the ground, headed straight towards the green sea monster.

Gorgo moved out curiously, meeting this new challenge with grim determination. Gorgo swung toward the elephant, and observed it for a moment. He moved his head sideways, indulging in an intellectual study of the strange, tusked pachyderm.

The elephant ran full blast into Gorgo, burying its tusks deeply in the massive green body. The monster staggered back under the impact, but immediately regained its balance, turned, and faced the elephant, beating the ground angrily with the huge, powerful lizard-like tail.

The elephant back off, stunned. For the first time in its life it had not succeeded in goring an enemy with its tusks. This enemy was a brand new one with a peculiar smell and a tough hide that did not damage.

The elephant charged again, coming in from the side to sink its tusks into Gorgo's throat, instinctively seeking the jugular. As it came running in, Gorgo shifted stance just the slightest, and flipped at the elephant head with its massive tail.

The elephant crawled to its feet, swaying and weaving, staring with unfocused eyes at the green monster eyeing it truculently. Clambering from the ruins of the oak tree, the elephant again mounted an attack, and rushed across the ground at the beast. In the do-or-die tactic, the elephant leaped off the ground in its last dozen yards, and hurtled directly at Gorgo's neck.

Gorgo's shifted stance again to sidestep the elephant's rush. The elephant tore into Gorgo's side, and as it did so, Gorgo turned and sank his own sharp fangs into the neck of the elephant. With a sudden flip of the body, Gorgo lifted the entire five tons of wriggling elephant into the air and threw him down to the ground.

We could feel the shock waves go through the earth at our feet.

An then, as the elephant lay twisted and bleeding on the ground, the monster of Nara rose to its full height and plunged its talons into the body of the elephant. Instantly the elephant was rent to pieces and moved no more.

There was a short hiatus to the violence. As Gorgo looked down at the kill, Joe signaled the flame-throwers again, and they rushed in toward the monster. Joe and I ran over with them. I saw Jack Finn come up behind us, the inevitable cigarette dangling from his mouth. He was charged with emotion, but on the surface he appeared as placid and expressionless as he'd ever been on the *Triton*.

The flame-throwers advanced on Gorgo from two directions. I could see the monster's red eyes staring at the flames. Gorgo's head moved from side to side. Actually, the monster looked as if he was in a mood to take on the whole bunch of us, and the circus animals besides.

Joe gave a whistle, and the flame-throwers tried a couple bursts of flame. Gorgo roared, and pawed at the ground. The talons grazed the two men. Joe moved in, waving the flame-throwers closer. They edged in, keeping a blast of flame steadily directed on Gorgo's tough hide. The flames touched Gorgo. He bellowed in anguish, and moved back.

"Oh, God!" someone cried beside me. I looked down.

It was Sean.

"Get out of here!" I yelled. "You little fool, do you want to be killed?"

Sean looked up at me with pain in his eyes. He was visibly suffering along with the monster.

Now the beast began to retreat, bellowing in pain, guided and urged on by carefully controlled bursts of flame. I saw Jack Finn move in to help the first flame-thrower.

Gorgo turned and saw the ramp. Avoiding the fire, he headed for the ramp, deciding that was where salvation lay. I began to feel a slight relaxation of tension. Gorgo was just about safely caged.

The, so fast no one could anticipate it, the great tail flicked. Jack Finn had just moved close to direct the flame-thrower. The tail hit him full in the body, a smashing blow. He sailed into the air and slammed to the ground, lying motionless.

I ran over there, disregarding the damned beast and the flame-throwers. I reached him first, Joe right behind me. I turned the terribly mangled body over. I saw the blood and the broken bones and the torn flesh and I was sick.

"Boats!" I murmured, and let the body settle to the earth.

Joe closed his eyes. "God," he said, almost a prayer.

I stared into the darkness about us. I saw Sean in the light of the flame-thrower. His eyes were on mine. There was no surprise in them. It was almost as if he had known from the first. Who was next. I wondered. Joe? Sean? Me?

In the distance I could see that the flame-throwers had now finished their job. Gorgo had finally climbed the ramp, and was moving uneasily about in the cage. Once inside the pool, he rose to his full height at the parapet, reached out and grasped the lowest strand of charged wire.

Instantly there was a bright ,crackling flash. Gorgo bellowed in pain, backed off, and climbed upon the rock in the center of the pool. Then he lifted his head and sounded a long, plaintive roar.

Sean watched with level, understanding, compassionate eyes.

# Chapter 11

WE DREW CROWDS. We broke records. People came from all over England to ogle the Eighth Wonder of the World. There wasn't enough room for everybody who wanted to see Gorgo.

I should have been the happiest man in the world.

I was the most miserable.

I'd stand out there and watch the shrieking, yelping fools as they peered and goggled at the monster in the tank. I'd watch them, and then I'd watch Gorgo.

Gorgo was bewildered and unhappy. The milling,

gaping crowd seemed out maneuver him. Every so often he would give a mournful, lonesome bellow, at which the stupid crowd would roar in delight. Then Gorgo would shrink from the sound, and try to get under the surface of the water.

But if course, there wasn't room.

Sean was as sick of the circus as I was.

Joe thrived on it. He counted the money with Dorkin every night, gave me my split, and then disappeared into London somewhere. Wine. Women. Song. And plenty more if I knew Joe. He'd bought himself one of those low-slung foreign cars, a cream white Frazer-Nash Targa Florio, and he'd red dog that through the London traffic. He bought himself about twelve new changes of expensive duds. He like to live it up big. He was in the chips now. More power to him, if that was what he wanted.

As for me, I was sick and tired of the whole damned business.

About a week after we'd opened, I was sitting inside the circus wagon with Sean, who was in bed asleep, when I heard Joe drive the jalopy up and get out. He was whistling jauntily, and when he opened the door I saw that he'd bought another suit of clothes. He appeared a little uneasy as he walked up to the table where I was sitting. He looked at the bottle of Irish whisky I was working on.

"I was going into town," Joe muttered hesitantly. "I saw your light."

I nodded, not looking at him. "Have fun."

"I thought you might like to go along," he said nervously. "Have a couple belts with me."

"Don't worry about old San, kid. I'm having a couple of belts myself." I looked up at him. "How's business?"

Joe expanded, his eyes lighting up, ignoring the needle I was giving him. "Great!" Then he deflated, like a broken balloon. "Sam, will you quit bucking it?" He looked around at the circus wagon disgustedly. "Get out of this dump! Live a little! I got a whole suite at Claridge's!"

I looked over at Sean. "This wagon seems to suit the two of us, Joe."

Outside there was a sudden commotion in the grounds. We could hear animals roaring, scuttling about in their cages. I got up and looked out of the window. I couldn't see anything, but I could feel it.

"The animals are going crazy. Something's going to happen, Joe. I can feel it. Boats is dead. Who's next?"

Joe shook his head and pounded the table with his fist. "I'm as sorry about Jack Finn as you are. It was a tough break, that's all."

"He's got a wife in Galway. That'll make it just fine for her, knowing it was only a tough goddamned break!"

"Maybe we can send her some dough," Joe suggested absently.

"Sure. That'll help a lot. But he's dead. And nothing's going to bring him back. There'll be more tough breaks before this is over!"

Joe took a deep breath and turned toward the door. "You've been listening to your new buddy too much." He squinted at Sean's sleeping form.

"No," I said softly. I've been listening to some I should have listened to before. Myself."

"See you, kid," Joe said, waving and stepping out into the night. I sat there and poured myself another drink. I could hear the Frazer-Nash start up. Joe threw it into gear and roared down the road toward London.

It was only about five minutes after the sound of the jalopy faded that I got the phone call from Professor Hendricks at Dinosaur Hall at the Natural History Museum. He seemed to be in a state of suppressed excitement, and wanted to see both Joe and me right away. I explained that Joe was out. He suggested I come over as soon as possible.

I left a note for Sean, and flagged down a cab on Queens Road. It was only a short drive across Chelsea Bridge and up to Cromwell Road. I walked up to the big terra cotta building with its distinctive Romanesque front, staring up at the high towers which seemed to loom two hundred feet in the air.

A guard took me to Dinosaur Hall where all the reconstructed reptiles of the Mesozonic Age stand about in shadowy darkness.

I found Professor Hendricks at the top of a fifteen foot ladder, holding a photograph in his hand and comparing it to the skull of the dinosaur skeleton beside him. At the foot of the ladder Professor Flaherty stood, studying three huge photographic blow-ups of Gorgo which he had taken several days before at the circus.

"Oh, hello," said Professor Hendricks, squinting at me in the gloom. He climbed down the ladder. "I'm glad *you* could come, at least."

That seemed to be a cut at Joe, but I let it pass. I shook hands with him and with Flaherty, who said nothing.

"You said there was something important."

"We think so," Hendricks said briskly. "Mr. Slade, the creature you've captured is not an adult specimen.

I looked at him. "You mean, Gorgo isn't full grown?" I glanced at Flaherty who would not meet my eyes.

"No. In fact we believe it's in rather early infancy."

"But how can you tell?"

Hendricks sighed. "It would be impossible to explain all our deductions to a layman. But I can say this. By comparative anatomy and by various measurements, we are almost positive of our conclusion."

"You mean there may be a full-grown Gorgo around somewhere?"

Flaherty joined in the conversation. "It's a fair assumption. Where there are offspring, there are generally parents."

199

"Perhaps the large ones were destroyed in the volcanic upheaval. In that case, Gorgo is the only one."

"Perhaps." Hendricks seemed dubious.

I rubbed my chin, looking up into the shadows at the dinosaur recreation looming above us. "How big would a full-grown Gorgo be?"

Hendricks snorted a moment into his mustache. "Well, I can give you only an approximate guess. Come along with me. The Brontosaur exhibit might give you a fair estimate."

We moved to another corner of the big room. I looked at the exhibit, a small skeleton about the size of a crocodile. This was mounted directly below a monster Brontosaur thirty feet high at the shoulder.

"That would make a mature monster of Gorgo's type nearly two hundred feet high!"

Flaherty nodded. "At the very least."

I wondered if Hendricks and Flaherty were pulling our legs, trying to dream up some crazy story that couldn't be checked out in a drafty attempt to squeeze Gorgo away from us.

"This is some kind of gag to put the heat on us," I said. "Why don't you admit it?"

Flaherty smiled with superiority. "The heat, Mr. Slade, may already be on." He turned to Hendricks. "Obviously the proper authorities must be notified at once."

That got me mad. "You mean you want to stir up a hornet's nest just because of a few calculations you've made on a piece of paper? The hell with that noise, gentlemen!"

Hendricks' tone dripped with scorn. "I am afraid Mr. Slade, that the decision is no longer in your hands. And you can tell Captain Ryan and that entrepreneur, Dorkin, I said so, If you wish."

"You bet I will!"

But in the cab headed back for Battersea Park, I had some second thoughts. I knew one thing: eggheads don't operate like other human beings. With them, everything is for science. The worst thing they could do would be to make a mistake and look foolish. They wouldn't say Gorgo was an infant unless the monster actually was. How they knew for sure, I couldn't guess. But I realized they were not lying.

In that case, I had a momentary qualm. Suppose Gorgo's parent, say the monster's mother, decided to look up her lost baby? Would this two hundred foot giant come striding up out of the water the same way Gorgo had? Had it, too, been released from the suboceanic depths in the same volcanic upheaval that had released Gorgo?

Sweat rolled off my face. I didn't want to think about a struggle like that one! Against a two hundred foot Gorgo? Impossible to imagine.

I thought for the first time in many days of the Island of Nara. I thought of the lighthouse, the radio shack, and McCartin's cottage with its grass-thatched roof. I thought

of Moira, and that undid me.

*Somhairle.* I could hear her voice. I could feel the touch of her hand, the velvet softness of her body. Why had I left her? Why had I tried to forget when I knew I couldn't? Even if she had tried to trick me, she was mine. My thoughts always turned to her, no matter how hard I tried to keep them in check.

Now I knew I had to go back to Nara to see her. She had a hold over me that I couldn't break. Even though I realized I was the biggest fool in the world, laying myself wide open to another doublecross, I had to go back to Nara. To Moira.

I rapped on the glass and told the cabby to take me to the nearest airport where I could get a plane for Galway, Ireland. He nodded and turned down Grosvenor Road at the Thames, and went on to Westminster Bridge, and directly to Croyden Airport, south of London.

At Croyden I caught the midnight plane to Shannon Airport and Galway. I got to Galway in the early hours of the morning. It was no trick at all to rent myself a launch, and I set out for the island along about noon, after packing two box lunches.

At sundown I caught sight of the odd baldpated outline of Nara in the distance, and I must say I was glad to see the old hellhole. Mostly, I guess I was glad to be so close to Moira again.

I pulled into the harbor, tied up at the dock, which seemed to be showing some signs of repair, and roused a villager at one of the sod huts along the beach.

"Moira McCartin," I told him, handing him a note. I gave him money. *"Amháin di Moira McCartin."* I said stressing *only*. He nodded. I knew he got the idea. Probably spoke English better than I did.

Then I ate the box lunch I'd brought along from Galway, and headed the launch out around the lighthouse point. I came into the cove, tied the launch out of sight in the cave, and went out on the beach.

And there I waited for Moira.

She came the way she had always come, like a wraith out of the darkness. And once there I held her tight in my arms, and I knew she was no wraith. Those lips, those eyes, and the feel of her against my body—all these things were very real.

"Somhairle!" she sobbed, and I could tell there were tears in her eyes." 'Tis really you, come back. I had given you up, I had."

I kissed her again. "You're in my blood, Moira. Even though you're as untrustworthy as all women!"

She disentangled herself long enough from me to look me in the eyes. " 'Tis a fine one you are to be talking 'untrustworthy' to me Samhairle!"

"I saw you in Joe's bunk there! I saw you kissing him, and enjoying it!"

"Why should I not go to another man's arms, when my own man does not even have the decency to tell me he's married!"

I held her in my arms, stunned, unable to think. Married? Did she mean me?

"Who told you I was married?" I asked abruptly.

"There, 'Tis said!" Moira whispered. "I never meant to bring it up, because I was too deep hurt, but 'tis the truth, and you know it, and now you know I know it."

"I'm not married!" I snapped out, and suddenly the whole scheme of Joe's was laid bare before my eyes. "Joe told you didn't he? He told you I was married. So he could make time with you himself!"

Moira's eyes were fiery. Her face was flushed. "I saw the picture of you and your wife! I saw them, Somhairle! How can you deny it?"

Anita! Sure. Joe had taken a snapshot of Anita and me at a beach party. He had it in his wallet. He'd shown that to Moira and told her I was married to Anita. No wonder she'd let him kiss her like that! No wonder. . . .

I held her tightly. "Moira, Joe lied. I'm not married. I swear it. I'm not married and I love only you. I've been with other girls, certainly, but it is you I'm in love with. I always will be! Now can you believe that?"

"Oh, yes!" she cried. "And 'tis you only I've ever loved. That in the ship's cabin with Captain Ryan was merely a woman's way. 'Twas spite, *Somhairle*. Spite against you for being married and leading me on the way you did!"

"And you and Joe," I said hesitantly. "The two of you—?"

"'Twas never a thing between us, *Somhairle*. Believe me, never a thing but a trick to turn you green with jealousy!"

I laughed. "I love you, Moira."

She sighed. "Oh, *Somhairle*," she said, and she leaned into my arms and we were one again for a long, crashing, breathless moment. And when we came out of it, she was weeping tears. "I would have gone with you on the *Triton*, if I'd known the truth," she said. "But when Captain Ryan cut the line to my father's launch, I thought I'd best come back to Nara and forget you. That's why I didn't board the ship, Somhairle. I knew we couldn't free the monster, no matter what, once you were discovered."

"It's all right now," I said.

"And Sean!" she cried suddenly. He is all right?"

"Right as rain, Moira. You'll be with him again as soon as we can get to London. Then we'll never be apart again, I promise you that."

"We can leave tonight? she asked, her eyes glistening.

"Yes Moira," I said, and I pressed her tightly to me. And as we lay there, I told her how Joe had misrepresented her motives for freeing the monster, how he had hinted that her father was trying to steal the monster and exhibit it himself.

Moira chuckled and was amused at my gullibility. She assured me there was nothing to it at all, and I laughed and felt like a kid again. I knew that Joe had been trying to play us, one against the other.

I felt her soft flaming hair pressing against my face, and I felt the warm soft curves of her body warm against mine, and I forgot all about the reason I had come to Nara. I kissed her again, and she closed her eyes, holding me to her with her arms twined about my neck. It was warm in the sand, and I gently slipped off her dungarees and unbuttoned her shirt so that her breasts fell free and gleamed in the starlight above us.

She lay there naked on the sand, a study of voluptuous curves and gentle planes, and her moist lips gleamed. She touched my belt with her hand and released its clasp, and then her hands were around my waist, clawing at my back, crushing me close. We struggled against one another, moving our bodies into the age-old position of duality and completeness, and her lips tasted of salt and tears and I touch the taut nipples of her breasts and she cried out in the night and dug her head into the sand, arching her back to me. She seemed to reach outward with every fiber of her being, and surround me, and then she twined her legs about me in one terrible last shudder of emotion and the world whirled about us and the sea pounded on the beach and the skies opened and we seemed to be in the middle of space somewhere, with absolutely nothing else in the universe but us, our two bodies, and the one love that held everything, universe, planet, and us, together forever.

Spent, we lay there naked in the sand, staring up at the clear night and the stars twinkling there, and we touched each other without a word, and let our sated , glowing bodies drink in the nourishment of our remembered pleasure.

"My wife," I whispered through the flaming soft hair, into her intricately formed, marvelously wrought ear.

"My husband," she said. "*Mo fear*," she repeated in Gaelic, and I said it after her. She laughed. "You say, '*mo bean*.' My wife."

"*Mo bean*," I said.

And the darkness moved over us and enveloped us and it was just like that until I could feel a vibration in the air, a strange uneasy phenomenon I could not explain, and I turned to Moira and I asked her, "Do you fell that, too?"

She sat up, her eyes wide and fearful. "There is something out there."

I looked into the cove. "Something?"

She shivered. "If Ogra were not already captured—"

With sudden shock I remembered why I had come to Nara. The two hundred foot monster!

Speechless, I turned to her. But as I did so I saw it in her eyes. Disbelief. Fear. Horror.

I turned. It was coming up out of the water, just as I had imagined it might, rising like a giant formless thing, weaving back and forth in the darkness, scenting out the island, towering closer and closer, moving with its giant tail through the water, coming to Nara, coming to wreak vengeance on the world, coming to destroy us all.

"Oh, *Somhairle!*" Moira cried, and hid her face in my chest.

I stared, petrified, as the monster towered high over the lighthouse, and then reached out with one talon, slapped at the striped tower, and sent it spinning in a million pieces into the waters of the bay, the waters that were now surging and flowing outward like miniature tidal waves from the monster's moving body. With a shuddering crash the lighthouse structure disintegrated, and the huge, unbelievable sea serpent came lumbering out of the water, looming over us like some avenging demon, its fiery red eyes focused on us.

## Part Three: ARMAGEDDON

## Chapter 14

IT WAS MOIRA'S quick thinking that saved us. The instant she comprehended what had happened—that this towering, two-hundred foot sea serpent was reality, she leaped to her feet, crying for me to follow her. Acting purely on instinct, I did so, and she led me to the only safe spot, the caves.

Naked, shivering, absolutely drained of all emotion by the sheer weight of the terror hanging over us, we clung to each other like frightened stone-age beings, hiding our bodies from the inhuman manifestation from below which thundered about us and threatened our puny existence.

The ground shook all about us. Huge waves crashed in through the channel joining the cave to the sea. The launch was hurled time and again against the side of the rock walls by the violent rocking of the water Spray shot toward us, draining off the impossibly huge body of the saurian beast. Its growl and snarls filled the air like the thunder of a tremendous electric storm.

In my numbed mind all I could see was the stunning sight of that immensely magnified approximation of our own Gorgo, slapping at the striped lighthouse at the tip of the cape, demolishing it with one swipe of the massive tail.

We heard other strident noises as well. The radio tower's collapse. The cottage's destruction. We heard boards and glass ripping and shattering on the open island above us.

Moira sobbed, unable to contain her grief. Obviously all the human population of the island of Nara would be dead or dying in a matter of moments. Everyone except us. We were in the only possible shelter anywhere. The beast was destroying everything in its frenzied search for Gorgo. Every minute or so the sound of destruction would cease. But only for an instant. A tremendous thumping would make the whole rock mass of the island shudder violently. I could imagine the big beast beating the island flat with its powerful tail, enraged and frustrated in its search for its young.

In my arms Moira sobbed and clung to me. Our naked bodies were shaking with fear. This was certainly the end of the world. I had one consolation. We would, at least, go together.

The bellowing continued amid the sounds of shrieking, terrified human beings coming to us as the sea monster bashed in more of the rock cottages down by the harbor.

After a long time we heard a tremendous splash, and then a silence like death descended upon the island.

"The beast has gone," I said. I hoped it was the truth.

"Oh God!" Moira sobbed, clinging to me, her breasts warm and soft on my naked chest. She buried her head and her lustrous hair on my shoulder.

"Come on," I said. "We've got to be sure."

I led her out of the cave. Outside we came upon a sight I shall never forget. Towering clouds of dust spiraled into the air from the wreckage of the lighthouse, the radio tower, and the McCartin cottage. There was no sound on the island.

I scanned the horizon of the sea. And there, like a telltale wake that was as obvious as a trade mark, gleamed a line of phosphorescence, exactly like the trail Joe and I had seen from the stern of the *Triton.*

The monster was gone.

But I had the uncomfortable thought that it was going exactly where the *Triton* had gone. The terribly unnerving premonition occurred to me that it was in pursuit of Gorgo; the beast was headed directly for London.

We gathered up our clothes and dressed hurriedly.

Without mentioning my fears to Moira, I helped her climb the cliffside. The island of Nara, to all intents and purposes, had ceased to exist as a human habitation.

Moira's cottage was completely destroyed. Only scattered piles of ripped-up planking and rubble remained. The rest of it was scattered to the four winds. The same was true of the cottages that had made up the stone village on the beach.

We ran to the twisted ruins of the McCartin cottage.

"Father!" screamed Moira. She scrambled from me.

It was inconceivable to me that there was anything left of Kevin McCartin, but I followed her anyway.

Under a pile of splintered planks, the big red bearded man lay, his eyes closed, his flesh bleeding and torn. Moira stooped over him, crying out his name in the lost, pitiful way of a distraught child.

He opened one eye, looking up at us through a film of pain. "Child," he whispered.

"You're all right! she cried hysterically. "You're all right!"

He tried to smile. It took courage. I gritted my teeth and bent over him. "Take it easy."

"Slade," he said stiffly. Then he winked. "Take care of my little girl and boy."

I reached for his hand, lying in the dirt, and squeezed it tightly.

"The Monster of Nara. The Monster I invented. It came and got me! he said. "All the gold. All McCartin Retribution for the death of Dorach Dolan."

That was all he said. He went limp then, the great body convulsing for one last time under the pile of timber, and then letting go, relaxing to death.

Moira crossed herself and lifted her face to the heavens, trying, in the only way she knew, to prepare the soul of Kevin McCartin for its ordeal to come.

We buried him quickly in back of the site of the cottage.

No one on Nara was alive. We searched the ruins. And then we hurried to the launch which I had tied up in the cave, possibly the only place on the island safe from the monster's destructive onslaught.

By dawn we were back at Galway, and I put in a telephone call to Joe in London. I gave him a brief report of the appearance of the new monster at Nara Island, and then Moira and I flew to Shannon Airport, and on to London.

When we landed at Croydon and walked across the big floor in search of a cab, we were approached by two burly Marine Sergeants.

"Mr. Slade," the bigger one of them said.

"Yes."

"You're to come with us." Each of them stepped to one side of me and took an arm.

"I'm not under your orders! What do you mean I'm to come with you?"

"Orders of the admiral," the big one said, stiff-lipped and unsmiling. There was under his urbane politeness a driving urgency which somehow unnerved me.

"The admiral!" I looked helplessly at Moira.

"'Tis best to be going, *Samhairle*," she said. I can take care of myself."

"No. You can't! I turned to the bigger sergeant. "Look.

I've got to get this girl to a hotel. Can we drop her off on the way?"

He nodded. "Yes, sir. We'll go along with you.

I considered. That was better than nothing. But the admiral—how had I gotten in bad with the admiral?

In the admiralty vehicle I pondered my situation. It didn't seem good. In a short chat with the two marines I discovered that Joe was on his way to the admiralty too. We were both in it together. It must have something to do with Gorgo.

Worried, and hardly aware of what I was doing, I installed Moira at the Berkeley Hotel near Piccadilly Circus, and then went with the silent, stolid, very British marine sergeants.

We drove to Whitehall, drawing up in front of a huge red brick and stone building with three tower corners and a campanile. It was one of those Italian palladian style buildings, imposing and in the grand manner. Naval guards stood sentry duty in front of the wide doorway, and passed us quickly through into the quiet doorway, and passed us quickly through into the quiet interior without any fuss.

The sergeants hustled me down a corridor and up a flight of stairs to a room marked *"Admiralty Communications."* It was a room with a long row of uniformed naval radio operators seated at what looked like an elaborate switchboard on one side. On the other side of the room a huge wall map of the British Isles hung from the ceiling to the floor.

I saw Joe. He was in conversation with a gray-haired, straight-backed man in his sixties, obviously the admiral. Joe saw me come in and waved me over. I left the big sergeant who caught a nod from the admiral and vanished.

"Admiral Hugh Brooks," said Joe. "This is my partner, Sam Slade."

The admiral stared at me with startling deep blue eyes. I felt as if he were reaching down inside me to see what made me tick.

"Ah, yes," The young man whose message alerted us to the trouble on Nara."

"Yes, sir," I said. "There are no survivors—except for a girl named Moira McCartin."

The admiral nodded briskly. "We knew the moment we lost contact with Nara that there was some difficulty there." The bright blue eyes probed me. "Your clear-cut report leaves no doubt in our minds now as to the fantastic thing that happened.

The admiral waved at the huge map on the wall.

"Her Majesty's Aircraft Carrier *Royal Oak* has proceeded to area N-3-4 to report any unusual sightings or conditions in the vicinity of Nara Island." He paused significantly and looked at Joe and then at me.

"Reconnaissance aircraft from the carrier, as well as one destroyer, have sighted a creature answering your description." The admiral turned to the map and indicated a spot in the sea south of Ireland. "In this area. The creature submerged when they approached. We are waiting a further report at this moment."

The admiral's icy blue eyes chopped to me.

"I feel you two gentlemen should be the first to know about this situation." I shivered. He had us by the short hairs, and he knew it. Business-like, he went right on. "Perhaps there is something you know about this creature which will help us to appraise it."

I nodded. "First off, sir," I said, "I'd say it isn't an 'it' or a 'him.' It's a 'her.'"

The admiral lifted an eyebrow. So did Joe.

"I'd guess it's the adult of the species. The mother. The one we've got quartered at Battersea Park is her child."

The admiral stared at me stonily.

"Check with Professors Hendricks and Flaherty," I said impatiently.

"I already have," the admiral said coolly. "They concur with you in your theory." The admiral shrugged. "Very well then. The monster—the second monster—is hereafter referred to as 'her.'"

Joe was staring up at the map on the wall. "Excuse me, sir," he said. It looks to me as though the thing's heading for London. That sighting's along the same route the *Triton* took."

"Definitely," said the admiral. "Which in itself calls for some kind of explanation. Do you have one?"

Joe frowned, looking a bit subdued. "Well, we were playing a stream of water over it—him—during the passage. That was Professor Flaherty's idea. We may have left some kind of a track in the ocean."

"Joe," I broke in. "The phosphorescence. When Moira and I looked out to sea after the thing had left Nara we saw a long trail of iridescence in the water."

"I see," mused the admiral. "Well, we don't really anticipate any great difficulties in controlling the monster. I have already taken notes from Professors Hendricks and Flaherty on the creature. Outstanding characteristics, vulnerable areas."

The admiral picked up a radiophone headpiece from the table in front of the map and slipped it on. He listened a moment, then pushed an intercom switch on the table. A squawk box beside it immediately came to life.

"We're in contact with the reconnaissance plane," the admiral explained briefly, taking the phones off. "That's the skipper of the destroyer speaking to the recon plane's pilot. Listen."

"Plane to Bridge. I see something now. She's four point off your starboard bow. Have you got that?"

"*Four point starboard.*" The skipper's voice repeated.

"*Don't you see her?*" The pilot's voice became suddenly agitated. *My God, she's massive! That head, weaving back and*

forth!"

"We see her now." The skipper seemed calm.

"She's looking for something. What's she want?"

"We'll never know. Fire number one turret."

We could hear the concussion echo from the shot.

"Plane to Bridge. I can see her. You've missed her! You're way off to the left."

"We can see. Fire number two."

Again we heard the concussion.

"You've hit her direct! She just staggered back. Can you see? She's impervious! Looks like she wants to throw the shells back!"

"Fire number three!"

Again the concussion.

"*Plane to Bridge! She's gone now!*" The pilot's voice went a bit slack then, apparently in reaction from the excitement.

"*Cease fire!* That was the skipper's voice. "*Cease fire!*"

"That did it, men. Good show!"

"*Port two points,*" said the destroyer's skipper calmly.

"*Whew!*"sighed the pilot. "*What a close thing that was! You can't see her from there, but I'm telling you—she was a huge thing! A great green lizard.*" The squawk box went silent.

The admiral turned to us. "At least two direct hits. I don't suspect the monster will be coming back for more now." There was just the hint of satisfaction in his voice.

"They killed it?" I asked. I didn't want to throw any cold water on his jubilance, but frankly I had my doubts.

"She disappeared beneath the sea, as you heard yourself. They are sweeping the area now, but I'm sure she has almost certainly been killed."

The admiral was about to reach across the table and flick the squawk off, when we all heard it at once.

"*She's up again!*" the pilot's voice yelled. "*Plane to Bridge. She's out of the water! Look out! Your starboard bow! She's reaching out for you!*"

"*I see her!*" cried the skipper.

"She's coming at you! Get out of there, fast! Move@ She's going to—"

"Fire Four! Fire fi—"

There was a crackle of static, and then silence, silence in the middle of a word.

In the Communications Room no one moved.

The pilot's voice came on again. "*Flight deck! Royal Oak! Plane to Flight Deck!* the voice cried, trembling, on the verge of hysteria. "*I've lost contact with the Destroyer Bridge.*" Now the voice broke. "*The destroyer has been turned over! I can see men swimming in the water. I can see—*"

There was another pause.

"*Oh, my God! cried the pilot's voice. "She's—she's breaking up the ship! She's smashing it in two! It's the most incredible thing I've ever seen! She's huge—vast—absolutely impregnable.*

A calm flat voice cut in on the air. *Flight Deck, Royal Oak, to Recon Charlie. Do you read me, Recon Charlie?*"

"I read you," the pilot's voice choked.

"Radio your position. We're on our way."

There was no answer for a moment. Then we could hear what seemed to be a sob. "It's no use. The ship is gone. The–the thing pushed it down into the–the water! She pushed it down and broke it to–to pieces under the water!" The pilot's voice soared to a thin tremor. "She ripped it to pieces like a kid with a toy!"

The Royal Oak Operations Chief's voice shook now. "But–the men–can't we save the men?"

"There's no chance. There's nothing afloat to save them. The thing has pushed the destroyer down under the water. No hope." The voice went dead.

"Report in," said the carrier's Operations Chief wearily.

"She's going under the water now," the pilot whispered. "No! she's rising! She's screaming, roaring out! She sees me up here! She's reaching up! But I'm too high for her. Too high!" The pilot began laughing hysterically.

Then there was a click, and the squawk box went dead.

Everyone in the room was frozen, and a deathly quiet settled down. The admiral was completely stunned. His face was white and he could not speak for a long while. No one would say anything until he did.

"Capsized," he muttered finally. "Sunk. With every man aboard."

I jumped up. "All right! Now what?"

The admiral shook his head. It's terrible."

Joe snapped it up. "But what'll you do now?"

"I know what we'll do!" I said, turning to Joe. "We're going to turn the thing loose! Take it back to sea and dump it! While we're still got a chance!"

Joe moved against me, gripping a handful of my shirt tightly. "What's the matter with you? This is the twentieth century! There's got to be a way to handle an overgrown lizard."

I flicked his hand away and stared at him. Then I turned and hurried over to the door.

"No you don't!" Joe cried out, and moved after me.

Angered by Joe's remark about the lizard, the admiral came to life. He shook himself, as if rousing himself from a bad dream. "There's no doubt we can stop the creature." He looked about him for support. Everyone was staring at him dully. "We'll call you if we need you again. Good evening, gentlemen."

Always the officer, I thought. I ran through the doorway and out into the quiet corridor.

Joe came right after me.

# Chapter 13

AS WE DROVE BACK to Battersea Park in Joe's Frazer-Nash, I told him in detail about what had happened on Nara Island. I told him that Moira was at the Berkeley, and that I was going to let her sleep through the clock before disturbing her again. She had been through a terrible ordeal and needed rest. Later, her brother Sean could move in with her. He would be much better off away from the negative influence of the circus people and the Gorgo crowds.

If, that is, Sean would be willing to leave Gorgo's side.

Joe drove me up in front of the circus wagon and let me out. As I stood there, about to mount the steps of the wagon. I could hear the rumbling, fearsome cry of Gorgo at my back. The sound of his roar had changed subtly in quality since we'd come to Battersea Park. It had taken on a kind of mournful note that made my flesh crawl.

"So long, Sam," Joe said, flicking on the ignition. "I wish you'd take my advice sometime and live it up a little! Do you good!"

I shook my head. "Not me, Joe. I like it here."

He shrugged, gunned the engine, and drove off as I stood there watching him. I climbed the steps of the circus wagon, opened the door and snapped on the light. Sean was all bundled up in his bed asleep. I didn't wake him. I didn't want to disturb him, and I thought Joe must have told him about his father's death already.

I crossed quietly over to the refrigerator and got out a fresh bottle of Irish whiskey. I poured myself a stiff one and sat at the table to toss it down. I needed some kind of bracer. That damned monster. Not Gorgo. The big bugger. She was the one to make you really sit up and take notice.

I finished two more shots and then got up and went to the window. I looked through the darkness toward Gorgo's cement tank. I could hear him out there, thrashing around restlessly, every so often letting loose that plaintive, mournful bellow.

I shivered.

I came back to the table, and almost knocked down Sean, who was standing in my path, his wide eyes watching me curiously.

"You knew," I said to him, my tongue suddenly loosened by the liquor. "You knew all the time, didn't you?" He just looked at me. "You knew it was more than just a big lizard! All their science. All their civilization. You knew more than the whole bunch of them."

Sean glanced at the half empty bottle of Irish whiskey on the table.

Come on, then! If we've got to free the Avenging Angel, let's go!"

Sean was puzzled. "Go, Sam? Go where?"

I shook my head and opened the door. I stumbled down the steps onto the ground, and I could hear Sean's steps coming after me.

"Come on boy! Come on!" I was really warmed up now. I wanted action.

"Sam, now," Sean wheeled, "what would you be doing?"

I grinned at him, ruffling his tousled mop of red hair. "Don't you know, boy? Don't you know?"

"Sam!" he cried, but I was already headed for the scrap lumber pile at the corner of the grounds. I pulled out a choice length of two-by-four, and turned toward Gorgo's tank. Sean grabbed hold of my arm. "*Somhairle!*" he cried. "*Ná déan é!*" "*Nëan déan é!*" "Don't do it! he pleaded.

I threw him off me, and continued determinedly toward the cement basin. I could see the shape of Gorgo ahead of me, staring out through the wires, his tiny red eyes gleaming in the dark.

"Sam!" Sean cried, getting to his feet and racing after me. "Don't! He'll kill you."

"What's the difference?" I snarled. "One more death or other.

I stumbled up to the first line of wires, the ones with the electric current running through them. Gorgo watched me, and moved closer, peering out at me. He raised his head and growled a spine-chilling warning, the echoes returning from the woodland of Battersea Park with an eerie wail.

Sean grabbed hold of me from behind, but I threw him to the ground and swung the two-by-four. I hit the first strand of wire. There was a crackling blue flash. The end of the two-by-four burst into flame.

Sean screamed.

Gorgo reared back, rising to his full height, bellowing frantically into the skies.

I swung the two-by-four again. A brilliant lightning flash followed. But this time the timber slipped from my numbed fingers and spun through the air into Gorgo's enclosure. The sharp claws reached down quickly, grabbed up the timber, and imitated me, flailing at the electrified wires. He poked the timber through the wires, bouncing it up and down. Instantly a blinding sheet of flame curtained up between the monster and me.

Before I could react, the flaming two-by-four shot through the wires and hit me a glancing blow on my shoulder.

I went down in a heap.

Stunned, I lay there. The monster howled and beat his tail on the concrete flooring. Sean was weeping, tearing off his shirt, trying to smother me in it. I realized in a sort of vague way that my clothes were on fire, and that I could not move.

The boy blanketed me with his shirt, and tried to haul me to my feet. I was too heavy, to sodden with alcohol. He knelt beside me then, and I could see the tears streaming out of his eyes. Over my shoulder he looked up at the beast's head, peering down at us, and shuddered.

Sean shook me again. I finally roused myself enough to get to my knees. Trying to support most of my weight, Sean moved me slowly toward the circus wagon. With the last vestiges of my fading strength. I pulled myself together. I staggered up the wagon steps and fell onto my bed. He undressed me and covered me. I was too drunk, too stunned, to really care.

I was so exhausted from the long events of the day before I slept through till noon. When I awoke, I found a note from Joe:

TOOK THE KID TO SEE HIS SISTER. SLEEP TIGHT. JOE.

I grinned, got up, shaved, and wandered over to the pub across Queens Road for breakfast. I was amused at the newspaper headlines. One of them suspected the whole monster story to be a hoax, a deliberate attempt to build up box office patronage at the Gorgo exhibit. Another accused the prime minister of using the monster story to cover up and attack on the navy by a "foreign power." Another claimed that Nara Island had been destroyed by a malfunctioning intercontinental ballistic missile.

No one believed the truth.

I shook my head. The gullible people. What fools they were.

I grabbed a cab and went into London to Piccadilly, where I waited for Moira in the lobby of the Berkeley. Soon she and Sean and Joe came in from shopping, and we split up. Joe taking Sean back to Battersea Park to collect his things preparatory to moving in with Moira at the Berkeley, and I taking Moira on a tour of the city. I had to admit Joe was quite decent about everything. I wondered if he'd really reformed.

It was dusk when we got through a short sightseeing tour of London. Moira, who had never been among people much before, was like a hick from the boondocks. I was amused at the way she gaped at the buildings and watched the Londoners with her wide, innocent, sea-green eyes.

I took her out to Battersea Park to see Gorgo, and she shuddered and held my hand tightly as we stood there. I could feel the chills running down my own back. I couldn't forget how easily, and how accurately, Gorgo had thrown that flaming two-by-four at me the night before.

We went to the pub on Queens Road for dinner, and it was there that Moira saw her first television set. She was fascinated at watching the moving pictures coming from the little box, and she observed everything with undisguised fascination. Finally the evening newscast began. I pricked up my ears, too, trying to hear the broadcaster's words over the din of the pub, which was now beginning to fill with after-work customers.

"It is now regarded as certain that the creature is approaching the Thames Estuary." the announcer said blandly. "Following the disaster early this morning—the loss of a destroyer with all hands—the admiralty has deployed major forces of the North Seas Fleet off the mouth of the estuary in an attempt to locate and destroy the monster before it reaches the coastal defenses.

I glanced at Moira. Her eyes were wide and she was gazing hypnotically at the newscaster. Her lips moved slightly. I could imagine her whispered words: an unvoiced prayer of some kind. For Gorgo? Or for mankind.

"As a special feature of the BBC, we now take you to the inside of the Submarine Net Control Room where naval officers are even now closing the underwater nets guarding the Thames approach."

The scene on the television screen shifted to the Net Control Room. We could see a sailor turning a large wheel mounted on a wall into "LOCK" position. Lights flashed on a panel nearby.

"All secure, sir," said the sailor.

A lieutenant nodded and spoke into a phone. We're just closing the last of the submarine nets now." He listened a moment, and then spoke. "Yes, sir."

The screen went blank and the BBC announcer's face appeared again. "We have established contact with one of our mobile television units aboard a submarine patrol operating outside the estuary. We now take you to the submarine patrol, sector two-eight.

The screen went blank and cleared again. We now saw the inside of a submarine. The captain, a radio operator, and a sonic technician were standing in front of a sonic recorder. I could see a squiggle, like an electrocardiograph, which emitted a noisy "beep-beep."

The captain of the submarine was standing at the periscope, slowly rotating it.

"Anything there , sir?"

The captain shook his head and continued his scanning.

The radio operator, on a phone, turned to the captain. "Captain, it's Admiral Brooks. He wants to speak to you."

The captain took the phone. "Yes, sir." He listened a moment, and then said: "No, sir, Nothing here."

The captain, carrying the phone, moved to the sonic recorder. At a signal from the captain, the sonic technician increased the volume. The "beeps" became more insistent, but still they continued in a regular, almost soothing, rhythm.

"The same, sir," said the captain into the phone. "No change." He handed the phone back to the radio operator.

The screen went black again and then we saw the BBC announcer. "Ladies and gentlemen," he said, "you have just seen a live on-the-spot report of the situation at the Thames Estuary. It is apparently obvious now that the monster—"

The announcer halted and turned, receiving a note handed to him from someone. The announcer raised his eyes quickly to the camera, signaling.

"We take you back to the Submarine Net Control Room—"

Instantly we saw the Submarine Net Control Room again. An ensign was speaking into a phone, his face intent and alert. "Yes, yes! Just one moment, please."

A loud gonging sound cut him off short. The lieutenant turned quickly to the ensign, startled.

"The nets!" he cried. "The signal for the nets!"

The ensign spoke into the phone. "Hello! Hello!" He put the phone aside and turned to the lieutenant. "The connection is gone. I had him there a moment and—"

"Well, what did he say?"

"He said the nets have been torn. And then the connection was broken."

The lieutenant turned and grabbed up another phone. "Admiral, sir! Admiral Brooks. The creature's got through. She's smashed the nets! There's nothing we can do now. Standing by for instructions, sir!"

The screen went blank. I could feel the tension about me in the pub. Everyone who had been eating and chatting and drinking a moment before now sat stunned and silent, looking about furtively and fearfully. There was an air of horror and disbelief in everyone's face.

Then the face of the BBC announcer flashed on, tense and strained. He read a slip of paper in his hand, now and then glancing up at the camera.

"Ladies and gentlemen, we have received a communication from Army Headquarters in London, from the Commander-in-Chief of Operations. It states that the creature is believed to be following the course of the River Thames. The decision to use atomic weapons on the creature would be out of the question because of the densely populated area involved. Tanks and missiles will be used to stop the beast's progress. The population is warned to remain indoors, however, to keep away from the river, and to remain calm."

Instantly the pub was filled with the sound of nervous chatter and the babble of hysterical voices.

I gripped Moira's hand. We stared at each other. " 'Tis what I have guessed, *Somhairle,*" She whispered " 'Tis the end of the world.

I shook my head. "No Moira. We'll be able to take care of it. You watch."

Now the screen of the television set showed a column of huge military tanks racing along the bank of the Thames River. At the had of the column a jeep, with a mounted siren screeching deafeningly, cleared the way. The streets seemed not overcrowded. Apparently the instructions of the government on the television had been followed.

"Ladies and gentlemen," another announcer said, "we are stationed here with our mobile unit just outside the Tower Bridge. It is this spot that the army has decided to mount its final assault on the monster."

As we watched, spellbound, the Tower Bridge flashed on the screen: two big fat Gothic columns of rock and masonry astride the Thames River, joined together at the top by footwalks, and at the bottom by movable twin bascules capable of swinging up and down to accommodate shipping.

We could see a naval ship of some kind passing through under the raised bascules, and then as the ship came clear, the two sections immediately lowered into place. The column of tanks, which had been waiting at the Tower Bridge approach, moved onto the stabilized span. Soldiers with bazookas and walkie-talkies leaped out of personnel trucks and took up positions on the bridge. Others ran into the two towers, and began the ascent to take up their places on the footwalks above.

The tanks moved in, facing downstream. Soldiers pushed huge searchlights into place on the bridge.

"There she is!" cried the announcer.

We all strained our eyes. Yes! We could see her! In the water past the bridge, a huge head, dimly visible, emerged from the murk. A murmur of tense excitement shot through the people in the pub about us.

We saw a soldier shoot off a flare-gun. The flare's parachutes opened directly above the shape in the river. The flare-lights fell slowly, illuminating the darkened river with bright burning red light. The huge, red-eyed head of the monster became clearly visible. A volley of shots rang out. Long trains of tracer bullets beat down into the water at the beast.

The beast vanished. One instant she was there, the next she had gone.

More flares zoomed into the air. Then, with unbelievable speed, the monster rose to her full height just beyond the bridge, roaring and waving her talons about. She reached up and grasped the steel girders of the bridge, ripping at the cables, smashing at the massive towers.

A moan of something quite like pain squeezed from the throats of all of us in that pub. No one moved. It was incredible, the strength and the ferocity of the beast! And we could see it clearly and vividly on that television screen.

The television camera kept on. Flares fell about the beast, lighting her grotesque form with a greenish light, showing clearly her fiendish grin, her pointed teeth, and her massive, destructive talons. She reared up, and swiped with her tail at the north tower of the bridge. Stones and rubble pelted down in a huge swirling cloud of dust. We heard screams and shrieks, and we saw soldiers struggle in the Thames, thrown there by the lashing force of the beast's attack.

Then, with terrifying suddenness, the monster backed up, raised her claws, and crushed them down on the bridge span. The footwalks split apart. Men went plunging into the water, screaming. Tracer bullets wove a crazy pattern in the air and then ceased. Flares fell into the Thames, burning brightly. The monster reached up and pulled apart the cables linking the towers to the banks. Then she grasped the two wide steel bascules and ripped them from their moorings at the tower bases. She flung them backwards under her into the water. Tanks and men tumbled out helplessly.

Standing there in the middle of the devastation, she then swung her two arms out wide like a man doing calisthenics, striking and buckling the two heavily-built Gothic towers, breaking them in the middle. They collapsed into two piles of rubble at each side of the river.

The immense obscenity turned and viewed the pile of masonry and steel which had once been the proud Tower Bridge. Then she turned toward us. She raised her hideous head in the air and let loose a shriek of triumph and warning. Then she dove into the water heading up river, pushing aside wrecked tanks, twisted steel, and broken human bodies like so many match sticks.

The television screen went blank.

"Ladies and gentlemen," a man's shaking voice croaked weakly, "due to technical difficulties, the program previously scheduled has been temporarily disrupted. We will now hear the London Marching Band in a special selection.

Nobody was listening to the music. Panic had erupted in the pub. Like a wild thing unleashed, the crowd rushed for the doorway. Patrons clawed at one another savagely.

I kept Moira clutched to me. We were sucked into a vortex of milling people and abruptly spewed out into the street.

Dazed and stunned, we stood there, watching the panic-stricken Londoners fleeing in all directions. To the east we could see a strange, ominous brightness lighting the sky. Something was burning.

"Has Ogra set the city on fire?" cried Moira, looking at the glowing sky.

"I don't know," I said, struggling to keep my own panic under control. I turned and looked around. I had no idea what to do now. Set the beast free? Possibly. . . .

Before I could act, I heard a screech of brakes, and there was Joe in his cream-colored Frazer-Nash. He leaned out and yelled at us. I was never so damned happy to see that lean, yellow-eyed face in my life before.

"Sam! Moira! The kid's gone! Sean! We've got to get him!"

I gripped Moira's arm. "Sean?"

She screamed. "You let him go? You—"

"I didn't let him go! He was there, packing, and a woman came and got him! I just got there and heard."

"A woman?" I couldn't follow that.

"She claimed she was his mother. Said she'd seen the write-ups in the paper, and knew he was Sean McCartin. She had blonde hair. Blue eyes. A mole on her left cheek, they tell me."

I stared at Moira.

"It was! she cried, "She's my stepmother! *Maighréad*. Oh God! Where did she take him?"

"To the Berkeley Hotel to find you. They want to meet you there.

I stared at the reddening sky. "The Berkeley! That's near the monster! We've got to get Sean! Come on! Push that pedal to the floor, Joe! See if she can do that one hundred and twenty-five miles an hour you've been shouting about.

We piled into the car and Joe took off like a bat out of hell.

# Chapter 14

THE LITTLE FRAZER-NASH roared along Grosvenor Road, on the north bank of the Thames, on to Westminster Bridge Road, and we could see the orange glow blossoming out into the sky ahead of us. Moira tugged at my arm suddenly, pointing out toward the river from Westminster Square.

I turned. It was a navy gasoline barge. On its side I could read the big red letters: DANGER—HIGH OCTANE.

"Joe!" I shouted. "They're going to try to burn the monster out of the river.

We turned and headed out into Westminster Bridge where we stopped. We saw the oncoming monster. We saw the officer on deck shouting to his men, waving his arms. Gasoline poured out of the opening on the side of the ship into the water.

"Oh my God in heaven!" cried Moira, pointing out into the murk of the river. " 'Tis she! 'Tis Ogra!"

It was she. The monster had reared out of the water and was now slapping along, glancing about unhurriedly, watching the tiny ants of people running about helter-skelter. She kept right on coming. More barges joined the first one, emptying more gasoline into the water. Then on signal, the sailors and officers jumped into launches and sped for the sides of The River.

The monster kept coming forward slowly, sniffing the air as if she were curious about the strange gasoline smell. The men from the barges hid down behind sandbags erected at the edge of the River. We could see an officer raising his hand.

A sailor on the embankment fired a flame-thrower into the water. The flames leapt from the thrower to the gasoline. Instantly  eentire width of the Thames was a mass of lames. The wall of fire moved swiftly toward the advancing creature. Now, for the first time, the monster came to a halt, and looked apprehensively in front of her. She stared down at the fire, now rapidly enveloping her, and then reared back.

With her tremendous tail she slapped the curtain of fire away from her. Flaming water enveloped the barges. The monster struck again, washing the barges with burning gasoline. The barges were now a mass of swirling flames. The crackling sound of the holocaust filled the air. Smoke billowed down over us like a blanket.

As we sat there in the Frazer-Nash, stunned by the sight before us of the burning Thames, I heard a strange far-off sound, coming from in back of us, coming from Battersea Park.

It was the anguished, lonesome cry of Gorgo, in his enclosure. Gorgo!

Now the huge monster in front of us, towering two hundred feet into the air, cocked her greenish head in the direction of Gorgo's sound, and emitted a howling screaming answer. With one more flick of her tail at the flaming barges, she turned, wading through the sheets of flaming gasoline, and started to come ashore on the north side of the river, a half block ahead of us.

All around sirens screamed. Fire trucks appeared from nowhere, playing jets of water on the blazing Thames. A wind had come up. It was carrying the flames onto rooftops nearby. The reddish glow in the heavens spread out like a nasty, noxious stain. The wreckage of the Tower Bridge had apparently caught fire, along with the countless broken electric power lines.

Joe gunned the Frazer-Nash and we backed up, heading for St. James Park and Piccadilly. We had to get to the Berkeley on St. James Street before the monster did. The general plan of the monster's progress was not quite evident. In wading ashore, she had definitely turned in a direction away from Gorgo's pen. She must have some reason. I couldn't figure it.

A sound truck approached us from the rear, blasting out with a deep roaring voice:

"The street must be kept clear for military and defense personnel! Repeat, the street must be kept clear for military and defense personnel. The Ministry of Civil Defense has declared a state of Emergency for all areas of London within three miles of the Thames River."

In the pandemonium of crying voices and running people, I'm sure no one even heard it.

"If you are without shelter, go to the nearest underground and stay there! Repeat. If you are without shelter go to the nearest underground! Please keep off the streets! I repeat. Military authorities request all persons to keep off the streets!"

We turned and headed up St. James. I could see the shape of the Berkeley at Piccadilly corner. "There it is, Joe!" I cried. "Not much further! Keep going!"

It was becoming increasingly difficult to drive. The street was a crawling mass of panic-stricken humanity. Cabs jockeyed about for position. Cars were abandoned. Policemen were rushing about trying to bring some semblance of order to the milling crowds. Out of upper story windows pop-eyed civilians peered down, staring frenziedly at the mass of close-packed humanity below.

The tide of humanity engulfed the Frazer-Nash. We were literally lifted off the ground, and turned half about. Joe pulled the keys out of the ignition.

"Come on! We've got to run for it!"

I grabbed Moira, and held tightly to her. We pushed through the screaming mass of people in the direction of Piccadilly. Around us sweating, hysterically screaming people were pummeling one another, crying out, shouting, and going nowhere. It was the end of the world.

And then, as we shoved and beat our way desperately against each other, trying to keep from being crushed, there was an instant's silence, and a terrifying scream of horror and fear.

I looked up.

The monster had turned aside from the Thames, and was now pushing its way into Piccadilly Circus, half obscured in the night by a cloud of dust and debris kicked up by her own destructive movements. Air raid sirens squealed about us. A man with a huge white beard stood on top of an automobile in the center of the ocean of panicked people shouting: stood on top of an automobile in the center of the ocean of panicked people shouting:

"It's Armageddon! Your sins have found you out! It's the prophecy fulfilled!"

As he stood there, screaming, the crowd surged and ebbed. A hand reached up out of somewhere. He went down. He did not appear again.

"Quick!" Joe yelled. Into the underground!"

He pointed toward a sign. We pulled along after him, fighting our way each step. I saw the big monster's form lumbering along Piccadilly. With enraged howls, the big beast would throw her talons into a building and tear the walls to pieces as she touched them. Bricks cascaded into the pavements, bloodying, screaming pedestrians below. Bodies hurled through the air, literally torn out of the falling buildings.

Fire broke out. Electric wires crackled with a sinister sibilant sound. Smoke and dirt boiled out of the destruction toward us. The crowd became a huge, coiling reptilian beast itself, whirling about like cattle in a mill.

I glanced up. The monster was holding a screaming human being in her talons, eyeing it curiously. Then, as I stared, fascinated, the big beast slowly crushed the life out of it as a man would an insect. Then she shrieked in triumph, and moved again toward us.

I could see the underground entrance now. I gave a frantic shove to get us into the doorway and to safety before the thing swooped down on us and crushed us all to pulp.

Nobody could breathe. Like a wave rolling onto the beach, the entire crowd on the sidewalk pushed and forced itself into the under ground passageway, just as the big beast smashed a building on the corner into rubble.

It was the Berkeley Hotel. I didn't say a word. Moira must have seen too. Sean and his mother, Maighréad, were surely dead.

A gas line burst in the shattered pavement. A geyser of flame shot into the air. I could hear the shrieks of the burning people near it as they tried to escape the flames. We were wedged in so tightly in the entryway to the underground that none of us could move. Dust and smoke beat down on us. We stumbled over the steps to the platform. As we did so, someone next to me cried out in horror.

I looked up at the ceiling. Bricks popped out of the vaulted archway, showering down into the crowd. I saw a woman's head split open. She sank out of sight. The crowd gaped upward.

I grabbed Moira and Joe and we forced our way through the crowd onto the subway tracks. Others followed. I could see the tunnel ahead, a vast cave of darkness. Bricks poured down around us. Cement peppered us. The crowd was battling itself now, trying to dodge the disintegrating ceiling, murderously insane in its struggle for self-preservation.

"Hurry up!" I screamed, literally carrying Moira with me. Joe needed no urging. An old man stumbled into me.

There was a ripping, tearing sound them, a strident mechanical sound above the shouts of the crowd. I looked back over my shoulder. A huge talon broke through the ceiling of the underground platform. It groped down through the hole toward the squirming crowd.

Down the tracks to our back, a headlight pierced the gloom. A subway train was approaching the platform. I could see the motorman's face as he looked up into the ceiling above him and saw the huge claw. He screamed and frantically tried to apply the brakes.

It was too late. As I watched, too stunned to move, the train was inundated by an avalanche of collapsing stone and dirt as the monster smashed against the tunnel from above with all the pressure of her body. The train vanished in a pile of brick and rubble.

Water burst from the ground. A water main had broken. A cascade of spray shot high into the air. Broken glass showered down onto the crowd of people now half on and half off the subway platform, fighting their way toward where we were.

We turned and ran ahead, the water from the broken main spreading about us rapidly, lapping at our ankles.

Moira went down. I cried out to her and tried to pull her to her feet. She shook her head, closing her yes in pain. It was her ankle.

I lifted her in my arms, the water swirling about my knees now. I pushed through the water, with Joe ahead of me, trying to clear the way. People in various stages of hysteria and emotional frenzy poured by on each side of us, desperately trying to keep above the water that was fast enveloping us all.

The ground shook again. I looked up, fearful that the entire tunnel was collapsing about me. But nothing happened. We kept pushing on until we came to a turn in the tunnel about a hundred yards further on.

The water piled up around us, first to the waists, then to the shoulders. I lifted Moira above my head, stumbling along, my head going under every other step. Joe was fighting the current that enveloped us.

Then, as I glanced up, I saw something that looked like a ventilation shaft.

"Joe!" I cried, gesturing upward.

He turned. He nodded, and came to us, where we were struggling against the current, and tried to pull the two of us along with him toward the shaft. Floating timbers collided with us, making movement almost impossible. A human body floated by, face up, eyes staring.

Joe found the ladder in the darkness and climbed up first, reaching back for Moira. I lifted her up to him, pushing her from below. The three of us scrambled upward. A man followed just behind us. The water rose about us as we ascended, almost as if it were reaching out to catch our ankles.

Cold fresh air poured down over us and Joe called back: "Here we are!"

Ten more rungs and I fell out onto the pavement of a cluttered street. Joe dragged me to my feet. Moira stood beside me, her dress plastered wetly to her body, her breasts and hips clearly outlined. A redness in the sky flickered and glowed. Fires were burning all about us.

"Where are we?" I asked, turning and looking around. Joe shook his head. "No idea."

" 'Tis cold I am!" Moira shivered, holding me tightly.

"We've got to get out of here," I said. "Where in hell's the car?"

"Way over to the north, I'd day," Joe muttered.

We moved slowly and stumbling forward in the street

cluttered with broken glass, split timber, and smoking rubbish. A huge searchlight beam flashed into the darkness ahead of us. The glare caught a gigantic green shape clearly. The monster!

She was moving down a street at right angles to us, heading toward the river and Westminster Bridge. I now know the street was probably Birdcage Walk. The searchlight held to her head, moving along with it. She roared out a challenge, and we could hear the far-off answering cry of Gorgo in his enclosure at Battersea Park.

This made the mother monster flail her talons about. The powerful tail thumped the pavement and shook the ground. The sky behind the monster glowed in a sudden flare of light.

A second searchlight joined in, covering on the head from another angle. And a third. And a fourth. They all centered on the monster's head. Smoke and dust poured up around her now, highlighted by the searchlights.

I recognized one landmark ahead. Big Ben. The monster was approaching Westminster Bridge at the House of Parliament. We ran forward. The monster saw the big tower. She moved directly toward it. The searchlights followed her.

An earth-shaking series of explosions made the buildings around us tremble. Huge fiery missile-like streaks shot into the air near the monster's neck. The missiles all missed except one. That one exploded directly in the monster's face.

"Missiles!" yelled Joe. "They're trying to bring her down with missiles!"

" 'Twill not bring Ogra down," Moira said softly.

She was right.

The monster roared at the tower of Big Ben, grasping it in her massive talons. The beams of light focused on Big Ben. Again another cluster of missiles sailed into the air, around the beast's head. Two of them hit the tower.

The big beast began shaking the tower now, somehow identifying it as the origin of all her troubles. Bricks flew out of the tower, showering the earth. Stones plummeted. There was a rending, snapping, final sound. The searchlights clearly outlined the big tower as it shook for one last time, and snapped in the middle. The top half, with the world-famous big clock, smashed down into the darkness of Westminster Square.

One searchlight abruptly swung to an awkward angle, it did not move. All four beams of light came to rest, pointed crazily in the sky, unaimed.

The monster moved away from us, going up along the river side of the Houses of Parliament. With a gigantic flip of her massive tail, she began breaking in the walls of the Houses of Parliament, flinging debris and broken bodies in all directions.

Dust and dirt poured back over us, combining with the

clouds of smoke already sifting onto us from the buildings as the remains began to burn.

Then suddenly, without the least warning, the beast slid down into the waters of the Thames near Westminster Bridge, and vanished.

Arm and arm, Moira and I waded through the murk and gloom after Joe, joining the hundreds of crazed people, wandering about without purpose in the darkened, rubbish-cluttered streets.

Bleeding and covered with filth, perspiration, and mud we pushed out into a demolished wasteland of pavement, and broken walls. Around us loomed the skeleton-like shells of dead and gutted buildings. Ghostly shadows of lost souls roamed about, pitifully picking at mountains of rock and wrecked household things.

Moira sobbed, covering her eyes with her hands. " 'Tis the end of the world!" she wept. "Take me from it!"

Joe plowed ahead, past St. James Park, searching for street names. Then he signaled us to follow him. In the gloom I tripped over broken window sashes and a cracked bathtub, perched crazily in a pile of wood splinters. I dragged Moira to the corner where Joe was grinning, pointing.

There, in front of our bloodshot eyes, stood the Frazer-Nash. We climbed in, exhausted. Joe flipped on the starter. It was a miracle. The engine caught instantly.

"Where to, kid? he asked, grinning wolfishly.

"Battersea Park," I snapped. "We're going to let that damned Gorgo out. Then maybe we can shake this monster."

Joe's eyes narrowed. He took a breath. "Sam," he said slowly, "you were right. You and Moira. I was wrong. I'd be a damned fool not to admit it now."

He started the car, turned around, and we shot through the street clogged with abandoned automobiles and strewn with piles of rubbish and an occasional corpse.

## **Chapter 15**

WE PASSED THROUGH the demoralized city, skirting the Thames on Grosvenor Road. The monster was nowhere in sight. She apparently had submerged temporarily.

Or perhaps she was off on another tangent wrecking her special type of devastation on the beleaguered city.

We crossed Chelsea, roared into Battersea Park, and came to a stop near the monster's enclosure. We were amazed at the activity around the place.

A kind of command post had been set up near Andrew Dorkin's office. Temporary telephone connections had been strung in, a field switchboard set up, and an army operator sat at work in front of it.

To one side stood an army colonel talking on a phone.

A huge temporary panel containing voltage and amperage dials had been erected in the open. A couple of electricians were showing the set-up to two men. I could see who they were: Professors Hendricks and Flaherty.

As we got out of the car and passed by the colonel on the phone, I heard him say: "The circuits have just been completed, sir."

The colonel nodded at something he had heard on the phone, and lifted his hand. Instantly the needles on the dials jumped into life. I could see one of them center on 50,000 volts. Then after a moment, it went to 100,000 volts. Then to 150,000 as another switch was thrown.

I whistled. That was a lot of voltage. I wondered where it all came from. Then I recalled having heard that one of London's biggest generation stations was located at Lots Road in Battersea Park. Perhaps the entire set-up here had been hooked in directly to the dynamos.

I motioned to Moira and led her over to the circus wagon. I wanted to gather up my stuff to get it ready for transport. I didn't care where I went, as long as I got out of that cursed area.

Over my shoulders I saw that Joe had gone to join the two professors. They were chatting among themselves.

I told Moira to wait for me and I mounted the steps of the circus wagon. When I pulled the door open I was greeted by a wild cry of delight.

"Sam!"

"Sean!" I cried in astonishment. The little guy jumped right up into my arms. I set him down, and Moira bent over him, hugging him, crying out with great gusting sobs.

"*Tú atá slánsábháilte!*" she grabbled at him in Gaelic. "You're safe and sound! Oh, Sean, Sean I thought you were dead!"

"No. 'Tis me. And I've a surprise for you."

Moira looked up, puzzled. I glanced around. "Surprise?"

Sean stood aside and called into the wagon. "*Máthair.*" He grinned back at me as a slender, blonde, gentle-eyed woman stepped out onto the steps and walked down to us.

"*Maighréad!*" cried Moira, and rushed into the woman's arms.

The moment we found you'd not gone to the hotel, we came out here to search for you," Sean explained seriously.

"The hotel was destroyed," I said. "By the monster."

Sean nodded. " 'Tis as we both said."

"I know."

"But these wires," Sean went on. " 'Tis like a machination of the devil. What is it all for?"

"To stop the monster, Sean," I said. "With electricity."

Sean shivered. " 'Tis not fair. They should both be let go. Ogra only wants her baby."

"You stay here,"" I ordered them. Moira nodded, chatting in Gaelic a mile a minute with her stepmother Maighréad.

I strode off across the field toward the command post. I joined Joe and the professors in front of the big board.

"Four million volts and full amperage," Hendricks was nodding. "The wires won't take any more."

I nodded to him and to Flaherty. "Whose idea was it to set up the net here?" I asked.

Hendricks looked at me a moment. "The generating station for the London Underground is located in Battersea Park. We've hooked it directly. The monster is sure to come here, with her you one inside the enclosure."

"I see. Do you think four million volts will do the trick?"

Hendricks shrugged and turned to the colonel. "It's the most we can provide."

"It has to work," the colonel whispered tensely.

Suddenly everyone turned to Gorgo's enclosure. The beast was lifting its head in a mournful cry.

Almost instantly, in the distance, came a powerful roaring bleat from across Battersea Park.

"Hit those light!" somebody cried, and the big searchlights went on, poking fiery fingers into the night sky. The ground began shaking, and then we could all see the awesome shape of the huge monster as she appeared above the silhouetted trees of Batersea Park, caught in the searchlight beams, moving forward with her steady, stolid plodding. Trees snapped in two, and branches crashed to the ground.

Around us now the circus animals roared and prowled restlessly. They could scent the danger in the air.

The monster roared out again, voicing her challenge to all of us, and telling Gorgo she was coming to him.

Gorgo thrashed about in his enclosure. He approached the wires lining the cage and beat his head against them. There was an instantaneous flash, and Gorgo reeled back, howling in pain. He slid down into the water of the tank, crouching and snarling, cooling off. Then he moved out again, eyeing the wires and the enclosure malevolently.

The big monster screamed out and moved closer. The shadowy body towered over us like a mountain. Trees continued to go down in front of the massive feet and tail.

The sound of fighter airplanes filled the air. I looked up. I could see them humming overhead like angry hornets. The first ship, the ladder of the V formation, went into a dive, heading straight for the huge monster. As it dove, it fired two missiles. Both miss the monster, exploding on each side of the big head.

The plane pulled out of its dive, turned, and climbed. A second plane followed it, loosing two more missiles. The earth shook as the missiles blew up in a tree nearby.

The big beast leaned down over us, reaching out her powerful talons toward the enclosure where she could now plainly see Gorgo. Gorgo was staring up at her.

She reached her talons out toward the high tension wires, and immediately blinding electric sparks cascaded up and down like a shimmering curtain of fire. Another plane dove at her from above, loosing two missiles which exploded with blinding intensity close to us.

Rearing back from the display of electricity in front of her, the huge mother monster reached out and slashed at the wires with the talons. A blinding sheet of lightning streaked from wire to tire and she cried out in pain. Her whole body shuddered with the terrific impact of four million volts. Gorgo joined in with a sympathetic scream

The huge mother beast reached up and began tearing angrily at a giant pylon erected near the enclosure to carry the wires in. The steel tower shook and trembled and then crumpled in the middle, bringing down all the high tension wires with it. The whole tangled mass exploded in a blinding flash of light, heat, and orange smoke.

At the same moment one of the diving planes loosed two more missiles at the enclosure, tried to pull out of the dive, but caught a wing tip against the top of one of the high power-wire pylons. The plane veered crazily spinning around in a horizontal circle, pinwheeling to the ground.

Its passage lopped off tree tops as it continued in its erratic course downward. It slid into the ground at the border of the London gas tanks nearby. The plane exploded. One instant later the city gas tanks went up, one by one, in a deafening roar that shook the ground and sent clouds of smoke pouring into the skies.

Flames shot upward, painting a vivid background to the dramatic conflict centered at Gorgo's enclosure.

I held my hand in front of my face. The heat was intense. The continuous flare of missiles and electric static blinded me. No one said a word. People about me were frozen into immobility by this amazing and titanic struggle of animal power against electric power.

The big mother monster became enraged at the fire and the noise all about her. She reached up into the top of the nearest extant pylon, grasped it tightly, and began rocking it back and forth. Electricity crackled and snapped, sending blue flashes out in all directions. The monster fathered together four of the pylons, and tugged at the bundle.

Electricity shot through her on its way to the ground, making her entire body tremble and vibrate. The greenish phosphorescence of her outer layer changed color to a dazzling glue, and then to a crimson reddish hue. But she still struggled. The pylons uprooted. She hurled them high into the air. Millions of live wires, torn from their insulators, wriggled about the park, like fiery snakes, burning and scorching everything in sight.

I turned just in time to see one of the hot wires uncoil and strike Joe's Frazer-Nash. In an instant the entire car disintegrated, blown into bits. It shuddered and became a mass of flames and smoke. I turned back to Gorgo's enclosure. The huge mother monster was ripping at the last of the power wires. All the lights about the area had one out now. Flames from the burning London gas tanks in the distance silhouetted the whole scene in an eerie red glow. I saw the big mother monster reach down and rip up the steel strands of wire that had been carefully constructed over the enclosure to keep Gorgo inside.

In the big monster's claws, the toughest steel snapped like thread. There was nothing any of us could do. We stood there, glued to the spot with disbelief, overawed by the tremendous evidence of power and force displayed by this ancient animal.

With her huge feet, she began crushing in the sides of the enclosure. Gorgo himself stayed inside the tank, waiting for the break-through. As he saw the big mother monster's talons reaching in through an opening in the steel wall, Gorgo climbed out of the water and started up the pile of twisted and smouldering metal and rubble that lay scattered about.

I turned just in time to see that Moira, Sean and his mother had joined me to one side. They, too, were watching the rescue of Gorgo with wide-eyed fascination. I must admit I saw something of satisfaction on their faces, as if they all three wanted this to happen, as if they all three always knew that this manifestation of man's greed and inhumanity would come to this end.

It was all over. The huge monster stooped down, lifted Gorgo's tremendous weight as if it were a feather, and deposited Gorgo in the middle of Battersea Park—or what was left of it after her previous advance through it.

Then the two of them began to move slowly through the woods toward the river. In the background behind them I watched the flames from the city gas tanks mounting higher into the air. Darkness lay beyond. London had no electric power left. Everything was silence and stillness in the biggest city on earth.

Someone moved beside me. I turned. It was Professor Hendricks, joined by Professor Flaherty. They were watching the departure of the two monsters, the same as I. They said nothing. At this point, what could they say?

Moira came to me. She took my hand in hers and pressed herself close to me. Her body was trembling. I gripped her and hard and reassuringly.

"They'll be going back now," she whispered. "Back to the island. Back to the sea."

Sean and his mother approached. The boy gazed up at me with his wide clear eyes. "Where he belongs, where they both belonged, and should never have been taken from."

I touched the boy's hair and ruffled it. "Maybe you're right, Sean."

The two unearthly, prehistoric figures had advanced almost all the distance across the Park and were ready to enter The Thames. Dust and fog swirled about them. The flames of the burning gas tanks bathed them both in a dull crimson glow. The big mother monster turned her huge head and gazed back at us there in the murk, her fiery red eyes gleaming.

Lifting her head to the heavens she loosed a final rumbling roar, like distant thunder, a warning to us all, to mankind in general, and turned and vanished in the fog and mist.

I felt Moira's eyes on me. I looked down at her.

" 'Tis a warning," she whispered. "'Tis a warning to mankind. This visitation must be heeded, or there will be worse to come. *Nuair atá tú go sóúil fulaing thú féin.*"

I squeezed her hand, remembering the quotation: "Let well enough alone."

H Bombs. A Bombs. Infinity. Space exploration. Unlocking the secret of life.

I wondered if mankind would heed the warning.

I doubted it.

Man has a way of facing up to even the toughest challenges of the universe—and of life itself.

That's why we're here.

But I leaned down and kissed Moira anyway. I knew she meant it in the right spirit.

## The End